Other Titles in the
Sic Transit Terra Universe

Lydia's Royal Ace (a Sic Transit Terra novella)
The Genius Asylum
The Otherness Factor
The Relativity Bomb

SIC TRANSIT TERRA 1

THE GENIUS ASYLUM

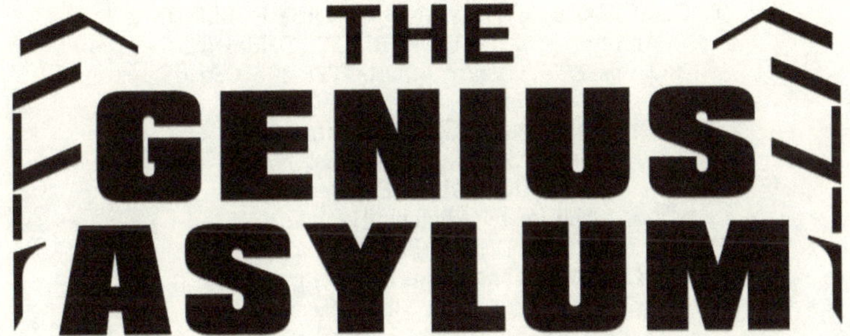

ARLENE F. MARKS

EDGE SCIENCE FICTION AND FANTASY PUBLISHING
An Imprint of HADES PUBLICATIONS, INC.
CALGARY

The Genius Asylum

Sic Transit Terra Book 1

Copyright © 2016 by Arlene F. Marks

This is a work of fiction. Names, characters, places, and incidents are the products of the author's imagination or are used fictitiously and are not to be construed as real. Any resemblance to actual events, locales, organizations, or persons, living or dead, is entirely coincidental.

EDGE SCIENCE FICTION AND FANTASY PUBLISHING
An Imprint of HADES PUBLICATIONS, INC.
P.O. Box 1714, Calgary, Alberta, T2P 2L7, Canada

The EDGE-Lite Team:
Producer: Brian Hades
Acquisitions Editor: Ella Beaumont
Edited by: Michelle Heumann
Cover Design: Ella Beaumont
Cover Art Elements: 1971yes, algolonline
Book Design: Mark Steele
Publicist: Janice Shoults

ISBN: 978-1-77053-123-9

EDGE Science Fiction and Fantasy Publishing and Hades Publications, Inc. acknowledges the ongoing support of the Alberta Foundation for the Arts and the Canada Council for the Arts for our publishing programme.

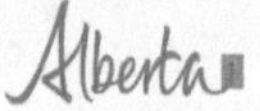

Library and Archives Canada Cataloguing in Publication
CIP Data on file with the National Library of Canada
ISBN: 978-1-77053-123-9
(e-Book ISBN: 978-1-77053-111-6)

FIRST EDITION
(20160727)
Printed in USA
www.edgewebsite.com

Publisher's Note:

Thank you for purchasing this book. It began as an idea, was shaped by the creativity of its talented author, and was subsequently molded into the book you have before you by a team of editors and designers.

Like all EDGE books, this book is the result of the creative talents of a dedicated team of individuals who all believe that books (whether in print or pixels) have the magical ability to take you on an adventure to new and wondrous places powered by the author's imagination.

As EDGE's publisher, I hope that you enjoy this book. It is a part of our ongoing quest to discover talented authors and to make their creative writing available to you.

We also hope that you will share your discovery and enjoyment of this novel on social media through Facebook, Twitter, Goodreads, Pinterest, etc., and by posting your opinions and/or reviews on amazon and other review sites and blogs. By doing so, others will be able to share your discovery and passion for this book.

Brian Hades, publisher

ACKNOWLEDGEMENTS

Building any universe is a complicated endeavor. *Sic Transit Terra* has taken shape over a very long time, during which I have been fortunate to have access to the encouragement and expertise of many good friends. Among them:

My husband David and sons Robert and Chris Marks, who always knew the ugly duckling "plague universe" would grow into a swan.

My mother, Mollie Lerman, who still has the first story I ever wrote (at the age of 6) and always knew that *I* would grow into a swan.

Bette Walker, my soul sister and partner in crime, and her husband Adde, who lets me pick his scientific brain.

Beta readers David Penney and Jody Schaefer, who laughed in all the right places and pronounced *The Genius Asylum* ready to meet the public.

James Alan Gardner, Julie E. Czerneda, Ed Greenwood, Suzanne Church, and Jane Ann McLachlan, whose generosity of spirit has nourished my own.

To all of you, I'm deeply grateful.

The Space Installation Authority (SIA) was first established in 2153 C.E. to provide civilian oversight of Earth's then-nascent colonization program. Its purview was expanded in 2190 C.E. to include the establishment and governing of Ares, the newly constructed settlement on Mars. To provide law enforcement on Ares, the High Council then created the Space Installation Security Agency (SIS), a fully-empowered police organization commanding a corps of officers who came to be informally referred to as the Rangers. These off-world officers were charged with keeping the peace, investigating criminal activity, and making arrests. In densely populated sectors of Earth space, Rangers were posted directly to colonies or space stations (known as hubs). In sectors where the Human population was sparse, Ranger detachments were headquartered in orbiting observation platforms. In 2308 C.E., following the bombing of a conference on Asimov Hub that claimed the lives of three representatives of the League of African Nations, the High Council approved the establishment of an off-world intelligence agency, called Space Installation Security Covert Operations (SISCO). Although they sometimes cooperated with one another, the SIA, the SIS and SISCO were separate and equal organizations, reporting directly and only to the Earth High Council.

— *Sic Transit Terra, An Unauthorized Planetary History* (2673 C.E.)

Chapter 1

The video clip came in from Surveillance shortly after 8:00 a.m. Drew Townsend had just arrived at his desk and was shrugging out of his jacket, already feeling weary at the thought of another day spent spinning his wheels. He could have shortened it by arriving an hour or two late, like the other Eligibles in the precinct, but he'd been a field investigator for too many years to feel comfortable about trimming his shift.

"We've got a body!" bawled Captain Romero, leaning out the door of his office. "Our friends in the Zone have apparently been at it again. Adult male, Emerson and Fifth. Lupo and Truman, get over there. And be careful. It may just be a body dump, but that's Warrior Kings territory."

The Kings? Romero *had* to let him take this one.

"Captain, if this is gang-related, two men may not be enough—"

"You're right, Townsend. Dinally and Gluckstein, you'll go as backup."

Dinally looked pained and Gluckstein threw Townsend a helpless shrug as they headed out the ward room door together.

"That wasn't what I meant," Drew protested.

"I know what you meant, and the answer is no. You're an Eligible now, which means I'm forbidden to put you in even potentially dangerous situations."

"We both know that a body dump is one of the safest places for an investigator to be," Townsend argued. "And I have a history with the Kings—"

"You used to *be* a Warrior King. There's a difference. In any case, you can stop wasting your breath, because I'm not sending you into the Zone."

"But if the vic is a King I may be able to ID him."

"Great. I'll have Lupo transmit a snap of the body to your desk screen."

Frustration hardened Townsend's voice. "Dammit, Captain, I'm one of your top field investigators!"

"Yes, and I was very sorry to lose you. But the moment the Relocation Authority took you back into the fold, you leaped to a higher plane of existence. Now you have to mark time, and I have to like it. And if you get so much as a boo-boo on my watch, they will come down on me and mine like a ton of high explosives. So it's desk duty for you, pal. Desk duty and java runs," Romero said, returning to his office and closing the door.

Drew Townsend was very good at a lot of things, but sitting around waiting for others to make things happen had never been one of them. He'd heard stories about Eligibles marking time measured in months or even years before being posted off-world. For Drew, the last three weeks had felt like an eternity, and he wasn't sure he could take much more.

So, he let the moment settle, then counted to fifty and punched the intercomm on his desk. "Hey, Cap," he said in his best casual voice, "I could use some java. You?"

After a beat, Romero replied, "No, thanks, Townsend." There was a smile in his voice. It figured. The captain was too smart to fall for a con this transparent, but smart enough to recognize deniability when it was offered to him on a platter, so Townsend forged ahead.

"In fact, since things are so slow at the precinct right now, I think I'll drink it at the cafe."

"If you put yourself in danger, you risk losing your Eligibility again, you know that."

The warning was *pro forma*. Drew knew that Romero would love to put him back to work in the field.

Don't wait up for me, Dad.

— « o » —

Romero had called ahead. As Drew steered his PV carefully along the cracked and rubble-strewn pavement of Emerson Boulevard, he saw Truman standing on the road a good block away from the scene, waving to him to pull over. Obediently Drew parked and waited for his former partner to stroll to the driver's side window.

"Captain warned me you might get lost on your way back from the cafe," said Truman with a grin, then laughed out loud as Townsend handed him a steaming cup. "Mm-hmm," he said after savoring a sip. "Black and extra sweet, just like my lady."

"I got one for Lupo, too. I wasn't sure which one of you would be heading me off."

"Lupo hates cold java, so we'll make this quick. The vic is light brown, mid-fifties, about five foot ten and medium build. No ID on him, but he's wearing a business suit and expensive shoes, and diamond ear studs, two per lobe. Whoever this guy is, he's not a ganger. And he still has his diamonds, so I'm pretty sure the Kings had nothing to do with this."

The mention of ear studs had set off alarms at the back of Townsend's brain. "Show me his face."

"It's been mutilated, Drew. We've transmitted the snaps to the precinct—"

"You can either show me his face here or back off so the PV door doesn't hit you when I get out to take a personal look," Townsend told him in the calmly authoritative voice he normally reserved for the suspect interrogation room. "Your choice."

Truman knew better than to argue. Wordlessly, he reached into his pocket and handed over his compupad. "You think you might know this guy?" he inquired softly.

Drew called up the image file and stared at the screen, feeling his jaw muscles work as his stomach slowly twisted itself into a knot. For a long moment he studied the snap, letting each grisly detail burn itself into his memory. Then, forcing himself to breathe normally, he closed the file. "I knew him. He was my friend. His name is Bruni Patel."

Truman had the grace to look uncomfortable while delivering the formula speech. "Drew, I'm really sorry for your loss."

"Yeah. I'll see you back at the precinct." He thrust the compupad and Lupo's java cup into Truman's fumbling hands and drove away before the rage beginning to boil up inside him could find its way to his mouth.

Townsend reached the urbanway in record time and joined the grid, programming his on-board computer to take him back to the 33rd Precinct. And, as Auto Traffic Control merged his vehicle seamlessly into the southbound stream, he came to a decision.

Bruni Patel had been much more than a friend to him. Bruni had bossed the wing of the detention center where Drew had been sent eighteen years earlier for possession of stolen property. Bruni's steady guidance during the next five years was the sole reason that Drew was able to complete his education while detained and have a decent life waiting for him upon his release. The job with Security had been a challenge Bruni threw at him. A slammer rat in Security was practically unheard of, but that only made Drew more determined to qualify. The day he was hired, Bruni brought a printout of the employment contract to his cell along with a bottle of wine and two juice glasses, and they toasted Drew's victory over adversity.

Approached years later by the Earth Intelligence Service, Townsend discovered by chance that Bruni had also been recruited. Bruni did a lot of traveling, but they'd managed to stay in touch off and on for nearly eight years. And now Bruni was lying dead in the Zone with empty eye sockets, deep gashes around his ears, and letters carved into his forehead.

Eligible or not, authorized or not, Drew owed it to his friend to do everything possible to solve his murder and bring to justice whoever was responsible.

— « o » —

The rest of the Eligibles had arrived and were sitting at their desks pretending to be busy when Townsend strode through the door of the ward room and immediately booted up his screen.

"Looking for something?" came Romero's voice from directly over his left shoulder.

"E-F-T. Those letters were carved into Bruni's—into the vic's forehead. What the hell is that, Captain? Someone killed him because they thought he was an amphibian?"

One of the Eligibles found that amusing. Drew silenced him with a look.

"Earth for Terrans," sighed Romero. "Just what we need right now, another bunch of crazies crawling out of the woodwork.

This group began taking out ads on the InfoCommNet a couple of weeks ago, warning that Earth's population has been infiltrated by alien spies. We've had no reason to take action against the EFT because up until now it's been nothing but talk. However, if they've upshifted to committing murder to make their point—"

"We need to haul in their leaders for questioning," Drew decided.

"I'm way ahead of you. And you need to step back from this and let us do our jobs. The M.E. is pushing this case to the top of her list. Gluckstein is combing databases to reconstruct the vic's last 24 hours, and Truman and Lupo are interviewing persons of interest as we speak. They're all good investigators, Townsend. They'll get whoever killed your friend, I promise."

Drew pasted a grateful smile on his face and kept it there until Romero had returned to his office and shut the door. The other Eligibles, meanwhile, were studiously avoiding making eye contact, even with one another, for fear of triggering an explosion of rage across the room.

Good, thought Drew as he reached into his desk drawer and palmed the device he'd concealed there. A small black tube ringed with ridges along half its length, it had been given to him by his Earth Intelligence handler. The encrypting comm was keyed to Drew's DNA. As he wrapped his fingers around it and squeezed gently, he could feel a soft tingling in the skin of his palm. He released his grip, then squeezed again, three times more in quick succession — a standard request for a meeting. There was no emergency, not yet.

The rest of the day went by with tortoise-like slowness and a suspicious lack of hard intel about the Patel murder crossing Drew's desk. To help take his mind off the case, Romero assigned him to Surveillance Monitoring — Sensitive Areas. These were the high-crime-rate blocks surrounding the Zone. His eyes roving constantly over a bank of twenty flat screens, in a period of four hours Drew witnessed — and forwarded video coverage of — fifteen muggings, more assaults than he could count, and the beginnings of two weapons deals, which were aborted when the parties involved realized they were being watched by remote vidcam. At the end of his shift, fighting an eyestrain headache that he was sure would have brought down a bull moose, Townsend found himself looking down the business end of a zapper as a ganger took careful aim at the surveillance drone that had followed him into an alleyway. Cursing, Drew punched the 'evade' button, a half-second too late. The screen went black.

"Bull's eye," he muttered darkly. *Good work, kid. One down and only about seven thousand to go.*

— « o » —

The EIS contact waiting for Townsend when he pulled into his half of the garage behind the octoplex on Lamont Street that evening was not Drew's handler.

"Where's Gow?"

The other man shrugged. "Otherwise occupied, so I'll have to do. What's on your mind, Townsend?" he asked, the patronizing tone of his voice suggesting that he already knew the answer.

"Bruni Patel was murdered last night."

"An unfortunate loss for all of us. He was a good agent."

"Save it for his eulogy," Drew snapped. "What's the EIS going to do about this?"

The man took a second to change expressions. Now he wore a superior, faintly feline smile on his face as he said in that same condescending voice, "Rest assured, Mr. Townsend, we are already doing it. We do not take lightly the murder of one of our operatives. An investigation has already been launched into the activities of the EFT."

"I want to be assigned to that investigation."

"Understandable — he was your friend."

"He was more than that. I owed him my life. And since I couldn't repay him by saving his, I plan to do the next best thing, which is to see to it that whoever killed him pays full price."

"An admirable goal, I'm sure. However, not a practical one. You have been entrusted with a very important mission, one with a narrow window of opportunity, and you need to devote your time and all your energy to preparing for it. Meanwhile, we will ensure that Mr. Patel receives justice, never fear."

This was the second time that Drew had been figuratively patted on the head and told to stay out of the way. Fighting to keep his voice steady, he pointed out, "My mission doesn't begin until I board a ship bound for Daisy Hub. Until then, be advised that I'm putting myself on this murder case. And you can tell the higher-ups not to worry about the mission — I'll be ready when that 'narrow window of opportunity' opens up."

"Excellent! I take it that you are fluent once more in Galactic Standard, then. All packed up? Ready to go at a moment's notice...?"

The threat implied by his words caused Drew's hands to curl into fists at his sides.

"Just because you have been forced into wait mode for the past three weeks doesn't mean the rest of us have," the man continued. "You're on the clock, Mr. Townsend, and we've been building you a credible backstory. Clearly, you've been too preoccupied lately to monitor your credit account. Perhaps you should check it out. And we're done here."

Without another word, the man strode past Drew, out of the garage and down the alley to the street, where a large black PV sat idling, waiting for him.

— « o » —

Townsend raced up the three flights of stairs to his apartment and went directly to the InfoComm unit on his desk.

There had been a lot of activity in his credit account over the past couple of months, none of it initiated by him.

Flowers purchased and ordered delivered to an address in Fairhaven Enclave six weeks earlier, and again two weeks ago. Dinner for two once a week at different restaurants. Box seat tickets to a low-grav basketball game. Pairs of admissions to the sim-arcade and the thrill park. A whopping big fuel bill. And that afternoon while on his way home from work, he had apparently stopped at a jeweler's shop and put a down payment on a ring. Drew called up a snap of his 'purchase'. The stone was modest but unmistakably a diamond.

All the relevant video footage had been expertly doctored. He didn't recognize the woman shown cuddling up to him in the various venues, but she had to be related to someone with influence. Someone who would do anything to prevent an ex-slammer rat from marrying into his or her family, including pull strings to have Drew's name put on the Relocation Authority's FIA list — For Immediate Assignment.

A chill trickled down his spine. He would need time to ferret out Bruni's killer. With luck, it would be a while before the 'narrow window of opportunity' opened. But if Drew had learned one thing in his 36 years of life, it was not to trust anyone's luck, especially his own.

Chapter 2

The next morning, with Plan B in place and eager to get started on his investigation, Drew put his PV in pursuit mode and overrode the grid. Traffic was light on the southbound urbanway. As he kicked his speed up to plus thirty, his comm unit suddenly squawked, startling him.

"Unidentified vehicle, it is a Class 1 moving violation to override grid control for the purpose of exceeding the speed limit on a four-lane city artery. Activate your transponder and discontinue manual operations immediately!"

Briefly, Drew considered discontinuing the comm unit instead. Then his common sense cut in, and he sighed and toggled the transponder switch. So, it would take him an extra fifteen minutes to get to the forensics lab. That wasn't necessarily a bad thing.

"Townsend, is that you?" demanded a voice he recognized. "I should have known. You just got your Eligibility reinstated, *amigo*. You want to lose it again for a lousy traffic citation?"

The thought had probably crossed his subconscious mind, Drew realized. Aloud, he replied, "Sorry, Miguel. I was a little preoccupied and forgot to switch over when I merged with the southbound."

"I believe you, but my captain says one warning only, and you've already had yours, several times. So no more fooling around, okay? Listen, I have to reprogram your on-board to take you to District Headquarters. The Chief wants to see you."

His heart reflexively filling with dread, Drew watched a series of lights blink across his control panel. "I don't suppose you have any idea why he's calling me in?"

"Not a clue, *amigo*. Have you taken any bribes lately?"

It was meant as a joke, but Drew wasn't smiling. A summons from the District Chief of Security was nothing to laugh about, especially when it came this early in the morning. Townsend had to be in some serious trouble. His cover could even be blown. If so, the usual betrayals of trust would hardly stack up in the Chief's mind against Drew's moonlighting as an agent for a black ops organization like the Earth Intelligence Service.

New storefronts and low-rise office buildings floated past him on both sides as the vehicle negotiated a series of broad, hilly downtown streets, finally turning off into a one-lane entranceway between two squat, gray brick structures. All downtown parking was underground, for security reasons. It was also gridded. As the control system neatly inserted Drew's vehicle into a numbered space and shut off the engine, he automatically checked the chronometer on the dash. It read 8:05.

Three minutes later, he was standing alone in the anteroom to the office of Melville Ridout, Chief of Security for the District of New Chicago, as well as voting member and Past Deputy Chair of SISCO — the covert security branch of Earth's Space Installation Authority. SISCO and Earth Intelligence had been working at cross-purposes practically from the day the EIS was formed, so keeping SISCO unaware of the EIS's existence was a top priority for every agent.

There were comfortable leather chairs in the room, and at any other time Drew might have found them inviting — but not this morning. This morning, his nerves were dancing. Something important had to have brought the Chief in to work at this early hour, and Drew had a terrible feeling he knew what it was. If his cover had been compromised, he would need to improvise a very convincing con. Try as he might, however, he couldn't get his thoughts to settle into any sort of coherent plan. It took him a few seconds to realize why: the anteroom was set up specifically to put anyone like Townsend off his game.

It made sense. The Chief had worked his way up through the ranks, and a good cop had to understand — and use — psychology. Drew gazed around the room once more, seeing it for the weapon that it was and admiring its effectiveness.

The receptionist's desk was a slab of real redwood, polished to a flawless and intimidating luster, holding an inlaid InfoComm screen and comm speaker and absolutely nothing else. Rich, impersonal, and cold in both senses of the word, since the air was also perceptibly below normal room temperature.

The pale gold carpet gave luxuriously underfoot, its deep pile casually swallowing the sound of his movements. And those stern-faced portraits of previous District Chiefs on the walls were real paintings in ornate wooden frames. Drew could feel disapproval glowering down on him from every direction, further chilling the atmosphere.

"Please come in, Field Investigator Townsend." The voice that rumbled out of the comm unit on the desk coincided with the soundless, automatic opening of the Chief's door.

Nice touch. Of course, now that he knew what game they were playing…

Drew took a deep breath, selected an appropriate level of confidence to display, and strode into the Great Man's sanctum.

Ridout looked up as Drew entered, and motioned him to one of the three guest chairs in the room. "Have a seat, Townsend."

Drew pulled the nearest chair a little closer to the desk and sat, his gaze riveted on the thick sheaf of printout with three datawafers on top of it that lay at the Chief's left hand. Ridout, he recalled from an earlier briefing, was very fond of paper. He even printed out reports and kept them as hard copy in an old-fashioned metal filing cabinet. That stack of paper on his desk could be anything. Under the circumstances, however, it was most likely Drew's criminal and service records.

Ridout cleared his throat and began briskly, "I won't waste time with pleasantries, Townsend. I've called you here because there has been a suspicious death at one of our space installations, and SISCO has asked me to choose our best investigator for an undercover mission. From what I've seen of your career file, you're perfect for the assignment. You're thorough and tenacious, with the most efficient murder-solving record in the District — except for my own, of course," he added, leaning back with a smile. "And you have a checkered past, so you'll fit right in on Daisy Hub."

Feeling as though the room had just skewed itself sideways, Drew struggled to keep his expression neutral. A suspicious death? An undercover mission? Had the EIS ordered a kill to get him shipped out to the Hub? Was that what the agent in his garage had been hinting at yesterday evening?

"So this is a mission briefing, sir?"

"Of course," snapped the Chief. "What the hell did you think it was?" Not waiting for an answer to his question, Ridout leaned forward again and continued, "The victim is Karim Khaloub, until two weeks ago station manager of the Hub. That's when his body was discovered in an airlock, in his pajamas, frozen stiff. The Relocation Authority is screaming foul, claiming that someone on the crew must have taken him out, believing that he was there to spy on them." Ridout paused, scowling thoughtfully, then shook his head. "Even if that were true, which SISCO doubts, Khaloub would have been a poor choice for the job. He was still in his twenties, fresh off desk duty at Data Management, and Daisy Hub was his first off-planet assignment. We decided that anyone we sent out there had better have a little more mileage on him, and a lot more savvy. I've been reviewing your biodata, Field Investigator, and you certainly fit the bill.

"It's lucky for SISCO that the Relocation Authority saw fit to reinstate your Eligibility. Most reformed criminals don't even bother applying, because they know how high the odds are stacked against them. But you're not just any ex-slammer rat, are you?"

"No, sir, I'm not," said Drew, straightening in his chair, assuming his best poker face and purposely looking directly into the Chief's eyes. If Ridout suspected him of being a mole, that was where the tell would be.

The other man didn't even blink. "Be warned, Townsend: you're going to need all your skills on this assignment, both criminal and investigative," he continued. "Daisy Hub is our farthest-flung inspection and resupply station. It's crewed by Eligibles, of course, but these people have eccentricities. Quirks. They aren't mentally ill — they wouldn't be Eligible if they were. Let's just say that they don't work well with others."

Inwardly, Drew permitted himself a smile. So, not a tell — a challenge, one that he felt certain would pique Townsend's interest.

Ridout picked up the pages of printout, jogged them up, and replaced them in a neat stack on the desktop. "And, of course, there are the Nandrians, who apparently don't work with others, period," he sighed. "The local Ranger detachment has already initiated an investigation, but their preliminary report is laughable, and SISCO doesn't believe they're getting much help from those mavericks and misfits on the Hub. That's what can happen, I guess, when all the bad apples end up in one basket. And that's why we've strong-armed the Relocation Authority into appointing an experienced field investigator — you — as the new station manager."

Drew's stomach tipped over into a barrel roll. Station manager? That wasn't the assignment the EIS had trained him for!

Ridout's expression flickered briefly. "We've built you a cover story and Security is already transmitting your new documentation to Platform Zulu and Daisy Hub," he went on. "Naturally, you'll be maintaining that cover by doing whatever it is the station manager does, including filing routine reports with the SIA; at the same time, you'll also be transmitting updates on the investigation to SISCO. The encryption codes have been embedded into your new biowafer. Say SISCO rapidly twice at the beginning and end of your report. The message will sound like static to anyone without the proper clearance. We'll keep silence at our end unless there's an emergency. In that case, you'll receive a request for clarification, your cue to use your biowafer to unscramble the static under the transmission. This case is a real mess, Townsend. We believe only an inside man who's also a bad apple will be able to sort it out."

A real mess? It was going to be a nightmare. SISCO had co-opted Drew's mission for the EIS, and there was no way he could turn down this assignment without raising a lot of red flags. So, he said the only thing he could under the circumstances:

"Yes, sir. When does my long-hopper leave?"

"In three hours. Don't worry about the formalities — your relocation paperwork is already in the system, and I'll notify your precinct commander personally. You should have just enough time to pack and report to the airfield."

Ridout scooped up the datawafers and held them out to him, across the desk. "Here is all the information we have on the case on Daisy Hub, the biofiles of the station crew, your revised biodata, and whatever we've managed to learn about the Nandrians. The Hub specs and deck layouts, along with certain other things you'll need, will be waiting for you on board the ship. You'll have plenty of time to study them en route to your destination. You'd better hurry home, Townsend. I'm depending on you to wrap up this investigation as quickly as possible."

"Yes, sir." Drew stood and turned to go.

"Oh, and, Townsend?"

One stride away from the door, Drew paused and looked back over his shoulder. Ridout sat motionless behind his desk, staring fixedly at the stack of hard copy on top of it.

"Yes, sir?"

The Chief took a deep breath and looked up. "Irene denies it, but evidence doesn't lie. A man with your past and your life experiences should have known that it would be a cold day in hell before I let you marry my niece."

For the second time that morning Drew's world took a sudden leftward tilt. Ridout's niece? Of all the people to pick! But now it made sense. The EIS had done such a good job of falsifying records to support his cover story that it had become a con, and Ridout had fallen for it. And Ridout wasn't just someone who knew someone who could pull strings — he was the one whose say-so got things done. Things like bouncing Drew's name to the top of the FIA list, making him immediately available for this conveniently-timed undercover assignment for SISCO.

The EIS had planned to slip him into a low-profile position where he could observe for a while before making any moves. SISCO was putting him into the hot seat straightaway as the station manager, negating weeks of training and preparation and forcing him to learn a whole new job on the fly. And in case that wasn't challenging enough, Drew had now graduated from mole to double agent, with two separate cover stories to keep straight and two covert agencies to report to, neither one of which would hesitate to kill him if it thought he had revealed its presence on Daisy Hub to the other one. It was like walking a tightrope while juggling knives.

Drew's gut was uncomfortably tight, but once again, there was nothing to say except, "Yes, sir."

"Dismissed."

— « o » —

Drew went to the precinct house first, to clean out his desk. Specifically, he needed to download all the available information on the Bruni Patel murder case and retrieve his encrypting comm. News of his off-planet posting had preceded him, so nobody was surprised that he was leaving. Romero wasn't happy about it but sincerely wished him luck and shook his hand. The other Eligibles cast openly envious looks in his direction. Everyone else was out in the field. There was a sour taste of unfinished business at the back of Townsend's throat as he walked out of the ward room for the last time, headed for his PV.

In a hurry to get home and pack, he programmed a more direct route than usual into his on-board, along the canal and past Fairhaven Enclave. He'd been offered an apartment in Fairhaven when his Eligibility was reinstated but had turned it down, preferring to stay in the one on Lamont Street. Thirteen years earlier, this had been the only building willing to rent to him when he was released from detention. Now, despite its proximity to the Zone, it was the only place that felt like home.

As the road curved left around a greenbelt area, Drew switched to manual control and bore right, away from the traffic grid, into a twisting maze of older residential side streets. The ride became progressively bumpier and more unsettling the closer he got to the Zone. Pavements were buckled, overhead lighting had been vandalized, storm drains were clogged with garbage and debris. At this hour the streets were quiet, but he knew from experience that silence could be deceptive. Drew gritted his teeth and focused on counting blocks, not wanting to miss his turn. Street names and speed limit signs were unreadable in this part of the city, PVs were extremely scarce, and other than the video drones that roamed the area during the daylight hours, Security was damn near nonexistent. That was why he barely paused when turning into the driveway beside his building and didn't stop until he was parked inside the garage behind it.

Today was the last time he would be doing this as well. Drew made a mental note to commconnect with Barry Novak. Security not being the best paid of occupations, Bruni had arranged for Townsend to borrow a personal vehicle from Novak's company, SecuriTech. The PV would have to be returned now that Drew had received his first off-world posting.

His first. Karim Khaloub's first. Both as station managers. He and the victim had that much in common. And Khaloub had ended up not only dead, but suspiciously so. The Relocation Authority refused to put even potential troublemakers in positions of power, so Khaloub must have been squeaky-clean at the time of his appointment. If foul play was involved and the EIS wasn't, then something must have happened on Daisy Hub, something that gave somebody a reason to kill the boss. According to Ridout, the Hub was crewed by "mavericks and misfits", so Drew had to consider the possibility that perhaps the target hadn't been Khaloub personally, but rather the position he held. If so, then whoever stepped in to replace him would be in danger as well.

Abruptly, he became aware that the vehicle's flatscreen had been flashing a question at him: *Commence lockdown procedure? Y or N*

Drew thumbed the screen and scrambled out of the vehicle, his mind already sorting through his transportable possessions. There would be luggage mass restrictions on the long-hopper and probably on Daisy Hub as well. He would have to leave a lot of his favorite things behind, quite possibly forever.

Drew shook off the sadness of that thought before it could sink in. There would be time later for separation anxiety. His ship was scheduled to leave in less than two hours and he still had to pack and get out to the airfield. Swinging through his front door, he slipped out of his jacket and knelt to open the leather trunk that had been serving as his end table for the past eight years. Not many items had found their way inside during that time. With one exception, they were gifts from Bruni Patel. All of them were precious. None of them were staying behind. A jar of curry powder, a box of jasmine tea, a tin of cocoa paste, a vacuum-sealed bag of dried figs — literally a taste of the world travel Eligibles like Bruni were able to enjoy, dangled in place of the proverbial carrot to keep Drew working on getting his own Eligibility reinstated. Ironically, Townsend was about to travel much farther than Bruni ever had, to a place where none of these delicacies would be available.

As he was emptying the trunk to make room for clothing, Drew noticed the area rug. It was blue, almost the same shade of royal blue as the piece of carpet under the desk in Ridout's private office. They had quirks, the Chief had said. Why not? This rug would have been replaced soon anyway. The pile was worn and pocked by at least twenty years' worth of furniture legs. It was perfect.

Drew found a length of rope in the bottom of his closet, then proceeded to roll and tie the rug into a sausage for transport. Ten minutes later, the trunk was filled, locked, and sitting beside the carpet roll just inside the apartment's front door. After arranging for his transportation to the airfield, Drew sent a comm note to the building super, who was usually unavailable but whose recording unit at least sounded apologetic about it. At SecuriTech, he spoke to a desk clerk who patched him through to Barry Novak's private message recorder. Finally, Drew palmed the encrypting comm, squeezed gently to activate it, then squeezed again twice to send a 'touch-base-all-green' message.

It wasn't the message he wanted to send. The one that most accurately described his current situation would be an eruption of profanity, followed by a string of exclamation marks. Unfortunately, his comm device provided a limited menu of tactile transmissions, none of them with frustrated or incredulous subtext. However, there was a 'green' aspect to report: Drew was in fact being sent to Daisy Hub, which was where the EIS needed him to go.

Turning the barrelful of bad apples on Daisy Hub into an off-planet EIS cell would, by definition, not have been an easy assignment even when it wasn't complicated by a murder investigation for SISCO. Now, it could very well be an impossible mission.

And yet...

Drew had already done a couple of impossible things. He was the only field investigator in all of Americas and possibly on the entire planet to be hired by Security while still serving time in detention. And he'd managed to get his Eligibility reinstated, despite having a criminal record. If he could do that, there might be no limit to what he could accomplish on Daisy Hub.

Organize the cell and solve the murder, without breaking his cover. It was a tall order, to be sure, but Drew loved a challenge; and the more he thought about this one, the more confident he felt about his ability to handle it. After all, he was thorough and tenacious, a gifted investigator, and an experienced and very talented con artist.

Sometimes, he even conned himself.

Chapter 3

The long-hopper did not lift off as scheduled. Something about waiting for a second passenger to board. Drew didn't bother asking for details. He had found a slender briefcase under his seat, containing the promised materials and a palm-held playback device. By now he was engrossed in scanning the contents of the datawafers Ridout had given him, checking to see whether anything had changed since his most recent EIS briefing on Daisy Hub and its crew.

When fully staffed, the Hub had a complement of 53. It was currently operating with a crew of 46. Most of the names and faces on the station's crew manifest were familiar to Drew by now, as were their reasons for being posted to the Hub: speaking out against the Relocation Authority, rocking the Earth Council boat, or just being an embarrassment to someone with influence, as described in both of Drew's cover stories. SISCO's version was almost identical to the one fabricated by the EIS, but the doctored video clips showed him picking out the ring for the daughter of a District Councilor. Nobody with any sort of clout wanted Townsend marrying into the family, it seemed. Ironically, although several of the Hub's crew had been arrested, not one of them had ever been formally tried and convicted of a crime; in fact, once he arrived, the only one aboard Daisy Hub with a criminal record would be the cop sent to investigate the suspicious death.

There were a couple of new additions to the crew besides himself, and Drew read their bios with great interest. Someone named Nestor Quan was now the Hub's Disease Control Officer. Evidently, there had been an outbreak of Angel of Death in that sector of Earth space. There was also a woman whose image on the screen stared back at him with an expression of mild reproach: Teri Mintz. According to her biodata, she had once been a well-known professional singer.

Gavin Holchuk was on the crew as well, listed as Chief Cargo Inspector. Drew had flagged that name the first time he'd seen it on the manifest.

Around the same time as Townsend was being in-processed by the detention facility, Holchuk became a hot CommNews item. An Eligible married to an Ineligible, he had been turning down off-planet postings for years, refusing to be separated from his family. Then Holchuk became the only survivor of a vehicular 'mishap' that killed both his wife and their young daughter. Crazed with grief, he loudly and publicly accused the Relocation Authority of engineering the tragedy in order to remove any further obstacle to his being posted off-world. More disturbing, however, was his insistence that his daughter was alive somewhere, that she had been stolen by the Authority and given to someone else to raise. He searched for her for more than a year before the Relocation Authority finally ended his investigation by shipping him off to Daisy Hub.

The settling-in period on the Hub had been "difficult and turbulent", and, eighteen Earth years later, he still apparently resented having to follow rules and regulations. Understandable. In his place, who wouldn't harbor a grudge against Earth's Authorities and anyone who represented them? Karim Khaloub's very presence must have been a daily reminder to him of what he had lost. Means, motive and opportunity, but especially motive, put Holchuk's name at the top of the suspect list in Khaloub's murder.

"Get your damned hands off me, you big ape! I'm telling you, there's been a mistake!"

The second passenger had arrived. A woman. Her voice was low-pitched and hauntingly familiar. He was still trying to place it when three people suddenly burst through the door, two of them muscle in gray Airfield Security uniforms. Drew watched with interest as they maneuvered the frantically struggling third person into the passenger cabin. At first, all he could see of her upper body was a tossing whirlwind of long auburn hair. Her shoes were auburn as well, with pointed toes that painfully connected several times with the guards' legs as she was dragged, pushed, and finally thrown, squealing and spitting, into the seat across the cabin from Drew's. The two men had to plant her forcefully twice before she would stay put, enabling them to leave.

She tossed her head and the curtain of hair parted at last, and Drew recognized her from the crew manifest: Teri Mintz. Great. Just what every space station needed — a resident wildcat with a two-octave range.

The wildcat shot a venomous glare at two retreating gray-clad backs before sinking into her seat with a sigh of pure disgust, her generous bosom heaving beneath a now-disheveled beige shirt and jacket.

A low vibration began rising through the deck plating and into Drew's boot soles. The craft was tilting into liftoff position.

Long-hoppers weren't passenger shuttles or interhub liners; they were government transport vessels, stripped down to the essentials and equipped with a combination of atmospheric and deep space propulsion systems — no, that was too flattering. Long-hoppers were basically reinforced metal buckets hitching rides on fuel tanks with engines attached to them. They violated several Fleet Control safety protocols and were consequently banned from docking at any of the orbiting transfer stations. That suited Earth Council just fine. Long-hoppers launched directly from the planetary surface, carrying classified cargo, diplomatic couriers, agents on covert missions, and the occasional councilor whose transportation allowance had run dry. So, there might be an announcement to buckle up or there might not be, depending on the mood of the pilot.

Suddenly, Drew realized what it was he'd been smelling ever since boarding the ship — antiseptic cleaning solvent. No-frills space travel wasn't everybody's cup of tea. Quickly he threw all the loose items around him into his briefcase and stowed it in the locker at his feet. Then he reached overhead, found the restraining harness and snapped it around his seat, noting with satisfaction that the wildcat had already done the same. Good. She might be angry, but she wasn't stupid.

And until the ship had escaped Earth's gravity field, she wouldn't be dangerous either. Recalling the instructions on his briefing 'pad, Drew forced himself to take long, deep breaths and did his best to ignore the strange, almost orgasmic sensation of blood rushing away from the front half of his body.

Several long minutes later, the long-hopper had broken free and they were on their way out of the solar system. The invisible rockslide that had pinned Drew to his seat was gone, up and down were back where they belonged, more or less, and the restraining harnesses had returned to manual control. A hardier and more experienced traveler than himself might unlatch at this point and try floating around the cabin like a fish; Drew felt his gorge rise and searched for the location of the washroom, and the spot on the bulkhead from which he would have to push off to launch himself toward it.

As he sat waiting for his stomach to settle, he watched the wildcat warily, half-expecting her to turn green and fill the cabin with globules of partly-digested dinner. Instead, her face crumpled into a portrait of frustration.

"Damn!" she muttered tearfully. "Damn, damn, *damn* you, Harry Mintz! I hope you rot in hell!"

Drew swallowed experimentally. It was probably safe to speak now. "You had a ticket for some other destination?"

She started at the sound of his voice. In an instant, her features recomposed themselves. Teri straightened her shoulders and tugged her jacket lapels square, but she was bobbing helplessly back and forth between her seat and the restraint, and must have realized her dignity was beyond recovery at this point. "Tell me you're not from one of the tabs," she pleaded.

Afraid of being misconstrued, Drew suppressed his smile. "I'm Drew Townsend, the new station manager of Daisy Hub."

Her face fell even further. Of course. There was only one thing worse than having your life splashed across the tabs, and that was to have a knockdown battle with Security in front of your brand-new boss. "Terrific," she moaned.

According to his briefings, this was going to be an interval-long spaceflight, through three Gates, with no amenities. He'd better at least try to put her at ease. "Well, I know what *I* did to earn this assignment. What's *your* story, Ms. Mintz?"

"Teri. One 'r', ends in 'i'," she added wearily. "My stage name is Teri Martin — used to be, anyway, before I married that slimeball, Harry, seven years ago. When I divorced him last year, I decided to try kick-starting my career with a comeback gig on one of the resort hubs. I told Arnie — that's my agent — I told him I'd take anything, even back-up singer to an opening act, just to get onstage, somewhere away from Harry. I warned him not to let Harry find out where I was going. He has friends, you know. Harry does. Big, important friends."

Her expression was darkening. Best not to let her dwell on Harry and his friends. "So, Arnie made the booking?" Drew prompted her.

She nodded wistfully. "I was supposed to open for Vic Stratton in the Starlite Lounge on Vegas Hub. A twenty-four interval contract. It was perfect." She paused, frowning. "Too damned perfect, now that I think about it. But it got me out to the airfield, with my luggage. Gawd, I'm such an idiot!"

Time to change tack again. "So, you're a singer?"

"Used to be."

"I think I've heard you sing. Not in person, but I recognize your voice—"

"—from the CommAd jingles," she supplied bitterly. "Right. That was a little bone Harry threw me the first time I threatened to leave him. Hell of a way for a career to die. Later, I cringed every time I heard one of those ads. For months, I couldn't even bear to look at the InfoComm screen. I missed Angela's wedding, Soledad's operation..."

"Excuse me?"

"U-Town," she replied, in a voice that seemed to add, 'and what cave have *you* been hiding in?' "It's my favorite interactive destination. I was a charter subscriber. All the characters knew me. Jake confided in me whenever he had a problem, even called me his second mother. And now, thanks to that rotten ex-husband of mine, the poor little tyke will have to carry on all by himself. And, worse, I'll be bumped off the jury at Brock's trial. Damn!"

Okay, enough, Drew decided. This woman was fretting at having to leave behind her a virtual town filled with fictional characters. Compared to some of the experiences described in the crew's biofiles, her life had been a seaside picnic.

"I hope you haven't forgotten all the other ways to use the InfoComm, Ms. Mintz."

The sudden formality in his voice made her glance up. Her eyes were large and golden-brown, and they widened with puzzled apprehension as they locked with his. "What did you say?"

"Daisy Hub is a working station," he reminded her sternly.

"So this is a placement interview, Mr. Townsend?" she asked, her chin acquiring a decidedly stubborn slant. "I hope the company can train me, then, because I very much doubt whether you'll have any use for my previous job skills."

Or her current attitude, Drew added mentally. But that was just a façade thrown up by fear. He'd erected enough of his own in the past to be able to see through them now, and what he saw in Teri Mintz had interesting possibilities.

She was Eligible, which meant she was highly intelligent; but she was smart, too, a survivor. He liked the fact that she was strong enough to stand up to a superior, albeit with a wobble in her voice. He liked even better that she couldn't possibly have killed Karim Khaloub. He suspected he would need somebody like her on the Hub once he began his investigation. And he knew exactly where to put her to best use.

"I don't imagine your skills will be an issue," he replied. "I've been reviewing the crew manifest and I think I know which would be the best position for you." He paused, and the angle of her chin increased perceptibly. Drew caught a flash of defiance in her eyes as well and for just a split-second sympathized with Harry Mintz. "I'm going to assign you to Gavin Holchuk's detail. He's the Chief Cargo Inspector, and—"

"—and what? He needs someone to sing him to sleep at night?" she bristled.

"That's enough! You're the one who mentioned job retraining. Do you want it or not?"

Still restrained by the harness, she collapsed and shrank, like a rapidly deflating balloon. "I want my life back, dammit," she said tearfully.

"I'm afraid that's not an option right now. Listen, I don't know whether you'll ever be a professional singer again, Teri, but I can tell you this: you'll find a lot of kindred spirits where you're going, especially Gavin Holchuk. You two have a lot in common."

That sparked her interest. "You're kidding. Someone else who ticked off Harry Mintz?"

"Not exactly. Holchuk ticked off the Relocation Authority."

"Ouch!" Then, switching to Galactic Standard, she asked, "So how long until we get there?"

For the moment that it took him to translate her question into Ameranglo, and his reply back into Standard, Drew was speechless. But she was right to begin using the off-world language now, he realized, since it would be the common tongue spoken on Daisy Hub; and despite his bravado yesterday in the garage on Lamont Street, Drew hadn't held up his side of an entire conversation in Standard in more than twenty years.

"We be — arrival — in one interval. That is ten plus one days of Earth," he said at last.

Teri's eyes were dancing. With visible effort, she managed not to laugh as she inquired, "Which Enclave are you from, Mr. Townsend?"

He was able to reply almost immediately. "No Enclave." *Not recently, anyway. Not since I was turfed out of Clearmeadow at the age of twelve and left to survive as best I could on the streets of New Chicago....* His jaw tightened momentarily at the memory.

"That explains it," Teri declared. "We speak — spoke — Gally all the time in the Enclave. Fortunately," she added, her lips now curving in a wicked grin, "we have ten plus one days of Earth to get you up to an acceptable level of fluency."

She was batting her eyelashes at him from across the cabin. Drew felt his face grow warm and his stomach lurch again, but not because of weightlessness.

It was going to be a very long interval.

Chapter 4

"Ten plus one days of Earth" later, the long-hopper finally docked at Observation Platform Zulu, just four hours by short-hopper away from Daisy Hub. Unaware of the situation, both Drew and Teri were out of their seats when the ship entered the platform's gravity field. They landed with a double thump, Drew on his side, Teri on her backside, both uttering the same angry expletive — in Gally — as they hit the deck.

"He did that on purpose!" Teri fumed.

Unfortunately, she was right. A councilor or a courier — somebody who could have lodged a complaint or made things difficult for the ship's pilot — would probably have received the courtesy of a warning.

Drew heard something knocking against the hull. Docking clamps, most likely. "Come on," he said, rubbing his hip with one hand as he pulled Teri to her feet with the other. "We have to debark now."

"Oh, no… Do people have to see me like this?" she moaned, pawing at her hair and her clothing. "I haven't showered in — gawd, I feel like something found in the wreckage."

She actually didn't look too bad, but Drew wasn't about to tell her that. After traveling together in a tin can for eleven Earth days, swabbing with pre-moistened towels, sleeping with the light constantly on, eating vacuum-sealed field rations, and sharing a single null-G toilet, he and Teri Mintz had reached an understanding, of sorts. She now understood that he could not be moved by any quantity of whining and complaining, and he now understood that nothing he said to her, regardless of its content or his manner while speaking, would get the desired or expected response. In part, that was because of his accent, which was apparently heavy enough to garble the meaning of some words. Still, even Teri had to acknowledge that his fluency and grammar had remarkably improved over the past week and a half.

Four men emerged from the cockpit then and busied themselves around the cabin. One of them paused to toss each of the passengers a silver-colored bundle and a transparent bubble helmet. The rest ignored them.

Teri had obviously done this before — she was suited up in about five minutes. Drew had been briefed about the exosuits but had never actually put one on. Teri watched him fidget and fumble with the unfamiliar fastenings for a while, then commented drily, "You really are a space virgin, aren't you, Townsend?"

Yes, he was. And he shouldn't have been, not according to his cover story. Eligibles went into space all the time. They vacationed on the resort hubs. They attended conferences on Mars and Luna. Drew felt his chest tighten and his cheeks grow warm. "I'm just clumsy, that's all," he muttered unhappily. "And if you really want to help…"

"Okay, okay," she sighed, putting her helmet down on one of the seats. "Stand still for a minute."

Behind her back, a crewman smirked knowingly at them as he worked on something around the entrance hatch. A choice comment sprang into Drew's mouth at that moment, but he forced himself to swallow it. He and Teri had probably been the in-flight entertainment for these guys, all the way from Earth. Fortunately, except for some profanity that had slipped out during one of their disagreements, Drew had been a perfect gentleman the whole time. And what was more important, he hadn't said anything that could compromise either one of his missions, or his ability to carry them out.

The crewman straightened up and backed away from the hatch, nodding satisfaction at his handiwork. "Whenever you're ready, professors," he tossed at them, then wheeled and headed back to the cockpit.

As it turned out, Drew hadn't done too badly with the suit. Teri only had to make a couple of adjustments. When she was satisfied that everything was airtight, she helped him lock his helmet in place before reaching for her own. He forced his gloved fingers through the handle of his briefcase and moved ahead of her to the exit.

The hatch had converted into an airlock. Fortunately for Drew, everything was clearly labeled. He cycled the air, then stepped off the ship — and froze.

He was standing on the curved 'floor' of an umbilical walkway, a flexible pipe about two meters in diameter. Somewhere ahead of him lay another airlock door. The walkway was opaque. Glow-bars stuck haphazardly to the metal ribs that hugged its walls and ceiling gave off a dim, sporadic light that seemed to drain everything of color. Suddenly, Drew's breathing was loud in his ears, and he could feel perspiration tattooing his skin like an icy shower. As a field investigator back on Earth, he would have called for support before venturing into an alleyway that looked like this. But this wasn't Earth, he reminded himself sternly — it was deep space. His only 'support' was Teri Mintz. And no matter how he tried to persuade his imagination that he was simply boarding the Inter-Union ferry at O'Hare, his imagination — and his gut — knew better.

"Keep walking," warned Teri's voice inside his helmet. "Or stand aside and let me lead. The air supply in this suit is good for about a minute, that's all."

Let her lead? He didn't dare. Drew tightened his grip on his briefcase and willed his legs to begin moving again.

They reached the platform's airlock in about a dozen steps. The door opened easily. Passing through it, the two travelers found themselves at the top of a long ramp. Drew paused to remove his gloves and helmet and heard Teri's sigh echo his own. After eleven days of weightlessness, his muscles weren't at all happy about having to walk in one G. The ramp couldn't have sloped more than fifteen degrees downward, but he may as well have been looking down the side of a mountain. And he never had been fond of heights.

"Don't stop now!" Clearly, Teri's sigh had been one of impatience.

There was nothing to do but grit his teeth and make his way to the bottom. Partway there, Drew glanced up and saw a tall, square-jawed man in a scarlet and dark blue uniform walking purposefully toward them across what appeared to be an empty warehouse floor. The man grinned broadly and waved without breaking stride. When he reached the bottom of the ramp, he spread his arms wide and bellowed heartily, "Welcome to the Zoo! I'm Ranger Captain Steve Bonelli. We don't get many visitors passing through here, so I have to tell you, we're really glad to see you folks."

"I can imagine," Drew replied wearily. "I'm Drew Townsend," he added, shifting the briefcase from right to left and extending his hand for shaking. Instantly he wished that he hadn't. Bonelli had a grip like a bear trap. "And this is—"

"Teri Martin," she cut in, her voice even throatier than usual. "I'm a singer. Perhaps you've heard of me?"

Bonelli's eyes lit up at the sight of her. "An entertainer! No, ma'am, I can't honestly say that I have. But I am very pleased to make your acquaintance." Bonelli swept his cap off, revealing a military buzz-cut of indeterminate color. Wisely, he chose not to shake her hand. But Teri's curves were announcing themselves inside that silver suit, and Drew could tell from the way the captain's eyes moved over her precisely what was going through his mind.

He could also tell from the way Teri fidgeted beside him that she was in no mood to be ogled this hungrily by someone who didn't even have the grace to pretend to be a fan. Her chin was rising, a dangerous sign, and the brown eyes were filling with storm clouds. Drew couldn't help noticing that Bonelli's nose had been broken in the past. If the Ranger didn't look somewhere else fast, it was probably going to be broken again. Back in New Chicago, an assault on a field officer would have got them both detained until charges could be laid. Out here in the boonies? Drew didn't really want to find out.

"Captain?" he ventured, bravely mustering his imperfect Gally vocabulary. "The travel has been long. I'm sure Ms. Martin has a desire to freshen her body before we continue on to Daisy Hub...?"

There was a scathing retort on her tongue, he was sure, regarding Drew's own "body freshness" at this point, but he was pleased to see that Teri was smart enough — or wanted the promised shower badly enough — to swallow her sarcasm and wait for the guide summoned by Bonelli to lead her off the landing deck.

Once the others were safely out of earshot, Drew turned to the captain and said, "We need to talk about the death research. Is your meanwhile report finished yet?"

Startled, Bonelli stared at him for a moment before replying, "Yes, sir, and as soon as Security passes it on to the Space Installation Authority, I'm sure they'll be transmitting a copy to your office."

"You don't understand. I have Security in my past time."

The Ranger shook his head, his patience, not to mention his decoding ability, clearly being tested. "They didn't give you much warning about this posting, did they? With all due respect, Mr. Townsend, I know you spent time attached to a District Security precinct, but that doesn't make you a field investigator. The Relocation Authority seems to enjoy putting round pegs in square holes. It sticks people in all sorts of places before assigning them off-planet. If you really were a cop, you'd have been posted to the Rangers, not given a make-work desk job like managing Daisy Hub. So, my advice to you is to stay clear and let me complete my investigation. I promise to keep you advised of any breakthroughs in the case."

Drew considered carefully before speaking again. After all, SISCO had falsified his biodata in order to establish his cover. It wouldn't do for him to blow it before he'd even had a chance to look over the crime scene. But Khaloub's death was weeks old, practically a cold case by now, and it would feel like such a waste of time starting the investigation completely from scratch if the Rangers had already questioned the mavericks and misfits working the Hub — and there was something disturbingly familiar about Bonelli that kept slipping just out of his mind's reach.

Suddenly, a comm speaker directly behind Drew blurted metallically, "We have a shuttle coming in, Steve. You'd better clear the deck."

Bonelli jerked his head in the direction of an access door and began leading the way. "That'll be the short-hopper from Daisy Hub," he tossed over his shoulder. "I alerted Mom as soon as we began tracking your approach."

"Mom?" Drew echoed, certain he must have misheard.

"Ruby McNeil, the assistant station manager."

"And she's your mother?"

Bonelli laughed. "She's everyone's mother. You'll understand when you meet her. Come on, desk boy. If you're still on the deck when those bay doors open, you'll be a flesh-flavored ice cube."

"Yes, sucked out into space," Drew supplied, already weary of the Ranger's patronizing attitude. "They do educate us before they send us out here, you know."

"Not about everything, son. Our landing deck and the one on Daisy Hub are equipped with Meniscus Field generators, courtesy of the Nandrians. A little bit of technology they slipped us under the table when the Great Galactic Council wasn't looking. Air can't get out, but ships can get in. Unfortunately, the field can only form in a supercooled area, which means the air is too cold and dry to be breathed by Humans. And you're better off not knowing how we learned that."

The Nandrians didn't work with anyone, period, the Chief had said. Interesting.

The two men had reached a heavy metal door that was taking its own sweet time about sliding open. Even though he knew the temperature hadn't changed, Drew shivered.

"Don't worry. The bay doors can't operate until all other accessways are sealed shut," Bonelli assured him. "Once the short-hopper is inside, it will take about ten standard minutes — fifteen Earth minutes, if you prefer — for the landing deck environment to normalize. Then we'll go back in and meet the pilot."

On the other side of the hatchway, Drew peeled off the silver suit, then found his eyes drawn to an overhead monitor beside the door. Bonelli hadn't exaggerated about the temperature drop. Drew watched in fascination as the room they'd just left frosted over, and a strangely configured vessel floated across the screen and settled onto the deck on three pairs of spidery legs.

"You can exhale now," the Ranger murmured into his left ear. Drew started, only that second aware that he had, indeed, been holding his breath. He started again at the sound of a buzzer going off directly over his head. "That tells us the doors to space are shut," Bonelli translated. "When the heat's been replaced, this hatch will return to manual control."

"So there's actually air in there now?"

Bonelli nodded. "You'll flash-freeze in there, but you won't suffocate."

"Incredible! Who else knows about this—" He paused, and a second later the word came to him. "—this technology?"

"Everybody but you, desk boy," chuckled the Ranger. "Earth Council put it here just over a year ago, and I'll bet you even credit that there's a team of physicists busily 'discovering' it as we speak. For obvious reasons, part of the deal is that we have to protect the identity of our supplier."

Drew watched the monitor screen for a long moment. The layer of white was slowly shrinking, like a dusting of light snow blown by a steady wind. Meanwhile, a tiny, twisting suspicion was setting off alarms at the back of his mind. "So this is highest level of secret?" Drew inquired softly.

"More or less."

"Are you not risking much, then, by telling me about it, since I've only just arrived?"

Bonelli's mouth puckered thoughtfully. "No, actually, I'm not," he replied at last. "Everyone who's posted here knows about it, since the short-hopper decks on Zulu and Daisy Hub are testing sites. As the station manager, you were going to find out about it anyway. Besides, let's face it, we all have a snowball's chance in hell of being recalled to Earth or reassigned, so why add stress to the situation by worrying about hypothetical threats to security? If a real one actually arose...? I'd say we're equipped to handle it ourselves."

For the second time in ten minutes, Drew forgot to breathe. So the Rangers were exiled out here, just like the crew of the Hub? An image flashed before his mind's eye of a man left stranded on a landing deck as the bay doors opened and the Meniscus Field generator kicked in. Perhaps because someone had discovered that he wasn't a bad apple like the rest of them, and that he could, in fact, be recalled and reassigned, and therefore posed a security threat?

The suspect list was growing by the minute. Earth Council itself might be involved; or, even worse, the Nandrians. And what about the man beside him, the patronizing lech wearing a Ranger's uniform? Drew was reasonably certain there were no criminals on Daisy Hub. What about the bad apples on Zulu? How bent did a space cop have to be to end up there?

"…desk boy." Pulled back to the moment by the sound of Bonelli's voice, Drew noticed that the Ranger was pointing at the screen of the overhead monitor. Someone was debarking from the short-hopper. It was time to return to the landing deck and meet the pilot from Daisy Hub. Bonelli had already thumbed the hatch control. The door was opening with agonizing slowness. With luck, the luggage would be transferred over quickly and they could depart Platform Zulu without delay.

"There now, that's better!" The voice and energetic footsteps approaching behind them belonged to Teri Mintz. No, Drew corrected himself, this was Teri Martin. Her hair now fell in thick, shining waves to her shoulders, her eyes and lips had been emphasized with makeup, and she was wearing a striking green outfit, a skirt with matching sequined vest over a filmy pale green blouse. There was sparkle all over the blouse as well. It looked like a stage costume.

It *was* a stage costume. Drew cursed under his breath. A wildcat he knew he could handle, but a singing star? On Daisy Hub, where his mission was to get everyone working together as a team?

All the way from Earth, Drew had done his level best to convince her that the showbiz phase of her life was over, that this posting was an opportunity for her to reinvent herself. Teri had listened attentively to him, frequently nodding agreement. Conning him, he now realized. Making him think he was getting through to her. And all along, she'd just been biding her time until she could make her grand entrance on Daisy Hub and be a star again.

Bonelli turned at the sound of her voice and looked her slowly up and down, the wolfish grin on his face making Drew wish he could have brought his own sidearm along on this mission. And — was that a fresh bruise under the second Ranger's left eye?

"Stevie-boy!" called another voice, a rich, full-bodied female voice, from the direction of the landing deck.

Bonelli lurched like a charging pit bull that had suddenly run out of leash. "Hey, Ruby!" he cried, making hasty repairs to his smile as he spun to greet the new arrival. "I wasn't expecting you to come all this way yourself."

"I know," she replied. Ruby McNeil was a tall, rangy woman in her late sixties, Drew guessed, with a cap of smooth gray hair, a stern mouth, and a devilish twinkle in her eyes. Not a mom so much as a mischievous grandma. She obviously had Steve Bonelli's number, for she continued, "You figured I'd send Ozzie and Sky, and the three of you could drink and play cards for a few hours while these weary travelers cooled their heels. Sorry, kiddo. Not while one of them's the new station manager and the other one is a woman." Ruby paused and stared expectantly at Bonelli, who finally, reluctantly, responded to the cue.

"Well," he sighed, "I guess I'll just go supervise the transfer of your luggage."

"Don't forget the other cargo," Ruby warned. "And my special order — five barrels."

"Five barrels, yes," he repeated, leaving the word 'Mom' hanging unspoken in the air. "It was a pleasure meeting you folks. I'm sure we'll talk again."

Drew waited until Bonelli had moved out of earshot to mutter urgently to Ruby, "Will we?"

"I'm afraid so. But whether you personally have to deal with Captain Bonelli depends entirely on you," she replied. "Karim felt it was his duty to represent the Hub in all interactions with the Rangers. But the manager we had before him, a fellow named Jovanovich, avoided contact with them at all costs. They don't call this place the Zoo for nothing, and some people get along with animals better than others. Part of the assistant manager's job is to run interference in situations like this. So just take your time and settle in. By the way, I'm—"

"—Ruby McNeil," he cut in. "I've already reviewed the crew manifest. I'm Drew Townsend. And this is—"

"Teri Martin!" gasped Ruby, her hands flying involuntarily to her cheeks. "I knew I recognized you from somewhere. I took my last vacation on Riviera Hub. You were the opening act in the Broadway Room. You were just a kid at the time, barely in your teens, but, what a voice! Honey, I knew you were going places, but I never expected to see you out here."

In the presence of a genuine fan, Teri seemed to grow taller. She smiled graciously. Her entire demeanor warmed and softened. Drew watched with a mixture of amusement and resignation as the last remnants of Teri Mintz melted away, revealing Teri Martin, star of hub lounges and InfoCommAds. "It was a surprise to me, too, Ruby. I thought I was going to Vegas Hub, but—"

"—but somebody with connections had other plans. Tell me about it. My son-in-law worked for the Relocation Authority for six Earth years, maneuvering himself into a management position just to be able to send me somewhere. Now I'm the perfect mother-in-law — healthy and productive, and three Gates away. Hold it!" she called to the deck crew. "I want to count those barrels before you close the hatch." Ruby turned back to Drew and Teri and said in a quieter voice, "Why don't you two climb aboard? As soon as I've finished giving these guys a math lesson, we'll go home."

The short-hopper's outer hull was shaped like the carapace of a kind of scavenger beetle Drew had often seen scurrying around the garbage bins behind his building on Lamont Street. He and Teri ascended a narrow embarkation ramp that extruded like a stinger from the ship's rear end, then had to duck to enter a cabin that seemed to occupy the entire length and width of the vessel, but only half its height. The ceiling inside was uncomfortably low. Drew had to stoop to protect his neck and shoulders from its bumps and protrusions, and Teri, though shorter than average, couldn't stand upright without hitting her head. Strange, then, that the shuttle's interior should feel so welcoming. No, Drew amended, it wasn't strange — it was the entire purpose of the decor. Soft amber light reflected off bulkheads plaincoated in warm autumn colors — rust, yellow, golden brown. The deck plating gave slightly under their footsteps, the carpet-like feel belying its metallic appearance. At the front of the craft sat a row of four generously-padded armchairs on pedestal bases, facing a broad, curving viewport.

Clearly, this was where passengers were meant to be — sitting, not standing.

As they eased themselves into two of the seats, Teri observed, frowning, "No control panels?"

She was right. If they were facing frontward, then one of these seats had to belong to the pilot.

"Everybody settled?"

Startled, Drew whipped around in his seat in time to see Ruby lie down on the deck behind them. She reached over her head and pulled a recessed lever in the bulkhead, and, slowly, a section of ceiling panel swung down on top of her, containing an array of colorful multifaceted knobs. "This is the original pilot's console," she explained, moving her hands over the controls. Then, as the engines hummed to life, she added, "You'd better buckle up, kids — I'm still driving with a learner's permit."

Without warning, the little ship sprang straight up and spun 180 degrees, then made a dash for freedom, banking steeply at the last second to avoid hitting the edge of the landing deck door on its way through.

If Drew's breath hadn't caught in his throat just then, he might have screamed. There had definitely been advantages to traveling in a metal bucket without viewports.

"All right!" Ruby whooped with exhilaration and banked again. "Now we're flying!"

Without warning, the shuttle breached the perimeter of Zulu's gravity field at full speed, hurling itself into space and its passengers into weightlessness. Struggling to swallow, Drew unclenched his right hand from the armrest of his seat and began prying open Teri's death-grip on his other arm. Her eyes were like saucers. Her lips were moving, but no sound was coming out. So much for not being a space virgin.

"This isn't an Earth-design short-hopper, is it?" he remarked unsteadily to their pilot.

"Very observant, Chief. It's Corvou," she called back. "We got it from a Nandrian ship that was passing through."

"The Nandrians gave it to us?" Drew recalled the description he'd skimmed from the datawafer in his briefcase: two-and-a-bit meters tall, green skin, jaws like a T-Rex...

"Well, they didn't exactly give it to us," she amended.

Drew thought for a moment that he would faint. "You stole it?"

"Steal from the Nandrians? Do I look suicidal?" she scolded. "We traded for it. One short-hopper in exchange for a standard year's supply of lemon juice."

Lemon juice? That didn't sound right. Even if it came from an off-Earth source…. "Aren't they allergic to our citrus products?" he asked.

"Is that what you've heard?"

"Yes. Did I hear wrong?"

"Not exactly. Citric acid affects Nandrians the same way that alcohol affects Humans."

Now he was sure he would faint. "They get drunk on citric acid? On the Hub?"

"They used to," Ruby confirmed with a smile in her voice. "But Karim pretty much put a stop to it when he imposed a five drink limit on them."

They couldn't have been happy about that, Drew realized. He hadn't wanted to put the Nandrians on the suspect list. Now it appeared they had a possible motive for murder, leaving him no choice but to question them. According to the datawafer, Nandrians spoke in riddles. How was he supposed to get a straight answer out of a huge sapient reptile that spoke in riddles? He heard a strange gurgling sound beside him. It was Teri, stifling laughter.

"Lemon juice is their favorite," Ruby went on, "although they've been known to settle for fresh limes or grapefruit juice. They're itinerant merchants, Mr. Townsend, buying and selling on hundreds of worlds. Whenever a ship of theirs docks at the Hub, they let us shop in their cargo holds. There's a lot of exotic stuff in there."

And, by extension, on Daisy Hub as well, he realized. This could be a very interesting assignment, indeed. "And those five barrels Bonelli put on board?"

Ruby chuckled wickedly. "Barter currency, Earth's finest. ETA Daisy Hub in two hours, Chief."

"Two? I thought it was four."

"On paper, maybe," she told him. "On *Devil Bug*, it's two. Let me show you what this little space bomb can do."

She spun and accelerated again, as though trying to escape the engines buzzing angrily behind them. It was like driving full speed through the Zone at night, without headlights — surrounded by blackness, the body aware of movement but the eyes denying it. Helpless to prevent the collision that his every instinct insisted was only a breath away, Drew stiffened in his seat.

Beside him, Teri was silent. Maybe she had been lucky enough to pass out.

As the universe continued to spin around him, Drew forced himself to think, about anything that would take his mind off his current predicament. Unfortunately, there weren't many memories he cared to recall. Louelle Truman, perhaps, at the Security barbecue where he'd first met her shortly after being partnered with her husband. She'd been wearing a bib apron over her hot pink bikini, flipping burgers one-handed and sucking lemonade-flavored punch through a straw.... Lemonade-flavored! Drew bolted upright in his seat, cursing himself for slow-wittedness.

There had been barrels — barrels! — of precious lemon juice in the hold of that long-hopper from Earth.

For the past several years, CommNews had been reporting massive citrus crop failures over most of the world. Only Isrusalem and Java still had healthy orchards, and their fruit was going to the highest bidders. In most places on Earth, even the wealthy and powerful were making do with chemically-flavored juice substitutes. But real lemon juice was being shipped out here by the barrelful, on demand and apparently without question, so that a bunch of bad apples could trade with the Nandrians. And, by strange coincidence, Earth was now secretly in possession of a piece of Nandrian technology for which the price could have been measured in only one thing.

Lies, he thought disgustedly. Earth High Council lied to the Great Council and to all the Regional Councils. SISCO lied to the High Council and to the Relocation Authority and to Earth Security. Anyone in power lied to the media, who then lied to the public. The Relocation Authority routinely lied to everybody. Lying convincingly had been a survival skill for

Drew on the streets of New Chicago, long before it became just another tool in his crime-solving kit. And he was pretty sure Ridout had purposely withheld information from him during his briefing for the SISCO mission. No wonder the EIS chose to remain a secret organization: it had been formed to gather and store — and take action on — truthful intelligence, which was in frustratingly short supply these days.

That was the reason for Drew's mission to Daisy Hub. If anything happened to compromise the position or integrity of the EIS on Earth, the organization would need a remote cell, a place to regroup, a base from which to launch an offensive if necessary.

In the words of Stephen Vincent Benét, truth had always been "a hard deer to hunt". Now it was an endangered species, needing to be protected at all costs. And the latest of many ironies in Townsend's life was that he, a convicted criminal and unregenerate con artist, was the man entrusted with the responsibility of laying the groundwork for its preservation.

Chapter 5

Zulu and Daisy Hub had been placed in high synchronous orbit on opposite sides of a gas giant circling a medium-sized yellow star on the edge of Earth space. Some puckish fellow had named the planet Helena, after a character with two unwilling suitors in a Shakespearean comedy. At the height of an Earth mania back in the mid-twenty-second century, the star had been named as well, for the wife of a philanthropist on the occasion of her hundredth birthday. The residents of the Hub, however, had changed "Marvella Labatt" to a name they considered more appropriate — Purgatory.

The Relocation Authority had planned Zulu and Daisy Hub to be completely self-contained and self-maintaining — it was officially labeled as an experiment in isolated deep space living. Purgatory and Helena had so far suited their purpose admirably. For half of each planetary day, one of the installations was exposed to Purgatory's stellar winds and radiation, providing an opportunity to recharge power cells. As well, being aligned lengthwise in stable orbit meant that minimal energy had to be expended for attitudinal adjustments, including the slow, constant rotation necessary to avoid sunburn.

"And what about the Meniscus Field?" Drew asked.

Sitting to his right, Ruby blew out a sigh and shook her head slowly. After half a standard hour of showing off *Devil Bug*'s maneuverability, she had activated the autonav computer and joined him and Teri at the forward viewport. "To be honest, I don't really think it gives us any kind of advantage. Airlocks are more effective at conserving our atmosphere and take less energy to operate. When the field generator was first installed, I thought somebody back home was simply gadget-happy.

Now, I wonder whether there isn't something else going on, something more sinister.

"You've studied Earth history, Drew. When we began mining the asteroid belt, back in the 2040s, it was common knowledge that Earth's government was crewing the operation with convicts, because the technology was buggy as hell, accidents were a certainty, and convicts were considered expendable. Nowadays, we're the expendable ones, and Earth wants to know whether this alien technology will work for Humans. Okay. But it's being tested under a blanket of secrecy, and I'll bet you anything they don't plan to install it on landing decks."

She was probably right, Drew realized. Back on the Zoo Bonelli had vaguely hinted that there had been at least one accident. He'd also made a thinly veiled threat, no doubt to discourage the new station manager from even thinking about blowing the whistle on Earth Council. Could that have been why Karim Khaloub died? And if so, how many cover-ups would Drew have to cut through to get at the truth?

"There are technicians aboard the Hub," he remarked casually. "Have they tried to—?"

"Probably, knowing this bunch, but not to my actual knowledge."

"You know I'm going to keep asking questions."

She smiled. "Honey, you wouldn't be out here if all it took to stop you was a warning. Just be sure you're asking the right people. Don't take it personally if they tell you to go swimming in Purgatory. And if you decide to talk to the Nandrians, get Gavin Holchuk onside first. They like him; if he vouches for you, they may even give you a straight answer."

Impressive, Drew thought, and puzzling. What was a woman as knowledgeable and as obviously respected as Ruby McNeil doing in the position of assistant station manager? She had certainly been on Daisy Hub long enough to know the place — and its crew — inside and out. There was nothing in her biofile to suggest that she couldn't have done just as good a job as Khaloub. Why hadn't she simply been promoted when his position had opened up?

Because SISCO had pulled strings to put Drew Townsend into it, that was why.

Great. Even 'Mom' had a motive now. This assignment was making him paranoid.

Drew glanced to his left, where Teri sat, curled in her chair and peacefully dozing after the stress of their journey.

"You'd better wake her up," Ruby advised, pointing at the viewport. "She's going to want to see this."

Riviera Hub, Vegas Hub, and Ginza Hub were vacation resorts named for popular tourist destinations in Earth's past. Shakespeare Hub was one of several communications centers, each named for a famous and prolific author. Patton Hub was a Ranger headquarters, named for a revered military leader. And Daisy Hub...?

Supposedly, the station was called Daisy Hub because the docking modules arrayed around the large comm dish at its north end had reminded someone of flower petals.

What a trivial and insulting way to name a space station, Drew thought as Ruby brushed past him.

Then a huge golden blossom seemed to ascend from behind Helena's curved horizon, its petals sculpted out of Purgatory's light and radiating an otherworldly glow, and Townsend had to remind himself to breathe. Unable to tear his eyes away from the viewport, he groped for Teri's shoulder, found her arm, and squeezed it.

"What—?" she gasped, startled. Then she saw. "Oh, my," she sighed, and fell silent. There was nothing more to say.

"That's what we think, too," said Ruby, by now on her back at the pilot's console once more. "But we can't stay out here all day admiring it, folks. Better brace yourselves. I have to remember how to park this thing."

They were approaching the Hub end-on, but the short-hopper landing deck was located behind the docking modules, a third of the way to its midsection. As Ruby veered out of orbit for her final approach, Drew was able to see the entire length of Daisy Hub.

It was a good thing he wasn't claustrophobic.

According to the datawafers, the average hub could run from one to five kilometers in length. The core of Daisy Hub was barely six hundred meters long, but still managed to contain living quarters, rec facilities, and evac pods for sixty people, along with the Med Services Unit, the kitchen and cafeteria, an automated life support system, thrusters, power cells, supplies storage, a hydroponic garden and meat lab, reclamation and recycling units, a landing deck, a utilities deck, an admin and communications deck, and a gravity field generator. It had looked like a tight fit on the schematics printout in his briefcase. It looked even tighter now that bay doors were visible apertures in the Hub's matted metallic skin.

Ruby banked the little ship to match their orientation, then set *Devil Bug* down with smooth precision in its own marked spot on the landing deck. The shift to gravity was expected this time, and Drew and Teri were comfortably cushioned by their seats. Auto Traffic Control couldn't have done a better job.

Still held by his seat restraints, Drew heard the hum of the pilot's console as it folded itself back into the ceiling behind him. "You may as well relax — it'll be ten or fifteen minutes before we can debark," came Ruby's cheerful voice.

Beside him, Teri stretched luxuriously, forcing him to duck her backhand.

"That was excellent parking, Ruby," he commented with a smile. "How long have you been practicing?"

"About four station years, or standard years, same thing. Technically, *Devil Bug* belongs to the Hub, but I seem to be the principal pilot."

"So all that — that—" Speaking Gally was hard work right now; but it was like riding a moto, he reminded himself. The extensive vocabulary he'd learned when he was younger had remained in his brain, filed away. With practice, a lot of it had already come back to him. As well, someone had thoughtfully included a bottle of somno when packing his briefcase. A little more of the drug and another night's sleep were all he needed to finish unlocking his long-term memory, making him once more as fluent in Gally as he'd been at the age of thirteen.

Drew smiled as the word he'd been trawling his brain for finally dropped onto his tongue. "All that showing off back there was for Steve Bonelli's benefit?"

Ruby pursed her lips before replying demurely, "Well, partly. Partly, I just like to cut loose once in a while. But I do have an image to maintain. Teri knows what that's like."

The wildcat nodded sagely.

Right. Drew sighed and leaned back into his seat. The Zoo was being run by a wolf. His assistant station manager enjoyed stunt flying an alien-built shuttle called *Devil Bug*. The cafeteria of Daisy Hub was now a citrus bar for Nandrians, but the huge aliens had to leave after five drinks. (Sure. Tell a T-Rex with a buzz on that he's had enough and it's time for him to go home now. That should work really well.) The crew of Daisy Hub had been trading with the Nandrians, probably through Gavin Holchuk, for at least four station years, possibly longer. Earth Council was beyond doubt supplying citrus juices to the Nandrians in payment for a piece of alien technology which it was secretly testing on the Zoo and the Hub for purposes not yet made clear — and that deal might have been brokered by Holchuk as well, since the Nandrians *liked* him.

His first report to the EIS was going to raise blood pressure, guaranteed.

Chapter 6

"Mr. Townsend?" The voice emanating from the comm unit just inside the door to his temporary quarters sounded tinny and nasal.

He wasn't able to answer right away. He'd been unpacking and had come across Bruni's gifts tucked in among the clothing and personal items inside his trunk, and a sudden powerful wave of remembered loss had swept through him, robbing him of speech and blurring his vision with unwelcome tears.

At the sound of his name, Drew forced himself to suck in a long, steadying breath. Then, once he could trust his voice again, he replied gruffly, "Yo! Who's there?"

"Jason Smith, Life Support Engineering Specialist. There's a problem with this piece of — of carpet you brought aboard, sir."

That wasn't what he'd meant to call it. In spite of himself, Drew was smiling as he gently extracted all the precious parcels from their hiding places in his trunk and arranged them in a pile on the bed. "Really? And what problem would that be, Mr. Smith?" he called over his shoulder.

Drew already knew what the problem was. He'd known what it would be even as he was rolling and tying the rug in his erstwhile apartment. 'Mom' had raised an eyebrow when she saw the thing emerge from *Devil Bug*'s cargo hatch but had said nothing, just stood aside to let the decon crew pounce on it. If anyone understood the significance of that piece of luggage, it would be Ruby McNeil.

An audible sigh preceded the engineer's reply. "Carpeting aboard a space installation is impractical and dangerous, sir. We're in a closed environment, constantly recycling atmosphere. Carpet fibers trap dust and debris, overworking the air purification system. Pumps can overheat, even burn out. I cannot in all conscience—"

"—obey a direct order, Mr. Smith?" Drew cut in imperiously. Part of him felt sorry for the young engineer. Smith was just doing his job. He was being logical and reasonable, and he was right; but Townsend was establishing his cover, and in the larger scheme of things that had to take precedence over everything else.

"Are you ordering me to install it, sir?"

"No, I'm ordering you to unroll it on the floor in my office and stick a desk on top of it."

"Because I want it understood that I'm doing this under protest, sir."

"Your protest is acknowledged, Mr. Smith. Now go away."

Another sigh. "Yes, sir."

Sir, sir, sir. Strangely polite behavior for a bad apple, Drew mused. Then he recalled the final entry in Smith's biofile: reason for reassignment to Daisy Hub — assault on a fellow officer. Jason Smith had graduated with honors from the Fleet training program. He evidently had no difficulty taking orders. He'd served for five standard years on a starship, working his way up to Assistant Engineering Specialist. And then something had happened. Smith had thrown a punch at a superior officer, and had promptly made things worse for himself by verbally assaulting the other man in front of witnesses. Clearly, he'd been provoked, but an officer should have been able to control his anger. So, Jason Smith had a hot button and had evidently been given a choice: return to Earth as an Ineligible or take reassignment to Daisy Hub. Might Khaloub have inadvertently pushed that button? Could that be why he had died?

Adding the engineer's name to the now-burgeoning suspect list, Drew realized it would probably be in his own best interests to find out more about young Mr. Smith.

Townsend pulled the last of his personal effects out of the trunk and pushed it aside with his foot. For a moment he regretted having brought the brass-studded, leather-covered box. In his apartment it had made an interesting piece of furniture; here, in a guest room only slightly larger than his bathroom back on Lamont Street, there was space for only a bed and a built-in desk. Everything else was concealed behind smooth, sliding panels in the bulkheads. The trunk was too bulky to hide behind a bulkhead. It was too high to conceal under the bed and too wide to fit under the desk. It was too long to serve as a nightstand and too low to double as a chair.

It was a damned good thing these were not his permanent quarters.

The station manager's suite was on the other side of Deck E, and, according to the station plans, was larger than three of these cubbyholes put together. That was where he should have been unpacking. However, the Rangers who had initiated the investigation into Karim Khaloub's death had designated the victim's quarters a possible crime scene and had sealed them off immediately to prevent evidence contamination. There was only one way for Townsend to claim the living space that was rightfully his, and that was by concluding the investigation and solving the case, precisely what SISCO had sent him there undercover to do.

In that respect, he wasn't sure whether to be grateful or annoyed that Steve Bonelli was a real cop. Drew not only understood the Ranger's attitude toward the man with the "make-work desk job", but prior to the reinstatement of his Eligibility he had also shared it. Trained Security officers had no patience for Eligibles marking time, and with good reason: the job was dangerous enough without an amateur getting in the way. In Bonelli's eyes, that was all the new station manager was — well-meaning, perhaps even talented, but an amateur nonetheless. A hazard. A liability. It was galling to be thought of this way. Still, Drew reminded himself grimly, he was working undercover for a reason. He would have to conduct his own investigation to the best of his ability — with or without the cooperation of the Rangers — and report his findings to SISCO.

That was where the upside came in. Bonelli, a seasoned professional, had obviously discerned more than one possible crime scenario, and had moved in quickly to protect potential evidence. It made Drew shudder to imagine what might have been awaiting him otherwise, Earth weeks after Khaloub's death.

Something buzzed sharply, twice. Drew carefully placed the containers of exotic foodstuffs on a wall shelf, then slapped the sliding panel shut. "Now what?" he wondered aloud.

A reply came through the speaker beside the door. "Are you decent, Chief? I'm here to take you on that tour."

Ruby had promised to show him Daisy Hub 'by the letters', from top to bottom, Decks A through M, introducing him to whichever crew members were on duty at the time. "They need to listen to you speak, see your face, shake your hand," she'd explained earlier. Now, as they rode the tube car to Deck A, she elaborated, "They need to get a sense of who you are and what you might do. For starters, they need to hear that improbable accent of yours for themselves."

"I'm working on it," he shot back, stung.

But she had already moved on. "You'll be invited to join the *tekl'hananni* pool. Pick any number except nine. That was Karim's number. When he died, it became cursed."

"According to whom?"

"The Nandrians. *Tekl'hananni* is their planetary sport. The standings are posted every couple of intervals, and the leading House gets free docking privileges for its ships at Daisy Hub until the next scoreboard goes up. So far, Trokerk is the House to beat — Nagor and his crew are regular visitors here. This is A Deck," she announced, as the tube car doors sighed open on a large circular area ringed by arching portals.

These were entranceways to the docking modules, he recalled from the deck plans. Inbound ships had to stop here for cargo inspection before being allowed to proceed into Earth space. And outbound vessels had to be checked for stowaways, now that the plague had hit their sector. Glancing around, Drew counted eight archways — wishful thinking for a hub this small and isolated, he realized, but perfect for a remote EIS base.

"There's a full set of auxiliary controls concealed under this floor plating," Ruby continued, "in case we have to evacuate the lower decks. We can even separate the Hub into three sections in an emergency. But you probably know that already."

He nodded. On purely technical matters his briefcase had briefed him quite thoroughly.

"All right, then," she sighed. "B Deck is Lucas Soaring Hawk's workshop. You met him when we first arrived — the fellow with the long hair and sweatband who was barking orders at the techs in the short-hopper landing bay? Hawk is our resident propulsion systems genius, so Jason put him in charge of maintaining and repairing the short-hoppers and Personal Life Support suits as well. Half of the suits are stored on B Deck, the other half are kept on L Deck. That way, exterior maintenance crews can exit the Hub near either end, using the airlocks."

Airlocks. Drew visualized the station plans. There were six airlocks altogether, three on Deck B, three on Deck L. He couldn't help wondering in which one Karim Khaloub's body had been found. There had been mention in the preliminary incident report of pajamas, but not of any Personal Life Support suit. Drew made a mental note to question Lucas Soaring Hawk about that.

"The short-hopper landing bay you've already seen. So, our next stop will be C Deck," Ruby declared, nudging him back into the tube car. "That's the Admin and Communications center, AdComm for short. Lydia Garfield's in charge of data management, InfoComm maintenance, and SPA programming. She's been looking forward to meeting you."

"SPA?"

"Shared Programmable Activities — it's a virtual reality playroom, on Deck D. Fools us into thinking we're in the mountains, or strolling through a forest, or quarterbacking a football game. Great for mental health. Not bad for physical health, either. And it can be customized. Lydia has imprinted personal SPA wafers for everyone on the Hub. Just tell her what you used to do for fun — or what you'd like to do for fun — and she'll set you up, no questions asked."

That one he couldn't ignore. "It sounds as if she's received some unusual requests."

"Unusual back on Earth, maybe. Not here."

"What if one went beyond unusual, to immoral, or even frightening, like wanting to play at being Jack the Ripper? Would questions be asked then? Would a report be filed?"

An ominous silence suddenly blanketed the tube car. "That sounds like a Ranger talking," Ruby said quietly. The door slid open at that moment, but she made no move to step onto the deck.

Strangely, he felt powerless to step past her. Which part of what he'd said was she reacting to? Had a Ranger already asked her the same question? Or did someone on Daisy Hub fantasize about being a serial killer?

"I'm not a Ranger, Ruby," he told her at last. "I'm just the dead man's replacement. If Khaloub was a target, I may be one too. So I'd really like to know what happened to him."

She thought for a moment, then slowly nodded. "And you probably don't like living in guest quarters, either. I guess that's fair. But there's something you need to understand, Mr. Townsend. The Rangers are not well liked on Daisy Hub. We try as much as possible to give them no reason to come here. Lydia even went so far as to design and install a SPA for them over on the Zoo, so they couldn't use ours as an excuse.

"Still, Bonelli insists on sending his new arrivals over here for 'orientation'. They strut around and play 'bad cop' for half a day. Then Fritz Jensen, our head chef, serves them two-day-old macaroni for lunch, to discourage them from hanging around until dinner. So you see, everyone on Daisy Hub knows what it's like to be interrogated by a Ranger, and no one enjoys it. You can still ask questions — but make certain they're honest questions. That way, you have a better chance of getting honest answers."

And he did want honest answers, Drew acknowledged, even if he had to lie to everyone on the Hub to obtain them.

AdComm took up all of Deck C and was, literally as well as figuratively, the nerve center of Daisy Hub. It was also the most haphazard arrangement of office trappings Drew had ever seen. Glancing around, he was able to identify an assortment of display consoles, several stacks of security monitors, a half-dozen or so InfoComm units, two work tables, a couple of desks, five or six stray chairs, and a sprinkling of shoulder-high gray metal filing cabinets.

"Where was Khaloub's workspace?" he asked.

"All of C deck," Ruby replied matter-of-factly. "Except for my console and Lydia's station, which is over there."

As his gaze followed Ruby's pointing finger, Drew realized why he hadn't noticed the other woman before. He could barely see her now.

Lydia Garfield sat, fortressed by furniture, in a pie-shaped cranny just large enough for one person and a row of monitor screens. She was slim and very blonde. And she was shrinking. From the moment Ruby had pointed her out and the two of them had begun walking toward her, Lydia had grown visibly shorter behind her desk. She was a data nerd, Drew guessed, more comfortable around numbers than in the presence of living people. Perfect choice for a virtual reality programmer. And she'd been looking forward to meeting him? Sure, she had!

As Ruby made the introductions, pretending to ignore the younger woman's anxiety, Drew couldn't help wondering how Lydia Garfield managed to function, let alone hold onto her Eligibility. Her eyes were darting all over the room, as though seeking out her next hiding place, a safer haven than the one in which she had just been discovered. Her shoulders shook. Her hands drew nervous figures in the air. And her discomfort was contagious. Drew had to stifle the impulse to grab her and hold her still — he was afraid she might die of fright, like a trapped bird. He shared her obvious relief when Ruby suggested continuing his tour on Deck D, maybe getting a bite to eat in the caf while they were there.

The crew of this hub had quirks, Ridout had said. Eccentricities. But Lydia's behavior went beyond eccentric. It strongly reminded him of those female vics who called Security after being sexually assaulted and then locked themselves in the closet. Clearly, there would be some further investigating to do once his mission for SISCO was accomplished.

Chapter 7

"What can you tell me about Karim Khaloub?"

In response, Ruby took another sip of her java, glancing up as Chef Jensen, a rotund man in his forties with a shock of frizzy brown hair, sank into the third chair at their small round table. The Daisy Hub caf was empty at this hour, and Jensen was obviously glad of the opportunity to get off his feet.

"The man was a saint," he declared.

"No, he was a manager," Ruby corrected him patiently. "Since I arrived here, there have been six individuals with the title of Station Manager, but only two of them have actually managed the station with any effectiveness — Nayo Naguchi and Karim Khaloub."

"Then Naguchi was a saint," Jensen decided. "If he hadn't made me a chef, I'd still be a grunt, inspecting airlock seals and replacing lightbars. He came in one day while I was fixing myself lunch, saw how much I enjoyed cooking, and asked if I would like to do it all the time. The very next day, I was reassigned to the kitchen and informed that I'd been enrolled to take Cordon Bleu courses via interactive Gate transmission."

Ruby was nodding agreement. "Nayo believed in order and discipline, but he also felt that people functioned best when they were working toward a goal. He organized the various departments, established protocols and duty cycles, and saw to it that everyone kept learning. That was his greatest gift to us. The man was brilliant. He had degrees in medicine, psychology, and engineering. He personally trained half the techs on this station, then designated them engineers and stepped out of the way so they could teach the other half."

"And Khaloub?" Drew reminded them.

"Karim was more into health and safety," said Jensen. "Order was his first priority, though. Had to be. He replaced Jovanovich, who had just spent four years hiding under his desk—"

"—after being traumatized by the Nandrians his first day on the job," Ruby cut in. "He was looking for Gavin, and found him negotiating a trade with some of Nagor's crew. Jo barged into the discussion and accused Gavin of being a black marketeer, which cast a slur on the Nandrians as well, who responded in typical Nandrian fashion by biting Jo, here and here." She indicated the midpoints of both thighs.

"Nandrian venom is actually a digestive enzyme," Jensen explained. "It's how they feed. See, the paralyzed prey begins dissolving from the inside out, and—"

"I get the picture," said Drew with a grimace.

"Fortunately, Doc Ktumba had some antivenin on hand. She got to him quickly enough to prevent any serious permanent damage to his body."

"He limped a little after that," Jensen clarified. "It was hardly noticeable, except when he walked."

"Mostly, he scurried."

"Scuttled, actually, like a crab."

"It was very sad," said Ruby, by now unable to keep a straight face. As she made eye contact with Jensen across the table, they simultaneously burst out laughing.

Drew looked from one to the other of them and sighed patiently. His first impression of Ruby McNeil had apparently been correct. "I can see you really sympathized with him; but tell me, what happened when Khaloub arrived?"

"Things were pretty chaotic around here, so he knew he had to lay down some rules," said Ruby, struggling to regain her composure. "Karim was no slouch in the smarts department. First thing he did was consult with Gavin Holchuk. Together they cooked up a plan. They waited until a shipload of Nandrians was aboard the Hub, celebrating their latest *tekl'hananni* victory. Then the two of them went down to L Deck and put on PLS suits with null-G microgenerators. They raised the gravity on the station to 3Gs, not enough to immobilize the Nandrians, but sufficient to slow them down a little. Then Karim circulated around the Hub and explained the new five drink limit. Gavin had coached him on how to say things without appearing to insult the aliens' honor. Finally, just to seal the agreement, Gavin and Karim presented the Chief Officer with a lifetime certificate entitling him to free drinks on Daisy Hub."

"A temptation?" The puzzled silence that greeted his question told him he'd better try again. "They gave him a — a bribe?"

"Call it what you like," said Ruby. "It worked. The Nandrians have followed the rules ever since."

"Of course, *our* crew was pretty upset about being flattened on the deck for nearly an hour," Jensen added, chuckling. "Karim hadn't warned anyone beforehand, but he did explain everything later on. That was another reason why I liked him. He never gave us the mushroom treatment — you know, keep 'em in the dark and pile on the manure? — and we never had to wonder about his priorities. Daisy Hub always came first for him."

Ruby had finished her java. As she moved the empty mug deliberately to the middle of the table, Drew summed up, "So, Naguchi was intelligent, but Karim was smart. Naguchi cared about discipline and learning, and Karim…?"

"Karim cared about morale," Jensen supplied. "He knew how important that was, especially to people like us — stuck all the way out here and incredibly overqualified for most of the duties available. Well, if you can't laugh, you're going to cry, right? So he did what he could to make life bearable, if not enjoyable. He encouraged us to develop our interests, use our imaginations, make our own fun. And it worked. Kept us all sane, at any rate."

"Speak for yourself," Ruby scolded playfully before adding, "Karim was into sports and fitness. He spent a lot of time in the SPA room. He even tried to organize virtual reality baseball games and soccer matches among the crew. He failed, unfortunately. Still, he cared enough to make the effort, and you have to respect him for that."

Drew's gaze wandered once more to the wall behind Jensen's seat, where someone had apparently painted a mural.

About one meter square, it depicted a deep space hub, much larger than this one, amid a swarm of docking and departing ships. The style was impressionist, and the colors were richly metallic golds, platinums, and bronzes, with the occasional splash of Chinese red or peacock blue. But the most impressive color was no color at all — it was utter blackness. The artist's depiction of space held not a hint of blue or brown. After staring at it for several minutes, Drew was half-convinced that there must be a breach in the hull. "And whose interest does that represent?" he asked, pointing.

"Nobody knows," said Jensen, shaking his head. "And no one seems anxious to step forward and take credit for it, either."

"There are pictures like it all over the Hub," Ruby added, "and they're making our Structural Integrity Specialist crazy."

"How does a painting affect structural integrity?" Drew wanted to know.

"It isn't a painting," Jensen replied. "Take a closer look at it. That isn't smart paint — it's plaincoated metal, and nothing has been applied onto it. Someone has found a way to change the refractive index of the individual molecules of that bulkhead."

Ruby pursed her lips. "It's probably the work of an alien device. Some kind of molecular paintbrush."

"The only way to know for sure is to catch the Midnight Muralist in the act." Jensen's voice lowered conspiratorially. "But you can never be sure where he — or she — will strike next."

"Well, we'd better let you get back to work, Fritz," said Ruby. "I want to show Drew the SPA room, and then take him down to Med Services to meet the Doc."

"Meeting the Doc on his first day? Her bite is even more venomous than the Nandrians'," the chef observed with a grin. "As a condemned man you're entitled to a last meal, Mr. Townsend. Any requests?"

Drew returned the smile. "As a matter of fact, yes. Does your—" He wrestled with his memory for a moment. "—your hydroponics unit. Does it grow citrus fruit trees?"

The other man stiffened visibly. "For consumption only, sir. My fruit is not for bartering."

"Good. Because it's been years since I had a fresh orange with my morning meal."

Jensen glanced uncertainly at Ruby. "Years, Mr. Townsend?"

"Citrus is scarce on Earth these days, Fritz. A Jaffa orange costs almost as much as a video wall."

Suddenly sober, the chef told him, "They're clementines, sir. I'll see that you get one every day."

"We had no idea, Drew," Ruby apologized as they left the caf. "We don't get much news from Earth out here. And anytime I've requisitioned lemon juice, it's arrived, no problems. What happened to the citrus crop?"

He wanted to tell her. He wanted someone else aboard Daisy Hub to be as angry as he was. As angry as Jovanovich had evidently been when *he* first arrived. But Drew had no hard evidence yet, only circumstances and conjecture, and it could be fatal to his mission if anyone aboard the station acted prematurely.

So he ducked the question. As they strolled along the gently curving corridor rimming D Deck, he asked Ruby instead, "When did the Nandrians make first contact with Daisy Hub?"

She shrugged. "It happened before my time, and I've been here longer than I care to think about. With all their comings and goings, they were bound to stumble on us eventually, I guess. But we didn't become a regular port of call until shortly after Gavin Holchuk arrived."

"Why then?"

"Naguchi was the station manager at the time. Nayo valued order and discipline, and Gavin was grieving and angry. Not exactly an ideal fit. My guess is that Naguchi wanted to give him something difficult to do that would distract him and maybe dissipate his rage. Learning all about the Nandrians was the perfect assignment for Gavin. He threw himself into the work and, over the years, has compiled an enormous amount of data on them. He can even speak a little of their language. Just the fact that a Human would devote so much time and energy trying to understand their culture seems to have impressed the dickens out of them. So when I told you the Nandrians liked him, I didn't mean—" Abruptly, she stopped walking. "Uh-oh!"

There was another mural on the wall, a moonscape with planet ascendant, this one just as artfully drawn as the last.

"Let me guess — this wasn't here yesterday?"

Ruby found a wallcomm and thumbed the blue button.

"Spiro? This is Mom, honey. Check out D Deck thirty degrees clockwise of the SPA room. The Muralist has struck again."

An agonized cry drifted out of the speaker as Ruby turned with a grin. "Like the man said," she reminded him, "we make our own fun around here."

Chapter 8

The SPA room looked like a torture chamber. Dimly lit, it was filled with metal frameworks resembling chairs, at least a dozen of them, each with a rainbow of wires cascading off its back and sides, some tethering it to the floor, some leading to a light-studded metal column in the center of the room, and the rest ending in interface plugs that seemed to sprout like bulrushes out of the armrests.

"So where's Doctor Frankenstein?" Drew wanted to know. "Out having a java?"

Beside him, Ruby was chuckling. "Doctor Petroff says this room sends a chill down his spine — reminds him of the examining lab at his old dental college. Nonetheless, he's in here for three hours every few days, playing a round of virtual golf. Lydia put together a SPA wafer for him, containing the twelve most challenging courses on Earth. Sometimes Devanan Singh joins him — he's our electrical and field maintenance expert. You know, I've heard that a lot of business gets conducted on golf courses. If you have questions about the Meniscus Field, going eighteen holes with Singh might not be a bad idea. The skins are stored in individual compartments in the bulkhead, and there's a change room, over there," she added, pointing to the wall right behind them.

"Skins?"

"The body suits that interface with the chairs. We call them skins because you have to strip down and wear them next to your skin to get the full effect of the program."

"Do you know whether Khaloub spent any time in here the day he died?"

Ruby frowned suddenly. "Why?"

"You said he was a sports enthusiast. If he had some kind of medical condition that contributed to his death, and if he perspired inside one of those skins close to the time of his death...?"

She shook her head wearily. "Are you sure you're not a Ranger, Drew?"

"If I were, I'd be working on Zulu. Answer my question, Ruby. Did Khaloub log any SPA time the day he died?"

"Yes, but you can forget about finding any evidence inside his skin. For health reasons, SPA suits are sterilized between uses."

"And who is responsible for making sure that happens?"

A beat, then, "The wearer. Each suit is custom-fitted to a single user. When it's replaced in its compartment, the lockpad activates an automatic decon cycle."

"What if someone isn't feeling well at the end of an exercise period?" he persisted. "What if he leaves in a hurry, still wearing his skin, and forgets the cycle?"

"Lydia doesn't let that happen. Her console monitors the vital signs of anyone wearing a skin, whether they're running a program or not, and alerts her at the first indication of medical distress. If the alarm goes off, she terminates the program and summons Med Services. She's programmed the monitor board to do that automatically if something happens while she's off-duty. And, to answer your next question, Lydia was at her console during Karim's SPA session that morning, and Karim was in no distress whatsoever. He pitched nine innings, then showered and went to the caf and had an early lunch. Several crew members have already testified to the Rangers that they saw him there, and that he appeared in excellent health."

Drew heard the unspoken warning in her voice and realized that this was why she was called 'Mom'. If the day ever came when he was wounded and in need of solitude, he hoped someone would protect him as fiercely as she was obviously shielding Lydia Garfield right now.

Poor Lydia. Had she been so easily rattled when she arrived on Daisy Hub? Or was her nervousness a recent development? Had she sensed that he was a cop? Perhaps the shy little nerd was more involved in Khaloub's death than anyone around here was prepared to admit.

Meanwhile, Ruby had pinned a smile back on her face. "Decks E, F, and G are living quarters, nothing interesting there," she declared. "Next stop, Deck H — Medical Services."

The tube car door opened for them as if on cue. Drew let Ruby step through first. She thumbed the pad beside the door and waited for the car to begin descending before she spoke again. "Marion Ktumba is a walking database. She knows more than the rest of us put together. So, word to the wise, whatever you do, don't argue with the Doc. She always turns out to be right, and the last thing a station manager needs while making a first impression is to look foolish."

"I'm not another Jovanovich," he assured her.

"You're no Naguchi, either."

"Yes, Mom."

She made an exasperated sound.

According to the floor plan, Med Services took up all of H Deck, at roughly the midpoint of the station. Unlike Deck C, however, it had a circumference corridor, with entrances leading off it to a variety of storage and work rooms in the central area of the deck. All the corridor walls were smooth and plaincoated pale green, and the air smelled clean and faintly antiseptic. As he walked with Ruby past closed doors labeled Radiography, Pharmaceutical Supplies, and Regeneration, hearing nothing but the humming of air purifiers and their own footsteps, Drew felt as though he'd been teleported back to the fifth floor of Mercy Hospital in New Chicago.

"Here," said Ruby, gesturing toward a door marked Clinics and Consultations. He paused and let her precede him into the waiting room.

Now they were in a triangular space that reminded him of the triage area of a family health clinic. The decor was definitely Earth Institutional, from the imitation rosewood walls to the beige falsahyde chairs with their bent-pipe armrests. Most striking, however, was the smell in the air. Drew sniffed experimentally. "Strawberries?"

"It's her favorite," Ruby confirmed.

There were four doors providing access to four different clinics, according to the lettering beside each one: Trauma, Rehab, Counseling, and Dental. Drew would have guessed that a medical professional who knew everything about everything would probably spend her time in Counseling; but it was the door marked Trauma that slid aside just then for the most formidable female he'd ever seen in a white coat.

Marion Ktumba was a tall, sturdy black woman with a helmet of densely curled hair, piercing dark eyes, and an air of authority that would have made a charging rhino stop and rethink its plan.

"Is this him?" she demanded.

Yes, Trauma was definitely the appropriate place for someone like this.

"Doc Ktumba, meet Drew Townsend, our newest fearless leader. He has many questions," Ruby added with an impish smirk.

"And I have many answers," said the Doc, her faint smile eloquent with disdain. Drew had seen the same expression cross his division commander's face five years earlier when he had informed her of his plans to reapply for full Eligibility status. Now, as then, all it did was stiffen his resolve.

He met the Doc's gaze with a challenging stare of his own. "And I would like to hear those answers. Let's begin by going into your office," he said, keeping his voice steady.

"Yes, let's do that," she agreed. As she turned to lead the way, Drew couldn't decide whose brand of condescension was more infuriating, Bonelli's or the Doc's.

The Doc's office was a doorless cubbyhole off one side of the Trauma room, little more than a desk and some chairs in a pale green alcove. After waving her guests into two of the chairs, she went behind her desk and sat down. "Now, how can I help you, Mr. Townsend?" she inquired.

He was her superior and she was treating him like a patient. Understandable, but unacceptable. Under Jovanovich and Khaloub there had clearly been a power vacuum that the Doc had moved in to fill. Now that Townsend had arrived, with "more mileage on him and a lot more savvy", according to Ridout, things would have to be different; and she needed to realize that sooner rather than later.

"Let's start with this place," he said briskly. "I've been looking over the deck plans, and you have an impressive arrangement of space here. A complete hospital, including a pharmacy, a burn treatment unit, and a state of the art medical laboratory. What do you do with it all?"

"I treat patients, Mr. Townsend," she replied tartly.

"Yes, of course, but how many Human patients can you possibly get here? One trained physician for—let's see, there are forty-six adults on Daisy Hub, and about fifteen Rangers over on the Zoo, assuming that their infirmary is only equipped for first aid. That comes to just over sixty people. There are places on Earth that are lucky to have one doctor for five thousand children and adults. And all your patients are Eligibles. That means they're genetically resistant to most of the common Human diseases and conditions. You can't be treating the passengers of arriving or departing vessels, since very few ships stop here for inspection, and the ones that do stop have their own doctor aboard. Aside from the occasional accident, then, since Khaloub put an end to the Nandrians' drunken violence aboard the station, you must have a lot of spare time to fill. I'm curious, Doctor — what do you do with it?"

That wilted the corners of her smile. "I stay up to date, Mr. Townsend," she informed him in a voice that could have doubled as a scalpel. "I read medical journals. I reproduce experiments that have been done elsewhere and confirm the findings for myself. I also conduct my own scientific research. I do what a mentor of mine once advised me to do — I never stop learning."

"That sounds like Nayo Naguchi."

"Yes. A great teacher. I knew him before he was assigned to Daisy Hub. He showed me his design for this Medical Services Unit and I came here hoping to work with him again, but he'd already—" Surprised, Drew heard a catch in her voice as she concluded, "He was a brilliant and very honorable man who cared about the future of Humanity."

"And so you took his place on Daisy Hub?"

"No, I took mine. I would never presume to be his equal in anything."

Humble words from the infallible Doc Ktumba? Perhaps Jensen was right, and Naguchi really was a saint.

Okay. Drew took a breath and zagged. "When you examined Karim Khaloub's body, what did you find was the cause of death?"

"I didn't get to perform an autopsy. The Rangers removed the body directly from the scene to the morgue on Platform Zulu."

"So they have a medical examiner over there?"

"No." A faint smile again.

"Are you saying there was no autopsy done? A man died under strange circumstances and the investigators simply took custody of the body and stored it, without ordering a medical examination?"

Still smiling, she nodded.

Prison mentality, Drew realized. No way are you moving up, so you do what you can to bring the warden down. Volunteer nothing. Make him drag it out of you, one detail at a time. One syllable at a time is even better. If he gives up in exasperation, you win. If he loses his temper and smacks you around, you win.

Drew had never been good at that game, in or out of detention. He'd never had much patience for anyone else who played it, either. But he'd spent enough time behind tall fences to learn the rules, and he had a possible murder to solve. As long as the crew of Daisy Hub insisted on acting like inmates, they gave him no choice but to behave like a cop.

"Did they give you a reason for that?" he persisted, applying his sternest expression and deliberately leaning forward in his chair. He was pleased to see the Doc sway slightly away from him, even if it *was* for just a second. "Did they mention calling in an expert from outside, for example?"

"They said they already knew what the cause of death was, and that it would violate Karim's religious practices to cut up his body without good reason. Then they told me not to worry about it, that their report would take care of everything. Finally, they left, taking the station manager's corpse with them," she concluded, her expression and tone of voice both freighted with warning.

Townsend ignored it. "And have they shared any information with you since then?"

Ruby had been sitting quietly to this point, listening attentively as Drew conducted his interrogation. Now she shook her head and replied with undisguised annoyance, "No. Not a byte."

"Well, I'm going to," Drew decided. Zagging had worked for him in the past. Perhaps revealing a lie could shake loose the truth. "In their report to Security, they said that the body was discovered, frozen solid, inside an airlock."

The two women gasped in unison.

"What?"

"That's not right!" declared Ruby.

"That's what I suspected," Drew agreed. "So, tell me, where *was* the body found?"

"You already know that, Drew. His quarters were sealed off to protect—"

Townsend got to his feet then and raised his voice, overriding the rest of Ruby's response. "I'm having trouble understanding why, if Khaloub died in his quarters and the Rangers already knew the cause of death, they wouldn't simply report it that way, instead of making up something about an airlock. They ignored standard Security procedure, and they lied. What I need to decide right now is, do we allow them to continue this — this farce of an investigation? Or do we take it over ourselves and do it properly?"

Ruby looked as though she was about to swallow her tongue. "Take over the investigation? Oh, I agree with you that we could probably do a better job, Chief. But exactly how do you propose we reassign the case? We can't simply elbow the Rangers aside. We need a trained field officer to head things up, and Bonelli would never—"

"We don't need Bonelli," Drew cut in, dropping back into his chair. "I'll head it up, and I'll write the report."

"Oh, you will?" The Doc crossed her arms slowly over her chest, fairly radiating skepticism. "And who will convince the Space Installation Authority to put any credence in that report, let alone pass it along to Security?" she demanded.

"That's easy," he replied. "We don't report our findings to the SIA. We go directly to the Security Agency."

"Bypass the Rangers?" Ruby wondered aloud.

"Not exactly. Is there anyone aboard who can fake Bonelli's thumbprint?"

Her eyes lit up. "I'll check," she promised.

The Doc flung her arms skyward and breathed an exasperated syllable. "Now you want to file a false report?"

"No, we'd be filing a completely truthful report," he pointed out patiently, "with a Ranger captain's thumbprint on it to make it believable."

"But the forgery would invalidate the report," she persisted. "Don't you understand? It's against the law."

"We're not using his print to defraud anyone, Doctor. We're putting it on the document that Bonelli himself would be filing if we allowed him to finish the investigation. That's only a crime if Bonelli complains about it, and since our report will be ten times better than anything he would produce on his own, and maybe even get him promoted off the Zoo, I don't think he will."

"Then you don't know Steve Bonelli. It isn't credit he's after, or a pat on the back from his superiors — it's the rush of adrenaline he gets from tracking prey. The Rangers don't have much opportunity to do that over on Zulu. When Ruby contacted him about finding a dead body, Bonelli was ecstatic. He'll protect his ownership of this investigation, Mr. Townsend, with deadly force if necessary. You'd better be able to match his firepower, or, mark my words, you'll wish you'd never started this," she warned, dark eyes flashing.

Beside him, Ruby was holding her breath.

Whatever you do, don't argue with the Doc.

It was too late for advice. He had a job to do.

Staring back at Ktumba with what he hoped was a match for *her* firepower, he leaned in and lowered his voice. "You may be right, Doctor," he said. "At the moment, however, I have just one more question for you. If I can arrange to get Khaloub's body back here, will you perform the autopsy, and then write up your findings in a form that can be attached to my report? Yes or no."

Unexpectedly, she sighed and turned away, and it was his turn to hold his breath. A forensics report was standard procedure in a case like this. Ktumba had to be aware that without her cooperation, his plan was doomed to fail. Well, at least she hadn't asked him how he planned to procure the vic's corpse.

"You're a lunatic," Ruby murmured, and squeezed his arm. "But you're my kind of lunatic. If you survive this, I'll teach you to fly *Devil Bug*."

At that, the Doc swung stormy eyes on him. "All right, Mr. Townsend," she said, rising to her feet. "I'm not convinced that the truth should ever come out about this, but since you are determined to go ahead, I can save you some trouble. It won't be necessary to retrieve the body. My medical examination is already on file."

By sheer force of will, Drew kept his voice calm. "I see. So you inspected the corpse before the Rangers arrived?"

"I saw it, naturally, but my detailed examination was performed before he died."

"Then you don't know the exact cause of death."

"Yes, I do."

This was too much. "How? Are you psych—?" The rest of the question died on Drew's tongue. In his experience, there was only one way a person could know, without an autopsy, the precise way in which another had died.

The thought must have reached his face, for Ruby commanded urgently, "Tell him, Marion, or he'll think you did it yourself!"

The portrait of disgruntlement, Ktumba settled back down in her chair and began reciting in a singsong voice. "Karim went to his quarters right after lunch, complaining of indigestion. An hour later, he contacted Med Services. I made the house call. He had a dangerously high fever, and I gave him something to bring his temperature under control. Then he told me what he'd eaten for lunch, and I went to the caf to get some samples for analysis. By the time I'd done that, the man. Was. Dead."

"Of whatever he'd eaten that caused the fever?"

That mirthless smile was back on her face. "No, actually, he'd frozen to death."

"Frozen to death?" he repeated, dumbfounded. "Without leaving his quarters?"

"Without leaving his bed," the Doc confirmed.

"So he didn't die of accidental poisoning?"

She shrugged. "He might have died of that. On the other hand, he might have survived, if the temperature in his quarters hadn't dropped to about 200 below zero."

All right. Now they were getting somewhere — he hoped. "Who actually found the body?"

The women exchanged a glance. Ruby looked distinctly uncomfortable as she replied, "Jason Smith's console monitors all the interior temperatures on the station. When it registered the variance in Karim's quarters, it set off an alarm. Several people arrived at about the same time."

"And they discovered the body?"

"The door to his quarters wouldn't open right away. People ran to get tools, they told others what was happening, more came to help..." Ruby spread her arms helplessly.

Drew sighed. If the Rangers had received the same runaround as he was getting now, that would explain Bonelli's preliminary report. Meanwhile, he could feel a tension headache building. Time was running out, and these people were playing games. Somehow, he had to convince the crew of Daisy Hub that he wasn't the enemy. Well, as Ruby had pointed out, he was no Naguchi; perhaps he could be a Khaloub.

"Ruby, how much time do you calculate we have until Bonelli's next duty shift?"

She glanced at her wristcomm. "About three and a half hours. If he's going to pay us a visit, that's when we'll hear from him."

"Then that's how long we have to determine the truth. I want a meeting of the entire crew, in the caf, in fifteen station minutes. And tell them I have to decide what it's safe to put into a report to the Space Installation Security Agency regarding Karim Khaloub's death, and I can't do that unless I have the whole story. No guesses, no evasions, and no excuses. That means everybody attends and everybody contributes. *Capisce?*"

Ruby grinned. "I love it when you talk dirty, Chief."

Chapter 9

Most of them looked just like their images on the crew manifest. Some looked older. None of them were smiling. Drew positioned himself beside the Muralist's depiction on the cafeteria wall and watched them all straggle in and find seats. There was Spiro Gouryas, the classically featured structural integrity expert. Several techs walked in together, and Drew mentally matched their faces up with names and checked them off: Raymond Oolalong, Jill Wing, Park Sun, and Mischa Arkady. The ones he had already met glanced once in his direction, made eye contact, nodded briefly. Then they turned and pointedly looked at something else. He consulted his wristcomm, impatient to begin. They were still five people short. More to the point, where was Gavin Holchuk?

Holchuk was more than the station's resident expert on Nandrians; he was the man who had helped Karim Khaloub restore order to the Hub once before. Drew wasn't normally superstitious, but he did trust his instincts. Right now, they were telling him that if he wanted to repeat Khaloub's success, then he needed to follow Khaloub's recipe, the main ingredient of which was the Chief Cargo Inspector.

There he was. Tall, balding, with broad shoulders and deep-set eyes and craggy features, Gavin Holchuk strode into the room. He paused and scanned the assembled crewmembers, acknowledging their greetings with a nod. Finally, he strolled over to stand beside Teri Mintz and another cargo inspector, Robert O'Malley. Only then did he turn appraising eyes on the new station manager. Drew cursed under his breath and stared right back at him, holding the eye contact for a full ten seconds, until Holchuk broke into a grin and turned away. In that moment, the whole room seemed to exhale.

Prison mentality, Drew reminded himself sadly. Staring contests, pecking orders... Khaloub had been right to be concerned about morale.

"All right, people, let's begin our business," he announced. "For those of you who are seeing me for the first time, my name is Drew Townsend, and I was sent here as Karim Khaloub's replacement." He waited for the swell of murmuring to subside before continuing, "In less than three station hours, Ranger Captain Bonelli will be on his way over here to continue his investigation into Karim Khaloub's death. It is my intention to present him, when he arrives, with a *fait accompli*, a concluded case, giving the Rangers no further reason to visit this station. To do that, I need all your help. You don't know me yet, so you're just going to have to trust me to do what's in the best interests of Daisy Hub and her crew. Knowing the truth and making a report are two separate items on my agenda."

The silence that deadened the air following his words was as much a challenge as Gavin Holchuk's stare had been earlier. Finally, Ruby asked, "Where do you want to start, Drew?"

"The cause of death is a good starting point. Doctor, you told me Karim had accidentally eaten something that disagreed with him. Have you been able to identify what caused his fever?"

All eyes turned to Ktumba, who stood beside the door, white-clad arms crossed over her ample chest. "Not from the food samples I took from the caf. But I drew some blood for analysis, and in it I found an organic substance of unknown origin with molecular similarities to Human adrenaline. I would need to conduct further testing in order to confirm my hypothesis, of course, but I believe that it was this substance that caused Karim's fever."

"I knew it! It's my fault! I'm so sorry!" Fritz Jensen shot to his feet as though launched from a pad and stood in the middle of the room, wringing his hands. "He told me it was seasoning. It looked like ground pepper and smelled like oregano. I poured some into a small shaker and put it on Karim's lunch tray as a surprise. Some surprise! I killed him!"

"Whoa, slow down! Who told you it was seasoning?" Drew demanded.

Jensen looked about to cry. "The Nandrian crewman. It was early. The caf wasn't open yet. He came into the kitchen and traded it to me for a glass of lemonade."

Behind the chef's tearful words, Drew heard Gavin Holchuk cursing.

"Holchuk? Something to add?"

"That stuff should never have left the Nandrian ship," declared the Chief Cargo Inspector. "The Nandrians carry live food animals aboard their vessels and breed them as necessary. Nandrian seasoning accelerates the reproductive cycle of those animals, bringing them into *season*."

"So the crewman took the 'seasoning' into Jensen's kitchen—?"

"—because that's where our food is prepared," Holchuk replied. "And we do use seasoning, just not for the same purpose as they do."

Drew considered for a moment. "Sounds like an unfortunate misunderstanding to me. What do you think, Doctor?"

Ktumba smiled. "Assuming that I could have kept the fever under control until the effects of the seasoning had worn off, Karim probably would have recovered fully from his — indigestion."

"All right, Jensen, you're off the hook," Drew informed him. "But from now on, stay away from alien foodstuffs, at least until the Doc has had a chance to check them out."

Speechless with relief, Jensen nodded enthusiastically and plopped back into his seat with a huge sigh.

"So, the cause of death was exposure to extreme cold?" Townsend concluded, glancing at the Doc. She nodded. "Okay," he sighed, "that's the hard part. How, in God's name, does a man freeze to death in his own bed? Mr. Smith, you're the life support expert. Enlighten us, please."

A tall, lean man in gray coveralls stepped forward and snapped to attention. Terrific. After eight standard years aboard the Hub, surrounded by rebels and misfits, Jason Smith still behaved like a regular Fleet officer.

Drew sighed. "At ease, Mr. Smith, and report."

The engineer took a deep breath and began, "Out in space, we have to keep warm air circulating constantly. Otherwise, a compartment will rapidly lose heat, eventually becoming as cold as space itself."

"So something — or someone — cut off the air circulation to Karim Khaloub's quarters?"

"Yes, sir."

"I assume you have already performed a thorough examination of the air circulation system?"

"And the ductwork leading off the mains and into the station manager's quarters, yes, sir. We've ruled out any physical blockage that might have diverted the airflow. End-of-shift readouts showed all manual controls inactive around the time of the — incident. We also did a full diagnostic on the life support console. Everything is working perfectly."

"No possibility of an accident, then?"

Smith shook his head. "There's no way this should have happened, Mr. Townsend. Not by accident, not by sabotage. The entire system is watchdogged. An alarm would have gone off the second anyone hacked into the programming."

Drew smiled ruefully. "So you've ruled out the possibility that the console or its programming might have been tampered with? I'm afraid that leaves us with only one alternative, Mr. Smith."

As the engineer drew himself indignantly erect, Drew heard a collective intake of breath. "Sir, if you're about to suggest that I—"

"When the impossible has been eliminated, my dear Watson, whatever remains, however improbable, must be the truth," Drew said, quoting from memory in Ameranglo. "If there's no way the system could have been sabotaged, then we must assume it was doing exactly what it was programmed to do."

"By someone with the necessary skill and authorization codes," Smith added hotly. "That still points the finger at me."

"Maybe it does. But I told you, knowing the truth and making the report are two separate items. At the moment, I just want to know what happened. Don't you?"

Smith hesitated a moment, then nodded thoughtfully. Meanwhile, a darkly scowling Gavin Holchuk began striding toward the front of the room. As he passed Jensen's chair, the sound of a woman's sobbing stopped him in his tracks.

It caught everyone by surprise. Drew scanned the room and finally found her, standing with her back to the wall, beside the entrance to the caf. Lydia Garfield. Unable to barricade herself with furniture, Lydia had hidden instead behind a wall of people.

"I shouldn't have left him," she wailed. Ruby hurried over to comfort her, but Lydia was inconsolable. "I would have felt the temperature going down. I could have saved him."

"You were in his quarters?" Drew demanded.

"Doc Ktumba asked me to check on him," Lydia replied tearfully. "There was no change. I was going to put his skin on him, monitor from my console. I went to the SPA room — it took only a minute or so — but when I came back — I couldn't get in!"

"Don't blame yourself, Lydia," Smith told her. "There was nothing you could have done. By the time you'd noticed the chill in the air, the door would already have been sealed shut, and we'd be talking about two deaths now, instead of just one. Be grateful that you weren't inside with him."

In the ensuing half-second of silence, forty-four Eligible minds leaped to the same conclusion. Then, all at once, the room erupted with shouted questions and denials.

"What's that about the door sealing itself? Doesn't the Meniscus Field—?"

"I didn't think there was any connection. I thought it must be a malfunctioning—!"

"Doesn't the Meniscus Field generator control airflow? Isn't that how it supercools the area where—?"

"Detmar, you and Vera were talking about putting on PLS suits and going onto the landing deck to—"

"We never touched the damn thing! All we did was—!"

"Isn't the life support console supposed to—?"

"But nothing happened, I told you! It just ran for a while and then it—!"

"I never programmed that routine. It was—!"

"It was the Nandrians, when they installed the—!"

"It was encrypted, for crysakes! How was I supposed to know—?"

"The Nandrians warned us, remember? They told us—!"

"Damn!" Gavin Holchuk crossed the remaining distance between them and planted himself directly in front of Drew. "You knew," he declared accusingly.

Instantly, the room went quiet again.

"I suspected," Drew replied. "When we stopped over on the Zoo, Bonelli hinted to me that they had had an accident involving the Meniscus Field. He explained in great detail how the field worked, dropping the temperature, sealing the doors…. The puzzle pieces were there," he continued, raising his voice to include the assembled crewmembers in the discussion. "I just needed your help to put them all together."

But Holchuk wasn't about to let him off the hook that easily. "So the Ranger *kommandant* was giving you a starting point for your own investigation, one cop to another."

Drew uttered a rueful laugh. "Not a chance. As far as Bonelli is concerned, my Security background is useless and so am I. That's why I'm going to close this case, file the report, and kick his sorry behind all the way back to the Zoo. And you're going to help me."

The atmosphere in the room lightened perceptibly as the meaning of his words sank in.

"So, are we agreed then?" said Drew. "If I overheard correctly, when the Nandrians installed the Meniscus Field generator on the landing deck, they also *very generously* supplied some encrypted security software, which was *unintentionally* activated when some *naturally curious* individuals got too close to the device. As a *totally unexpected* result, a field formed outside the landing deck — in Khaloub's quarters, in fact — where he had the *bad luck* to be sleeping, and he *accidentally* froze to death because access doors *automatically* seal shut when the generator starts up, making rescue *impossible*. Does that about cover it?"

The room rippled with muffled laughter.

"Is that what you're putting in the official report?" Holchuk wanted to know.

"I wish it were," Drew replied grimly. "Unfortunately, Earth Council got this technology from the Nandrians illegally. They probably chose these locations to test it in order to give themselves deniability with the Galactic Council in case of an accident just like this one. After all, you've been trading with the Nandrians for years. Thanks to a nonstop flow of lemon juice, there's alien technology all over Daisy Hub."

Beside him, Ruby hissed angrily, "Those bastards set us up!"

"Don't worry, Mom," he assured her. "Deniability is a double-edged sword. When they set us up, they set themselves up as well."

Chapter 10

SISCO SISCO.

Time of report: Year 6040 G.C.E., Interval 37, Day 5, 2240 hours, station time.

I have been able to determine that the death of Karim Khaloub was, in fact, accidental. I repeat, there was no foul play. However, the circumstances leading up to the death of the station manager were unusual and may have involved an alien species. Any reports filed through official channels must therefore be regarded as incomplete, as I am covertly continuing to investigate. Details will follow as soon as I have confirmed them beyond any doubt. Especially if they implicate an alien species, it is essential that all information pertaining to this matter be both completely accurate and classified top secret until further notice. Do not send additional personnel. I am well placed to conduct the investigation alone and will keep my cover for as long as necessary.

SISCO SISCO.

Chapter 11

The countdown had begun. Bonelli would be arriving in under two station hours. Departments had met to discuss the situation. It was time for Drew to start doing his job.

In the first hour of night shift, lights were dimming in nonessential areas all over the station. The twilight illumination in AdComm cast worried shadows on the faces of the small group assembled there. Drew had mentally checked them off as they arrived: Gavin Holchuk, Jason Smith, Doc Ktumba, Ruby McNeil, Landing Deck Supervisor Lucas Soaring Hawk (stern-faced, taciturn), Dockmaster Orvy Hagman (muscle with attitude), and Generated Field Wizard Devanan Singh (smirking, superior). His war council, Drew thought wryly. He still didn't have an office. He'd pulled the available chairs into the middle of the room, but Ruby was the only one actually sitting. Everyone else apparently preferred to perch on tables or lean against filing cabinets. And once again, Drew was in a meeting, the outcome of which could determine his own fate and affect the lives of millions. But, hey, no pressure...

"As I see it, we have a couple of major problems to resolve," he announced. "Our first is Bonelli's report to Security. I understand why he lied about the circumstances surrounding Khaloub's death. Unfortunately, we have no choice but to corroborate the lie."

"What? Why?" demanded Smith. "That generator is dangerous. We need to let Earth Council know about this or they'll never take it off the station."

"What makes you think they don't already know about it?" Hagman replied hotly. "Wake up, boy! Earth doesn't care what happens to us."

Drew sighed. "Maybe I didn't make this clear to everyone earlier. The Meniscus Field generator is forbidden technology, acquired by Earth from the Nandrians without the knowledge of the Great Galactic Council. It's classified top secret. If it were mentioned in a Security report on an accidental death and the Great Council were to find out about it—"

"Earth Council would get what it deserved for dealing under the table," declared Smith. "I don't see the problem."

Of course, he wouldn't. Smith's biofile had been bang on. For that matter, so had Hagman's.

"The problem?" Holchuk cut in grimly. "The problem is that Earth made a promise not to reveal the source of the technology, and we would be breaking it, betraying the Nandrians' trust. The Nandrians have a very strict code. Betrayal demands retribution. The last time something like this happened, they destroyed an entire home world."

Into the silence that followed his statement, Ruby whispered incredulously, "They would attack Earth?"

"Attack it and, as a point of honor, eliminate it. There's a reason why they're the most feared warriors in the galaxy."

'Mom' swallowed audibly. "I guess we'd better figure out how a man could have ended up inside an airlock in his pajamas, then."

"Sleepwalking," the Doc piped up .

All turned to stare at her in disbelief. "Sleepwalking?" Drew echoed. "Isn't that a little too simple?"

She shrugged. "Possibly, but stranger things have happened out here. Besides, the simpler we keep it, the easier it will be to keep it straight."

There was some wisdom to that, he had to admit. Still...

"There are security vidcams on all the Utilities Decks," he reminded them, "and flatscreen playbacks available for review at the end of each shift. What if someone asks for proof? Shouldn't there be a visual record of Khaloub stepping into the airlock? Shouldn't someone have seen him doing it?"

"Not on L Deck," replied Singh. "There's sporadic interference from the gravity field generators down there. Video transmissions originating south of J Deck have been iffy for some time."

Drew glanced sharply at him. "Have they? And how long has this been going on?"

The engineer's smirk became positively Cheshire Cat-like.

Khaloub had encouraged them to use their imaginations, make their own fun, Jensen had said. Somehow, Drew didn't think this was what the previous station manager had had in mind. But it suited *his* purposes just fine.

"Okay, so we have that covered. But he still had to get from his quarters down to Deck L," he pointed out. "It would help if we had an eyewitness to some part of that."

"He used the tube door nearest his quarters," said Ruby quietly. "I had the watch in AdComm and was on my way there. When he crossed the corridor, I assumed he was going to the kitchen to get a snack. He did that from time to time. And everyone knows that sleepwalkers never actually look as though they're sleeping."

Drew nodded. "That works. And you'll swear to it? In a tribunal chamber if necessary?"

She flashed him a grin. "Cross my heart and hope to fry, Chief."

"All right, then. Doc, we'll need a medical report...?"

"Already done."

"Good. Ruby, how about the thumbprint?"

"No luck, Chief," she apologized. "It was kind of short notice."

"Not a problem — we'll switch to plan B. When Bonelli arrives, direct him to one of the docking modules on A Deck, but don't let him onto the station. Keep the archway sealed."

"You're going to try to convince him to thumbprint your report, aren't you?" Ktumba demanded. "How?"

"I have about an hour to figure that out," he told her. "But it has to be his word against mine. No audio or video record, anywhere."

Singh and Soaring Hawk exchanged a significant look. "Leave that to us, boss," said Hawk. "It's about time the microgenerators on the PLS suits got checked out."

"Diagnostic testing," Singh added, his smile even wider than before. "You know how touchy that kind of technology can be if it sits idle too long."

Everyone was grinning conspiratorially now. The mavericks and misfits were planning mischief. Making their own fun. Drew had a sense of *déjà vu*, as though if he closed his eyes and opened them again, he might find himself back in New Chicago, at a strategy meeting of the Warrior Kings. But, of course, he wasn't — and problem number two remained to be dealt with.

"Okay, moving along, then..." He paused and blew out a worried breath. "This one's a prizewinner, people. I don't expect us to solve it here and now, but I want you all thinking about it. Smith is right about one thing — the Meniscus Field generators on the Zoo and the Hub are a constant danger to us. That's why we have to find a way to get rid of them. I don't suppose we can simply ask the Nandrians to take them back...?"

Holchuk shook his head. "Asking a Nandrian to renege on a deal is tantamount to suicide."

It figured that they would have a no-returns policy. "What about asking them to help us disable the generators?"

"That would be sabotage. They would consider us to be traitors to our own government and summarily execute us, on Earth's behalf. And leave the Meniscus Fields installed on both stations," Holchuk added, his brow quirking sardonically.

"What if the generators malfunctioned on their own?" Drew persisted.

"The Nandrians would replace the defective merchandise. It would be the honorable thing to do."

Of course, it would, Drew thought sourly.

"Mr. Townsend, what's the real problem with these field generators?" asked Smith. "It's the failsafe, right? If we could figure out how to disarm the failsafe without damaging the rest of the mechanism—"

"Forget it!" Hagman declared loudly, his face twisted in disgust. "If we could just figure out how to get a look inside the damn thing without setting it off and killing someone else on the Hub, it would be a flippin' miracle!"

Deep down, Drew found himself agreeing with the dockmaster. There were at least two trained engineers in the room, neither of them ready even to guess at a solution.

Perhaps none existed. If they couldn't return or disable the alien technology, they might simply have to work around it.

Drew glanced curiously at Ruby, who had gone very quiet; she was staring at the toe of her boot, her expression shifting from concentration to bemusement and back. A moment later, she inhaled deeply, raised her eyes to meet his, and said in a firm, clear voice, "I think I know how we could look inside the casing. But I'll need to convince him."

"Him?"

"The Muralist. He'd have to give up his molecular paintbrush."

Chapter 12

It was show time. For a bunch of bad apples who didn't work well with others, the crew of Daisy Hub was beginning to pull together with promising speed. The EIS would be pleased with his next report. Together, Singh and Hawk had figured out a way to generate a jamming field from Deck B that would encompass Bonelli's short-hopper. Ruby had promised to get the Muralist to hand over his alien device for study. Even the Doc seemed to be coming around, slowly. It was a start.

Drew blanked the screen of his compupad and punched up a channel on his wristcomm. "I'm ready," he announced to whoever was on watch in AdComm. "Release the archway to docking module 3."

Bonelli had been kept trapped inside his ship for nearly twenty station minutes. He wouldn't be happy. That was all right, thought Drew grimly. He'd finally managed to place the Ranger's voice and was less than ecstatic about seeing him again as well.

Doors slid aside. Townsend stepped through them into a passenger area set up like a small conference room, just as Bonelli emerged from the short-hopper's cockpit with a sour expression on his face. "So, you finally came to your senses? About bloody time!"

Drew dropped the compupad onto the conference table. "There's your final report. We've corroborated your findings with medical evidence and a witness's sworn statement. All you have to do is print it and send it on, and the matter is closed."

"I'm not thumbprinting anything without personal verification, desk boy," the Ranger informed him. "I'm the law here, and you're not authorized—"

"Stuff it, Bonelli. As station manager, *I'm* the law on Daisy Hub. And since we're backing you up on a Kings-sized lie, I've just given you all the verification you need."

Bonelli's expression changed as though controlled by a switch, from threatening grimace to knowing smile. "Well, since you put it that way... You don't mind if I read it over first?" Drew nodded stiffly in reply. "I wondered when your memory would click in. How have you been, Snooper?"

The Ranger stepped forward and extended his hand for shaking. Drew pointedly ignored it. "We were never friends, so don't go warm and fuzzy on me. The only reason I allowed you to dock was to give you that report, and a message for your boys."

Bonelli chuckled indulgently. "Quite the tough guy you've turned into. It's a shame you don't have any firepower to back up that attitude, kid. We'd make a great team."

"Sure — until I turned my back."

His grin instantly erased, the Ranger shook his head sadly. "You've become cynical, Snooper. I guess the years can do that to a person."

Yeah, five years in particular, Drew thought. Bonelli, on the other hand, hadn't changed a bit.

"Okay, *Captain*, here's the bottom line. Unless I specifically request your help, I want the Rangers to stay away from Daisy Hub. You and your boys are not welcome here."

Bonelli was shaking his head again. And smiling.

Drew leaned closer and purposely lowered his voice. "Oh, and if I hear so much as a rumor that one of your people laid a finger on one of mine, I'll personally come over there and dispense some street-style justice," he promised. "Remember what the Warrior Kings used to do to nest-raiders in the Zone?"

Bonelli raised his hands in a gesture of appeasement. "Okay, that was unfortunate. They got excited, they crossed the line. But she shouldn't have—"

"What? She shouldn't have worn those clothes? She shouldn't have smiled at anyone?"

"Listen, it's past. The men responsible have been disciplined."

"Really? Are they still breathing? Because I can fix that."

The Ranger fell back a step. "Hold on! Cripes, Townsend, what the hell did she tell you?"

Bonelli's forehead and upper lip were glossy with perspiration. It looked good on him, Drew decided.

"You're making a big mistake, kid. You need us. Your friends in high places can't protect you out here."

"You're talking garbage. I don't have friends in high places."

"Oh, yeah? How do you think you managed to get back your Eligibility? Somebody liked you, Townsend. But they're back on Earth and you're out here on your own, and I'm the one with the guns."

More threats? He had no idea.

Aloud, Drew said, "Be that as it may, Bonelli, as station manager I'm warning you to stay off my turf. If any of your boys try to dock here uninvited, they're in for a nasty surprise."

Without waiting for the Ranger's reply, Drew wheeled and left the shuttle. He stepped through the archway, hit the intercomm button on the wall and announced, "I'm clear, AdComm. Seal the doors and blow the clamps. Let's speed him on his way."

The answering voice was so filled with elation that he scarcely recognized it. "Yes, *sir*, Mr. Townsend!" said Lydia Garfield.

Chapter 13

The lights in AdComm were coming back up. Night shift was ending, and Drew finally had his office. Following his exact orders, Jason Smith and two of the maintenance crew had brought the carpet in, unrolled it where he'd directed them, and "stuck a desk on it". Then they had walked away, muttering to themselves about station managers and their stupid blue rugs.

There were no interior walls on C Deck, and even if there were, Drew's aim had been to define his workspace, not barricade himself inside it. Lydia had already claimed her corner of AdComm, and Ruby's console took up nearly a fifth of the deck, directly in front of the observation port. The spot Drew had picked for his desk was just off-center, facing a piece of bulkhead halfway between two tube car doors. The blank wall was plaincoated in solid beige and already boring to look at. Maybe, if he dropped a hint or two, the Midnight Muralist would decorate it for him.

The tall gray metal filing cabinets, Drew had discovered, were filled with records left by his predecessors. They would make interesting reading if he ever got a moment to review them; meanwhile, the cabinets, banked together in an 'L' shape, made a passable office partition.

"It must be a station manager thing."

Drew turned at the sound of her voice and saw Ruby McNeil walking toward him, smiling, as the tube car door closed behind her. "I heard you were into interior decorating," she commented. "Not bad." Lips pursed, she surveyed the fruit of his considerable labors. "You know, that is one sorry piece of carpet, Chief. I didn't think it would survive decon. But now that I see it lying there like the skin of some repulsive alien beast, I must admit it pulls the room together."

"Don't try to talk me out of it," he warned her.

"Wouldn't dream of it. I came by to ask if I could buy you a cup of java in the caf."

"A second cup of Fritz's brew in one day? That would probably keep me up for the next five with indigestion."

"Drew, trust me," she said, all the laughter gone from her voice, "you're going to want this cup of java."

They were the caf's first customers of the morning. Drew let Ruby shepherd him to a table in the far corner of the eating area, his curiosity deepening as she hollered into the kitchen in passing, "Java, black, and keep it coming!"

Jensen personally brought them two large mugs and a pot of his most potent blend. Ruby waited until he had filled their cups and disappeared back into the cooking area, then asked, "What's this I hear about you having friends in high places?"

Drew cursed silently. He hadn't wanted anyone to overhear his conversation with Bonelli, but Ruby and the Doc had insisted that the confrontation be monitored from AdComm 'just in case'. Now questions were arising, and he would have to obfuscate like mad to control the damage.

"That was just Bonelli, blowing smoke," he told her. "I did something he couldn't have managed without someone intervening for him, so he assumed I had help. He was wrong."

"Are you sure of that?"

"Ruby, if I had friends with that kind of pull, why would I be here?"

"That's precisely the question I've been asking myself ever since we met. There's something about you that makes my brain itch, Mr. Townsend. But never mind, I'll figure you out. Meanwhile, drink your java."

"Yes, Mom."

There was good news and there was bad news. Ruby waited until he'd taken several swallows of Jensen's sludge before breaking either one to him.

"The good news is that the paintbrush turned up on Devanan's desk this morning. He and Spiro are already checking it out. If we're lucky, we might be able to use it to turn the casing around the Meniscus Field generator transparent without setting anything off."

"I hope you told the Muralist thank you for us."

"I had nothing to do with it, Drew."

Right. Of course, she didn't. "Well, thank him anyway."

There was a long pause until Drew prompted her, "You said there was bad news?"

"Yes," she replied reluctantly. "You'd better not plan on sleeping for a while, Chief. The latest *tekl'hananni* scores have been posted and the *Krronn* is on her way. In less than thirty-four station hours, this hub will be full of Nandrian warriors. You'll need every minute of that time to prepare for the First Meeting ceremony with their Chief Officer, Nagor."

Despite the hot mud in his stomach, Drew felt instantly clammy inside. He took another gulp of java.

"There's a ritual speech you have to recite," Ruby continued. "Gavin is waiting on A Deck to teach it to you."

At least she let him finish his java first. When Drew arrived on Deck A, half an hour later, Gavin Holchuk was standing in the middle of the room, looking grimmer than death.

"I don't have time to give you a crash course on Nandrian culture and customs, Townsend," he snapped. "Just get us through this ceremony without delivering a mortal insult to anyone and I'll be happy. Here," he added, thrusting a compupad into Drew's hand. "It's the invitation speech. Read it aloud, exactly as written."

Too tired to take offence at the other man's attitude, Drew began to read.

"Stop!" Holchuk blew out a disgusted sigh. "Damn!"

Drew could feel his patience giving way, one strand at a time. "Now what?" he demanded raggedly.

"You're going to get yourself killed, that's what." Holchuk spun away and spread his arms, as though imploring heaven. "We have a station manager who can't even speak Galactic Standard!" he announced to the ceiling. Then he turned to face Drew once more, his eyes cold with rage. "What the hell kind of Eligible are you, Townsend? Is the Relocation Authority so desperate to replace plague casualties off-planet that they're lowering the bar and granting postings to marginals? Or did you simply not bother qualifying for one, knowing that you could depend on someone high up to take care of you?"

Even caffeinated up to the eyeballs, Drew knew he didn't dare rise to the bait.

He zagged. "Look, I'm doing my best. If I'm mispronouncing words, swearing and shouting at me isn't going to help. Just tell me how to say them and give me a chance to practice. I'm a quick study, promise!"

Holchuk's anger drained away. He glanced upward once more and shook his head sadly. "Do you know what you just called yourself? A burrowing insect. Call Nagor that and he'll gut you without a second thought. When you give this speech, you can't mispronounce a single word. You can't stammer. You can't even hesitate."

"All right," Drew conceded wearily. "You wanted to frighten me — it worked. So why don't *you* invite them aboard?"

"I would if I were the station manager. Feel like stepping down, boss man?"

Drew sighed, wishing he *could* step down. That had been the original plan, after all — to get him assigned to a low-profile position like hub maintenance that he could use as a blind while he observed and orchestrated.

"Not today, Holchuk. Okay, tell Jensen to send us up some breakfast and lots of java. Then walk me through the ceremony."

While the Chief Cargo Inspector was talking on the wallcomm, Drew scanned the rest of the invitation speech. It was a brief history of Daisy Hub — or pretended to be. Some of the colorful and glorious battles it described couldn't possibly have taken place there.

"Is there a problem?" Holchuk asked, scowling.

"No, but it's—" *a bunch of lies*, he'd been about to say, before realizing just in time that the other man had probably written it himself. "It's very creative. Do the Nandrians actually believe this?"

"Lord, I hope not. It's posturing, that's all. The Nandrians are warriors. Posturing is part of their culture. Besides, it gives the Hub some ambience."

Ambience and Daisy Hub in the same thought? Drew shook his head slowly.

Meanwhile, Holchuk went on, warming to the subject, "Listen, if all you wanted was to get toxed, you'd pick something up at a liquor store on your way home. But if you wanted to celebrate, you'd go to a tav. Why?"

"The company?" Drew guessed.

"Exactly. A tav is a gathering place. Its history invites you in, its atmosphere makes you feel welcome. History and atmosphere — that's what this speech creates."

"So Daisy Hub was never actually attacked by dragons?"

"Only in one of Naguchi's nightmares. He figured it was a dream-metaphor for a fleet of hostile ships." Holchuk glanced at his wristcomm and winced. "Less than thirty-two hours left," he said, becoming brisk and purposeful once more. "All right. Trokerk is leading by four, so they'll ask to dock at module 4. Nagor will step through the archway, followed by his second and third. You will be waiting here, flanked by Ruby and me. Once the three of them are facing the three of us, you'll deliver the invitation speech, from memory. Then, assuming you've given them no reason to kill you on the spot, the introductions will begin.

"As the one arriving, Nagor will introduce himself first. He'll tell you his name, his father's name, and his position within the House of Trokerk. You'll respond by introducing yourself the same way, as Drew, son of…?"

"David and Caroline."

"Just David. Nandrian lineage goes through the male parent. Drew, son of David, Third Shield of the House of Americas. Say it."

"Why Third Shield?"

"Nandrian First and Second Shields are essential to the defense of the House, so they hardly ever leave the home world. The Nandrians already know that we have six different Shield levels represented on the Hub. The station manager has highest authority and would therefore have to be part of the highest possible Shield. Third Shield. Now say it."

"I am Drew, son of David, Third Shield of the House of Americas."

"You could sound a little prouder," Holchuk chided. "Nagor commands a starship and is only Fifth Shield."

"And what about you?"

"I'm Fifth Shield as well. Ruby is Fourth. Hagman is Eighth. You're the only Third Shield on the Hub. There, are you happy?"

Holchuk was deathly serious. Drew managed somehow not to smile.

"All right. Nagor will then introduce his second the same way, and wait for you to introduce Ruby."

"Then his third, and you?"

"Exactly. Then each leader describes his most recent battle victory. I've already begun scripting yours."

He reached over and scrolled down several pages on the compupad. Curious, Drew scanned the first paragraph. "Bonelli?" he protested, glancing up in disbelief. "That wasn't a battle. It was barely a skirmish."

"Once I've finished embellishing it for our Nandrian guests, they'll think it was a historical milestone. It doesn't have to be the truth, Townsend. All it has to do is keep you alive. Just remember that Nagor goes first, and that it's an insult if your victory is not equal to his. So pay attention to his account. If he fought single combat, you fought single combat. If he fought ten opponents, you fought ten Rangers, and won."

"But—!"

"Townsend, think of this as the Nandrian equivalent of saying please and thank you at a tea party. If your victory is greater than his, you make him appear inferior and are a poor host. If it's lesser, you make yourself appear inferior, and then he won't respect you as a leader. And, Third Shield or not, if he doesn't respect you he won't take orders or even suggestions from you. And neither will his crew. And then we're all fried."

"All right," Drew sighed. "I fought a whole battalion of Rangers and sent them home defeated and disgraced. What next?"

"Then he has a speech praising you for being a gracious host and a mighty warrior, and thanking you for the invitation."

"And then?"

"Then his crew swarms into the caf, Jensen starts setting up tall ones, and after my people have inspected the cargo holds, you get to go shopping. Unless you've mispronounced a word and gotten yourself killed. Then Ruby belongs to the highest-ranked Shield on the Hub and has the privilege of going first."

Chapter 14

All alone in AdComm, Drew sank down wearily in the chair behind his desk, his entire body aching with tension. Fortunately, a previous station manager had declared C Deck off-limits to aliens. Everywhere else on the Hub, jubilant Nandrians were chug-a-lugging lemon punch, loudly bragging about their exploits, reenacting them with whatever props came to hand, and generally giving new meaning to the phrase 'party animals'.

Humans liked to party, too. *Devil Bug* kept spinning past the observation port as 'Mom' showed off her skills to Nagor's officers, two at a time. Drew imagined they were debarking from the little shuttle a shade or two greener than when they'd boarded it. In the caf, Jensen was gleefully experimenting with new ways to mix lemon drinks. Lydia Garfield had opened up the comm system Hub-wide, and everyone who owned a musical instrument was down on L Deck, jamming. Everyone who appreciated good music was consequently up on B Deck, jamming in a different sense of the word. The Muralist's work was on display, of course, and the Nandrians were making quite a fuss over it — in their own hissing, snarling language, not Gally. And Orvy Hagman and the dock and maintenance crew were circulating quietly, identifying guests who had overstayed their welcome and politely but firmly escorting them back up to A Deck and onto their ship.

Night shift was beginning. Again. Not counting naps stolen behind Gavin Holchuk's back, Drew had now been awake for two-and-a-half station days. He had found the comm system controls on Lydia's console and used them to silence the speakers in AdComm. As the lighting dimmed, he felt the chill of fatigue and knew that he really ought to be getting some sleep. But now, while the past few hours were still painfully fresh in his mind and the rest of the crew were distracted by their 'guests', now would be the best time to log his first routine report as station manager.

The highlight of that report: Drew had finally met the Nandrians, face to razor-toothed face. Two meters of evolved carnosaur. Warrior-merchants. Players of a 'sport' in which final score and body count were synonymous. And in perfect Galactic Standard — and frozen to the deck in mortal terror — Drew Townsend had actually invited the top-ranked ship's crew to hold their victory celebration aboard Daisy Hub — and they'd accepted.

If this was what happened when the Nandrians liked you, it was no wonder Naguchi had had nightmares.

Drew didn't know whether it was demanded by the ceremony, but the Nandrians had stood still as statues, allowing him to negotiate the five hundred perilous words of his speech undistracted. As he finished, Ruby and Holchuk heaved audible sighs of relief. Then, in a spasm of nervousness, Drew managed to forget his own father's name, blurting out instead the first thing that came to his mind. ("Well, it could have been worse," Ruby consoled him later, grinning mischievously. "It could have been my name you forgot.") The rest of the ceremony had gone reasonably well, he thought. At its conclusion, as Nandrians poured through the archway to get to the tube cars, Ruby congratulated him specifically on keeping his credibility as the Hub's fearless leader by not wetting his trousers. (Jovanovich had apparently disgraced himself more than once in the Nandrians' eyes.) By then Holchuk had already hurried off without saying a word, but the three of them were still alive and the station was being overrun by huge alien warriors, so he must have been happy.

Yes, it was the perfect time to make his report, Townsend thought. Yawning, he leaned back in his chair and—

"Huh!"

Suddenly he was wide awake and the lights were up full. His neck and shoulders ached miserably. His mouth tasted the way a three-day-old corpse smelled. He checked the time on his wristcomm. It was nearly twelve hundred hours. Day shift was half over. "Dammit!" he spat.

Familiar laughter rippled into his office from just the other side of a tall filing cabinet. "I don't think your father can hear you from there, Chief," Ruby sang out.

"Don't be too sure of that," he muttered, shifting his body in the padded falsahyde chair and wincing at the popping and creaking sounds they both made.

"Oh, so we're talking about *those* kinds of friends in high places?" Ruby's grinning face appeared around the corner of Drew's improvised room-divider. "While you were snoring, your dance card was filling up," she told him. "Gouryas and Singh need to see you on L Deck. No rush. Just something about our hull integrity dropping. And Holchuk says there was a problem with the cargo inspection on the *Krronn*. He wants to meet with you in Med Services as soon as possible."

Drew halted in the act of finger-combing his hair and scowled. "Med Services? Is someone hurt? Did one of the Nandrians—?"

"No. But as soon as you've changed your clothes, I think it would be a good idea to go down there." A pause, then, "Lydia dropped by, as well, to thank you for what you told Bonelli the other day. And she was curious…"

"…to know how I knew?"

She nodded.

Drew eased himself out of the chair and carefully straightened his spine, wondering how thirty-six years could suddenly feel so *old*. "Something you told me the other day, about Lydia going over to Zulu to install their SPA room, plus the way Bonelli and the other Rangers looked at Teri when we arrived at the Zoo earlier, and your decision to come and pick us up from there right away because one of us was a woman. It doesn't take a genius to put those pieces together. Is Lydia getting counseling?"

"She was, and she was improving. Then Karim died, and suddenly there were Rangers all over the Hub, and, well, you saw the state she was in."

Yes, he had seen it — and the more he thought about it, the more it bothered him. For starters, what the devil was someone that traumatized doing working shifts in AdComm? That was assuming, of course, that Lydia's distress was genuine. After all, Ruby hadn't shown much compassion for her during his tour, and Doc Ktumba, flying in the face of common sense and the Hippocratic Oath, had apparently decided not to send the patient back to Earth for psychiatric help after her relapse.

It was a con. Had to be. And he was the mark. Tempting though it might be to simply out the players and shut the operation down then and there, Drew was curious to see just how far his crew of bad apples were capable of taking this charade. Was there a common goal at the end of it? He decided to play along and find out.

"Tell her from me that she won't have to worry about dealing with any more Rangers until she's good and ready to fry their butts herself," Drew promised, on his way to the tube car. As the door slid open for him, he turned and added, "But also tell her that Bonelli is mine."

Ruby flashed him a proud smile. "Yes, sir, Chief!"

Then the tube car door closed between them and her earlier words sank in: "Hull integrity dropping?" Drew pressed the button for L Deck. Gavin Holchuk would have to wait.

Chapter 15

"Where the hell is he?"

Doc Ktumba glanced up briefly, shook her head, and returned to examining the patient. "He'll be here when he gets here, Gavin. Meanwhile, perch somewhere, will you? You're wearing a trench in my floor."

But he couldn't stop pacing. "When will you know?" he demanded.

"Where is Teri?" she countered impatiently.

"She's finishing up in the aft cargo hold."

The Doc turned and stared at him incredulously. "Her first inspection, and you left her alone on a ship full of Nandrians sleeping off a victory party?" she scolded.

"You know me better than that. Robbo and Lu are with her. And Yoko."

The Doc stifled a laugh. "The Überrat will protect her, all right."

"Hey, never underestimate an Eligible rodent." A pause, then, "Well?"

Ktumba breathed an exasperated syllable. "She isn't Madeline, Gavin."

"Are you sure?"

"The first thing I did was a DNA comparison. You're not even distantly related. Now go away and let me work." In a more charitable voice, she added, "I'll have the results of the biotests in half an hour. Townsend should be available by then. Why don't you go check on Teri?"

He looked past her, at the girl lying so pale and still on the examining bed. Only a quiet chorus of electronic beeps emanating from various monitors indicated she was still alive.

Teri had found her in the forward hold of the Nandrian ship, bound and gagged and slung like a hammock from one of the duct pipes. The girl's clothing had been torn and there were scrapes and bruises all over her body. Tears had dried on her cheeks. Tendrils of dark hair were sweat-plastered to her face. A slight Human female, caught in the insanity of *tekl'hananni* — it was a miracle she'd even survived. Holchuk's first thought on emerging from the shock of seeing her there had been to talk to Nagor, but the Chief Officer had been sound asleep. Then he'd contacted AdComm, and learned to his disgust that the station manager was dead to the world as well.

At least Teri hadn't fallen apart on him. He'd feared she might, mainly because she claimed to have been some kind of celebrity in her previous life and seemed to resent having to tote her own luggage; but she'd surprised him, bless her. Together, they'd lowered the girl to the deck, removed the bindings from her wrists and ankles and the tarry substance from over her mouth, and brought her to Med Services.

The girl had been so light in his arms, so sweet and young, with an innocence that he hadn't seen, or even dared to think about, in far too many years. She was somebody's precious daughter. She looked the right age to be his daughter. And she'd been through so much...

"Gavin, it isn't her," the Doc repeated firmly.

Of course, it wasn't. After all this time, how could he still believe in those kinds of coincidences?

"Then who is she, Doc?"

"I promise you, we'll find out. But not if you don't let me work."

Holchuk raised his hands in surrender and headed back up to A Deck.

— « o » —

Teri was waiting for him beside the archway to docking module 4, hugging her compupad to her chest and frowning uncertainly.

"Trouble with the Nandrians?" he asked. There shouldn't have been — knowing that she might have to deal with members of Nagor's crew, Holchuk had introduced Teri as his mate, giving her Fifth Shield status and himself the right under Nandrian law to take action against anyone who harmed her.

"No," she replied. "But you'll never guess what the cargo is in the aft hold."

The aft hold wasn't as well-lit as the forward hold, nor as clean, although it seemed to contain just as many stratium storage cubes. Their pale, squat shadows hugged the deck, freckled by pieces of dirt and scattered bits of debris. As he followed Teri through the gray-on-gray maze, Holchuk could feel things flatten under his boots with a soft, almost apologetic crunch. It was a discomfiting sensation.

There was also a pungent smell in the air, as though something had broken open or spoiled, and he was opening his mouth to ask Teri what it was when they suddenly emerged into an area containing a dozen cages.

Some were constructed of metal bars and mesh, some of a bamboo-like material. None of the cages was taller than his waist, and all but a couple were occupied. He could feel the sad eyes of the Nandrians' silent captives on him long before he could see them.

"The Nandrians are transporting animals to be sold as pets," said Teri. "Rob is looking them up on the database right now. According to the manifest, this shipment is to be delivered to an exotic animal broker on one of the alien worlds."

Holchuk could tell from the glance she threw him then that they had both had the same unsettling thought.

"And look," she said, dropping abruptly to one knee. She plucked something off the deck and handed it to him. It was a splinter of the bamboo-like material, trailing a long fiber that had become trapped in a crack at one end.

"The deck is littered with these," she explained. "We figure they're what's left of one of the cages. And those fibers? They look an awful lot like cloth strands, don't they? The girl's clothing was in tatters when we found her. What if the Nandrians tried to cage her, but she broke out, destroying the cage — and her clothes — in the process? Gavin, what if—?" Her voice failed as she looked up at him.

Slowly he shook his head, feeling as though a wormhole were trying to open inside his stomach. This wasn't right. The

Nandrians were warriors, yes; but, as Nagor had told him on more than one occasion, they were traders, not conquerors, and certainly not slavers. The Great Council would never have approved Nandor's application for membership if its citizens preyed upon other worlds, other sentients. Members also had to have a peaceful home world. That was why the Nandrians had *tekl'hananni* — forty Houses continuing a millennia-old power struggle out in space with full-contact contact, regulated by officials on neutral observation ships. Holchuk shuddered as the thought occurred to him: If the Nandrians could make war and call it a sport, what was to prevent them from having another name as well for the buying and selling of slaves?

"Gavin? Are you okay?" Teri was watching him, her brows knitted with concern.

Holchuk met her gaze and felt his heart constrict. It had been a long time since anyone besides the Doc had given a damn about his welfare.

"Yeah, I'm fine," he growled. "If she had to break out of a cage, that could account for a lot of her scrapes and bruises." For a moment, he tried to visualize himself attacking one of those cages from the inside, with his shoulders, hips and feet. "All right, let's gather up some evidence," he concluded. "The boss man has delusions of cophood, so nobody's going to be shopping in here for a while. He'll probably order both these holds sealed off until everything in them has been inspected and analyzed seventeen different ways."

"That poor girl isn't going to die, is she?"

"Anything is possible, Tiger."

"Good news, people!" Robbo called to them from the hatchway. "They're pets. None of those specimens belong to any species classified dangerous or sentient on the Galactic Database." One of them chose that moment to yawn, and Holchuk found himself staring at an impressive array of sharp teeth. That explained why Robbo was keeping his distance. Yoko had probably shredded his shoulder trying to get away. Überrat, indeed!

"O'Malley, get in here and help Teri gather evidence," Holchuk decided. "I'm going down to AdComm to file our reports."

"Copies to Disease Control *and* Customs? Townsend's going to love that," Robbo commented wryly as they passed each other.

"Yeah," Holchuk muttered. O'Malley was right, of course. Was the girl a stowaway, or was she contraband? Until either Nagor or the girl was awake and willing to talk, there was no way to know what had actually happened aboard the *Krronn*.

As the tube car started its descent, Holchuk activated his wristcomm. "AdComm, this is Holchuk. Is the boss man awake yet?"

"Walking and talking," came Ruby's reply. "Isn't he with you? Okay, sorry, stupid question. He's probably gone to L Deck."

Cursing under his breath, Holchuk punched the override button on the tube car control pad and selected Deck L instead. What was 'Snooper' up to now? he wondered darkly.

Chapter 16

L Deck was a hodge-podge of workshops, lockers, warehousing, and factory floor, where parts and 'hot spares' were stored for all the technology on the Hub, and where the engineers and tech-types tended to spend much of their time. Sandwiched between the gravity field generator and the primary utilities deck, it was also the Achilles heel of the Hub. One direct hit to L Deck would not only knock out all the primary life support systems, it would also pretty much destroy any chance of repairing them. Worse, anyone caught on L Deck during the attack would either be blown out into space or, if the gravity field held, be crushed as the remaining decks collapsed onto him.

Naguchi had wandered all over Daisy Hub, including to L Deck, but Naguchi had been an engineer. Townsend was nothing definite yet, except a proven liar. So what the hell would he be doing down here? Holchuk wondered as the tube car slid past the stenciled letter L on the wall of the shaft and gently came to a halt.

The door slid aside, revealing some sort of meeting taking place. Townsend and two other men were involved in an animated discussion in the center of the deck, occasionally gesturing toward something that looked like a door panel, painted in colorful stripes. The molecular paintbrush thing? That was what had been so damned important?

"Hey, boss man!" Holchuk called out, striding angrily toward them. "Didn't you understand my message? I've got an emergency waiting in Med Services and—"

They turned as one to look at him, three faces so somber that at the sight of them he almost misstepped. Townsend, Spiro Gouryas, and Devanan Singh. If even Singh had lost his smirk, there had to be something seriously wrong.

"What's going on?" Holchuk demanded, suddenly feeling less certain than he sounded.

Townsend nodded briefly to the engineer, as though giving him permission to speak.

"It's our hull integrity, Gavin," said Gouryas. "In the past standard year, overall hull strength has dropped by nearly twelve percent. We're currently holding at 88.35, but unless we do something to get it back up close to a hundred, the damage will become irreversible." The engineer let out a long-suffering sigh. *I kept warning you about this*, it seemed to say. *Now will you listen?*

"Come have a look at this panel, Gavin," Singh said, gesturing him closer. "It's made of the same alloy as the exterior hull plating on starships. All we used on it was the Muralist's paintbrush and an ordinary hammer, in that order."

Holchuk stepped forward, and stood staring in disbelief. The alloy had been specially engineered for space travel. It was many times stronger than steel and shouldn't even have registered the simple kinetic force of a hammer. But this door panel was wrecked. In places, it was only dented, in others almost punctured. And, he couldn't help noticing, the worst-damaged parts had been 'painted' the deepest color — the color of space that the Muralist was so fond of.

"Damn," he whispered.

"The atomic composition of the material hasn't changed," Gouryas explained, "but the molecular latticework has been altered. Metaphorically speaking, the device turns diamond into coal. They're both pure carbon, but they deal with light in different ways. And whereas a diamond is one of the hardest materials in existence..."

"Scary, isn't it?" Singh added.

"Thanks to the Muralist, there are a total of twenty-five soft spots on the Hub, fifteen of them on perimeter bulkheads," continued Gouryas. "Nobody knows at this point whether the effect can be completely reversed, but I have all my techs working around the clock to determine how the device operates. My theory about this is that the color change is coincidental. I think the 'paintbrush' could have been originally intended as an industrial tool, or even a weapon."

It had come from the Nandrians, Holchuk realized. No wonder they'd become so excited about the Muralist's little masterpieces. What he'd done was the equivalent of turning a laser rifle into a lamp stand. And of course, the Nandrians would never insult a customer by pointing out that he'd made such an error. Instead, they'd probably set up a betting pool, giving odds on how long it would take their Human friends to discover the mistake themselves — and whether they would survive the lesson.

Townsend's face had acquired a strange, lopsided smile. "Monkeys with typewriters," he murmured.

"Typewriters?" asked Singh.

"Antiquated text printing devices, manually operated," Townsend explained.

"Why give them to monkeys?"

"To see what they'll do with them, Mr. Singh. Maybe compose poetry. Or maybe use them to bash in the heads of other monkeys. Either way, they'll be showing you just what kind of monkeys they are."

Abruptly, Holchuk went cold all over. "Are you suggesting that the Nandrians purposely traded a potentially lethal device to us in order to test us?" he said.

"It wouldn't be the first time one group of people has covertly taken the measure of another, Mr. Holchuk. Assume for a moment that I'm right. You're our expert on Nandrians — what would they be most interested in knowing about us?"

Quickly, Holchuk reviewed his mental database. The Nandrians already knew a great deal about Humans. They knew that Humans were intelligent and curious, and compulsively drawn to unravel mysteries. They had had occasion to witness Human courage and resourcefulness. They had also seen and heard examples of Human creativity, which they respected, just as the crew of Daisy Hub respected the Nandrian code of honor and the numerous rituals that went along with it. What, besides that, did the Nandrians truly value, highly enough to test for it without another's knowledge?

"Loyalty," he said at last. "They're warriors, and the most valuable thing to a warrior, next to his own strength, is being able to depend on his allies."

"But they've been trading with Humans for years. Why, suddenly, would they feel the need to test our loyalties?" Townsend wondered. "Unless— Holchuk, could they be planning an offensive?"

"Absolutely not. The Galactic Council would revoke their membership if they became aggressors in a conflict."

"What if they weren't the aggressors? What if they were expecting an attack and—?"

Holchuk stifled a laugh. "You're joking, right? The Nandrians?"

Townsend sighed. "Point taken. All right, then, someone must have done something to make them doubt us. Gouryas, you said that the Muralist began using the device about a station year ago. What else was going on around that time?"

"Khaloub arrived, and—"

"The Meniscus Field generators were being installed," Singh cut in. "The first mural appeared just after they came online."

Townsend's expression became thoughtful. "Interesting. The generators weren't purchased by anyone on Daisy Hub. Earth Council bought them and placed them here and on the Zoo. Had anything like that ever happened before?"

"No, and with luck it'll never happen again," declared Singh with a vehemence that surprised the new station manager.

"Is that how everyone feels?" Townsend asked.

"It is now," said Gouryas. "We welcomed it at first. We thought we'd get to play with it, you know? Learn how it works, maybe even improve on it. Then the Nandrians warned us about the security protocols. And, Mr. Townsend, I can't speak for the others, but I felt cheated. Not by the Nandrians. By Earth. As you said earlier, we've been trading with the aliens for years. Anything they've sold us has always come without strings — no restrictions, no warranties. Then Earth does a deal with the Nandrians, and suddenly, we're not allowed to touch. It's not right. Aliens might not be aware of that, but Earth Council should have known better."

"He's right," Singh chimed in. "Somebody should have realized that you can't install a new technology on a hub full of techs and engineers and expect them not to at least be curious about it."

Feeling even more cynical than usual today, Holchuk found himself entertaining a sudden thought. "Maybe someone did realize it, Dev. Maybe that's why it was put here."

"What are you saying?" demanded Singh. "That Earth Council *wanted* us to play with that field generator?"

Townsend was nodding now, his face a grim mask. "I think that may be precisely what they had in mind, Mr. Singh."

"Then why did they put on the bloody failsafe?"

"They didn't," he stated flatly. "Earth had no idea there were security protocols on the device."

Alarms were going off in the back of Holchuk's mind. "And you know this because…?"

"Security's response to Karim Khaloub's death was to investigate," Townsend told him. "Bonelli's preliminary report arrived on Earth shortly before I left. If the Council had been aware of the failsafe, the incident would have been ruled accidental immediately and swept out of the way before it could attract any more attention. It wasn't." The hardness of these last words was a clear warning not to question him any further.

But Holchuk needed to raise a point. Obviously, the boss man didn't realize how sensitive the Nandrians could be. "These aliens have a strict code of honor, Townsend. They don't lie. And they tend to take it very badly if anyone implies that they would."

The station manager grew a faint, infuriating smile, almost as annoying as the one Singh customarily wore. "I'm not suggesting that. I'm sure the Nandrians delivered exactly what Earth Council had ordered. Then, out of the bigness of their hearts, they tacked the security programming on as an extra. A gift."

Gouryas blanched. "But it turned the generator into a lethal weapon," he protested. "It killed Karim."

"Accidentally," Townsend pointed out. "Don't forget, it was an aberration that Khaloub was even in his quarters at the time."

And that made sense too, Holchuk realized abruptly. The Nandrians might not be experts on Humanity as a species, but they knew the crew of Daisy Hub very well. "Spiro, in your home, there are knives and laser guns. Which do you lock up for safety?"

"You've been spending too much time with Nagor, my friend," Singh observed. "You're beginning to sound like him."

"You answer the question then. Which do you lock up?"

"Both, if there are children in the house. But if I must choose, then the guns, of course. An accident with one of those is almost always fatal, whereas with a knife—" Singh's eyes widened suddenly with comprehension. "So you think the Nandrians locked up the more dangerous device to protect us?"

"Or perhaps they did it to protect everyone else. Maybe the lethal weapon here isn't the field generator or the paintbrush. Maybe it's us."

"Now you're frightening me."

Holchuk grinned.

"I think we should all be frightened," Townsend cut in impatiently. "Our own government put an alien technology on the Hub knowing the crew wouldn't be able to resist tinkering with it. Am I the only one here wondering why?"

"Who do you suggest we ask, boss man?"

"We don't," Townsend replied, ignoring the challenge in Holchuk's voice. "Even if we knew which arm of Council had ordered the installation, you can be certain they wouldn't give us a straight answer. We'll have to figure it out ourselves."

Yeah, right, thought Holchuk darkly. Townsend already knew the answer, just as he had known before calling the crew meeting precisely how Karim had died. It was just what Holchuk would have expected from a plant. Only he'd helped them uncover the truth instead of leading them away from it. And now it appeared he was doing the same thing again. Couldn't speak Gally, former street gang member — if Drew Townsend was a government agent, he was a damned strange one.

"We can safely assume that Earth wanted the device modified," Townsend was continuing. "Gouryas, Singh — you two are the Engineering Specialists. What changes would you make to the Meniscus Field generator if you could?"

"It takes up nearly a quarter of the landing deck. I would definitely see about making it smaller," declared Singh. "And lighter."

"Making it portable?"

The other man shrugged. "If it's possible, why not?"

Gouryas added, "I've never liked the idea of sealing off the landing deck from the rest of the Hub. Trapped oxygen is a fire hazard. If a short-hopper came in with an engine malfunction, the whole deck could go up in flames and none of us would be able to help."

"Could you modify the generator to reduce the risk?" Townsend wanted to know.

"Perhaps. Assuming we could gain access to its internal workings, we could try to make the entire process more controllable: install manual overrides, add a kill switch, calibrate a range of field strengths, maybe even figure out a way to limit the size and location of the field."

Singh was getting excited — Holchuk could practically hear wheels whirring inside the engineer's head. "You know, if we could point and shoot the field generator, we might not even have to keep it inside the Hub. We could mount the device on the hull and control it remotely."

A shiver crept across Holchuk's shoulders. Were these techno-geniuses listening to themselves? Point and shoot, remote control…

"It sounds as though you're describing a weapon." Townsend's voice fell like a lead weight into the middle of their discussion. Holchuk saw startled looks pass between the other two men.

"Well, yes, I suppose it could be used that way," Gouryas stammered.

"You don't actually believe it was Earth's intention that we discover offensive capabilities in this alien device?" demanded Singh incredulously.

Townsend heaved a martyred sigh. "Gentlemen, forget about what I believe. What we have to worry about here and now is what the Nandrians will believe. Remember the Nandrians?" he reminded them patiently. "Betrayal? Retribution?"

Holchuk nearly smiled. It was good to know that *someone* had been listening to him earlier on.

"This must be their test — not the paintbrush," Townsend declared, and, reluctantly, Holchuk had to agree. "The Nandrians probably put the failsafe on the field generator because they already knew it could be turned into a weapon. Hell, for all we know, that's how they score points in *tekl'hananni*. So, they mustn't ever find out that we're trying to bypass their security measures. We can't even let them know that we think we know why those measures are in place. This is important, gentlemen — it could mean all our lives. I need your solemn promise that nothing we've just discussed will be shared with anyone else."

Silenced by the expression on his face, the three of them nodded agreement.

"Gouryas, keep your techs working on that device. At the moment, our prime concern is hull strength. We need them to learn how the paintbrush works and whether its effect can be reversed. Let me know the minute you have an answer to those questions."

"Yes, sir."

"Holchuk, I'm creating a new position just for you — Alien Liaison Officer. Choose a member of your detail to take over as Chief Cargo Inspector whenever there are Nandrians aboard the Hub. If they're testing us, that means they're also checking up on us. We can't suddenly become secretive, or they'll know we're onto them. I want you to make a point of telling Nagor about the reduction in hull integrity, and that we've connected it to the paintbrush. Tell him the device has been confiscated for analysis and that we're trying to learn how to reverse the effect. Be specific about that. And don't tell him anything else, even if he asks. They talk in riddles — you answer them in riddles."

So, Townsend wasn't just a liar, thought Holchuk, nodding mechanically, he was also a schemer. Once the Nandrians were off the station he'd probably order Singh to draw up plans for a 'space weapon', just in case the aliens already had one. Wasn't that Humanity's standard operating procedure?

"Singh, is there any way you could adjust the gravity field to lessen the amount of stress on these twenty-five soft spots? Even a slight reduction would help."

The other man looked thoughtful. "Perhaps, if I were to dampen some of the field amplification relays north of H Deck. I'll run a sim and see what happens."

"Good idea. And if you think of anything else that might work, let me know immediately. Oh, and there mustn't be any record of this meeting. Find and erase the shift feed from the surveillance vidcams on this deck. Better yet, find us a way to turn them off when we need privacy, without waking any watchdogs."

Holchuk watched the engineers scatter to do Townsend's bidding. They would have to keep an eye on this new station manager. For someone so compulsive about getting at the truth, he was awfully damned good at covering it up.

Chapter 17

"Now, what's this emergency waiting for us in Med Services?"

As they headed for the tube car, Holchuk felt a brief spasm of annoyance. He'd wanted the pleasure of reminding Townsend about the other matter, but the boss man was too quick. "It's a girl we found in the forward hold of the Nandrian ship," he replied. "Might have stowed away, might have been kidnapped. Either way, she was in pretty bad shape. She was unconscious, so couldn't tell us who she is or where she's from, but the Doc's been running biotests."

Ktumba threw them both a sharp look as they came through the door. Holchuk watched with interest as Townsend met the look, then threw it right back at her. Playing the macho game. Clearly, this man liked living dangerously.

She crossed her arms deliberately over her chest and leaned back against the edge of a vacant examining table. "He's told you?" she asked Townsend, who nodded wearily. "All right, then. I ran the full battery on her, and this is the result: Jane Doe is one hundred percent Human, and aside from all the superficial contusions and abrasions on her skin, she's in good physical health, with no serious pathology anywhere in her body. Your estimate of her age is a little on the high side, Gavin — I'd say she's no more than seventeen, if that. Muscle and skin tone are near optimum, body mass is a little light but nothing to worry about. Except for her cerebral cortex, which is marinating in an alien substance I'm still trying to identify, every system checked out perfectly."

"She's still unconscious?" Holchuk demanded.

"She's in a drug-induced coma. I'm willing to bet it's reversible. And once the Nandrians are awake, I'm going to consult with Stran Dakin to find out how.

"There's no sign of any internal injuries, but I noticed that her gastrointestinal tract scanned clean, indicating that she hadn't eaten for at least thirty-six hours before the drug was administered."

Anger hit Holchuk like a battering ram. "You're saying they starved her?"

"No. I'm saying she didn't eat. That might have been her choice, Gavin. It isn't uncommon for prisoners to refuse food."

"Prisoners?" Townsend echoed.

"We have reason to believe that she was kept in a cage for some time before being strung up in the hold. Teri and Robbo are delivering the evidence to your desk right now," Holchuk told him. "Go on, Doc."

She watched them both quietly for a moment before going on.

"There's a naturally produced antitoxin in her bloodstream."

"Meaning...?"

The Doc briefly pursed her lips. "I've seen similar antitoxins in the bodies of plague survivors. This looks to me like an immune system reaction following exposure to one of the strains of Angel of Death."

"So her home world was probably hit by plague? That doesn't exactly narrow the search," Townsend pointed out.

"I'm analyzing the antitoxin right now. Give me a day or two in the lab and I should be able to tell you with reasonable certainty which strain caused it. Knowing that, we should be able to guess which planet the carrier might have come from," the Doc added briskly. "And that in turn should point us to some possible locations for the girl's home."

"What about Nestor Quan?" asked Townsend.

"What about him?" Ktumba challenged.

"Well, he's on the crew manifest as the Hub's Disease Control Officer. Since this investigation focuses on the plague, isn't he supposed to be involved in...?"

Impaled by her diamond-hard stare, Townsend dropped the subject. "Is there anything else?" His voice was taut, although his posture hadn't changed.

"We still need to establish Jane Doe's identity," replied the Doc. "I've taken DNA samples for a database comparison.

Meanwhile, if anyone has reported her missing, the Rangers on Zulu should have a copy of the file, so I'd like to—"

"If you're about to suggest that we ask them for help, the answer is no."

She was stunned. "I beg your pardon?"

Holchuk could only shake his head in wonderment. The boss man must be suicidal. *Nobody* ever said no to the Doc.

"Not too many days ago, I told Bonelli never to darken our doorstep again. Find another way to get the data. It's too soon for us to be asking the Rangers for any favors. And keep me advised of the girl's condition." With that, Townsend pivoted and left Med Services.

All right, he wasn't suicidal, Holchuk decided, just a little obsessive. And delusional, if he honestly believed Earth would waste a perfectly good Disease Control officer on an outpost like Daisy Hub.

Meanwhile, the Doc was fuming. "Don't access the Rangers' database? The only other source of DNA and Security records would be Earth's InfoCommNet, which we can't access anyway without going through Zulu. And if Jane Doe is a resident of our sector, the reports might not even have *made* it to Earth yet...!"

Ignoring her fussing, Holchuk punched up a channel on his wristcomm. "Lydia, patch me through to Jensen."

A moment later, the chef was on the line: "Holchuk, I'm busy. What do you want?"

"In a short while the caf will begin filling up with Nandrians looking for a hair of the proverbial dog."

"It already is. I repeat, what do you want?"

"Has Nagor shown up yet?"

"Half an hour ago," growled Jensen. The channel closed with an audible click.

"What are you doing?" the Doc demanded quietly.

"What the boss man said. I'm getting the information a different way."

"By questioning a hungover Nandrian? You must have a death wish."

"Maybe. But I also know exactly what Jane Doe's father is going through right now, and I've made myself a promise to cut that short any way I can."

She stared at him for a moment, with sadness in her eyes. "Her father may not be alive, Gavin. The plague, remember?"

"All the more reason for someone to care what happens to her. The way you care about the rest of us," he added softly. "Ruby's not the den mother on this hub, Doc — you are. I'll bet you've even begun worrying about Townsend."

Every part of her seemed to stiffen. "If you tell anyone, I'll deny it."

Holchuk grinned. "I have to get up to the caf before Nagor reaches his limit. I'll be all right. You know how good I am at digging up facts, even from reluctant sources."

The Doc was the first to break eye contact. "Go on," she sighed. "Go interrogate your friend. I'll let you know if there's any change in the patient's condition."

— « o » —

There were already several of the big aliens in the caf, each one jealously guarding a table with five tall drinks on it. Ktumba's warning hadn't been exaggerated — however mellow citric acid made a Nandrian, withdrawal from citric acid made him several times more irritable. Fortunately, a hungover Nandrian was easy to spot: his green skin developed a yellowish cast, an unmistakable 'stay away' sign that not even another hungover Nandrian could miss.

Holchuk found Nagor at a table for two in the corner farthest from the entrance, noisily sipping a glass of lemonade. His skin might have been yellow when he came in earlier, but it wasn't anymore — there were four empties in front of him, and he occasionally bobbed his head and bared his lower fangs at them, as though they were paying him compliments.

This was good, Holchuk told himself, carefully following a path to Nagor's table that kept him as far away from the *Krronn*'s other crewmembers as possible.

As prescribed by Nandrian protocol, Holchuk stood quietly at Nagor's left side, waiting to be noticed. He breathed shallowly, grateful that the air purification system was able to confine the strong citrus smell to D Deck during the Nandrians' visits.

"You are late," Nagor informed him. "I expected you—" He scanned the table with bleary orange eyes. "—ten drinks ago."

Holchuk opened his mouth to reply and immediately shut it again.

Years ago, on Naguchi's orders, he had worked up his courage and opened a conversation with the big alien. Now they were friends — or as close to it as any Nandrian and Human could probably be — and now, for the first time, Holchuk would be testing the strength of that relationship. He paused for a moment and prayed that he'd been right about Nagor.

Slowly he sat down, careful to keep the table between them. If this interview went south, he wanted to be able to leap out of reach of the Nandrian's sinewy arms. "I was in Med Services," he said, "getting a report on the condition of the young female we found in your forward hold."

Nagor nodded sagely. "She is yours. We are not fit to keep her."

Holchuk sighed, recognizing the speech as part of a ritual — the property-relinquishment script. Now Holchuk was supposed to reply that Nagor was, indeed, fit to own and use her and that it was an unprecedented act of generosity for him to give her up — and it was making his stomach churn just thinking about having to form those words inside his mouth.

"That's very generous of you, Nagor," he managed. "We accept her. And now we have some questions that need answering."

The Nandrian's eyes briefly widened, then narrowed again. Holchuk could practically hear the gears grinding inside his head.

"The female is Human. We bring you the female. She lives. What questions can you have?"

"The female's body appears to have been beaten."

Nagor shook his massive head. "No one beat the female."

"Drew, son of... *Dammit!* is not pleased with her condition. He demands an explanation from me. I request one from you."

Nagor inhaled and exhaled noisily, his features darkening. The lemonade on his breath was overpowering. Holchuk leaned as far back in his chair as he could without openly insulting the big alien.

"He demands?" growled the Nandrian.

"From me."

"And what do you wish?"

Holchuk paused. He would have to be careful now. As expected, Nagor was asserting his own right to honor by choosing to favor a request from a friend over the official claim of a higher-ranked stranger. In Nandrian society, a friend did not ask to be given anything specific; he stated his need and allowed the one granting the favor to decide how best to meet that need. Honor accrued to both sides that way.

Nagor waited patiently as Holchuk searched his mind for the correct words. At last, he was able to put them together: "I wish truth and justice. Truth to help you. Justice for the female."

Nagor slumped a little in his seat. "Wishing cannot bring back the dead."

"The female isn't dead, Nagor, just unconscious."

The alien made a sound between a snort and a wheeze. "She grieves for her animal."

After years of conversing with Nandrians, Holchuk knew he should be accustomed to this by now. Non sequiturs, leaps of logic... The more they talked, the worse his confusion generally became.

"Her animal is dead?"

"Eaten."

"So you're saying that justice for the female is impossible, because her animal can never be returned to her?"

Nagor nodded with ponderous finality.

"And what of truth, Nagor ban Nagoram?" Holchuk persisted.

"I have shared my truth."

"By itself, it does not help you or me," Holchuk pointed out.

Nagor sighed sonorously. "You wish us to wake the female."

"So your truth can be confirmed."

"This would be unwise. She is *hartoon*."

A new word. Great. "Can you translate that?" Holchuk asked.

Nagor was silent for a moment. "No."

"Then can you give me another example of someone who is *hartoon*?"

The alien tilted his head in surprise. "I know of no one else who is *hartoon*," he pointed out reasonably.

Holchuk forced himself to sit absolutely still. He counted slowly to five. Then he gave it one more try.

"Nagor, what would have to happen to me to make me *hartoon*?"

He thought for a second. "If your mate were tortured to death by an escaped criminal who then took his own life, then perhaps…"

"…I would become *hartoon*?"

"Perhaps."

"And what would I do, being *hartoon*?"

"You might attack the prison, killing every creature you found there."

Suddenly, pieces of meaning began to fall into place. "Because the criminal I really wanted to kill would already be dead," Holchuk mused aloud, "so I would shift the blame to those who had let him escape, and take my revenge on them."

"You understand."

"Was she *hartoon* when you brought her aboard your ship?"

He shook his head. "She came aboard. No one brought her."

"She stowed away." Nagor nodded. Encouraged, Holchuk continued, "To avenge the death of her animal?"

"To retrieve it."

"She didn't know it was dead?"

"Only the *mishta* knew."

Another new word. And they'd been doing so well!

"Who or what is the *mishta*?" Holchuk asked wearily.

"Spaced. It died."

Conversing with a Nandrian was hard work. Holchuk could feel sweat beginning to trickle down his back and sides.

"Died of what, Nagor? What killed the *mishta*?"

The alien did something with his shoulders that vaguely resembled a shrug. "Her animal."

"But you said her animal was dead."

"The *mishta* ate it," Nagor said patiently. "The female saw…"

"...and became *hartoon*." Holchuk sighed, feeling as though the Nandrian were leading him in circles, ignoring his larger questions. "Nagor, how did the female's animal come to be aboard your ship? Did you trade for it?"

Nagor nodded. "With her nestbrother. He was glad to see it gone."

"So, her brother trades away her pet behind her back. She stows away to try to retrieve it, but by the time she reaches the aft hold, one of the other animals has already killed and eaten her pet. She sees... what? Little hind legs sticking out of the *mishta*'s mouth? A little carcass lying on the floor of its cage?" Nagor nodded. "She goes berserk. She kills the *mishta*?"

"Already dead. She attacked the *mishta*'s cage. Destroyed it. Then she crawled inside the ventilation shafts and began attacking the ship. She was *hartoon*. She broke into the crew quarters, damaged our environment control system, even tried to sabotage the engines."

"She was seen doing all this?"

Nagor nodded. "By my crew. They reported it to me."

Of course. Holchuk swallowed the next question, rather than appear to cast doubt on the veracity of Nagor's crew. Instead, he asked, "Was the female aboard during a *tekl'hananni* match?"

"Four days ago? No."

So her condition was not the result of the primal bloodlust released by *tekl'hananni*. Some of the bruising might have been self-inflicted by someone who'd gone a little crazy and was bouncing off the walls. But the rest of it — the scrapes and scratches, the tattered clothing, not to mention the obvious lies told to Nagor by his crew...! Holchuk could feel his own rage swelling inside his chest.

"Nagor, she is one little Human female — a child!"

He made that snorting, wheezing sound again. "She was *hartoon*, Holchuk. Filled with wild strength. We tied her. She struggled. We put her into a cage. She threw herself against the bars, injuring herself. Finally, we had to put her to sleep."

His choice of words sent icy tentacles straight down Holchuk's back.

"She belongs with her own clan, Nagor."

"And so we brought her here."

"And she needs to be awakened. Nothing less will satisfy Drew, son of… *Dammit!* He has told me that if you refuse his request, you will be dishonoring both the female and this station."

It was strong language for a friend to use. Hopefully Nagor's 'hair of the dog' had mellowed his senses, and he wouldn't take exception to it.

Nagor nodded sadly. "Our Medical Officer will cooperate with your Doctor Ktumba," he promised.

Chapter 18

"Do you believe his story?" Teri demanded, frowning.

Holchuk shrugged. What he believed or disbelieved was immaterial at that moment.

They were standing in Med Services and Doc Ktumba was on the comm, in quiet discussion with the Nandrian Medical Officer. Holchuk couldn't make out any of her words, but her expression looked relaxed enough. They were probably arranging for the delivery of the antidote to the alien stasis drug.

Meanwhile, Teri stood beside him, darting uneasy glances around the room. "Shouldn't someone have notified Townsend?" she murmured.

Holchuk shook his head. "We can handle this. The boss man's got a bigger problem on his plate right now." *And a huge mess on his desk*, he would have added, if the Doc hadn't thumbed the comm switch to 'off' and leaned back in her chair with a gusty sigh.

"It'll arrive in ten minutes," she told them. "Jane Doe should be all right until then."

Teri wandered over to study the young girl's face. "She looks like such an angel, doesn't she?"

"They all do, honey," the Doc chuckled. "Ask any parent. Children look all sweetness and innocence when they're sleeping. Then they wake up and they're hell on wheels."

That was what Nagor had said, too. Hell on wheels. Lashing out. Seeking revenge. Holchuk purposely kept his distance from the examining table. He wanted to believe his friend; and yet, from the first time he'd seen Jane Doe, it had seemed inconceivable that this slight Human female could be anything but a helpless victim.

Had he misunderstood the meaning of the term *hartoon*? How could anyone, bound hand and foot and thrown into a cage by Nandrians, still be wild with grief over the death of a pet? At that point, it seemed far more likely that she would be cold sober and terrified about her own possible fate.

"I think there's more going on here than anyone is telling us," he remarked quietly.

Suddenly, the Med Services door hummed open and a Nandrian crewman lumbered into the waiting area. He glanced around curiously, finally spotted the Doc beckoning him into the Trauma Clinic, and ducked his head again as he came through the entrance to join them. Holchuk had never spoken to this alien, but he did recognize the science insignia on the front of the brown and yellow uniform. And he noticed the crewman's eyes. They were green, an unusual color for a Nandrian.

Wordlessly, the alien scanned the little group for a moment. Then he reached out and deposited a small purple vial in the Doc's hand. "Five, then five, then two. Wait for changes before proceeding," he told her, turning to leave.

"Wait a minute," she said sharply. "Are you sure this is the correct dosage for a Human female with her body mass?"

Her tone of voice was a challenge, just short of an insult. The Nandrian locked eyes with her and bared his upper fangs. Unimpressed, Doc Ktumba stood her ground, her chin jutting stubbornly, and after a moment the alien growled and backed down.

Involuntarily, Holchuk smiled. Right or wrong, nobody argued with the Doc.

"This dosage will counteract the amount of sleeping drug she was given," the Nandrian snarled. "Body mass does not matter."

"The hell it doesn't," she retorted, her voice stopping him from leaving once again.

Holchuk heard Teri's soft gasp echoing his own. He held his breath, his skin prickling an urgent warning. The Doc had had plenty of dealings with the Nandrians and knew how they reacted to real or imagined slurs. What the hell was she playing at? Did she really want to bait this big alien into attacking her?

The Nandrian spun to face her. Holchuk's heart began sledgehammering his ribs and pounding in his ears. He had never actually taken down a member of this species, but if the crewman went for the Doc, he would have to try.

Holchuk glanced at Teri, the pit of his stomach telling him that the expression on her pale, frightened face probably mirrored his own.

"You are not the Medical Officer of your ship," said Doc Ktumba, her voice teetering on the edge of scorn.

Grudgingly, the Nandrian tilted his head to indicate a negative response.

"Well, I hold a Human life in my hands right now, and I'm told it was your Medical Officer who put it there. I want him present when the antidote is administered."

"Then the female *hartoon* will continue to sleep," he declared sullenly. "Stran Dakin's time is filled with more important matters."

"And you speak for Stran Dakin? I find that difficult to believe."

The alien lowered his head like a bull about to charge. Holchuk calculated the distance between them and slid closer to the Doc. He was unarmed. He was also coiled tight and full of adrenaline. He hoped it would be enough.

"Doc..." he muttered, but she waved him silent, never taking her eyes off the Nandrian's face.

"I know Stran Dakin," she went on, each word dagger-sharp. The alien's expression grew even uglier than before. "I don't know you, and I doubt whether he knows you either."

It was raining ice in Holchuk's stomach. "Doc...!" Again she waved him silent.

He pressed the send button on his wristcomm and raised it to his lips. "Holchuk to Security," he said, just loudly enough for the alien to hear. "I need a team in the Trauma Clinic right now." It was posturing, that was all. Security on Daisy Hub consisted of two uniforms and a nightstick. But posturing sent a message the Nandrians understood.

The crewman scowled at Holchuk and thrust his huge, clawed hand, palm up, toward the Doc.

"Give it back and do without," he growled.

They heard the soft hum of the Med Services door working.

"Oh, I'll give it back," she said with a mirthless smile. "But not to you."

On cue, the Trauma Clinic door sighed open behind the big alien, admitting four more uniformed Nandrians. Holchuk recognized Nagor as he stepped forward and took the vial from the Doc's hand.

"You understand much," he said, then turned to address his crewman. "Rostol, go with these officers to your cell."

Evidently, they had him dead to rights for *some*thing. Rostol dipped his head to his superior, then went quietly.

When the three Nandrians had left, Nagor bowed ceremoniously to Doc Ktumba. "I am deeply indebted for your assistance."

She bowed back and replied, as scripted, "I am honored to accept your gratitude."

Holchuk's jaw had dropped open. He closed it.

"Son of a gun," Teri murmured beside him. "There *was* something going on."

Nagor beckoned the fourth Nandrian forward and introduced him. "This is our Medical Officer, Stran Dakin. It will be his duty and honor to assist you in awakening the female."

More bowing. More "duty" and "honor" and "privilege", while Holchuk, near to bursting with curiosity, waited impatiently for the formalities to be over so that he could open a script. "Nagor ban Nagoram, I have many questions."

The alien made a sound between a snort and a wheeze. "And I have answers, Gavin son of Samuel. But my throat is dry."

A friend stated his need and allowed the other to determine how to meet it.

Holchuk smiled. "Why don't we continue our discussion in the caf?"

— « o » —

At this hour of the afternoon, the caf was virtually empty. Nagor sighed as a mouthful of cold lemonade trickled down his throat. "So much has happened. Where to begin?" he wondered aloud.

"Let's begin with the scene I just witnessed in Med Services."

The alien tilted his head. "But you were there. You saw."

"I *think* I saw you and the Doc spring a trap on Rostol. That wasn't the real antidote he was delivering, was it? It was meant to kill her."

"Stran Dakin and the Doc," Nagor corrected him, nodding. "You understand."

"How did they know?"

"They suspected. They came to me. It was enough."

"But what made them suspect?" Holchuk persisted.

"The fluid sample," he replied after a pause.

"From the girl?" Nagor nodded. "The Doc must have sent a sample of the girl's cerebral fluid to Stran Dakin for analysis." He nodded again. "And he discovered...?"

"The stasis drug."

"Wait a minute. Didn't Dakin administer the drug in the first place?"

Nagor tilted his head no.

"Then who put her to sleep?"

"Rostol is Stran Dakin's assistant."

"With access to all the drugs, of course. But if he wanted her dead, why put her in a coma? Why not simply give her something lethal in the first place?"

"Rostol is ignorant and impetuous. That is why he is a failure."

Suddenly a light went on upstairs. Holchuk could see Rostol, anxious to kill the girl immediately, rushing to Dakin's pharmacy and hastily grabbing a vial of something he thought would do the job. Except—

"He gave her the wrong drug," Holchuk exclaimed. "Only by accident, it was the right drug, the one Dakin would have used."

"You understand," said Nagor, his measured voice giving a solemn weight to the words.

For the first time, Holchuk realized what a huge compliment Nagor was paying him. Their conversations were a lot of work for a Human. The big alien spoke in riddles, made leaps of logic, and threw obscure clues and Nandrian vocabulary at him, forcing him to puzzle out the meaning. Nor did the Nandrian accent make following Nagor's speech any easier. Holchuk had always assumed the alien didn't care or didn't notice what an effort it took for a Human to comprehend him. He'd been wrong.

Holchuk felt a rush of heat to his cheeks and realized with a start that he must be blushing, something he hadn't done since high school. Nagor gave him the Nandrian equivalent of a smile, baring his lower fangs in approval.

"I don't understand completely," Holchuk told him, "but I think I'm getting there. If the Nandrian criminal mind operates anything like the Human criminal mind, then Rostol probably wanted to silence the girl, to prevent her from talking about something she knows or something she saw."

Nagor nodded his agreement. "When she awakens, she will tell you. You will tell me."

— « o » —

Stran Dakin had already returned to the Nandrian ship when Holchuk arrived in Med Services with Yoko.

It was probably best that Dakin not be present. There was no telling what the girl might do if she woke up and saw a Nandrian standing over her.

To be honest, Holchuk wasn't sure what she would do when she woke up and found a large white rat staring down at her. Nonetheless, they had to take the chance, just in case Nagor had been right and she was still *hartoon*. Yoko was the closest thing they had aboard the station to her own lost pet.

The crew of the Hub joked incessantly about Robbo and the Überrat. Holchuk could understand why. Yoko had to be the most intelligent animal he'd ever encountered. And she'd picked to care for her one Robert O'Malley, who could at times be the most obtuse Human he'd ever encountered. Give him credit, though — O'Malley was astonishingly even-tempered. When the razzing began, he just smiled like the proverbial cat with a feather hanging off its lip and walked away.

Robbo often claimed, to the derision of his crewmates, that Yoko could understand spoken Gally, that she considered herself nobody's pet, and that she cooperated much better when people said please. Today, Holchuk could believe it. Normally, the Überrat hated being behind bars; she generally traveled perched on Robbo's shoulder. However, once O'Malley had explained the situation to her and what they needed her to do, she had voluntarily gone into her cage and begun grooming herself, like a performer getting ready for a show. There she was, in her dressing room on the green enameled table against the Med Services wall: Lady Yoko, patiently awaiting her cue.

The Doc's eyes were glued to her scanner readouts. After what felt like an eternity, she turned and announced cautiously, "The drug seems to be neutralized, and I'm reading rapid eye movements. She's experiencing normal sleep. We ought to be able to wake her up now."

Holchuk filled his lungs and blew out a sigh of relief, but there was a sudden lump in his throat that refused to be swallowed. He couldn't stop thinking about Jane Doe's father. Holchuk knew exactly what he was going through — how the heart slowly turned itself inside out, the agony worsening with each day that a child remained missing. If only there were some way to let him know…!

Madeline had been fourteen Earth months old when she'd disappeared. Thirteen standard years later, Holchuk still dreamed about that night, the sickening smell of blood and smoke filling his nostrils in the moments before he blacked out. Over and over, he dreamed about waking up in the hospital, making the numbing pilgrimage to the morgue to confront Risa's death, and urgently demanding of a sea of blank faces what had become of his daughter. That had been the worst ordeal of all — knowing in his soul that she was still alive but being unable to find anyone who would admit to having seen her.

Teri gripped his arm. Holchuk drew in a steadying breath and patted her hand. "I'm all right," he reassured her. And he was, for the moment. Madeline was an adult now, almost 21 Earth years old. If she was Ineligible, then she'd grown up tough and resourceful, like her mother. If she was Eligible, then the Relocation Authority had made a huge investment in her, one that would cause them to think twice before harming her. There was time. When everything was in place, Gavin Holchuk would wake up Daisy Hub and teach the Relocation Authority what hell on wheels was all about.

"I always wanted kids," Teri murmured. "Harry had three, from a previous marriage, and they all hated his guts. I thought, if he and I could raise just one together, it would be worth giving up my career. Stupid, huh?"

Holchuk swallowed hard, thinking of other sacrifices, other times, and gave her hand a comforting squeeze. "Not stupid," he told her, his voice suddenly thick in his throat. "Not stupid at all."

As the Doc disconnected the scanner and removed the arterial drip, Holchuk took Yoko out of her cage and placed her on the bed. She sat back on her hind legs and cocked her head to stare curiously into the girl's face. According to Robbo, first impressions were very important to rats. Holchuk hoped Jane Doe wouldn't scream and swat the animal across the room the second she came awake.

Once the equipment was stowed, Doc Ktumba positioned herself at the side of Jane Doe's bed and gently took her hand.

Stran Dakin had made sure the procedure was on track and then returned to his ship. Holchuk probably should have delivered Yoko and disappeared as well. But he needed to see for himself that the girl was all right.

She awakened with a gasp, nearly leaping off the examining table in panic.

"Hey, take it easy! You're all right now. You're safe," Teri assured her.

"What's your name, honey?" cooed the Doc.

Holchuk's heart lurched as he watched her visibly screw up her courage to answer the question. "Alison. Alison Morgan. Where am I? And what is *this*?" she added, grimacing involuntarily as Yoko scrambled onto her collarbone and began busily licking salt off her cheek.

"We heard you'd lost a pet," he told her. "This is a loaner."

— « o » —

A while later, once Alison had calmed down enough to talk about her experience aboard the Nandrian ship, she confirmed some of Nagor's story, and most of Holchuk's suspicions.

Yes, she had stowed away to try to rescue her animal, a young *scurra* she'd raised from a pup. And yes, she had flown into a rage when she'd found it half-eaten inside another animal's cage. But she'd taken to the ventilation ducts, not to sabotage the ship, but to get away from the three angry Nandrians she'd surprised near an open storage container in the forward hold. They'd come after her with weapons, terrifying her. She remembered knocking out some gratings to get into crew quarters to use the washroom, but— damage the environmental controls? She didn't even know what one looked like. The engine room? Where was that?

Tired and hungry, her skin scraped and her clothing shredded by the rough, raised seams inside the ductwork, Alison had finally given herself up to a crew member after nearly two days as a fugitive. She'd expected to be turned over to the captain. But she'd been taken instead to the aft hold, where the green-eyed Nandrian, one of the three she had seen earlier, was waiting. Almost before she knew what was happening, she was bound and gagged and stuffed into a cage. That was when she realized she must have surrendered to one of his two friends.

As she spoke, in a tear-filled, quavery voice, Alison cuddled and stroked her loaner pet, which the Doc was letting her keep with her in the Rehab ward. Yoko had never had it so good. She lay melting in Alison's arms, eyes closed, with an ecstatic expression on her little rodent face. Holchuk had to smile. So Alison's brother had thought the *scurra* was a pest? He hadn't met the Überrat.

"This doesn't make sense," said Teri, frowning. "Rostol and the others were acting as though you'd seen them with something they didn't want anyone to know about. And yet, we inspected both holds, and the only contraband we discovered in either one was you."

"What were they doing when you interrupted them?" Holchuk asked.

Alison shrugged. "Just taking some dark-colored sand out of a barrel."

He and Teri exchanged a look. There was only one thing that resembled sand aboard this Nandrian ship.

"The seasoning?" she wondered.

He nodded slowly, perplexed.

Their job as cargo inspectors was to look for stowaways and contraband, not evidence of theft. They identified cargo and verified its origins. They weighed it only to confirm that it wasn't heavier than it ought to be. If Rostol and his friends had been seen stealing from the ship's hold, that would explain the need to silence a witness. But if Rostol and company were going to steal, why steal seasoning? Why not lift a handful of precious stones, or a few pigducats of rare metal? There had been plenty of both in the *Krronn*'s forward hold.

"I think there's something going on here—"

"—that nobody is telling us?" sighed Teri, wearing a here-we-go-again expression.

"That Nagor can explain," he corrected her, already on his way out the door.

— « o » —

Nagor and five of his crew were in the caf, tucking into huge platters of macaroni and cheese. Fruit-flavored gelatin was another of their favorites. According to the menu, the color *du jour* was green.

Holchuk stood respectfully at Nagor's left side until he was noticed, then spoke the scripted line: "I beg to disturb your solitude."

The alien bared his lower fangs and gestured to the Human to take the chair across the table from him. "I was only waiting for your company, my friend."

He couldn't help noticing that Nagor's drink was brown. Cola, probably, with just enough citric acid added to give it a kick. The instant Holchuk was seated, the Nandrian asked, "Is the female awake?"

"Awake and talking." Holchuk summarized for him everything Alison had told them in Med Services, ending with the question, "Why would they steal seasoning, Nagor, when there was so much more valuable stuff in the hold?"

The big alien paused before replying, "Lemonade."

Holchuk sighed wearily. Nagor was talking in riddles again. "You mean, how is the seasoning like lemonade?"

"Lemonade is readily available in Earth space, Gavin son of Samuel, but it is outlawed on Nandor. The penalty for smuggling is severe."

"Well, sure," Holchuk agreed. "Because of your body chemistry, lemonade has an intoxicating effect on Nandrians. It acts like a drug."

Nagor watched him silently, as though willing the Human to make a connection.

Finally Holchuk's brain clicked in. "It *is* a drug. And the seasoning — does it also have… interesting effects on certain species?"

Nagor bared his lower fangs. "You understand. My government strictly forbids the trade of seasoning to off-worlders. The penalty for breaking this law is death."

"That's why Alison had to be silenced," Holchuk declared. "Rostol must have known that if she told you what she'd seen, he would be killed."

Nagor made that snorting, wheezing sound. "They told me she was *hartoon*. I saw her in the cage, acting *hartoon*. I ordered her put to sleep for her own safety. Rostol has confessed that he intercepted the order and injected her himself."

"The girl is lucky that he made the mistake he did."

"We are all lucky, Gavin son of Samuel. And I am shamed for believing his lies."

The scripted response popped into his head: "The shame belongs to the liar, my friend. Your heart is unstained by his guilt."

A strange expression crossed Nagor's face, and suddenly the air was thick with the scent of cinnamon. Smoke and cinnamon, Holchuk amended. It wasn't distasteful, or even unpleasant to his nose. However, under normal conditions, and even some abnormal ones, Nandrians had almost no body odor. What was going on here? Had the big alien just 'let one go'? Was there a script to cover that sort of social gaffe?

Before the Human could speculate further, Nagor solemnly said, "In a thousand generations of travel, the Shields of Trokerk have met many off-worlders, but none that any of us have wished to call brother, until now. Gavin son of Samuel, I offer you the honor of carrying the Fifth Shield beside me in defense of the House of Trokerk. Be my brother and claim the undying loyalty of Trokerk which by your honorable ways you have earned."

It was an enormous and unexpected compliment. It took his breath away. And if he did the Human thing and acted modest, he was dead.

Holchuk smiled weakly and nodded, not trusting himself to speak.

Chapter 19

Drew was getting a familiar sinking feeling in his stomach. Was this going to be the pattern on Daisy Hub — everything going crazy the moment he'd filed a ho-hum status report with the Space Installation Authority? "You'd better run that past me again."

Seated on the other side of his desk, Ruby sighed, re-crossed her legs, and folded her arms over her chest. "Which part, Chief?"

"All of it, starting with the drug dealing ring."

"That's an internal matter, not our concern. There were no Humans involved, and the Nandrians have already taken care of it."

"Oh, really? What about the crewman who traded seasoning to Jensen a couple of intervals ago? Indirectly, that deal resulted in the death of the station manager."

"True. But that crewman is on his way back to Nandor as we speak, where he will be executed for dishonoring his House — assuming that Nagor, the Chief Officer he also dishonored, hasn't already spaced him by then. It's a dead issue, Drew. Literally. Besides, do you really want to create a diplomatic incident and derail Gavin's adoption, which we are all looking forward to so very much?"

Her eyes were sparkling merrily.

No, Drew decided, he didn't, especially after what the Chief Cargo Inspector had put him through for that welcoming ceremony. Time had a way of bringing everyone down a peg or two, and anxiety was looking very good on Gavin Holchuk right now.

Apparently, Ruby felt the same way. "I can't remember the last time I saw him so worked up," she chortled. "One of the prerequisites for joining a Shield is to score points in a *tekl'hananni* match. Gavin has asked Lydia to design him a SPA simulation program, but he knows that won't be much real help. He's probably hoping that you'll render the whole issue moot by following procedure and not letting him off the station. Will you?"

She was right about his having to follow procedure. Daisy Hub was officially classified as an experiment, meaning that none of its residents were permitted to leave the system until the experiment was over. If Earth High Council and the Relocation Authority had their way, that would be never. However, part of Drew's assignment for the EIS was to forge as many covert alliances as he could, any way he could.

So, he grinned back at her. "Let him off the hook? Absolutely not. When does the initial ceremony take place?"

"Three days from now. Until then, Gavin is supposed to sequester himself and 'discover his inner warrior', whatever that means. When Nagor returns with the *Hak'kor*'s representative, Gavin boards the ship, alone. As I understand it, there are speeches and arguments and then he swears an oath of intent. Only the adoptee and members of the House of Trokerk are allowed to attend. But, Chief, wouldn't you love to be a fly on the wall?"

"Forget it, Ruby. And tell the rest of the crew to forget it as well," Drew warned her. "The last thing we need right now is for anyone aboard Daisy Hub to be violating the privacy of a Nandrian ritual. If Holchuk wants to talk about his experience later on—"

"—assuming he survives it—!"

He leaned forward and said, in a soft, deliberate voice, "Notify the crew that by order of the station manager, there will be no monitoring devices of any kind either placed on or directed at the *Krronn*. Anyone who disobeys and gets caught by me will be turned over to the Rangers. Anyone who disobeys and gets caught by the Nandrians will no longer be my concern. And anyone who thinks I'm not serious about this is welcome to be incredibly stupid and try me."

Ruby's eyes widened. It took her a moment to find the words to reply, "All right, Drew, whatever you say."

He'd rattled her. Good. Geniuses or not, these people needed to learn how to follow an instruction when it mattered.

Drew leaned back in his seat and continued conversationally, "Now, on to the girl in Med Services?"

"Alison Morgan. Long story short, she woke up and told us who she was and where she was from. We've already found and contacted her parents. The Morgans live three days from here, on an Earth colony called Ventrana. They are, of course, deeply grateful to us for rescuing their daughter. They've asked us to send her home as soon as possible, which we're doing, since Doc Ktumba says she's okay to travel. You made it clear you didn't want any communications with the Rangers, so we've rerouted the nearest long-hopper traversing the sector. It'll be stopping here to pick her up in about four days."

That was the part of Ruby's report that his mind had tripped over. Aside from the multiple breaches of safety protocol that would occur the second a long-hopper docked with an orbiting station, Drew was dying to know, "How, exactly, did you manage to reroute a government spacecraft?"

Ruby's gaze darted away and back. "I'm not sure of the details, Chief. Robbo took care of it."

Robbo took care of it. She said this so casually. Drew made a mental note to debrief Mr. O'Malley at the next opportunity.

"...but since the alternative was to go to Bonelli with hat in hand, so to speak, and you'd already ordered the Doc not to ask the Rangers for any favors, we figured you wouldn't mind."

"Wouldn't mind what?"

She shrugged, as if to signify that it was a triviality, beneath his concern. "Our using your Authority codes to validate the route change. We weren't defrauding anyone," she added, cheeks dimpling mischievously. "It was the request you would have made yourself if you hadn't been so busy with—"

Drew recognized the argument and sighed philosophically. "Okay, I had that one coming. So, which of my illustrious predecessors decided that the assistant station manager should have access to confidential SIA codes?"

"I'm not sure, Chief. It must have been before my time. All I know is, we needed them, and there they were."

"I see," he said. Drew leaned forward, studying her face. "'We' refers to you and O'Malley?" She nodded brightly. "And was Khaloub aware that the codes were no longer secret?"

"No. I meant to tell him, but somehow it never came up in the conversation."

Of course not. "And he never mentioned changing them, as a routine security precaution?"

She shifted her weight uncomfortably. "No. But then, like you, he sort of hit the ground running when he first arrived here. Are you planning to change the codes, Drew?"

"They're supposed to be changed by each incoming station manager, so yes. But I can't see any harm in the assistant manager knowing how to access them, in case of an emergency."

Ruby relaxed visibly and sat back with a satisfied grin.

"Now, what happened to the evidence Holchuk said he left for me?"

"I wouldn't know about any evidence, Chief. But it looked as though Robbo had emptied out Yoko's cage onto your desktop, and—"

"Bottom line, please."

'Mom' gestured dismissively with both hands. "It's gone away."

"No evidence, no crime? I guess that works for me..." he decided, "...this time. Final item: Nestor Quan."

She tilted her head, frowning quizzically. "Who's Nestor Quan?"

"Our forty-sixth crew member," Drew explained patiently. "The only one I haven't met yet. According to the manifest, he's our Disease Control Officer."

Ruby shook her head slowly. "This is the first time I've heard of him, Chief. And why would a hub this far out need a Disease Control Officer, anyway?"

Good question. Townsend paused, remembering his earlier exchange with the Doc. He'd thought at the time that she was challenging his decision to involve the DCO, but perhaps he'd misread her reaction. Perhaps—

"Are you sure the crew manifest is correct?" Ruby asked, barging into his thoughts.

"I *was* sure," he sighed.

Ironically — but not surprisingly — Earth's 'best and brightest' tended to do only mediocre work while waiting for their off-world postings. If the Hub's crew manifest had been prepared by an Eligible marking time in Data Management, then it was quite possible that Nestor Quan was actually assigned elsewhere, or not assigned at all. In any case, Drew decided, he had more important things to worry about right now.

"Okay, then, Ruby. If there's nothing else we need to discuss...?" She shook her head. "Then this meeting is over. If anybody needs me, I'll be on E Deck, moving into my permanent quarters."

Chapter 20

This was more like it. Drew stood just inside the entrance and gazed around him with satisfaction at a suite of furnished rooms that comfortably held his leather trunk along with all the worldly goods that he had brought with him from Earth. And it had only taken him four days to move into the space: one and a half to solve the mystery of Khaloub's death and officially close the case; two to survive the Nandrians' ceremonial arrival and victory party; half a day to gather Khaloub's effects and package them for shipment back to Earth; and a matter of minutes to throw his own belongings into the trunk and have it transferred in from guest quarters. When he'd put everything away, reprogrammed the smart paint on the walls to a pale pastel blue, and put his own voice and thumb prints on the door lock, the place was finally his. Drew Townsend was home — in the middle of a former crime scene.

Well, why not? He was a former cop, after all. Drew was glad that Ruby had arranged with Orvy Hagman and the decon team to clean out the station manager's quarters before he moved in. They'd also switched the vic's bed with another and rearranged the furniture, all without having to be asked. Of course they had, he mused — they were Eligibles. When people routinely made intuitive leaps of logic, many questions simply never came up.

Not for the first time since coming aboard the Hub, Drew had to remind himself that he was Eligible too. Actually, he'd never stopped being Eligible, even when the Relocation Authority had deemed him undesirable.

Little Drew had been screened at school at the age of eight, like all the other offspring of Eligible parents. He had passed every test and been awarded the magical label that would get him the best education, the promptest access to health care, the choicest foodstuffs, and a ticket to explore the galaxy. None of those things had mattered to him, of course. All he knew at that young age was that he was no longer allowed to have fun. He had to study. He had to behave. He had to look and smell and sound just so. He had to fulfill his potential, or at least meet the daunting list of expectations that the Relocation Authority placed on him.

Being Eligible, Drew rebelled. He racked his brain for a way to escape from this cage that the Authority had dropped over him, and could find only one — acquire a juvenile criminal record. So, shortly before his twelfth birthday, Drew Townsend began misbehaving in earnest. The plan worked perfectly — the Authority revoked his Eligibility. His parents became sad and quiet, but he figured they would get over their disappointment eventually.

And then he awakened from an unusually long sleep to discover that his family had been posted off-world during the night, leaving him alone in an empty house; and a stranger with an eviction notice was banging on the door. That morning the word 'Ineligible' had instantly acquired a host of unpleasant meanings.

A sudden beeping just behind him nearly launched Drew out of his skin. In a single motion, he spun and pounced on the comm button beside the door. "I'm here. What?" he snapped.

A startled pause, then, "Mr. Townsend, this is Gouryas. You wanted me to let you know if we made any progress with the paintbrush? Well, I've got good news and bad news for you, sir."

— « o » —

When Drew stepped out of the tube car minutes later on Deck L, he saw Gouryas and Singh standing to either side of their experimental door panel in the center of the deck. At their feet lay a flashing, gurgling object with horn-shaped handles that could only be the molecular paintbrush. It was a very dramatic presentation. Either the good news was miraculous or the bad news was devastating.

"All right, gentlemen," he commented without breaking stride. "You said you'd made some progress?"

They exchanged an uneasy glance.

"We're not sure it is progress, actually," said Singh after a pause. "We still don't know how or why the device works, but we do have an approximate idea of how to operate the controls."

Drew shook off the uncertainty in the Engineering Specialist's voice. "Have you found a way to undo what was done to the bulkheads?" he wanted to know.

Gouryas shared another meaningful look with Singh, then replied, "I'm afraid not, Mr. Townsend. If this thing has a reverse button, it's well concealed. However, we have found a way to do the other thing you were interested in."

He nodded to Singh, who picked up the device and aimed it at a turquoise-'painted' section of the door. As Drew watched, Singh depressed and slid a panel on the side of the paintbrush. Meanwhile, Gouryas was quietly counting off the seconds. When he got to five, a visible beam shot out of the device, showing purple where it splashed against the metal and apparently 'painting over' the first color. When he got to ten, Singh reversed the control, killing the beam.

Drew opened his mouth to speak, but Gouryas raised a silencing hand. "Just watch what happens."

Before their eyes, the overpainted swatch of door metal darkened to black, then changed again. It seemed to soften and deepen, revealing straight lines and shadowy, shifting forms, almost as if an artist's sketch were rising to the surface of the metal. For a moment, Drew stared, mesmerized. Then, suddenly, he realized what it was he was looking at — the legs and lower torsos of the techs moving around at the far end of the deck. The alien device had created a serviceable window in the middle of the metal panel.

Drew grinned and turned to face the two engineers. "Transparent supersteel?"

"Acrylic," Gouryas corrected him regretfully. "Overpainting not only alters the refractive index, it also changes the atomic composition."

That was the bad news. Clearly, they didn't dare let the Muralist get his hands on this device again. Acrylic couldn't withstand the cold of space, and it couldn't protect them from

Purgatory's radiation. However, Drew reminded himself, there was another, more urgent use for the device. "How controllable is this effect?" he asked carefully.

"I can restrict the beam to the width of the casing on the Meniscus Field generator," Singh replied, "and I believe I can restrict it to the thickness of the casing as well. That is what you wanted to know, isn't it, Mr. Townsend?"

— « o » —

AdComm was deserted. Good. Drew sat down at his desk, took the encrypter out of his pocket, and activated the device with a squeeze. Then he inserted it into the port of his InfoComm unit and keyed in a series of coded passwords. The report followed, touch-typed as rapidly as he could move his fingers. For security reasons, Drew tried to keep his updates to the EIS brief; unfortunately, the situation on Daisy Hub seemed to change hourly, making that difficult.

A moment later it was done. Townsend's next routine status memo to the Space Installation Authority would be carrying a little extra baggage.

"So it's true."

Startled, Drew glanced up and saw Lydia Garfield standing at the end of his partition. The woman not only looked like a ghost, she evidently moved like one.

"Gavin predicted this, you know," she continued, walking slowly toward him.

Drew blanked the screen and leaned back in his chair, in one motion palming and pocketing the encrypter. "Predicted what?"

"He said that if enough bad things happened to enough station managers, they'd give up the pretense that this was anything but a detention center and send in a real warden."

Her voice sounded flat and weary. Drew gave her a sympathetic smile and motioned to her to sit down. "Lydia, I promise you, I'm not a warden."

Lowering herself carefully into the offered seat, she remarked, "Well, you're using SIA reports as carriers for encrypted messages to Earth, so you must be here spying for somebody. Who is it? The High Council? The Relocation Authority?"

"Neither. But how did you know…?"

"…about the messages?" The corners of her mouth curved slightly, just short of a smile. "I spend a lot of time around InfoComm gear. Hardly anything worth reporting to the SIA ever happens around here; but you've sent three fat signals in five days, Mr. Townsend. That tells me you're a man on a mission."

"In a way, I guess I am," he replied, nodding thoughtfully.

"Ruby told me about your meeting earlier today. She said that for a moment you sounded as though you were talking to Bonelli."

"She wanted me to approve eavesdropping on Gavin's adoption ritual."

Lydia shrugged and pointed out, "You did allow us to monitor your confrontation with Bonelli."

"I know. It was a mistake."

"Only because it blew your cover."

He had been expecting this eventually. And he'd evidently been correct about Lydia Garfield. The 'basket case' had made a miraculous recovery; in fact, the woman sitting across from him right now was cool as an autumn breeze in New Chicago.

"Mr. Townsend, I'll be blunt. You're a good man. And you were probably an excellent field investigator back on Earth. But as a secret agent…?" She sighed eloquently. "Listen, whatever your assignment is on the Hub, if you want to complete it successfully, then you're going to need help."

"No doubt, the kind of help *you* can provide."

She nodded. "I'm in charge of data management and communications. Day in and day out, I sit in my little corner, screening incoming and outbound transmissions and monitoring all activity aboard the station. Nobody really notices me, but not much happens on Daisy Hub that I don't know about. I was Karim's eyes and ears. If you'll let me be yours, I'll try not to fail you."

Drew heard the catch in her voice and began to understand. Lydia's show of grief at the meeting in the caf may have appeared a little melodramatic, but it hadn't been faked. As Karim's 'eyes and ears', she had good reason to feel she had let him down. If she wanted forgiveness, a cop was the last person she should be asking for it. Still, he realized, she'd put so much on the line at this point that it would be cruel to turn her down, not to mention foolish. After all, he'd come to Daisy Hub essentially to form a gang. And what was a gang without a snoop?

Lydia sat quietly across from him, her eyes wide and shining.

"How did you know I was a cop, Lydia?"

"Simple. Your original biofile popped up when the system received your documentation from Earth."

"And just how did your local InfoCommNet happen to have my original biofile?"

Slowly, her lips curved once more. "Do we have an arrangement, Mr. Townsend?" she wanted to know.

"We do."

"Then you'd better have a talk with Robert O'Malley," she said. "Tell him I sent you." And without another word, she got up and left.

— « o » —

He'd been meaning to do it anyway, after what Ruby had told him. Now Townsend was doubly intrigued.

He pulled up the crew manifest on his screen and found O'Malley's duty schedule. He had to smile when he saw 'Care for Yoko' on it, five times per day. It figured. But something else didn't: O'Malley had been classified as a cargo inspector; and yet, he was assigned to work shifts on half a dozen other details during the current interval, including waste management and hydroponics maintenance. Admittedly, it made sense. There wasn't a whole lot of work for a cargo inspector in this sector of Earth space.

However, if this was typical scheduling, then it seemed to suggest that everyone not actually in charge of a detail was being treated as an interchangeable part, working at and becoming familiar with every job on the station. A quick look at several other duty schedules confirmed his suspicion. Techs were suiting up and learning how to perform exterior maintenance. Dockworkers were learning how to adjust attitudinal thrusters.

According to Ruby, the duty cycles had been established by Nayo Naguchi, the great teacher who had insisted that every crewmember continue acquiring skills and knowledge. Naguchi must have known that it would take a lifetime and more to get to know Daisy Hub inside and out. It was a brilliant way to keep everyone busy.

And, as a side-benefit, it ensured that the station could continue to operate even if half the crew were lost in an attack. That could come in very handy if Earth Council ever twigged to what Townsend was actually doing out here.

"Drew?"

He glanced up. Lydia was standing in front of his desk again.

"You're needed in Med Services, right away," she told him.

Chapter 21

"All right — what's the problem?"

As if on cue, everyone in Trauma froze in place. They made an interesting tableau: Doc Ktumba, rigid and smoldering, stood over a girl he assumed was Alison Morgan, who was sitting curled up on a medbed, defensively hugging the largest white rat he had ever seen, while Robert O'Malley hovered to one side, his hands clasped in a conciliatory pose, concern written all over his face.

Which of them had called him down from AdComm?

"Well," said Drew after a moment, "don't all talk at once."

O'Malley spoke up first. "We loaned her Yoko, and now she won't give her back."

As if he'd unpaused a video recording, the argument resumed.

"You're not even allowed to have a pet on a hub," shrilled Alison, tightening her grip on poor Yoko. O'Malley said nothing, but his knuckles were beginning to whiten.

The Doc uttered an exasperated syllable. "I told you before, Yoko is not a pet."

"It doesn't matter what you call her," the girl declared haughtily. "Article 17 of the Space Installation Protocol categorically states that no live animals are permitted on ships or hubs." *So there!* She hadn't had to pronounce the words. The tone of her voice had said them for her.

Eligible kids could be such insufferable brats. Drew wasn't surprised that the Nandrians had bound and gagged this girl. He would probably have stuffed her into a PLS suit and *towed* her all the way to Daisy Hub.

Making his face as stern as possible, he stepped closer to the medbed and cleared his throat to get everyone's attention.

"Young lady," he said softly, "my name is Mr. Townsend, and you are a guest aboard my station. Please act like one. If anyone is going to quote chapter and verse of the Protocol to these people, it will be me. Understood?"

She nodded and leaned back on the cushions with a gleam in her eye and a triumphant tilt to her chin. *So there!*

Drew spun and met the Doc's jaundiced gaze. In his most officious voice, he declared, "Doctor Ktumba, I am ordering you and Mr. O'Malley, under Article 17, Section 3, Paragraph 9 of the Space Installation Protocol, to return this rat to the laboratory immediately." She opened her mouth to protest, then evidently thought better of it.

Meanwhile, Alison gulped audibly and murmured, "Section 3?"

"Paragraph 9," he supplied, adding in the same stern voice, "Exceptions may be made for laboratory specimens, provided they remain confined to the laboratory and are handled only by authorized personnel. Doctor Ktumba and Mr. O'Malley are running the experiment, and are therefore authorized personnel. They have also been properly immunized. You, however, present a problem." The girl's eyes widened to the size of saucers. Good. Drew pretended to think hard for a moment, then come to a difficult decision. "Doctor Ktumba, we need to confer on what to do about Ms. Morgan. She probably hasn't compromised the experiment, but—"

Without missing a beat, the Doc cut in, "You're thinking she might have been infected? It's doubtful, Mr. Townsend. Those pathogens have never jumped species in the past."

Alison went pale and practically threw Yoko into O'Malley's waiting hands. "Pathogens?" she wailed. "You gave me a sick rat to play with?"

O'Malley's features were contorting strangely. Fortunately, he and Yoko escaped from Rehab before he could blow the con.

"Yoko will have to be tested for anything the girl might have transmitted to her," Drew told the Doc, ignoring the whining child on the medbed, "and vice versa. You'll have to quarantine her in the meanwhile."

Reluctantly this time, the Doc went along. "I'll arrange to put her into Isolation immediately, Mr. Townsend."

"Good. When you're done, I want to see you and O'Malley in my office."

Drew left Med Services, nodding perfunctorily at a stricken Alison Morgan on his way out.

His mother had been right — children who fought over toys deserved to lose them.

— « o » —

"Admit it, Townsend — you enjoyed that."

"And you didn't?" he countered.

O'Malley just shrugged and grinned broadly at him.

On the other side of the filing cabinets, Drew could sense Lydia, hovering just out of sight.

"All I can say is that you're lucky Gavin Holchuk wasn't there to see you torture that child," declared the Doc.

"I tortured her?" Drew returned. "You're the one who brought up pathogens."

"Nonetheless," she continued with a dismissive wave of her hand, "Gavin feels very protective of her."

"Would he have let her leave the station with O'Malley's rat?"

"Yoko isn't mine," O'Malley corrected him.

"Then whose is she?" Drew wanted to know. "Who brought her aboard?"

Ktumba hesitated before replying, "Nayo Naguchi did."

"Rats live two standard years at most, and Naguchi arrived on the Hub at least fifteen years ago," Drew pointed out. "Are you saying you've been cloning Naguchi's pet?"

She gave him a faint smile. "Not necessary. This is the original rat. And although Nayo named her, Yoko was never his pet."

Suddenly, Drew was feeling a little light-headed. "So we have aboard this station a rat that has lived for more than twenty Earth years?"

"A very intelligent rat that has lived in excellent health for more than twenty-*five* years, and counting," she confirmed with a nod. "Her DNA is gumbo. My guess is that she was in the final generation of a genetics experiment and Nayo… relocated her. He left detailed instructions for her care and monitoring. Robert gives her companionship and mental stimulation. And every three intervals I biotest her and record my findings. She's already lived the equivalent of eight rat lifetimes, and shows no signs of slowing down. Theoretically, she could be immortal."

And the longer she lived, the more she would learn, becoming more and more intelligent. It was the perfect gift from a great teacher: Yoko, the role model.

"Who else knows the truth about her?" Drew asked, trying to sound casual.

"Not many on the Hub. Robert, of course, and Ruby and Lydia. Most of the crew think, as you did, that I've been cloning Nayo's pet for sentimental reasons."

"What about Khaloub?" Drew wanted to know.

She shook her head in response.

"Jovanovich?" Drew persisted.

"Not a chance!" blurted O'Malley. "He ordered me to space her."

"You're the first station manager since Nayo Naguchi who's expressed any interest in keeping Yoko on the Hub," the Doc explained, "so you're the first I've told. At my request, none of the others reported her presence to the Earth authorities; and up until now, we've managed to keep her a secret from the Rangers as well."

"And yet, you allowed Alison Morgan to play with her?"

"Gavin's idea," O'Malley piped up.

"He has a soft spot for kids in trouble," said the Doc.

Yes, he had, Drew thought disgustedly — it was in his head. And the Doc clearly had a soft spot for Gavin Holchuk, in the same location.

He completed his thought aloud: "So now Alison, who knows about Yoko, will be leaving the Hub in four days, and that could be a problem, especially since we've had the breathtaking audacity to deny her something she wants. Okay, let's assume that she's vindictive as well as spoiled, and that she makes a complaint to the authorities that the crew of Daisy Hub are breaking the rules and keeping a live animal on the station. Considering who and where we are, is anyone on Earth going to give a damn?"

"Of course, they will," replied the Doc tartly. "And I suggest that we hedge our bets by ensuring that the child leaves here as happy as possible. We could start by removing her from Isolation, since she really hasn't done anything serious enough to warrant four whole days of solitary confinement."

She was right, of course. Never argue with the Doc.

A beat, then, "Agreed," said Drew. "But I don't want her roaming the station. We'll need to keep her busy until her transportation arrives. Ms. Garfield," he called over the partition, "have you got any SPA programs that'll wear out a teenager?"

A moment later, Lydia appeared with a smile and a trio of datawafers. "I've got a few that wear out Orvy Hagman: rock climbing, white water rafting, and extreme skateboarding."

Drew paused, mouth open. Skateboarding? He would have to try that one himself some time. Then he recomposed his face and sighed dramatically, "All right, Doctor. Go release the prisoner. And hope she stays out of my way."

"I don't think you have to worry about that, Mr. Townsend," she said sweetly as she got to her feet. "She'll probably avoid you like the plague."

Drew gestured to O'Malley to remain seated.

When Doc Ktumba had left AdComm, Drew leaned forward across his desk. "Lydia says you and I ought to have a talk."

O'Malley was a slight man with swarthy coloring, an up-tilted nose, and a mop of unruly dark hair. He widened his eyes ingenuously and wondered, "Oh? About what?"

"You know about what," Lydia scolded him from across the deck.

O'Malley gazed thoughtfully at Drew for a few seconds, then seemed to reach a decision. "All right, Mr. Townsend. What do you want to know?"

"First of all, how did my original biofile come to be on the Hub's intranet?"

A slow grin spread across O'Malley's face. This was a story he would clearly relish telling. "We don't have an intranet anymore," he said after a pause. "Shortly after I arrived here, I figured out how to hack into the database on Zulu."

His nonchalance was astonishing. On Earth, hacking had been a capital offence for some time.

"You stole the Rangers' database?"

"Copied it," O'Malley corrected him.

"How did you get past their system watchdogs?"

"I knew they had to be the same as ours. I practiced for a while."

That simple statement left so much unsaid that it boggled the imagination. "You practiced?" he echoed.

"Lydia set up a sim for me using the SPA system."

Of course. How could he have forgotten O'Malley's accomplice?

"Wait a minute — are you saying my original biofile was in the Rangers' Net when you copied it over?" There was a sudden icy prickling across Drew's shoulders. Had his mission been compromised from the outset?

"Not exactly. See, once I knew the Zoo was receiving regular updates from Earth's InfoCommNet, I put us in the loop. Each time the Rangers sent data, I made sure a data request from the Hub was piggybacked onto it. Each time Earth sent an update, it came through us first. So far, I've copied just over sixty percent of the InfoCommNet's data bank into our on-board system. Including your original biofile." The grin broadened. "And I've begun copying the Galactic Database as well, in case the aliens ever decide to freeze us out," O'Malley concluded.

"And all these databases are kept current?"

O'Malley nodded.

"And you're sure the Rangers haven't twigged to this?" Drew persisted.

"Absolutely, boss."

Drew blew out an admiring breath. "That's impressive," he commented, nodding. "But you're talking about an enormous amount of data. Where have you been storing it?"

"Here and there." A shrug. "Primarily here for now, but we have storage over there as well, if we need it."

Over there? Suddenly Drew's thoughts were racing. There was only one 'there' in the vicinity — Platform Zulu. Lydia had installed a SPA system on the Zoo, Ruby had told him. What if—?

"The SPA room?"

"It can hold nearly twelve terasecs of data," Lydia supplied, wandering over to join the discussion, "with capacity left over for a doubles tennis match or a golfing foursome."

Of course. Space for four programs to be running simultaneously, but no more than four. That would rule out team sports, wouldn't it? So Khaloub could pitch nine innings, but not with his own people backing him up. It was a shame, Drew mused. Sports would have been such a natural way to pull this crew together. At the very least, it would have made mission planning a lot easier.

"Was Karim in on your little secret?" Drew asked, in a sharper voice than he'd intended.

Lydia and O'Malley exchanged a startled look.

"We weren't sure he would approve," she explained. "I was going to tell him, right after we returned from installing the SPA on the Zoo, but—"

"Lydia became ill," O'Malley cut in.

"Rob, it's okay," she assured him. "He knows."

The pieces were coming together, and Drew didn't like the picture they were making. Worse, Bonelli's voice had begun to repeat on him, like onions: *Cripes, what did she tell you? They got excited, they crossed the line. But she shouldn't have—*

No, she shouldn't have, Drew realized. Not on the Zoo. Not unless she'd had no other choice.

"You went with her to the Zoo, didn't you, O'Malley? Whose idea was that?"

He shifted uneasily in his seat. "It was Lydia's. She told Karim she wanted me along to protect her in case the Rangers made trouble."

"So as far as Karim knew, you were there to fend off Bonelli's boys while she installed the SPA. In reality, the two of you were there to co-opt the SPA as storage space for your stolen databases. Hey, I'm just keeping the facts straight," Drew told them pleasantly. "It's what I do."

Staring narrowly at him, Lydia leaned back in her chair.

"So, let me guess," Drew continued chattily. "You'd practiced slipping past the watchdogs, so you knew they wouldn't be a problem. But Bonelli didn't trust you, did he? He assigned a couple of guards to watch you. You knew this was your only chance to link the two SPAs together, and you couldn't do it unless the guards were distracted. So you sent Lydia out to flirt with them for a few minutes. Was that how it went down?"

"Actually," said O'Malley, "the flirting was Lydia's idea too."

"Really?" Drew crossed his arms over his chest and swiveled his chair so that he was facing her. "And was it also your idea to be assaulted? I'll bet that made one hell of a distraction for Bonelli's boys. How much extra time did it buy him, Lydia?"

She drew herself up, her eyes flashing.

"Hey, don't go blaming the victim," O'Malley protested angrily, rising out of his seat. "She was attacked by three guys. Doc saw the bruises—"

"Sit down, Rob," she told him.

He sat, instantly silenced. Inwardly Drew smiled, glad to know that his street instincts were still sharp. Whatever else Lydia Garfield might be, she clearly was not, nor ever would be, a helpless victim. Good for her. And good for the EIS.

"Twenty minutes," she finally replied.

Drew nodded thoughtfully. "And how badly hurt were you?"

A shadow passed quickly over her face. "Let's just say I've been hurt worse, in less worthy causes."

Drew didn't pursue the matter. According to her biofile, she'd grown up in Atlantica, an area rife with juvenile gangs. They tended to draw Eligible teens like magnets, pulling them out of the Enclaves and into the Zones for a little weekend 'fun'.

"You do the wounded bird thing very well," he remarked.

She accepted the compliment with a nod and returned, "And you do the cop thing very well, Mr. Townsend."

Lydia turned I-told-you-so eyes on her partner.

"Does Doc Ktumba know what really happened?" Drew asked.

"No," said Lydia, frowning. "Nobody does except Rob and now you. And the Rangers, of course, but who around here is going to believe them?"

"Then why didn't she send you away for treatment once Khaloub's body had been discovered and Bonelli's men began investigating?"

"She tried to," said Lydia.

"But...?"

The smugness of O'Malley's expression gave Drew his answer. The ratkeeper and Lydia were a matched pair, between them having complete control over the Hub's data and communications systems. If they didn't want to be split up, nothing and nobody aboard the Hub could make it happen.

"All right," Drew decided, "here's the deal. The two of you are going to be my intelligence team. My eyes and ears. You," he said, pointing a finger at Lydia, "are going to make a full and rapid recovery from your ordeal and put it behind you. A miracle cure. Doc Ktumba may even want to write a paper about it — let her. And you," he added, shifting the finger to point at O'Malley, "are going to continue stockpiling data. I'm giving you both clean slates, from this day forward, on one condition: from now on, you're to be absolutely straight with me and your crewmates — no more lying, and no more cons unless I'm running them."

"How come *you* get to run them?" O'Malley challenged.

Drew leaned across his desk on carefully placed knuckles and said in a lowered voice, "Because I've been doing it a whole lot longer and am a whole lot better at it than either of you. Now, do we have an arrangement?"

The other man grinned up at him. "Whatever you say, boss."

Lydia said nothing. On her way out of his office space, however, she turned and gave him an appraising look. Drew almost didn't recognize what he saw on her face. It had been a long time since anyone had shown him that kind of respect.

And speaking of respect...

"O'Malley, before you go, there's something I need you to do for me."

Cocking his head curiously, the ratkeeper resumed his seat.

"A good friend of mine was killed the day before I shipped out, and I want to follow the murder investigation. Can you request information about a specific open case file from Security Data Management?"

"Not without tipping our hand to the Rangers. They generally request larger packages of data — all the crimes of a certain type committed during a specified period or in a particular location, that sort of thing. When and where did this murder take place, boss?"

"New Chicago, about two intervals ago. The victim's name was Bruni Patel. When I left, all they had was snaps from the body dump scene. The file should be a lot fatter by now."

O'Malley nodded thoughtfully. "Okay, I'll see what I can do. Meanwhile, we may already have something in our system about Bruni Patel, so I'll search our on-board databases and let you know what I find."

Chapter 22

Gavin Holchuk had found his 'inner warrior', and it was *hartoon*.

The grieving husband and outraged father that the Relocation Authority had summarily boxed up and shipped out to Daisy Hub thirteen standard years earlier had finally broken free. Holchuk's senses were drowning in remembered pain. Every dream was a nightmare of blood and smoke, filled with Risa's screams and ending with her blackened, agony-contorted face in the morgue.

Holchuk couldn't sleep, couldn't rest, couldn't even sit. For three days now, he had prowled his quarters like a caged animal. On the second day, Jensen's assistant had taken one look at his face, dropped a food tray onto the desk and run out of the room. By the third, the need for vengeance was like a roaring furnace in Holchuk's brain.

Then, just when he thought he could no longer control the berserker raging inside him, he heard over the intercomm the voice he had been waiting for.

"Gavin Holchuk, son of Samuel," said Nagor, "the House of Trokerk has arrived. Prepare to join with us."

An honor guard of warriors from Holchuk's own House had to escort him to Nagor's ship. Fortunately, Gavin had thought to leave instructions with Ruby before going into seclusion. When his cabin door slid aside, there they were: Jason Smith, wearing the dress uniform of a Fleet officer; Lucas Soaring Hawk, dressed in buckskin breeches and a bone breastplate, his face painted in red and black stripes; Lu Xensiu, covered to his eyes in ninja attire, complete with nunchucks; and Orvy Hagman, who had apparently reached back into a previous life and come up with a black leather jacket with matching trousers and peaked cap, all bristling with metal studs and bearing the insignia of The Devil's Henchmen.

Despite their motley appearance, the four men were all stern-faced and deathly serious. Human warriors, ceremonially garbed.

As prescribed by Nandrian tradition, the honor guard marched him in silent formation to the tube stop, two behind him, two in front. They held formation inside the tube car, and walked him right up to the docking hatch of the Nandrian ship, where Nagor and three others stood in similar formation, waiting. The four aliens were also ceremonially garbed. Their upper bodies were encased in jointed armor, under long black tabards bearing the symbol of Trokerk worked in metallic thread.

"Welcome, Gavin Holchuk," announced Nagor. "Are you prepared to join us?"

Holchuk was sucking in long, steadying breaths, willing his mind to focus on the ritual. "I am ready, Nagor ban Nagoram," he declared hoarsely.

Nagor bared his lower fangs in approval. "A warrior burns within you."

"He thirsts for the blood of our enemies," Holchuk replied, following the script.

"He defends the honor of the House of Americas?"

"He does." A guerrilla memory triggered a surge of adrenaline; suddenly his skin was clammy and it was all Holchuk could do to stand still and upright.

"And he defends the honor of Daisy Hub?"

"He does."

"And he would defend the honor of the House of Trokerk?"

Through gritted teeth, Holchuk replied, "He would die if necessary in the cause of honor."

The big alien nodded. "Then enter."

With that, the Nandrian guardsmen strode forward and surrounded Holchuk. Then, in formation, all five boarded the *Hak'kor*'s ship.

The *Pet'silliar* was not like any of the Nandrian ships Holchuk had visited in the past. Those had been cargo vessels, rigged out for years-long trading voyages. Consequently, most of their on-board areas had been devoted to storage of one kind or another. The air inside them had been cool and dry. And both ship and crew were armed, of course, in case the opportunity arose for a *tekl'hananni* match. This ship was different.

As he was escorted through the entry port, the first thing Holchuk noticed was the air. It was warm and humid. Too humid. Moisture was penetrating his clothing and settling on his skin. Good. It would mingle with the perspiration that already covered him and provide an excuse for any other sweat that happened to break out during the next day or so.

Holchuk had worked shifts under Jason Smith and knew how energy-consuming it was to maintain a subtropical atmosphere aboard a spacecraft. The *Pet'silliar* was clearly not designed for long voyages. But it was incredibly spacious, for a shuttle. Its broad corridors were misty, bathed in soft light from concealed sources that lent the air itself a rosy or violet glow. Tall plants with round, multicolored leaves lined the bulkheads, seeming to grow directly out of the deck plating. They clung to the wall surfaces, curving with them into long and lofty ceilings.

Holchuk followed Nagor a short distance along one corridor, to a high arching door that slid aside soundlessly as they approached. The rectangular room into which the Human was now ushered was large enough to hold AdComm at least twice. A plant-free zone, it had a pale overhead vault and muraled walls depicting the historical victories of Trokerk in living — and dying — color. And stationed in the spaces between those battles stood uniformed warriors, their black tabards lined in blood red and fastened with silver, their blades already in their hands, their watchful eyes glittering like beacons.

These were the *Hak'kor*'s private guard. If Holchuk said or did anything that offended the *Hak'kor*'s representative, one of them would instantly avenge the honor of the House.

Involuntarily, Holchuk's eyes went to the painted image of a huge Nandrian warrior, holding aloft the severed head of an enemy of Trokerk — and inside his Human stomach, it began raining ice pellets.

Somewhere out in space sat a heavily-armed Nandrian ship of the line that had brought a member of the First Shield from the home world to meet him. The First Shield never left the planet unless on a matter of utmost importance to the House. The adoption of an off-worlder was evidently such a matter. And the retribution exacted for any perceived betrayal associated with that adoption would escalate proportionately. The *Hak'kor*'s guard would not stop with executing Gavin Holchuk. His House would be wiped out as well. Daisy Hub would be destroyed, and if the insult were sufficiently grievous, maybe even Earth.

Holchuk could feel a cold sweat popping out on his forehead, tattooing his stomach, trickling down his back. All those lives... All those Human lives depending on him.... Suddenly his inner warrior was only a memory, and his legs were trembling again, wanting desperately to carry him away from this place.

Just then, a door slid open at the far end of the room. Holchuk felt a hand on his shoulder, urging him to his knees, and abruptly the realization hit him: from the moment he'd smelled that smoky cinnamon in the caf, he'd been fried. Running had never been an option.

Every being in the room had dropped to his knees, to show respect for the arrival of the *Hak'kor*'s representative.

This Nandrian wore brow armor, signifying membership in the First Shield of the House. But he wasn't the *Hak'kor* — he was the *Kalufah*, next in honor to the *Hak'kor*. And next in line for leadership if anything should happen to the 'owner' of the House. His facial protection consisted of a band of intricately worked yellow metal that covered his forehead and curved downward over his cheeks, and he wore a richly embroidered tabard, loosely belted around his hips, over a breastplate that appeared to be made of the same metal. In his right hand he carried the living staff, a long piece of wood with leafy branches sprouting out of it. According to legend, the staff was several hundred years old and still putting out twigs. As long as it lived, the House of Trokerk could not fall.

One of the guards brought over what appeared to be a piece of metal sculpture and placed it directly behind the

Kalufah. With a long exhalation of breath, the Nandrian sank down onto it, shifting the staff from his right to his left hand.

"What do you offer to the House of Trokerk?" he demanded in heavily-accented Gally.

"A Human, *Kalufah*," said Nagor without changing position. "He has shown himself worthy."

"To you, perhaps, Nagor ban Nagoram. Let him prove his worthiness to me. Human, your line!"

The last three words struck Holchuk with almost physical force.

This was it, he thought miserably. Nagor had spent hours preparing him for this ritual. All he could do now was his best — and pray. Feeling the weight of billions of Human lives resting on his shoulders, Holchuk got slowly to his feet and took the prescribed step forward. He met the eyes of the *Hak'kor*'s representative, held his gaze for exactly two seconds, then began the speech he had so carefully rehearsed:

"I am Gavin Holchuk, son of Samuel the Bold, Fifth Shield of the House of Americas. I am the twenty-fifth generation of a clan of warriors, beginning with George the Righteous, who fought with others like himself to free the House of Americas from those who would have controlled it."

As he had once advised Townsend the Terrible, the object of the exercise was not to tell the truth; it was to stay alive long enough to achieve one's purpose. The Nandrians wanted to hear about the warriors in his family, so that was what he would tell them. In fact, most of his relatives had been posted off-planet, where they'd been killed by the plague. But warriors didn't succumb to disease. There was no honor in that. They also didn't get toxed and fall off the roof, or swerve their PV to avoid hitting an animal and smash into a tree instead, or choke to death on a piece of apple core. No doubt there were Nandrians whose lives had ended in similarly ignoble fashion, due to bad luck or foolishness; they just didn't advertise the fact. And neither would he.

Posturing, he reminded himself grimly, that was all it was.

"...and I, Gavin the Rebel, fought for years for the freedom of others like myself on our home world to choose our own mates and lead our own lives, until I was overpowered and exiled to Daisy Hub."

The *Kalufah's* eyes remained on him for several seconds more, gleaming like sentient gemstones. Holchuk gulped hard and felt icy claws walk across his shoulders. He hadn't let himself think about it before, but what if the *Kalufah* was one of the few Nandrians in existence who didn't *like* posturing?

Finally, the *Kalufah* broke eye contact and demanded, "And who swears for this Human?"

Nagor stepped forward then, and began to speak. He gave the history of his relationship with Holchuk, praising in glowing terms Gavin's unswerving honesty and righteousness. Finally, with much gesturing and many different voices, Nagor dramatized for the *Kalufah* the apprehension of Rostol, and the part Holchuk had played in saving everyone's honor.

That seemed to make up the Nandrian official's mind.

He thumped the living staff once on the floor and asked, "Gavin Holchuk, son of Samuel, what is your intention?"

The response to this had been scripted as well. "I wish to be a warrior in the cause of honor and justice," Holchuk declared. "I wish to join with my brother Nagor in defense of the House of Trokerk."

"A warrior's greatest strengths are his courage and his honor. Before you are joined, these must be tested. Are you, an off-worlder, prepared to risk your life to join the House of Trokerk?"

Risk it? He felt as though he'd already forfeited it.

Holchuk gulped a lungful of air, then let it out slowly. "I am prepared," he replied.

The *Kalufah* pounded the living staff three times more on the floor. "Seal the entry ports," he commanded. "Instruct the Chief Officer that we are returning to the *Hak'kor's* ship for *tekl'hananni*."

Chapter 23

Drew now had his eyes and ears, and a voice. He had plenty of muscle, and a foreman to manage it for him. He had in-house technical and scientific expertise, a fully equipped medical and forensic laboratory, and the Fleet Academy training of Jason Smith. He even had a getaway shuttle, and a berserker pilot to fly it.

If he didn't know better, he might be tempted to believe that someone had equipped the Hub specifically for his purposes.

Once Holchuk had been adopted into Nagor's Shield, Drew would also have the most feared warriors in the galaxy as backup if he needed it. And sooner rather than later, he knew, the Hub would need defensive weapons as well. In the meanwhile, thanks to Gouryas and Singh, Drew finally had the mission that would pull all these mavericks and misfits together into a working team. The briefing meeting would be held once Holchuk was back on the Hub. Before then, Townsend had some groundwork to lay.

Teri Mintz was pivotal to his plan. He found her having lunch with O'Malley in the caf, exactly where Lydia had told him to look. Teri's expression was sober, almost sad. Seeing the way she and O'Malley leaned toward each other across the table, so deep in discussion that there may as well have been a wall around them, Drew couldn't help wondering what scheme the ratkeeper was hatching now.

O'Malley clearly had no idea who he was dealing with, and why should he? From the moment she'd arrived on Daisy Hub, Teri had been a perfect lady. Townsend had earlier seen her wildcat temper — and evidence of a strong right hook — but decided to wait for Holchuk's first report on her before mentioning them to anyone. It was a good decision. Teri had obviously taken Drew's advice to heart after all and made a fresh beginning, for, according to Holchuk, the newest cargo inspector was a model employee: careful, hard working, and eager to please. Of course, someone like O'Malley might look at that and see a potential mark. If so, and if Teri realized she was being conned, the wildcat inside her would probably reach out its claws and tear a strip off him.

"I hope I'm not interrupting," said Drew. He wasn't. They had broken off their conversation as soon as Teri had noticed the station manager walking toward them.

What had been hopeful anticipation on her face morphed into an expression of dread. "It's bad news about Gavin, isn't it?"

"There's no news yet," he told her, pulling a third chair over to their table and sitting down. O'Malley's expression flickered annoyance. Three was a crowd. Too bad. "I just wanted to run an idea past you that I thought you'd be interested in. You too, O'Malley."

About to get up and leave, the ratkeeper sank back onto his chair with a sigh.

"I remembered how upset you were about not having a singing career anymore," Drew continued, "and I was wondering — how would you feel about doing shows for your crewmates?"

She looked skeptical. "The Daisy Hub Lounge presents…?"

"A hub is a hub," he pointed out, "and it has to be better than doing InfoCommAds. For one thing, you'd have creative control."

"You'd let me produce?"

"Co-produce." He was still the station manager, after all. "Or would you rather just leave all the decisions to me?"

"Absolutely not," she declared. Then, tilting her head curiously, she added, "You're really serious about this?"

"I am. It'll be great for everyone's morale. Will you do it?"

"Have you ever staged a show before, Mr. Townsend?" she asked, cheeks dimpling.

"No, but I suspect you can teach me all about it. As I recall, you're pretty good at that. So, do we have a deal?"

She nodded happily. "Deal."

"How much time do you need to get the first one ready?"

She leaned back thoughtfully in her chair. "The first one is always a lot of work," she told him. "But since it's going to be a one-woman show and I already have all my costumes and music with me, I won't need much rehearsal to get back up to speed," she decided. "Give me an interval."

"Perfect. And I know exactly where to set up the stage — K Deck. It's being used for storage right now. We can move all those containers to the secondary utilities deck, and that gives us plenty of room for you and your appreciative audience."

"…and a glitzy backdrop, a backup band, and a ton or so of electronics," she added, smiling. "What do you think, Rob?"

O'Malley frowned briefly. He opened his mouth to say something, thought better of it, then settled back in his chair with a speculative gleam in his eyes. "I think it's a terrific idea," he said. "Everyone loves a show."

He caught up with Townsend in the corridor outside the caf. "It's a con, isn't it? Who's the mark?"

Drew feigned indignation. "A con? How can you suggest such a thing, Mr. O'Malley?"

"Because you're setting up this stage directly over an arsenal of jamming gear. Now, who's the mark?"

Drew stopped walking and said with a sigh, "Not Teri, and that's all I'm prepared to say at the moment. Coincidentally, I have another special job for you."

"Part of the con? Name it."

"When will you be requesting the next parcel of data from the InfoCommNet?"

"The next transmission goes out tomorrow at 1100 hours, the one after that in three days' time. Is there something extra that you want me to get for you?"

"Not for me. For Teri."

O'Malley's eyes began to twinkle. "You sweet on her, boss?"

No, Drew thought wearily, *I just don't want her to kill me when she finds out who I'm inviting to this concert.* But his only reply to O'Malley was a smile.

Chapter 24

***Tekl'hananni* was a** Nandrian word meaning, literally, 'test of strength'. As a Human, Holchuk associated it with only one thing — open warfare in space, pretending to be a sport. The Nandrians, however, had other, older meanings for *tekl'hananni*, as Nagor finally explained to him en route to the *Hak'kor*'s flagship.

The Nandrians didn't always speak in riddles, Holchuk discovered. This manner of speech stemmed from the Nandrian belief that the value of a conversation was measured by the extent to which it made one think. When pressed for time, however, and if the subject matter was important enough, they could communicate information quite clearly and succinctly.

In ancient times, *tekl'hananni* had been a rite of passage into adulthood, the nature of the test to be determined by the *Hak'kor* or his representative. Not every Shield bearer had to be a warrior, and not every *tekl'hananni* had to involve combat — there were healers and spiritual leaders on the home world as well, who had earned their place in their respective Shields without ever picking up a weapon. Feeling almost limp with relief at having passed the *Kalufah*'s first inspection, Holchuk devoutly hoped that his would be a nonviolent *tekl'hananni*. For an adoption, it was the only thing that made sense. Any being with eyes could see that the only possible outcome of a Human-Nandrian combat would be a bloodied Human corpse.

At last, the *Pet'silliar* came to rest on a landing deck that dwarfed anything Holchuk had ever seen, in person or on vids. It should have been filled with shuttles and fighting craft. Instead, it appeared gray, cavernous, and incongruously empty. Holchuk didn't have much time to wonder about this, for an honor guard wearing the livery of Trokerk met him and Nagor as they stepped off the shuttle and escorted them directly to the *Hak'kor*'s reception room.

"Cling to your rage, little warrior," advised Nagor quietly as they marched through a maze of gray metal corridors, flanked by a squadron of Nandrians even larger and more heavily armed than before. "Let it burn within you."

Actually, Holchuk's rage had had an attack of common sense and yielded to a much stronger emotion — fear. But he wasn't about to tell that to a Nandrian. Being *hartoon* kept the fear at bay, but it also increased his chances of making a fatal mistake in the presence of the *Hak'kor*. Fear was controllable, Holchuk told himself. He just needed to distract his mind, keep it busy with details and observations and questions.

For example, the spacecraft they were now on was clearly a battleship. It was utilitarian, unadorned. Hard and flat as far as the eye could see. Nothing shone but the blades of the weapons all around him. It made excellent sense for the *Hak'kor* to travel this way. He was too important to his House to be running around the galaxy unprotected. But didn't his presence make the ship he was on just as important and just as much in need of protection? And that brought Holchuk back to the question of the day: Why were there no fighter craft in the landing bay? Were they being kept on another deck? Was this ship so large that it could reserve an entire hangar for just one ship — the *Hak'kor*'s private launch?

Actually, that might be the answer, he soon realized, for the reception room he was now entering made the one on the launch look like a closet. Holchuk had never been especially religious; in fact, his stubborn agnosticism when he was younger had slowly estranged him from most of his family. Nonetheless, as he stood now in the middle of this immense vaulted space with its restlessly flowing terra-cotta-colored walls, richly grained wooden floor, and illuminated pillars, the very air around him glowing amber, Holchuk felt as though he were in a great cathedral, surrounded by unfathomable power. In a sense, he was. This huge spacegoing fortress was carrying the *Hak'kor*, the most important person in the House of Trokerk, and a small army of handpicked palace guards.

A door slid open at the other end of the room and a phalanx of six Nandrians, metal-plated and heavily armed, marched in. In their midst walked the *Kalufah*. He wasn't carrying the living staff this time. And, Holchuk couldn't help noticing, nobody brought him a chair.

"There are many ways to fight for honor, and there are many kinds of courage. The *Hak'kor* has decided on a test," he announced.

So it would be a nonviolent *tekl'hananni* after all. Holchuk blew out a sigh of sheer relief.

"The Human will step forward," said the *Kalufah*.

He obeyed, just as another door slid open to admit four more huge Nandrians, leading a prisoner this time, hooded and in chains. The Human watched, fascinated, as the captive was dragged before the *Kalufah* and pushed to his knees.

"Human, you wish to defend the honor of the House of Trokerk?" demanded the *Kalufah*.

"I would die in the cause of honor," Holchuk replied, still following the script.

"This *lorssh* has betrayed our House and brought dishonor to the Fifth and Seventh Shields. You will avenge them."

There was no time even to utter a squeak of protest or confusion. Suddenly a sharp, bladed weapon was thrust into his hand; his fingers closed automatically around the leather-wrapped hilt. Clearly, some planning had gone into this test. The sword was light and perfectly balanced for a Human. In the next second, the hood was yanked off the prisoner's head, and Holchuk found himself staring into a familiar pair of malevolent green eyes.

It was Rostol.

Several seconds later, Holchuk remembered to breathe. Somehow, he had managed to hold onto the sword; but he was pointing it downward, leaving himself open to attack. This was not a wise thing to do when facing a desperate criminal twice his size.

Consciously filling his lungs, Holchuk raised the tip of his sword and held it centimeters away from Rostol's neck. The Nandrian should already be dead. He had confessed to committing a capital crime, and Nandrian justice was swift and unrelenting. Many criminals were summarily executed on the way to their trial. And yet, here was Rostol, kneeling before Holchuk, very much alive. Clearly, a great deal of thought and planning had gone into this moment of vengeance.

Perfect vengeance for a *hartoon*. The Relocation Authority had murdered his wife and stolen his child. Rostol had tried to kill a Human child. The Relocation Authority was beyond Holchuk's reach. But Rostol was close by, an easy and deserving target for his wrath.

Cling to your rage, little warrior.

Holchuk could feel the Nandrians' eyes on him. This was *tekl'hananni*, he reminded himself, a test of strength. They were watching him, judging his worthiness to join the Fifth Shield. And if he failed, millions of his people might die.

No, not might die. *Would* die. Suddenly he knew, with gut-twisting certainty, where all the Nandrian fighter craft had gone.

"Go ahead, kill me, Human," snarled Rostol, rattling his chains. "Are you afraid? Look! I cannot harm you."

Holchuk's blood was roaring in his ears. He forced himself to breathe steadily, to focus on the moment. He willed his sword hand not to waver. There was no room for error here. He would have to reason this through as if he were a Nandrian, behave as a Nandrian would. Remember, as a Nandrian would, that strength was nothing without honor.

Remember that the cold-blooded killing of a helpless captive was still considered a crime on Nandor.

"What is wrong with you, Human? Are you a coward?" Rostol taunted, his green eyes flashing.

"I would be, if I killed you," Holchuk replied softly.

He dropped his sword arm to his side and turned toward the *Kalufah*. "I wish justice for the House of Trokerk, and for the Human female this *lorssh* tried to kill," he said, in as firm a voice as he could muster. "But I also wish honor. Where is the honor for me in slaughtering a helpless prisoner? And where is the honor for Trokerk in allowing an off-worlder to take its vengeance?"

For an endless moment, there was silence in the room as the *Kalufah* considered his words. Holchuk waited tautly, not even daring to breathe. At last, the Nandrian official drew himself up and declared, "The Human understands."

At that, a storm of wheezing and snorting broke out. Lower fangs were bared in approval. Rostol was hustled out of the room. Holchuk had survived *tekl'hananni*. Overwhelmed with relief, he would probably have collapsed to the floor if Nagor hadn't reached out just then to give his shoulders a congratulatory squeeze.

Then, abruptly, the assembly went quiet again. Another honor guard had entered, escorting a very old Nandrian, his proud posture belying the sagging skin on his face and neck. His facial armor was more ornament than protection, a band of gemstone-encrusted leather that covered his brow and hung down both cheeks. He was wrapped in a floor-length brown leather cape and carrying the living staff, and he gave off an aura of irresistible power. The *Hak'kor* of Trokerk. In the same instant, everyone in the room, including the *Kalufah*, fell to their knees.

"The Houses will be joined," decreed the *Hak'kor*.

"They will be joined," chorused all the Nandrians present.

"Nagor ban Nagoram, you ask to be partnered with this Human?"

Nagor rose, stepped forward and replied, "I wish it, *Hak'kor*."

"Gavin ban Samuel, come before me," said the *Hak'kor*.

Holchuk hurried to his feet and obeyed, wondering at the *Hak'kor*'s choice of words. According to Nagor, there had never before been an interspecies adoption by a Nandrian Shield. Perhaps neither Nandrian nor Gally had a word to describe accurately the relationship that would result. But — partnered?

The *Hak'kor* looked him over carefully. "You have a mate," the *Hak'kor* observed.

For a second, Holchuk blanked. A mate? No. Risa was dead and he'd never— Suddenly his heart dropped, as he recalled: he'd told Nagor that Teri was his mate to give her Fifth Shield status and ensure she wouldn't be bothered by drunken crewmembers. A harmless lie, but a lie nonetheless. He didn't dare confess it now. If the *Hak'kor* had any reason to doubt his honor, he was a dead man.

Swallowing hard, Holchuk stammered, "I— Yes, *Hak'kor*."

The *Hak'kor* looked displeased. He tilted his head and spat and snarled something at Nagor, who spat and snarled something back. This went on for a couple of minutes, as a tide of dread rose in Holchuk's chest.

Finally, Nagor stepped back, and the conversation resumed in Gally.

"The Houses of Trokerk and Daisy Hub have enemies in common and therefore must *ssalssin*," declared the *Hak'kor*. "Gavin ban Samuel, you wish to be partnered with this Nandrian?"

Holchuk had no choice but to reply, "I wish it, *Hak'kor*."

"Then it will be. Nagor ban Nagoram of Trokerk, and Gavin ban Samuel of Daisy Hub, you will *ssalssit essendi* at the next full cycle."

Then the *Hak'kor* pounded the daylights out of the living staff on the floor, and it was done. Or begun. Holchuk had no idea what *ssalssit essendi* meant, or how long a full cycle was supposed to be. Clearly, however, his adoption wouldn't be finalized until he and Nagor had performed this ritual activity.

"Nagor ban Nagoram, I have many questions," said Holchuk.

"And I have many answers, Gavin ban Samuel. Unfortunately, there is no lemonade on the *Hak'kor*'s ship, so this will have to do." His lower fangs bared, Nagor handed him a large mug filled to the brim with an amber-colored liquid that smelled strongly of vanilla.

Holchuk took an experimental swallow and felt a river of fire flow down his throat and into his stomach. It was all he could do not to choke.

"What is this called?" he asked Nagor as soon as he could speak again.

"Whisky," the Nandrian replied, tilting his head in puzzlement. "It is the *Hak'kor*'s favorite Human beverage. We trade for it on Carvellis 7."

Holchuk nearly laughed out loud. Vanilla-flavored whisky. Would wonders never cease?

"Drink, my brother," Nagor urged. "The feast begins when these are empty."

Holchuk glanced around the room and realized with dismay that he and Nagor were the only ones holding mugs. There looked to be nearly half a bottle of liquor in each one. On the other hand, he thought, this was a Nandrian feast; considering what and how he was liable to be served, it would probably be better for everyone if he were toxed to the rafters before sitting down at the table.

Chapter 25

For hours after regaining consciousness on the *Pet'silliar*, Holchuk was sure he was dead and on his way to Hades. Once Nagor had managed to convince him that he was only on his way back to Daisy Hub, a single thought seized Holchuk's mind and wouldn't let go: Teri was going to kill him.

Teri was going to kill him and the Doc was going to help her. Unless this hangover beat them both to it. Or something he'd eaten at the feast. He'd impressed the *Hak'kor*, Nagor told him, by fearlessly consuming whatever was put in front of him, including a couple of delicacies from the home world that were an acquired taste even for Nandrians. The whisky had apparently done its job — Holchuk's memories of the evening were spotty at best, although he did have a vague recollection of something trying to escape from his plate. From the volcanic roiling in his stomach, he guessed that it was still trying to escape. And each time he burped, an unspeakable taste lingered in his mouth.

Nagor accompanied him part of the way, to a moon where the *Krronn* was waiting to rendezvous. That left Holchuk alone for the remaining few hours of the journey, with sandpaper eyelids and a desert in his mouth and a stomach that hated his guts, running scenarios through his mind. Every last one of them ended with Teri cussing him out and then stomping out of the room.

Not since Risa's death had he met a woman who affected him the way Teri Mintz did. She was strong and smart and vulnerable, all at once. And she cared, about things and about people. Specifically, she seemed to care about *him*. Just knowing that gave him hope for the future. Perhaps, eventually, they could have had a relationship together — if Nagor hadn't made him an offer he didn't dare refuse, dragging him and Teri into *ssalssit essendi*. He hated the thought of even having to tell her about it. He wouldn't blame her a bit if she refused to cooperate. She would probably turn her back on him because of it. And then, he wasn't sure what he would do. Go *hartoon*, most likely.

By the time the *Pet'silliar* had docked at Daisy Hub, Holchuk was perspiring all over and had a head that pounded like the bass drum in a marching band. He had hoped he might sneak aboard unnoticed, but it was not to be.

Townsend and Ruby and the Doc all stood waiting for him as he stepped through the archway of docking module 2.

Townsend was the first to speak. "Welcome back, Mr. Holchuk. You look—"

"—terrible!" Ruby cut in. "What did those Nandrians do to you?"

Her voice went like an electrical jolt directly to the pain centers of his brain. "Please, don't shout," he moaned. "I'm all right, really. It's only a hangover. And something I ate."

"Uh-huh. Death by partying," Ruby commented, exchanging an amused look with Townsend.

"He needs to go directly to Med Services so I can check him out," said the Doc briskly. "Come on, Gavin. You'll feel a lot better with an antacid in your stomach."

With Ruby hanging onto one arm and the Doc gripping the other, Holchuk managed to get his legs moving again. "If you decide to pump my stomach, be careful," he warned. "I think there's something still alive down there."

"If they fed you, they must consider you family," observed Ruby. "So, did they give you a new name?"

He shook his head. "I need to talk to Townsend."

"I'm right here, Mr. Holchuk." The station manager stepped into the tube car behind them and pressed H on the keypad.

"And Teri. And you, Doc," he continued miserably. "You're all involved in this."

"Involved in what?" Ktumba demanded.

"Did something go wrong out there?" asked Ruby.

He drew in a long, shuddering breath. "It's not finished. We have to talk."

Now Townsend was standing face to face, scowling fiercely at him. "Were you adopted? Yes or no."

"It's a long story, boss man."

"Then cut to the bottom line, Mr. Holchuk. Are the Nandrians still our friends?"

"Not exactly," he sighed unhappily. "They're our in-laws."

Beside him, Ruby stifled a laugh.

After a moment of shocked silence, the Doc said wonderingly, "You got married? To a Nandrian?"

"Actually, we both did. Nagor told the *Hak'kor* that Teri was my Human mate."

"And now you're a threesome," remarked the Doc drily. "Lovely."

"Gavin, I'm surprised at you," Ruby scolded, still suppressing laughter. "You should at least have brought the bride back some wedding cake."

— « o » —

"Let me understand this," said Townsend, frowning. "When a Nandrian says 'brother', he really means 'spouse'?"

Holchuk sighed wearily and lay back on the pillow Ruby had kindly plumped for him. It was the only sympathy he would get for the next while, at least. He knew he looked awful; he felt even worse. Having determined that the alien food hadn't poisoned him, Doc Ktumba had given him something for the headache and an antacid for his stomach. She had no magical cures, she told him reprovingly, for people who abused their bodies with alcohol.

Teri had arrived in Med Services moments earlier and taken up a position near the foot of his medbed. Now that they were all assembled, he could begin the explanation.

"It's a translation glitch. Nandrians aren't a gendered species. But we can't call them 'it' because that would be an insult of the worst kind. So, Gally has made them all masculine. When two males create a family-type bond between them, in Ameranglo as well as in Gally, they become brothers. That was what I thought Nagor wanted to do — adopt me into his Shield as his brother."

"But you were mistaken," Townsend summed up. "So what have we got here? Define the problem for me."

Holchuk nearly laughed. Define the problem? This Townsend fellow was no spy — he was a bloody bureaucrat.

"It doesn't fit into a box, boss man," he growled. "We have a joining of two Houses, in accordance with Nandrian tradition. An alliance between the House of Trokerk and the House of Daisy Hub, which will be officially sealed by the brotherhood between Nagor and myself, as soon as we have completed the final ritual, *ssalssit essendi*."

Townsend's eyebrows rose in disbelief before dropping into a scowl. "The House of Daisy Hub?" he repeated. "Can they do that? Simply declare that we're a House and form an alliance with us?"

"Apparently they can, since they just did. The *Hak'kor* seemed reluctant, but he said it was necessary because we share common enemies."

"Aww! And here I thought we didn't have an enemy in the galaxy," declared Ruby with a mocking grin.

"There are some aboard this Hub who would call Earth an enemy," the Doc added quietly.

"Enemies, plural," Holchuk pointed out.

Townsend had begun to pace. "Earth *will* be our enemy if the Council ever learns that we've made an independent alliance with the Nandrians," he pointed out.

"Earth wouldn't waste any ammunition on an outpost like this," countered Ruby.

Townsend shook his head. "They wouldn't have to — all they'd have to do is cut off our supply of lemon juice. Face it, people, what else do we have that the Nandrians might want? I mean, yes, it clearly benefits us to be allied with a much stronger power — but how can it possibly benefit the Nandrians to join with *us*?"

Holchuk bit back the first answer that came into his mouth and said instead, "The Nandrians see an advantage in it, boss man, besides the lemonade, and that's all that matters."

Teri had been standing quietly at the foot of Holchuk's medbed, listening to the discussion with visibly growing impatience. Finally, she blurted out, "I think we should complete the ritual and cement the alliance. Earth Council has left us hanging out here like laundry on the line. If the

Nandrians are looking for allies, that probably means there's going to be a war, and if there's going to be a war, we'll need all the friends we can get."

"Even if it means making ourselves a target for the other side?" Ruby challenged.

Holchuk opened his mouth to point out that Daisy Hub had always been a target, and an easy one at that; but the woman he'd nicknamed 'Tiger' leaped in ahead of him, claws unsheathed.

"Would you rather just waste away out here, doing routine maintenance and playing I Dare You with the Rangers?" she retorted. "The Nandrians are giving us the opportunity to stand for something, to make a difference. I say, let's take it, and damn the consequences."

Townsend stopped pacing and exchanged a look with the Doc. "Okay," he said, nodding. "So, what exactly does this ritual involve, Holchuk?"

This was the part he'd dreaded telling them. He'd spent much of the voyage home trying out and rejecting introductory lines. *Hey, Teri, remember how you said you'd always wanted to be a mother?*

Holchuk took a deep breath and dived in: "Traditionally, when there is an alliance between two Nandrian Houses, a member of each one's First or Second Shield is chosen, and they partner up and exchange eggs. All Nandrians have ovulation cycles. Once every ten standard years or so, a Nandrian produces an egg, which must then be fertilized by another Nandrian. The cycles are staggered, so that some of the adults in each House get to reproduce every year. The next egg that Nagor produces will be presented to me for fertilization, and he will expect me to have an egg ready for him to fertilize as well. Once they've both hatched, the alliance will be sealed, and the living young will symbolize its fruitfulness."

The Doc was frowning now, and shaking her head. "Gavin, they must know that this is impossible. They're oviparous. Humans are viviparous. Besides, and most importantly, you can't ovulate."

"They know that. But they also know that we're a gendered species, and they believe that I'm mated with a female, who *does* ovulate."

The air in the room went dead. Holchuk risked a glimpse at Teri's face and felt his own fall. Her features were hard, her eyes like daggers. Bad news — her inner warrior was emerging. But she had to agree to this. The offerings had to match. A fowl egg simply wouldn't do. Only a Human egg, fertilized by a Nandrian, would seal the alliance. And, of course, Doc Ktumba would also have to figure out some way for him to fertilize the Nandrian egg. They couldn't fake it. Nagor's egg would have to hatch out a living infant, and Teri would somehow have to deliver a living baby, or Daisy Hub was doomed.

Finally Townsend said, in a tightly controlled voice, "Let's see if I understand this correctly. You told the Nandrians that Teri was your mate. And now your Nandrian... brother?... will be expecting to have—" Teri started and whipped around, her expression daring him to complete the thought. The station manager knew he was on dangerous ground, for he closed his eyes and inhaled once, deeply, through his nose before resuming softly, "You're supposed to be our expert on Nandrians, Holchuk. How is it that you didn't see this coming?"

The Doc made an exasperated sound. "Gavin, you said 'Nagor's next egg'. Just when is this exchange supposed to take place?"

"In about eight standard years."

Her eyes lit up. "So we have a reasonable amount of time to work out the genetics? That's not so bad. And isn't it fortunate that I happen to have a fully-equipped, state of the art medical laboratory at my disposal?" she added, shooting Townsend a triumphant look.

Holchuk saw that and had to suppress a smile. Never argue with the Doc.

As Nagor had finally explained to him aboard the *Hak'kor*'s shuttle, this was what they had been arguing about in their own language during the ceremony. Realizing that the species were too different, the *Hak'kor* had been about to abort the alliance; however, Nagor had convinced him that, given enough time, Humans were resourceful enough to make the ritual possible.

"Anything might happen by then," the Doc was saying to Teri. "I should extract some ova now and put them into cryostorage."

"Okay, fine, whatever saves our butts," she snapped, shooting Holchuk a poisonous look. "Just don't expect me to carry it inside my body."

"You won't have to, honey. I'll get the engineers to design a crèche. Or, who knows, you might change your mind. Eight standard years is a long time."

Yes, eight years was a long time. Holchuk hoped it would be enough time. Not for the Doc to decode and splice the Nandrian genome — he didn't for one second doubt her ability to solve this puzzle — but for him to break the news to Teri that in order to complete the ritual, she would have to give up her own baby and adopt instead whatever hatched out of Nagor's egg.

Suddenly he realized that Townsend had been standing at the foot of the medbed, staring at him. "Would you like to hear some good news, Mr. Holchuk?"

Good news from the boss man? That was an oxymoron. Holchuk pasted on a weary smile and said, "Sure, why not?"

"We're finally ready to do something about the Meniscus Field generators. Be in AdComm tomorrow morning at ten o'clock for a strategy meeting."

Slowly, Holchuk nodded, his gut tightening with dread. His first instincts about Drew Townsend had been correct, he decided. Whatever scheme the boss man had cooked up to "do something about" the Nandrian technology, things could only end badly. And there wasn't a thing Gavin ban Samuel could do about it without breaking Nagor's confidence and betraying the House of Trokerk. So either way, they were all fried. Terrific.

Breathing a sigh of resignation, Holchuk leaned back into the cushion and closed his eyes. A moment later, sensing a presence beside him, he opened them again. Teri was standing a meter away, arms crossed, chin tilted upward, clearly determined to look angry no matter what emotions played behind her large brown eyes.

"Go ahead, Tiger, take a swing," he said. "Nobody aboard the Hub would blame you."

"That wouldn't solve anything," she murmured at last. "I just want you to look me in the face and tell me honestly that you had no choice."

"You've met the Nandrians, Teri. Trust me, under the circumstances there was nothing else I could have done. I'm sorry."

She nodded thoughtfully. "It's a start," she said, then wheeled and left the room.

Chapter 26

Never mind raising blood pressure — Drew's next transmission to the EIS would probably give someone a stroke. That was assuming, of course, that the mission was still a go and that Townsend was around to lead it. At this point, neither was a certainty. Just thinking about all the different ways he might blow this assignment was enough to give Townsend permanent indigestion.

For example, suppose SISCO tired of his stalling and sent out another operative — a regular — to wrap up the murder investigation. This second agent would have to be intercepted and either turned or terminated. The EIS had been quite clear during his briefings — there were no other options. Or what if somebody at Data Management figured out that Earth's entire database was being moved piecemeal into orbit around Helena, and raised the alarm? Bonelli would realize that the SPA on the Zoo was nothing more than a hacker's data stash and would undoubtedly follow through on his earlier threat to board and occupy Daisy Hub at gunpoint. Naturally, the House of Trokerk would then have to avenge the honor of the station by annihilating the Rangers. All of them. Everywhere.

As well, just in case Townsend needed something else to stress over, appearances were so deceiving on this station. Every time he thought he'd gotten a handle on something, it dissolved into unanswered questions. They nested in the corners of his mind, waiting for him to let his guard down, then "made his brain itch", as Ruby had put it.

Yoko.

Nestor Quan.

And Karim Khaloub, who posed the most troubling questions of all. If, as Ridout had told him, Khaloub couldn't possibly be a spy, then why had the previous station manager needed Lydia to be his eyes and ears? And if the vic was, in fact, working undercover for one of the Earth Authorities, why hadn't the EIS included that information in Drew's mission briefing? It seemed inconceivable that they wouldn't have known about it.

Chapter 27

Townsend waited as long as he could to begin the meeting. Just as he had given up and was opening his mouth to call for silence, he spotted Holchuk exiting the tube car and slipping quietly to the back of the assembled group.

They all knew why they were there, or thought they did. Orvy Hagman, Jason Smith, Ruby, Lydia, O'Malley, the Doc, Gouryas, Singh, and Teri. All sat or stood gazing expectantly at their 'fearless leader', who had promised to answer their questions if they could just be patient until the Nandrian-elect had returned from *tekl'hananni*. And now Holchuk was back, and the moment of truth had arrived — and Townsend knew with terrible certainty that he couldn't give it to them. He didn't dare.

So, it was a good thing that the Hub crew saw a payoff in this mission for themselves — freedom from the threat of the alien field generator. And if Teri had been voicing the popular sentiment when she declared that it was better to get involved in a war than to waste the rest of their lives doing busy-work, then Townsend was just giving them the opportunity to do what they wanted to do anyway, right?

(It was flimsy, but he'd take it. One way or another, he had to face himself in the mirror each morning.)

"Okay, people, I trust everyone knows why I've called this meeting?" he began.

"The Meniscus Field generators," piped up Jason Smith.

"So we're finally going to do something about those beasts?" Hagman cut in, grinning.

"Yes! And Drew has a genius plan. Right, Chief?"

"Yes," said Townsend, perhaps a little overenthusiastically, but at least it brought everyone's attention back to the person running the meeting. "The techs and engineers have been working around the clock to figure out the molecular paintbrush," he went on, making eye contact with Singh and Gouryas. "Gentlemen?"

"We still aren't sure how the device works," Gouryas apologized, "but Dev has figured out how to use it to turn metal transparent, and he's been practicing."

"I've calibrated the controls so we can target an area measured in hundredths of millimeters," Singh continued, smirking as archly as ever.

"Measured in two dimensions, or in three?" O'Malley wanted to know.

"In three," Gouryas replied. "We're going to make a window in the casing around the field generator and take a look inside it."

"That's your wonderful plan?" demanded Holchuk, frowning. "You're going to tinker some more with that device on our landing deck and maybe get someone else killed?"

"Actually," Townsend corrected him patiently, "we're going to practice with the generator aboard the Zoo first. Then, once we know exactly what we're doing, we're going to shut down the one on the Hub."

"Their generator *is* identical to ours," Smith agreed. "All we have to do is infiltrate the Ranger station wearing PLS suits and taking the paintbrush with us, and—"

"Hey! Whoa!" said Hagman, looking the way the adult lion always did in the vidclips when an overexuberant cub stepped on his tail. "All this secret agent stuff — is this on the level, Townsend?"

"I'm afraid so, Mr. Hagman."

Now Hagman was looking more like someone who went rock-climbing, white water rafting, and extreme skateboarding in his spare time. "So, we sneak over to Zulu, screw around with their field generator, maybe flash-freeze the whole rotten bunch of them? Sounds like it could be fun."

Indignantly, Ruby leaped to her feet. "Drew, you're not seriously considering—"

"—murdering fifteen people? No, of course not. I have a plan to get all the Rangers off Zulu at the same time."

Into the silence that followed his words, Ruby ventured, "Off Zulu to where, Chief? And how?"

Keeping one eye on the station's resident wildcat, Drew explained, "To here. We invite them over here for a concert."

Nine jaws dropped at once. The tenth, Teri Mintz's, began rising defiantly. He'd known she wouldn't like it. With luck, however, the first installment of her bribe had already arrived on the station.

"You're joking," said Ruby.

He shook his head slowly.

Doc Ktumba had been standing quietly near the tube car door. Now she lowered her head and charged through the crowd, stopping just short of colliding with him. "You are out of your mind," she stated, "if you think this flawed plan of yours is going to work."

Expecting nothing less from her, Drew stood his ground. "Flawed how, Doc?"

"All right. 'Never darken our doorstep again,' you told them. Suddenly you're inviting them over for tea. Bonelli is bound to be suspicious."

"So, I've had a change of heart, realized I was wrong and want to make up."

"While I'm certain you've had a lot of practice at apologizing, you don't strike me as the sort of man who grovels well, Mr. Townsend. And Bonelli will want to see you on your knees, holding an olive branch, before he accepts this invitation of yours."

"Not if the featured act is Teri Martin. You should have seen the way he looked at her when we stopped over on the Zoo."

"He's right, Marion," said Ruby thoughtfully. "We're not asking them to come here for amateur night. People used to pay upward of 100 credit units for tickets to her shows. And we're charging nothing. They'll all want to be here, every last one of them. They'll mutiny if Bonelli even tries to assign any of them to duties that shift."

"And Teri has agreed to this?" the Doc wanted to know.

He glanced over at the wildcat just as O'Malley bent to whisper something in her ear. Suddenly, her face lit up, eyes sparkling with barely contained joy. Townsend nearly sighed with relief. U-Town had arrived on Daisy Hub, and not a moment too soon.

"Ask her yourself," he suggested. But the Doc had caught the byplay and deduced what was going on. She shook her head disapprovingly.

"Excuse me, Mr. Townsend, but what's the timing on this mission?" Smith now inquired.

"If we're able to coordinate the incursion team's approach to Zulu to coincide with the Rangers' approach to Daisy Hub, then you'll have the length of Ms. Martin's show, probably two or three hours, to complete the mission and start back home."

Doc Ktumba uttered an impatient syllable. "That's all well and good," she cut in, "and I'm sure Teri will be a smash success, but aren't you forgetting something? Won't the Rangers notice when they return to Zulu that something has been done to their field generator?"

"Perhaps," Drew told her. "But if they can't actually pin anything on us, they'll probably let the matter drop. In the first place, there is reason to believe that the field generator on the Zoo has already acted up, causing an accident very similar to the one that killed Khaloub."

"Reason to believe?" The Doc's face was the image of skepticism. "And what reason might that be, Mr. Townsend?"

"Something Bonelli said to me the day that I arrived here," he replied, warning her with a look not to interrupt him again. "In the second place, assuming that he was telling me the truth, Bonelli is a cop. His knee-jerk reaction when there's a clear and present danger is to restrict access to it. So it's possible that only a handful of Rangers have even seen what the field generator looks like. Any who have, and who happen to notice that it looks different now, will probably assume that the device acted up again, during their absence."

"And you're willing to risk their lives and ours, on a probability?" the Doc challenged him. "A supposition?"

Drew paused. The answer was yes, of course. That was his job. But the Daisy Hub crew didn't know that, and so the decision couldn't be his alone. Ruby had told him when they first met that the crew of Daisy Hub was considered expendable. He'd disagreed with her then, and he disagreed with her now. In his mind, there was only one expendable person aboard the station, and that was Drew Townsend himself.

"Mr. Townsend, I'd like to volunteer for that mission," said Jason Smith.

One by one, others stepped forward as well.

"Me too, Mr. Townsend."

"Count me in, boss."

"I'm with you, Chief."

"Let's do this."

The Doc looked around at their resolute faces and sighed. "You're all out of your minds. However, if you are determined to go ahead with this, then I'll do what I can to help."

"Even if the Hub fills up with Rangers?" Ruby teased.

"Hey, we outnumber them three to one," Hagman pointed out. "They'll mind their manners. My boys will see to it."

Townsend took his first full breath in several minutes. "Okay, then, the mission is a go. Teri has already begun putting the show together. Lydia, you'll have to watch it from AdComm. You'll be up here with me, coordinating the operation."

"There'll be other shows, Lydia, I promise," Teri reassured her.

"Now, the incursion team…" He paused, letting his gaze sweep the assembled volunteers. "…will consist of: Ruby, who will be piloting the shuttle; Mr. Singh and Mr. Gouryas, who have familiarized themselves with the alien device we'll be using; Mr. O'Malley, because of his technical expertise; and Mr. Smith, who has Fleet Academy training and will be leading the mission."

"Wait a minute," Holchuk cut in. "You're going in blind? What about the watchdogs on the landing deck? Have any of you even seen a schematic of Zulu?"

"That's why O'Malley is on the team," Townsend told him. "He's getting us the access codes, landing deck authorizations, deck plans — the whole package."

Holchuk turned reproachful eyes on his fellow cargo inspector. "So, in spite of what we discussed, you're going to hack Zulu?"

"I've already done it," O'Malley informed him, then crossed his arms over his chest and leaned back in his chair, grinning like the fool that Holchuk seemed to think he was. That Townsend would have thought he was too, if the ratkeeper hadn't presented him earlier with a *fait accompli*.

Holchuk cursed under his breath. "I want to go on this mission, boss man."

Drew understood the request, even sympathized with it; however, "What could you do on Zulu, Holchuk?" he sighed. "Besides, now that you've been adopted, you may need deniability if this little excursion goes sour."

"And you may need a witness that the Nandrians will trust," the other man pointed out.

Townsend had been afraid of this. He had purposely picked four people besides the pilot so that they'd be able to run mission sims in the SPA room. Four was the limit, now that Lydia and the ratkeeper had filled most of its memory with stolen data. One extra body could blow that secret sky-high.

As though reading his mind, Lydia said, "I can program an observer into the sim, Mr. Townsend, no problem."

Against his better judgment, Drew relented. "All right, then, Holchuk, you're in. I'll want to meet with the incursion team in three hours, to work out the details of the mission."

Chapter 28

"You can't be serious."

Sitting across the desk from Townsend, O'Malley shrugged helplessly and replied, "I'm afraid I am, boss. There's no record of anyone named Bruni Patel in Earth's population database. We've got all of it, dating back to the last pandemic, and he isn't there."

Drew's thoughts had already begun to race. The population database had been the first one the ratkeeper copied, years earlier. Original biofiles popped up on the system anytime there were changes or discrepancies contained in updated information. That was how Townsend's cover had been blown earlier. If there was no current record of Bruni Patel, that meant that there had never been anyone born with that name. If Bruni Patel were a shell identity, the organization he worked for would have given him a full set of creds, including a verifiable biofile. So the name had to be an unrecorded alias.

"Check again. The man I knew was a correctional officer at Dearborn Detention Center, Block C, from 2380 to 2385. His real name could have been different than the one I knew him under."

O'Malley worked his compupad for a couple of minutes, then handed it across the desk so that Drew could inspect the seven biofiles he'd sifted out of the database. None of the images was the face of his friend. Not one was even close. And if the murder victim couldn't be identified using Earth's databases...

"What about the murder investigation?"

"The file wasn't as fat as you were hoping it would be," O'Malley apologized, handing him a datawafer. "No snaps, just the Medical Examiner's report, a membership list for a group called Earth for Terrans, and an order from District Council to halt the investigation, dated three days after your departure from Earth."

So much for Romero's promise. Using Drew's ID as a starting point, Gluckstein's search of the databases would have hit the same dead end as O'Malley's did. And Truman and Lupo's investigation records had either been wiped from the system or prevented from reaching it.

That left Earth Intelligence. Patel was supposedly an EIS operative, but the only commitment that organization had made was to look into the activities of Earth for Terrans. If the EFT could be turned and exploited, Patel's death would probably be written off as nothing more than the cost of doing business, regardless of who had actually killed him. This was possible only because Drew Townsend, with his thoroughness and his tenacity and his passionate desire to get justice for his friend, was now safely tucked away out of sight and out of mind on Daisy Hub.

Checkmate.

Townsend exhaled noisily and leaned back in his chair. "Thanks, O'Malley," he sighed.

"I can put a watchdog on this, boss," the other man offered. "The Hub's net can alert us if Patel or the murder get mentioned in any future updates."

"I'm pretty sure they won't be. Thanks for your trouble — I appreciate it."

O'Malley opened his mouth to say something, then apparently thought better of it. With a nod of acknowledgement, he got to his feet and left Townsend sitting alone, staring at the datawafer as though by concentrating hard enough he could read it with his naked eyes.

He was still at his desk, reading the M.E.'s report and regretting his decision to open the file, when the sound of the tube car door signaled that he was no longer alone.

Wordlessly, Lydia dropped into a chair across from his and stared at him until the silence together with the feeling of eyes boring into the side of his face became too much to ignore, and he finally turned his attention away from the screen and met her sympathetic gaze.

"We're worried about you," she said. "Rob told me about your friend. What can I do to help?"

"Nothing. I'm fine."

Leaning forward, she informed him in a low, urgent voice, "You've just lost someone twice — first when he was murdered and again when he was wiped from the InfoCommNet. Nobody on Earth is lifting a finger to find out who killed him and you're stuck out here with no way to do it yourself. Drew, I know a lot about grieving. Trust me, you are *not* fine!"

Inwardly, Townsend cursed. This was not the time to be revealing weakness. "Okay," he snapped. "You're right — I'm not fine. I'm feeling angry enough to punch a hole in the bulkhead with my fist. Is that what you wanted to hear?"

"It's a start. We're not bits of data in a computer, Drew, and we're not defined by the labels assigned by monolithic organizations like the Relocation Authority. We're real, warm-blooded Human beings, with emotions, and when we suffer a terrible loss, we need to allow ourselves to feel it so that we can accept it and get on with our lives. Bruni Patel meant a lot to you. Maybe you need to stop looking for answers on that datawafer and start finding them inside yourself." And without saying another word, Lydia got to her feet and left.

Drew glanced at the M.E.'s report — ID inconclusive, cause of death inconclusive — and felt something sharp and warm rising in his throat. Lydia was right. Bruni Patel was nowhere on that document. Townsend would have to look for him elsewhere.

— « o » —

A box of tea, a jar of curry powder, a tin of chocolate paste, vacuum-sealed bags of dried figs and shredded coconut, a bottle of amber-colored maple syrup — this was all that remained of Bruni Patel. As Drew gently removed each item from his trunk and placed it on top of the dresser in his bedroom, he tried to conjure a remembered image of his friend's face. But all he could see in his mind's eye was the ruined features of a pale and eyeless corpse.

Bruni Patel had been his best friend, maybe even his only friend. He had shown an angry young man what was possible and had helped him to reach it. Drew owed him everything that was good about his life. Now Bruni was gone, and nobody seemed to care. And, worse, Drew was having trouble visualizing what he looked like before he was murdered. It was like losing him for a third time, and that was just too much to bear...

At last, in the privacy of his quarters, Townsend sat on the edge of his bed, dropped his face into his open hands and let his tears flow. When they finally ran dry, the heavy weight he had been carrying around inside his chest felt much lighter, and he was able to see the foodstuffs lined up along the top of his dresser for what they really were. Drew gathered them up and carried them to Fritz Jensen in the caf.

At dinner that evening, there was a special dessert: chocolate layer cake with fig jam filling and coconut frosting, enough to serve every member of the crew a generous portion. When asked where the ingredients had come from, Jensen simply pointed in the direction of Townsend's table. It was probably just his imagination, but the resulting smiles and waves of gratitude seemed to fill up an empty space inside him.

Chapter 29

Townsend had never been good at waiting. He could do it if he had to, but it took a degree of effort that he resented. Normally, once he had worked out the details of a plan, he was like a greyhound at the starting gate, impatient to run.

That was how he was feeling right now. The meetings and briefings were all done. Everyone knew the part he or she would be playing in the mission to Zulu. Townsend as strategist was no longer required, and Townsend as mission coordinator had nothing to do until the team was on its way to the target. All that remained was the waiting, and he hated waiting, especially when he was the only one doing it. That was when he started second-guessing himself. His mind was never at rest, hadn't been since he was a child. In times of forced idleness, it reexamined decisions already made, problems put aside, plans set in motion. It criticized and analyzed, and made him wonder whether he could have done things better, sooner, faster, and with at least a decent chance of success. It painted worst-case scenarios and made him doubt himself, and in his current situation, self-doubt was something he simply couldn't afford.

Drew craned his neck and saw the top of Lydia's blond head bobbing beyond the wall of filing cabinets beside his desk.

"Lydia, I need the most recent crew status report," he called out.

"It should be on your unit," she replied. "I transmitted it this morning."

Unable to think of a way to draw her into conversation that didn't make him sound either incompetent (*I can't work the InfoComm. Come talk to me.*) or pathetic (*I'm assailed by uncertainty. Come talk to me.*), he sighed and pulled up the report on his screen.

Most of the crew, it revealed, were busy getting ready for the show. O'Malley was on K Deck with Hagman, Tate, Flanagan, and DeVries, installing the sound system. Other teams had spontaneously formed to take care of the lighting and build the stage and specified sets. Ruby had put herself in charge of Teri's costumes. Even the Doc was helping out, making props. And there was a backup band, presumably hand-picked by Teri and led by Soaring Hawk, rehearsing on A Deck.

"Soaring Hawk plays an instrument?" he wondered aloud.

Lydia poked her face around the corner of the farthest filing cabinet. "Tenor sax," she informed him, adding in a playfully scolding voice, "and if you'd joined the party instead of sequestering yourself the last time the *Krronn* paid us a visit, you'd know that. Hawk has picked a name for them, too — The Daisy Hub Powwow. It's kind of catchy, don't you think?"

They'd all gone stage-crazy. So much for Khaloub's morale problem, Townsend thought as he leaned back in his chair, shaking his head indulgently. "Tell me, is *anyone* working on the mission?"

Lydia sighed and flopped down into a seat across the desk from him. "The mission?" she echoed, brow furrowing and head tilting in a parody of puzzlement. "The mission..." She spoke slowly and licked her lips, as though the words she was pronouncing had left a taste behind and it was the taste that finally jogged her memory. "Oh, right! The mission. Let's see. Jason Smith is on L Deck with Spiro and Dev, learning how to use the paintbrush, just in case. When they're done, Dev and Hawk are going to set up the jamming gear on L and J Decks and the vidcams on A Deck, as you ordered," she continued. "Gavin is in his quarters, looking over the schematics for the Ranger station. He's asked not to be disturbed. Meanwhile, Ruby has discovered the joy of sequins, and Rob's probably finding creative ways to avoid climbing ladders." She made a wry face.

"He's afraid of heights?" Drew guessed.

"Only in the presence of gravity. Unless you plan to add Yoko to the team, I believe that's everyone."

"Everyone except Nestor Quan." He hadn't meant to say it aloud. "Sorry."

"Don't be. He's not available for missions," she told him flatly. "Our Disease Control Officer spends all his time being invisible."

"What?" Drew started erect in his chair, smelling a con in progress. But Lydia's smile was broad and open, and she *had* so far kept her earlier promise to be truthful with him. "Why invisible? Because he's not supposed to be here?"

"Actually, he is. He was apparently posted to the Hub when Angel of Death broke out in our sector about five years ago. The biodata arrived, but the man never showed up. Well, protocol aside, you and I both know why and how people get sent out here. I waited for an error correction from the Relocation Authority, never received one, and figured that Mr. Quan had somehow found a way to give them the slip."

"So you just left the name on the crew manifest?"

"Sure, why not? If they think he's on Daisy Hub, they won't be looking for him anywhere else. And for good measure, every once in a while I send a report over his name to Disease Control back on Earth," she said, confirming Drew's worst fears by adding gleefully, "Wherever he is, I hope he's having as much fun as I am."

Townsend closed his eyes for a moment, his heart dropping as his imagination leaped into overdrive. "Who else knows about this?" he demanded urgently. "O'Malley?"

She shook her head. "Just me. And Jovanovich, I guess. Or maybe not. When I told him about the biofile arriving, he was in Med Services. The Doc had dosed him rather heavily with pain medication, so I don't know whether he actually heard me."

Probably not, thought Drew grimly, but it was a safe bet that the Doc had been somewhere in earshot at the time. That would go a long way toward explaining her reaction to Quan's name earlier on.

So, they had a ghost on the Hub. An 'invisible man', according to Lydia. Most of the crew were completely unaware of his existence. Drew hoped that Lydia's theory was correct: that Disease Control hadn't questioned any of her forged reports because they honestly believed the transmissions were coming from Daisy Hub's assigned DCO, and that the real Nestor Quan was tooling around in alien space somewhere, enjoying his freedom. Because the only other explanations that fit the facts were disturbing to contemplate.

First, it was possible that someone had fabricated this identity and planted it on the Hub. Like the Meniscus Field generator and the paintbrush. Like Drew Townsend himself. They were all there to further someone's hidden agenda. Whose purposes might it serve to have Nestor Quan's biofile aboard Daisy Hub? Not Earth Intelligence's, he was certain, nor SISCO's. In either case, Drew would have been briefed about the shell identity. Quan had to have come from one of Earth's Authorities — Relocation or Space Installation. Or perhaps there was an agency even darker than the EIS, infiltrating Earth's outposts and no doubt delighted to have found a creative, unwitting ally in Lydia Garfield. That was assuming, of course, that she *was* unwitting. Drew felt a chill trickle down his back and decided he really didn't want to go there. Not yet.

The other possibility, equally painful, was that there had in fact been two deaths aboard Daisy Hub, one years earlier and one just intervals ago. The investigator in Drew Townsend immediately began sketching possible crime scenarios. Disease Control Officers were itinerant, regularly patrolling the inhabited planets in their sector; Quan would normally have spent most of his time away from his base of operations. However, the Hub would have been the first place he certified as plague-free, so the entire crew should have known who he was — unless he was killed before anyone but his murderer even knew he'd arrived. It could even have happened on Zulu.

More loose ends. As if Townsend didn't have enough to keep him awake at night!

Chapter 30

It was show time. Townsend stepped off the tube car on C Deck and looked for Lydia at her station. She waved. He nodded. And his gut kept right on twisting. Damn. He'd hoped that having her there as back-up would calm his nerves.

Drew had run literally hundreds of cons, but never one involving this many people. Now, the stage was built and the band was in final rehearsals. Teri was humming non-stop, overjoyed at returning to showbiz (and U-Town). The interference field surrounding K Deck and surveillance cams on A Deck had been thoroughly tested and pronounced ready. The incursion team had spent days doing sims in the SPA room and felt prepared for any contingency. Lucas Soaring Hawk had performed a complete overhaul and tune-up of *Devil Bug*'s Human-made components, and had put the PLS suits, toolkits and paintbrush aboard. O'Malley had downloaded all the necessary programming and data for the mission into a compupad. And now it was Townsend's turn. Drew sat down at his desk, stared at the blank screen of his InfoComm unit, and felt a chill wrap him like a blanket.

In detention, he had once seen an old flat-screen video of a novelty act that used thousands of dominos, placed on edge so that as each one fell, it would knock over one or two more. It had taken hours for the artist to arrange the dominos and about three Earth minutes for all of them to fall over. The dominos had been plaincoated so that as they fell, seen from above, they created a replica of a famous painting by some French artist, either Monet or Degas, he couldn't recall exactly. But as he watched, the thought that had kept running through Drew's mind the whole time was how powerless the artist was once those dominos began to fall. If even one of them spun the wrong way, the entire act would fail, and there wasn't a thing he could do to salvage it.

That same thought was running through his mind again, only this time, Drew was the artist. His dominos had all been carefully positioned, awaiting the flick of a finger that would set the con in motion. The only sure way to prevent failure was to walk away and leave them all standing. And that simply wasn't an option. Never had been.

"Lydia," he sighed, "hail Zulu, please. I need to speak with Bonelli."

There were comm relay satellites sharing orbit with Zulu and Daisy Hub. As he waited for Lydia to set up the connection, Drew remembered something Ruby had said to him the day he and Teri had arrived on Zulu: "They don't call it the Zoo for nothing, and some people get along with animals better than others." Drew had never thought of himself as an animal-lover; but the timing was right and the mission had to take priority. Always, he reminded himself firmly, the mission had to come first.

"Captain Bonelli on-screen, Drew," Lydia announced. "I'm sending the signal to your unit."

Drew had prepared himself to face the Ranger in a variety of moods. Friendly Bonelli. Arrogant Bonelli. Wrathful Bonelli. Disgusted Bonelli. Never had he expected to see the face that now appeared in front of him.

Bonelli's left eye was purple and swollen almost shut. His lip was cut, and his nose had definitely been broken again. Drew stared at him for a long moment, speechless. The Ranger finally broke the silence, in a voice that nearly made Drew wince, it sounded so weary. "Well?" he sighed. "You're the one who called *me*, Townsend. Is there something we can do for you?"

"Actually, Captain, there's something we'd like to do for *you*."

Bonelli's lips twitched briefly. "Does it involve an explosive device and an escape pod?"

Not that the thought of blowing up Zulu had never crossed Drew's mind. The EIS had trained him well. They would not have sent him out here if they weren't confident of his ability to take whatever actions were necessary, up to and including the destruction of Daisy Hub itself, in order to accomplish his mission. Naturally, he hoped that matters would never spiral that badly out of control. But the pragmatist in him recognized that if the time ever came for desperate measures, destroying the Zoo might be a useful, not to mention an extremely soul-satisfying, thing to do.

With an effort, Drew cleared the fiery image from his mind. "This is on the level, Bonelli. You know that we have a former singing star on our crew manifest. Teri Martin."

"We've met," came the terse reply.

"Well, she's agreed to give a concert tomorrow at 1900 hours, station time. You and all your men are invited."

"And how much are the tickets for this little shindig going to cost us?"

"Nothing. It's a free show. Think of it as a gesture of good will. An olive branch. I may have overreacted a bit the last time you were here."

Bonelli's attempt to chuckle ended in a grunt and grimace of pain. "A bit? You practically tore my head off."

Drew shrugged. "I was establishing my turf. You understand."

"I'm afraid I do." Bonelli nodded thoughtfully, his eyes narrowing in a way that effectively killed any sympathy Drew might have begun to feel for him. "You said we're *all* invited?"

"All of you."

There was a pause, during which Drew's stomach began slowly tying itself into a knot. This was the make-or-break moment for the con. All the Rangers had to make the trip, or there was no point in inviting any of them. *Come on, Spike*, he prayed silently. *Let your people go.*

"Okay. We could certainly use the break. And Zulu can operate for a few hours on automatic. Thanks, Townsend."

"Don't mention it."

"So we're a go?" Drew glanced up, startled, and saw Lydia hovering beside him, gnawing her lower lip. He didn't have to wonder what she was thinking. She was Eligible. She'd seen Bonelli's battered face on the screen and realized, as Drew had done, that there had probably been a mutiny on Zulu.

"We're a go," he sighed. "We'll have to be careful, though."

"Do you think he won?" she asked in a small voice.

Fresh out of reassuring lies, Drew told her, "I'm sure he didn't. Cops never joke about blowing up their own precinct house. That crack about explosives was his way of warning us that he's no longer in charge."

She frowned delicately. "So if not Bonelli, then who?"

"I guess we'll find that out tomorrow evening, won't we?"

Chapter 31

Officially, it took four hours to travel by short-hopper from Daisy Hub to Zulu. In fact, any competent pilot could make the trip in three; and if the pilot was Ruby McNeil, and the shuttle was Hawk's pet project, *Devil Bug*, that number dropped to two. Unfortunately, the Rangers en route from the Zoo to Daisy Hub were traveling in standard-issue Earth-made shuttles, forcing Ruby to slow to half-speed in order to keep Helena's bulk between *Devil Bug* and their convoy.

Holchuk had taken an end seat in front of the viewport. He turned it ninety degrees, putting the bronze-colored bulkhead at his back, and alternated between watching the activities of the incursion team and gazing at Helena, rotating serenely beneath them. That was what he was supposed to do, after all — observe. He was the reliable witness, the only one aboard *Devil Bug* who carried no responsibility for the ultimate success or failure of Operation Shutdown. The rest of the team had practiced every move and nuance of this mission, every predictable error and emergency. They were as ready as they could possibly be expected to be. But they were at least another hour away from Zulu. All they could do for now was wait. And waiting, Holchuk could clearly see, was proving to be the most difficult part of the operation.

Singh had tethered himself to the deck at the far side of the cabin and sat cross-legged, his upper body surrounded by a small swarm of parts and fasteners. He was checking out the paintbrush, for about the twentieth time — the components of it that he knew how to put back together, anyway, and therefore dared to take apart. The engineer's concern was understandable — the paintbrush was the linchpin of their mission. If it malfunctioned, all their planning and hard work was for nothing. On the other hand, the alien device was a machine, and even alien machines were assembled from parts that could get lost or wear out. What if the paintbrush failed aboard the Zoo because Singh had checked the thing out once too often before their arrival?

Jason Smith occupied the seat farthest from Holchuk, at the other end of the viewport. His eyes were closed, and at first glance he appeared to be sleeping; then Holchuk noticed that his lips were moving. The Fleet officer was reciting something to himself, over and over and over. He was making mistakes, too, jerking his head and cursing himself each time and then starting again from the beginning. Smith would be leading the mission. How reassuring.

O'Malley was sitting next to Smith, fondling the sides of his compupad and wearing an insufferably confident grin. O'Malley viewed life as a game of chance — the bigger the risk, the larger the payoff — and he'd so far been luckier than he deserved. *He doesn't understand*, Holchuk realized sadly. Eventually, the kid's luck would run out, and people would die, perhaps in great numbers; and O'Malley, if he survived, would still not understand. That alone made him the most dangerous person on the mission. They may as well have brought an armed warhead aboard the shuttle with them.

Gouryas, bristling with recording devices, was sitting directly in front of Holchuk, testing and retesting them as compulsively as Singh was doing with the paintbrush. Had he tried out his gear while wearing a PLS suit? Holchuk was willing to bet that he hadn't.

Ruby, meanwhile, had her hands full flying the shuttle — not so much controlling the ship as controlling herself. It was difficult for a speed demon like 'Mom' to fly slowly. Her impatience kept threatening to flood the cabin. Holchuk undid the restraint around his seat, maneuvered his face close to her ear, and murmured, "Make sure you match their speed, Ruby. If their sensors detect us while they're in transit, it's game over."

It was probably game over anyway. Everything about this mission was a disaster waiting to happen. That was why Holchuk had been so insistent about going along — if

O'Malley's luck held, and Townsend's crazy plan worked, and the alien gear behaved itself, and the team actually managed to return to Daisy Hub undetected by the Rangers, it would be nothing short of a miracle.

And if there was going to be a miracle, Holchuk wanted to be there to see it.

Chapter 32

"I've got them on the screen, Drew," Lydia sang out from Ruby's station. "Two short-hoppers, point of origin Zulu. They'll be asking for docking instructions in about ten minutes." She turned and shot him an inquiring look.

The dominos were falling now in rapid succession, each one a tiny missile capable of blowing the con to kingdom come.

Fighting the urge to mop his brow, Drew dragged in a deep breath. His gaze wandered involuntarily toward the viewport, but there was nothing to see there. The Rangers were approaching the Hub end-on, as Ruby had done the day he and Teri had arrived. And as long as they continued to approach the Hub, then it was a safe bet that they hadn't detected *Devil Bug*.

Mentally crossing his fingers, he told Lydia, "Direct them to A Deck, modules 2 and 3." *No point in letting them see that vacant parking spot on the shuttle deck.* "Tell them not to debark until I've spoken with their commanding officer. Then seal the archways and activate the surveillance vidcams. And send about a dozen of our biggest and strongest up there, just in case."

"I hope you're wrong about this," she observed, frowning.

"So do I, Lydia. Just follow my instructions, please..." ... *and hope the Rangers do the same.* Drew would have preferred to turn away their shuttles, deny them docking privileges, until he knew what had recently happened on Zulu. But he couldn't. The mission had already begun, and the mission had to take priority. Besides, as had already been pointed out to him by both Bonelli and the Doc, the Rangers were armed. "Once the shuttles have docked, watch the surveillance screens carefully. If you see anyone forcing the archway doors or drawing a weapon, evacuate our people from A Deck. Then seal it off and send out a mayday to any Earth ships in the sector."

"Now that Gavin's been adopted, wouldn't it make more sense for me to send a mayday to any Nandrian ships in the sector?" Lydia suggested. "I know some of their comm codes."

Drew shook his head vigorously, his imagination leaping from one scene of mayhem to another, much worse one. "That alliance is a secret," he reminded her. "We can't afford to tip our hand. Besides, the Nandrians wouldn't just rescue us — they'd kill all the Rangers and then blow up Zulu to emphasize their point. I guess we'll just have to wait and see who steps off the lead shuttle."

"I'll compose the message anyway," she persisted. "You can decide whether to send it once we have a better idea of what we're dealing with."

He couldn't very well argue with that.

Ten minutes later, the leading short-hopper identified itself as the *Tripoli* and requested docking instructions. Two minutes after that, the second shuttle, the *Bonaventure*, contacted them as well.

Drew's thoughts turned briefly to *Devil Bug*. If they were on schedule, the incursion team ought to be approaching Zulu's short-hopper docking bay by now.

Gazing over Lydia's shoulder at a two-by-two bank of surveillance screens, Drew saw Orvy Hagman and ten other men pile out of the tube cars on A Deck. The resolution of the vidcam images was sharply defined — Drew could see the steely glint in the eyes of the dockworkers as they took up their positions around the deck's circumference. They looked as though they'd been posted to guard duty at all the docking arches, not just the ones the Rangers were using. That was good. It suggested that the Daisy Hub crew was vigilant and prepared to deal with intruders. With luck, it would make the Rangers think twice before they tried anything.

Lydia pressed a button on the comm console, listened for a moment, then swiveled in her seat. "Mr. Townsend, I have the new commanding officer of the Ranger detachment on the comm. In compliance with your instructions, he's waiting to speak with you, in the airlock of docking arch 2."

"Did he give you a name? A rank?"

"Major Cisco."

Drew felt a sudden chill. Cisco? Or was it SISCO? This couldn't be a coincidence. Had Ridout decided to stir the pot a little? Or was it someone else on the Security Committee, grown impatient with Townsend's lack of progress? Either way, it appeared that things were going to become very interesting on Daisy Hub, very fast.

"All right. Inform him that I'm on my way up. And copy to Orvy Hagman. If anything nasty happens up there, you know what to do."

"Yes, *sir*," said Lydia, throwing him a mock salute.

As Drew stepped off the tube car on A Deck, all the dockworkers snapped to attention. Surprised, he paused momentarily, wondering whether someone besides Lydia was watching them. Then he realized: they'd been rehearsing. Teri's concert had introduced a whole new mindset to the rebels on Daisy Hub, and appropriately so, because it was show time, and not just for Teri Martin and the Powwow.

Drew turned to face the nearest vidcam and announced, "All right, Ms. Garfield, unseal the archway and let the major through."

As the doors slid aside, Drew assumed his most uncompromising stance and expression. Behind him, he could sense Orvy's men forming up, preparing for trouble. He imagined Lydia down in AdComm, anxiously gnawing her lower lip as she watched events unfold on her surveillance screens.

As they all stood there, adrenaline-pumped and braced for conflict, a short, slight man with straight black hair stepped hesitantly past the archway doors. If this was a Ranger officer, he was completely out of uniform. In fact, his navy blue business suit looked stained and slept in, suggesting a very hasty departure from wherever he'd been before Zulu. He blinked a couple of times, then smiled and walked up to Drew, his hand extended for shaking.

Stunned, Drew accepted it, alarms going off at the back of his mind. He'd already seen this man, on the Daisy Hub crew manifest. Either Nestor Quan had an identical twin brother, or their Disease Control Officer was leading a double life.

"Major Cisco, I presume?" he said at last.

"Greetings, Mr. Townsend." The rumpled little man appraised him with cold, dark eyes that belied the warmth in his voice. "I thank you for your generous offer of hospitality to me and my men. I see that you have chosen not to underestimate me — a wise decision. However, we are guests on your station, and I promise you, we shall behave with all decorum."

Or else? Drew couldn't help thinking of Bonelli, with his broken nose and black eye. If they'd been dealt to him by the new commander, then, clearly, 'Cisco' was not someone to be trifled with. If SISCO had sent him, he'd probably been trained in several martial arts. In any case, Drew was certain that the Zulu detachment would do precisely as he ordered. The question was, what exactly had he ordered them to do?

The dominos are falling. Enter the Trojan horse.

Drew pinned on an answering smile. "I appreciate that, Major. These gentlemen are here to assist in the orderly debarkation of your men. They will escort them down to K Deck, where our chef has set out a buffet supper. Following the meal, they will be ushered to their seats for the concert."

Cisco bowed deeply and said, "You are too kind, Mr. Townsend. And while this is going on, perhaps you and I could have a word in private?"

Privately, Drew wanted nothing more than to return to AdComm and check on Lydia — it must have been a shock for her to see Quan's face on the surveillance screen — but he trusted his instincts. Right now they were telling him not to let 'Major Cisco' out of his sight; so, Townsend nodded and gestured toward one of the tube cars.

Chapter 33

Zulu was a stumpy cylinder clad in energy conversion panels, with a dish antenna at one end, a gravity field generator at the other, and landing deck ports in its middle. Seen through the viewport as *Devil Bug* approached it, it distinctly resembled a mushroom wearing an overcoat.

Holchuk wasn't the only one who made the association with food. Beside him, O'Malley's stomach had begun to growl.

"Hey, we've been out here for hours," he pointed out. "My tummy's entitled to a grumble or two."

"I've got dinner on board for everyone after we complete the mission," Ruby announced. "Meanwhile, brace for gravity: In three, two, one..."

Forewarned, her passengers all made sure they had stowed their gear and were right side up when *Devil Bug* entered the Zoo's gravity field. This was the part of weightlessness that Holchuk hated, even when he was cushioned by a well-upholstered chair. It wasn't his back or his legs that he worried about — it was the fact that the Human body was mostly water. If the mighty oceans on Earth could be moved side to side by gravitational flux, it chilled him to think what might be happening inside him right now, to his stomach and kidneys and intestines. The Nandrians didn't have to put up with this; all their ships were equipped with artificial gravity. Maybe, when this excursion was over, he could negotiate a retrofit for *Devil Bug*.

Ruby halted the shuttle a hundred meters from the landing bay doors. "Okay, Rob," she called out. "It's time for you to work your magic."

Rubbing his hands together gleefully, O'Malley activated his compupad and began punching keys, as everyone else in the cabin crossed their fingers in unison and held their breath.

If the codes were wrong or out of date, the AI minding the Zoo would lock the platform down and begin transmitting an 'under attack' message, and the mission they'd trained so long and hard for would have to be aborted. But that wasn't the worst that would happen. The jamming field would prevent the Rangers from receiving the distress signal only as long as they remained on K Deck. As soon as they left the concert hall, they would know that someone had tried to board their station. They would realize at once that the show had been nothing more than a diversion. And then...

Holchuk shuddered. He had been an agnostic most of his life, but now he prayed: *God help this cocky kid if his luck runs out tonight.*

"Done," declared O'Malley, sounding very pleased with himself.

The incursion team stared for a long, silent moment at the landing deck doors. Nothing.

"Done what?" Holchuk demanded.

"I've put the AI to sleep. Even if I convinced it we were a passing long-hopper with a parcel to deliver, it wouldn't let us remain aboard Zulu longer than half an hour. This way, we can take our time, get the job done, and put the AI back online as we're leaving."

"That's great, O'Malley," said Smith, and clapped him on the shoulder, hard enough to make him flinch. "But the job doesn't start until we're inside. So why don't you see what you can do about those doors?"

As O'Malley worked, the tension in the cabin grew thick enough to spread on a slice of bread. It seemed to be taking him forever to force-feed Zulu the right codes. Finally, however, he leaned back in his seat with a sigh of satisfaction. "We're in," he announced. "We just have to wait for the Meniscus Field to form."

Sure enough, less than a minute later, the shuttle bay doors began to slide apart. The mission team could see the slight bulge of the Meniscus Field, like a delicate silver veil billowing through the opening.

"Good work, O'Malley," said Smith. "All right, people — we've practiced this a hundred times. Let's do it."

Ruby focused on the task of parking *Devil Bug* while the others installed their earmikes and prepared to suit up. As the little ship settled onto the deck, the bay doors slid ponderously shut behind them.

Suiting up for space was serious business, demanding total concentration. A PLS suit was more than just a shiny one-piece garment. It was an entire life support system, providing twenty-four hours' worth of breathable air, warmth, and hydration. Every connection had to be solid and correct. Every fastening had to be airtight. Once on, each suit had to be inspected by two other people and pronounced space-ready before its wearer was allowed near an airlock. From start to finish, the process could take half a standard hour. With practice, the mission team had cut their time down to less than twenty minutes. Holchuk's time was even shorter, since he was one of the few crewmembers tall enough and broad enough to simply step into a PLS suit without having to adjust it for size. By the time the air temperature in Zulu's shuttle bay had normalized, the team was ready to go into action.

Singh was carrying the paintbrush. O'Malley had the compupad tucked under his arm. Gouryas had both hands full of recording devices. Smith had taken charge of all the charts and specs. Ruby, their getaway driver, remained aboard the shuttle, monitoring the mission over the comm system and ready to lift off at a moment's notice. Holchuk briefly considered volunteering to carry something, then thought better of it. He was the one who would have to explain this little escapade to the Nandrians if things didn't go as planned, and that was burden enough.

Loaded down with their gear and hampered by the bulk of their PLS suits, the team filed out of *Devil Bug* and down the narrow ramp, then began making their way across the landing bay. Smith had ordered them to hurry; unfortunately, there were strong magnetic plates in the soles of the PLS boots, making it hard work to walk, and impossible to run. As they slogged along, all conversation ceased. Holchuk heard nothing inside his bubble helmet but the heavy breathing of five people and the muffled syncopation of their footfalls. Casting monster-like shadows against the deck and bulkheads, the mission team lurched and staggered in an uneven line toward a large black object — the Meniscus Field emitter — that glittered like a pile of glass shards at the far end of the shuttle bay. The Doc had once referred to it as "obsidian with acromegaly." In fact, the emitter did resemble an overgrown crystal, with dozens of chaotically positioned facets of various sizes. Almost touching the wall, it sprawled asymmetrically over at least ten square meters of deck space. Beside it sat the mission's actual objective, the Meniscus Field generator. Like the one on the Hub, it was a featureless black cube about as high as Holchuk's waist.

Suddenly, a loud metallic blurt from an unseen speaker reverbed right through his helmet, yanking his heart up into his throat.

"It's about bloody time you got here!" said a familiar, angry voice.

Holchuk turned and met four incredulous stares. "Rat's ass," he muttered, "it's Bonelli."

Chapter 34

Not having a private office to which he and Major Cisco could retire, Drew had opted for the caf. AdComm was out of the question — Lydia was there, listening for messages from the incursion team.

Hagman had hovered at Drew's elbow until dismissed, a detail that hadn't escaped Cisco's notice. Now, as they sat across from each other at one of the caf's round tables, he commented, "You seem to have whipped these people into fine shape, Mr. Townsend. My compliments."

It was an unfortunate choice of metaphor. Remembering Bonelli's battered features, Drew dropped all pretense of cordiality and got straight to the point. "We're alone, Major — or should I say, Mr. Quan? — as you requested. Now, what can I do for you?"

"You don't mince words. I like that," Quan said with a mirthless grin. "I won't mince words either. What you can do for me is surrender your rat."

Drew nearly choked. "My what?"

But Quan was not amused. "Yoko. She is aboard Daisy Hub, and I want her."

"I'm sure you're aware that SIA protocol prohibits live animals aboard—"

"Townsend, you disappoint me. Does the name Alison Morgan mean anything to you?"

So, the worst-case scenario had happened after all. Playing for time, Drew sighed and pretended to jog his memory. "Morgan. Yes, I remember Miss Morgan," he said at last. "A very ill-behaved child who spent almost her entire stay with us in Medical Services. She arrived here in a coma, in fact. Is she the one claiming that we have a rat on the Hub?"

At that moment, the caf door hissed open. "Mr. Townsend, there you are!" exclaimed the Doc, charging into the room. "We need to have a word about—" She pulled up short at the sight of Nestor Quan and screwed her already formidable features into an eloquent expression of distaste. "You! I should have known."

If Quan was surprised to see her, he didn't let it show.

"Doctor Ktumba," said Drew, carefully measuring his words, "have you met—?"

"Unfortunately, I have," she replied, her eyes shooting daggers at the unflappable man across the table from him. "So, you've finally weaseled your way onto the Hub. Under an assumed name, I would imagine."

"How are you, Marion?" said Quan, as though greeting an old friend he hadn't seen in a while.

"How can you ask that so casually, after what you did to Nayo?"

"It isn't a crime to be a realist, Marion. A lucrative opportunity came up and I took it. End of story. In any case, should we be airing our dirty linen like this, in front of a stranger?" he said reprovingly.

The Doc paused, her expression morphing from disgust to determination. She turned to Drew and said, "Nayo and Quan were partners in a research laboratory. Nayo wanted the results of their experimentation to benefit all of Humankind. The 'lucrative opportunity' he refers to was an offer from a privately owned corporation to purchase all their research notes and patents. Instead of benefiting everyone, their discoveries would be reserved for those who could pay exorbitant prices. It was a betrayal of everything that Nayo valued."

"May I remind you," said Quan matter-of-factly, "that I'm not the one who unlawfully removed an entire experiment from the laboratory one night and concealed it? You see, Mr. Townsend, Yoko is not just any rat. She is the property of a major genetics lab in the Greater European Union, and they are very anxious to recover her."

So, once again, Drew was in possession of stolen property? It figured. However, he was eighteen years older now, and there was so much more at stake than the anxiety levels of a European gene broker. The mission had to come first. No matter how much Drew wished he could simply kick Major Cisco and his shady dealings right off Daisy Hub, Quan had to remain, with all his men, until the end of Teri's show.

Townsend swallowed the sour taste rising at the back of his throat and said quietly, "I see. And I sympathize, I really do, but—"

"You're about four years too late," cut in the Doc. "A previous station manager ordered Yoko spaced. The order is on record."

Quan scowled. It was the first sign of real emotion Drew had seen on his face all evening. "Alison Morgan was on your station less than two intervals ago. There is a rat here!"

The temptation was almost too much. Drew had to bite his tongue to keep silent.

The Doc, however, declared, "You're right, there is a rat. I made it myself out of an old exosuit, and Teri's using it as a prop in her show. Come down to K Deck and see for yourself."

"You seriously expect me to believe that Miss Morgan cannot tell the difference between a live rat and a replica?"

"No," replied Drew, rapidly losing patience. "I expect you to understand that sometimes a spoiled brat will lie to punish someone who won't give her what she wants. In short, if Alison Morgan filed a complaint against Daisy Hub, it was both frivolous and malicious. Now, how about keeping your earlier promise to be a good guest while you're on my station? Your dinner is waiting for you on K Deck."

A calculating look darted across Quan's face. "I could order my men to search the Hub. However, in the interests of maintaining friendly relations between your crew and mine, I will refrain, for this evening. Yoko isn't going anywhere. I can always come back for her. And, by the way, your friend Bonelli...?"

Drew stiffened in his seat. "What makes you think he's my friend?"

"It turns out that Captain Bonelli is not what he claims to be."

"Really? And just what is it that you think he is, Mr. Quan?"

Quan smiled, evidently feeling that he was on solid ground once more. "Once I have Yoko, I'll be taking Bonelli back to Earth with me as well, to stand trial for treason and espionage. I realize that your invitation was intended for every man on Zulu, but under the circumstances, I'm sure you understand why I couldn't allow him to join us this evening."

Chapter 35

Holchuk cursed under his breath. They were fried. Of all the people who could have stayed behind on Zulu!

"Answer me, dammit! Say something!" There was an edge of panic to the words that not even five millimeters of high-density plexi could filter out.

With a sigh, Holchuk stepped away from the rest of the team and removed his bubble helmet. "Bonelli?" he called out. "Where are you?"

The Ranger's reply sounded breathy and distorted. "Landing deck control room," he said. "You'll have to come get me. I'm hurt."

This did not smell right. Not right at all. Holchuk turned and looked into Jason Smith's worried face. He was mouthing the words *private channel* and pointing to the comm flap on his sleeve. Holchuk nodded understanding. He put his helmet back on and switched his comm to the pre-arranged frequency.

Once they were certain Bonelli could not overhear them, Smith said urgently, "What if it's a Ranger trap? What if he stayed behind to spring it on us?"

Holchuk shook his head. "We still can't leave him here. I'm supposed to be the only witness. You go ahead with the team — I'll take care of Bonelli."

Smith opened his mouth to say something, thought better of it, and nodded sharply.

As he watched Smith hustle the others back into motion, Holchuk recalled what Townsend had told them at their final briefing: there had been a change of command on Zulu. If Bonelli was actually hurt, it had probably been the result of a mutiny. The Doc had earlier expressed concern over the Rangers' discovering that their field generator had been tampered with. Now they would be returning to discover their former captain missing. Not even Townsend would be able to explain that away.

Of course, it could all be moot if the Rangers currently visiting Daisy Hub were a gang of mutineers.

"A miracle," he muttered to himself as he turned and began walking toward the access door nearest the control room. That was what they needed right now and what he had come along to see; instead, everything was falling apart at the seams.

It was a good thing Holchuk had spent time studying Zulu's floor plans, because whoever had designed the station had clearly not wanted to make it easy for intruders to find anything. Just past the access port, he turned right, down a short corridor that dead-ended at an unmarked door. It was not that door but the one to its left, also unmarked, that led to the landing deck control room. Beyond the door stood a flight of metal stairs with just enough bent-pipe handrail to conform to safety protocols. Placing his feet carefully, Holchuk climbed half a floor, stopping before yet another featureless door. He could feel sweat popping out on his scalp and sliding down his cheeks and forehead. It wasn't just the exertion that was making him perspire: PLS suits had been designed to withstand the cold of space. They weren't meant to be worn at room temperature.

Holchuk paused to remove his helmet again. "All right, Bonelli, I'm here. Open up," he called, making no effort to disguise the irritation he felt.

Slowly, the door slid aside. Holchuk stepped through and halted just inside the threshold, staring at what had apparently been the scene of a violent struggle. Most of Zulu was made of metal and riveted in place. Consoles, monitors, and storage compartments all stood around the small oblong control room like chrome-plated guards refusing to desert their posts. Meanwhile, everything that was not permanently attached in the room had apparently been thrown, hard, at something that was, at least once and probably more. A surveillance screen spiderwebbed with cracks sat at an awkward angle on its mount. There were fist-sized dents in the console cowlings, and several of the pressure-sensitive surfaces were shattered.

The floor was littered with datawafers, small gadgets with their guts spilling out, and a variety of maintenance tools. Holchuk saw blood spatters all over the room. Someone had definitely been injured here. But where was Bonelli?

"I'm down here."

The voice was faint and thready. Holchuk bent slightly and saw Bonelli, lying on his side in a puddle of red and grimacing in pain, beneath the far console. He was partly concealed by an overturned metal chair, which he was now unsuccessfully trying to push out of the way. He looked as if a wall had fallen on him.

"I was beginning to think Townsend hadn't understood my message," he said, enunciating with obvious difficulty. Then, noticing that Holchuk hadn't moved since entering the room, he added, "This *is* a rescue operation, right? You're not here just to finish me off?"

The thought had crossed Holchuk's mind — and Jason Smith's as well, come to that — but there could be no honor in killing a helpless prisoner. "You weren't number one on our to-do list today, Captain, but I think we can squeeze you in. Can you stand?"

Most of the blood on the floor had come from a nasty gash on the Ranger's arm. Bonelli had been applying pressure to the wound. Now his shirtsleeve was stuck to his skin with dried blood, and he winced with pain as Holchuk pulled him to his feet. He winced again as he tried to walk, limping badly on his left leg. Noticing that he and the Ranger were about the same height and mass, Holchuk fastened his helmet to his utility belt, then propped himself under Bonelli's left arm, wrapping his own arm around the other man's waist.

"Take it slow," gasped Bonelli.

Holchuk nearly laughed. "Have you ever tried to hurry in one of these suits? Just don't pass out on the stairs or they'll have to come rescue both of us."

It was a painful journey in more ways than one. Bonelli did his best not to be dead weight, but his left ankle was visibly swollen, and it seemed to take forever to get him down those dozen steps and onto the landing deck. By then, his wounds had opened up again. The two men left a crimson trail on the deck as Holchuk half-dragged, half-carried Bonelli toward *Devil Bug*. Then they had to climb that narrow ramp. By the time he was able to deliver the Ranger to Ruby inside the shuttle, every muscle in Holchuk's body was aching, and his exosuit was a motley of silver and red. 'Mom', however, focused her sympathy and attention on the one who was actually bleeding.

"My gawd, Stevie, you're a mess," she fussed, giving his wounds a quick inspection before pulling out the medkit. "If I didn't know better, I'd say somebody tried to kill you."

He managed a faint grin. "Somebody did. If it hadn't been for that Teri Martin concert, he would have succeeded, too."

"He? One man did this to you?"

Bonelli nodded.

"He also inflicted some serious damage on the control room," Holchuk added.

"That is one scary little man," Bonelli agreed. Holchuk couldn't help noticing how shallowly the Ranger was breathing. He looked as though he was having difficulty keeping his eyes open. "I couldn't fight him. He was too quick... too strong. Blocked every move. All I could do was dodge... not too successfully. Finally found something that was harder than his fists... tried to keep it between us." He sighed. "He left before killing me... didn't want to miss the concert."

Ruby's hands moved quickly and skillfully, closing the gash on his arm, along with several other lacerations Holchuk hadn't noticed, and clamping the regen unit onto his ankle. When she glanced up from her work, there was a worried expression on her face.

In a perceptibly weakening voice, Bonelli continued, "That little ninja... disabled the long-range comm panel before he left. Warned me not to try calling for help. Said he could deal with me when he got back... since I wasn't going anywhere. Boy, is he in for a surprise."

He wasn't the only one, thought Holchuk sourly. To Ruby, he said, "Listen, I have to go join the others. Play nice, you two."

By the time he'd crossed the landing deck and rejoined the incursion team, Holchuk had broken another sweat and was disgusted beyond words. When they got back to Daisy Hub, he decided, he was going to suggest that the boss man spend a few hours in a PLS suit — just in case Townsend had any other crazy plans inside his head.

The four men had all removed their helmets and were standing around the field generator in various poses of indecision. Holchuk's was evidently the deciding voice, for his arrival seemed to unpause the scene.

"I'm glad you're here, Gavin," said Singh. "We have a— good grief! What happened to you?"

Smith cut in before Holchuk could reply. "That's Bonelli's blood," he told them. "Stay focused, people, and remember what we practiced. We're on a tight schedule here."

Holchuk looked over the engineer's shoulder and saw the top of the Meniscus Field generator. At least the paintbrush had worked according to plan. The generator's upper casing was completely transparent, revealing a tangle of glowing tubes, and a row of mechanisms that might be switches. And in the middle, an empty space, surrounded by connection nodes. "There's a component missing," he remarked to Singh. "But the Meniscus Field—"

"—worked exactly as we expected it to," Smith agreed. "So the Rangers haven't removed anything. This must be the way the generator was delivered to them — and to us."

"That indentation is exactly the same size and shape as the paintbrush," said Gouryas. "And the connection nodes correspond precisely. Clearly, this device is meant to fit inside the generator. The problem is, we don't know what will happen if we actually put it there. Remember what Townsend said, about this potentially being a lethal weapon? We have only a rudimentary understanding of how the paintbrush works. We don't even know how to reverse what it's done to the bulkheads on Daisy Hub. What if it turns the Meniscus Field into a molecular disruptor field? What if it turns all the metal on Zulu into acrylic?"

"But what if it gives us full manual control over the Meniscus Field?" Singh countered hotly. "What if it lets us shut down the failsafe and make the modifications we were discussing earlier? Isn't that what we came here to learn how to do?"

"Dev's right. We have to try," Smith told them. "It's why we're here. If anything goes wrong, we're all wearing PLS suits, and Ruby's safe inside the ship."

O'Malley broke in then, his voice half an octave higher than usual, "But what if it changes the atomic composition of our exosuits? What if it turns *Devil Bug* into plexiplast?"

"All right," Smith decided. "We'll do it this way: everyone get into the shuttle and remove to a safe distance from the station. I'll wait until you're out of range, then I'll open the casing and slip the device into the generator, and we'll see what happens."

"No, I'll do it," sighed Gouryas. "We need an expert observer inside the station. No disrespect, Jason, but I've already hooked up my recording gear, and I've spent more time studying the paintbrush than you have."

"Are you sure about this?" Smith demanded. "It's alien technology, remember. Against all logic, it could blow up in your face."

"In which case, we're all equally expendable, aren't we?" Singh pointed out drily.

"All right, then," said Smith with a grim nod. "Gouryas, it's your show. The rest of us will fall back to the shuttle."

Ruby watched them file back up the ramp and into *Devil Bug*, then wordlessly closed the hatch and lay down at the controls, preparing to leave the docking bay.

"As soon as we're clear of the gravity field, open a comm channel to Gouryas's suit," Smith instructed her.

Still wearing their exosuits, the rest of the team sat down at the viewport and fastened their restraints. Then Holchuk remembered Bonelli. He glanced backward and saw the Ranger's motionless form, tethered to the deck at the rear of the cabin. He was unconscious. That wasn't good. He'd lost a lot of blood, and they wouldn't be returning to Daisy Hub for several hours. Any threat that Earth had posed to the Hub in the past would be nothing compared to what they'd have to deal with if a Ranger captain died on their shuttle, especially if the Authority ever found out what they'd been doing on Zulu in the first place.

Monkeys with typewriters. Nandrian tests. *Tekl'hananni.* The words spun and blurred together inside Holchuk's head as he stared at the Ranger station through the viewport. Gavin ban Samuel had already passed his Nandrian test. Now, all he could do was watch as the others took theirs. He mustn't share what he suspected, what he knew, what Nagor had told him. Cheating on a test would bring dishonor to both their Houses.

The mushroom wearing an overcoat was revolving lazily in space, looking more and more like a chunk of scrap metal trapped in orbit. Whatever happened now, whatever Zulu became, it would be what the Nandrians wished for Daisy Hub; and what the Nandrians wished, Daisy Hub didn't dare reject.

Gouryas was wearing his bubble helmet. His voice echoed slightly as he replied to Ruby's hail, "I hear you, *Devil Bug*. I'm about to lift the lid of the generator casing and insert the paintbrush. Recording devices are active. Let me know if you see anything interesting out there."

In the silence that followed his words, Holchuk kept his gaze fixed on the viewscreen. So did everyone else. Nothing.

Abruptly, Gouryas gasped with surprise. "Hah!" the engineer crowed. "Hey, out there, are you seeing this?"

"Seeing what, Spiro?" asked Jason Smith.

"The emitter gave off a flash of purple light, and now the entire landing deck is purple. Deck, bulkheads, everything. It's as though the paintbrush has become a paint sprayer. If *Devil Bug* were parked right now, she'd probably be purple too."

Singh's lips were moving. At first, Holchuk thought he was praying. Then he realized that the other man was counting down: three, two, one. Right on cue, the image of the station on the viewport went gray and grainy, then began to waver... And before their eyes, Zulu seemed to burst into purple flame before abruptly winking out.

The Zoo had disappeared.

O'Malley was in shock. "Oh, my gawd," he breathed.

Singh sat grinning happily at the space on the viewport screen where Zulu had been.

"Son of a—!" Smith reached over and tapped him on the shoulder. "Was that what I thought it was?" he demanded. "Has the paintbrush just made Zulu and everything on it transparent?"

Singh shook his head. "Not transparent. If Spiro were transparent, he would be blind, and we haven't heard him screaming, have we?"

Holchuk could think of many possible reasons for not hearing Gouryas scream. Before he could share any of them, however, Ruby got on the comm.

"Spiro, are you all right?" she demanded urgently.

"I'm fine," he assured them. "Still seeing purple. Has there been any change out there?"

"You might say so," Singh replied. "From our perspective, the Zoo is invisible. A purple flash and it was gone."

"Are you serious?" Gouryas demanded excitedly. "Our theory was correct? Excellent!"

"Actually, it was *my* theory," Singh corrected him.

Smith was visibly losing patience. "Would one of you be good enough to let me know what the hell is going on here?"

"The color purple was the key," Singh explained. "Back on Daisy Hub, I hypothesized that the generator would create a field around Zulu, and that the paintbrush would establish its parameters," said Singh. "Apparently, I was right. The paintbrush creates its palette of colors by altering the refractive index of whatever it's aimed at. If the refractive index is such that it bends light around the affected surface, then the color becomes—"

"—invisible!" Smith's face lit up with understanding. "So it's an invisibility field. And we can recreate it on Daisy Hub?"

Singh nodded.

"Not so fast, Jason," warned Gouryas. "Invisibility may come at a price. Remember what the paintbrush did to our bulkheads? Let's see what happens when I disconnect it from the generator."

Chapter 36

Teri Martin was still a star. The transformation from resident wildcat to visiting celebrity that Drew had witnessed on Zulu had been no more than a tantalizing glimpse. Onstage, in a succession of sequined and feathered costumes and spot-lighted against a cleverly designed moving set, she was clearly in her element. Teri Martin glittered. She sparkled. She sang and danced and joked and strutted. She radiated an energy that was positively contagious. And for two and a half hours, she had fifteen Rangers and thirty-three of her crewmates eating out of her hand.

In AdComm, Drew, Lydia, and the Doc watched the show by remote vidcam. Even on a forty-centimeter surveillance screen, it was impressive. Quan might suspect that the invitation was part of a con, but he would still have to admit that Teri's performance that evening had been worth the trip.

She had planned to do one encore. As it began, Lydia sent a signal to the incursion team. They would have to coordinate their return to Daisy Hub with the departure of the Rangers' shuttles in order to remain undetected.

Ten minutes later, Teri's encore was over. As she took her final bow, the audience rose to their feet, applauding enthusiastically. All but one — Nestor Quan. Major Cisco remained firmly seated, arms crossed over his chest, an expression of mild annoyance on his face.

"He's just a ray of sunshine, isn't he?" Drew muttered, only half to himself. "We feed them, we entertain them..."

Beside him, the Doc snorted, "He's probably upset because there really was a stuffed toy rat in the show."

"You said earlier that they were research partners, Doc," said Drew thoughtfully. "Equal partners?"

She nodded. "Nayo shared everything with him. He was a very generous man."

"So the patents were jointly owned. That means Quan couldn't have sold them by himself; Naguchi had to sign them over as well. I'm curious, Doc."

She gave him a regretful smile. "You have many questions. I wish I had the answers, Mr. Townsend. All I know is that three representatives of the purchasing corporation paid Nayo a visit at home one evening. When they left, they had his thumbprint on a sales contract. Nayo wouldn't talk about what had happened that night, and I would rather not try to imagine it. He meant a lot to me. One week later, he was on his way to Daisy Hub, with Yoko. I never saw him again."

Now, finally, the pieces were starting to fall into place. "So, when you learned that Nestor Quan had been appointed as Daisy Hub's Disease Control Officer…?"

"I knew exactly what he was after," she said, her lips a hyphen of remembered determination. "Nayo Naguchi was deeply respected by his colleagues in the scientific community. I called in some favors on his behalf and got that little predator detoured before he could arrive here."

Interesting. So Drew Townsend wasn't the only one on the Hub with friends in high places.

"I would still like to know how a research scientist representing the interests of a Greater European genetics corporation ended up in command of this particular Ranger detachment. That took connections."

"He's using an assumed name," the Doc reminded him. "Maybe he conned someone."

Or maybe, just maybe, Quan's appointment had come from the same place as his own — the covert security branch of the Space Installation Authority. *Turn him or terminate him.* Drew's instructions had been clear. But the timing, the timing was everything.

"Maybe. And maybe he ran the con because after five years of trying, he finally realized that Nestor Quan was being actively prevented from reaching Daisy Hub," Drew remarked. "However he did it, Doc, he's here now, and he's given us a major problem."

"Drew!" Lydia cut in excitedly. "We just received a commburst from *Devil Bug*. The team found Captain Bonelli on Zulu, gravely wounded. Ruby managed to stop the bleeding, and they're bringing him back here for treatment, but she's afraid he may not make it. Before losing consciousness he told her that a ninja tried to kill him."

So much for taking the "spy and traitor" back to Earth for trial.

Drew and the Doc exchanged a meaningful look. "You know," he said, "if Quan does have the authority to search the station, we're going to have to find another hiding place for Yoko, and probably for Steve Bonelli as well."

"First things first, Mr. Townsend," she advised him. "First, I have to get some of Bonelli's stem cells out of cryo and save his life. Then we can worry about hiding him from Nestor Quan."

Behind them, Lydia cleared her throat. "Our guests are leaving, Drew, but Major Cisco is hanging back."

"Waiting for the host to say a formal goodbye, no doubt," he sighed, heading for the tube car. As the Doc had said, first things first. First, they had to send the ninja back to Zulu so that the mission team could return, hopefully undetected.

Quan was waiting for him on A Deck, either unaware or unconcerned that he was being closely watched by ten burly men and several surveillance vidcams. As Drew stepped out of the tube car, the little man bowed and said, "On behalf of the entire detachment, I wish to thank you for your hospitality, Mr. Townsend. It was a delicious dinner and a very entertaining performance. Please give our compliments to your crew for a fine evening."

He certainly knew the right words to say. It was a shame that was all they were to him — words.

"We're glad you enjoyed yourselves, Major." Automatically, the rest of the formulaic response rose into his mouth — 'Please come back again soon.' — but Drew bit down and swallowed it.

"The next time I visit, I'll come alone so that we can conclude the business that remains between us."

"There is no business between us," Drew corrected him pleasantly. *And therefore no need to visit.*

Quan began again, in a sterner voice, "The people we both work for—"

"Wrong again, 'Major'," Drew informed him coldly. "I answer to the Space Installation Authority, and I can't imagine you working for anyone but yourself." Behind him, he sensed Orvy Hagman and his men, sniffing trouble and forming up once again to head it off. If necessary, this guest would be bodily delivered into the airlock of his ship.

The ninja spent a moment considering his options. Drew could practically hear him mentally checking them off. Then, "What a shame that such a cordial evening must end on a discordant note," sighed Quan. "Good evening, Mr. Townsend, gentlemen..." And he wheeled and stepped through the docking archway.

First things first, Drew reminded himself. First, get Quan off the station and on his way back to Zulu. Get the mission team back on the Hub and Bonelli into Med Services. Later, there would probably be hell to pay. Right now, however, Townsend had other things to worry about.

As the archway door slid shut on their final guest, Drew heard noisy exhalations behind him. *And the dominos keep falling.*

Chapter 37

Lydia spun in her seat as Drew stepped off the tube car in AdComm.

"They're away," she told him. "And *Devil Bug* is on its way back home. Ruby sounded excited. They must have discovered something besides Captain Bonelli." A pause, then, "You look tired, Drew. It'll be a three-hour wait, at least. Why don't you go grab a nap? I'll let you know the second they dock."

He didn't even have to think about it. Sleep? Not a chance. When Quan returned to Zulu and discovered that Bonelli was gone, he would put two and two together — and probably get twenty-two. Lydia might have to send that mayday to the Nandrians after all.

"I think I'd rather grab a java," he decided. "Have the shuttle dock first on A Deck — Bonelli may not have the time it'll take for the Meniscus Field to cycle."

It had been a very long day for everyone on Daisy Hub; and for anyone involved with Teri's show, it wasn't over yet. K Deck had to be transformed back into a storage area. All those seats had to be returned to the caf. If Fritz and his assistants had been in Teri's audience, they still had to clean up after the buffet dinner and prepare the kitchen for breakfast. Fortunately, Drew was the boss and could ask for a cup of java whenever he wanted. Of course, he would probably have to drink it standing up, but under the circumstances, standing would probably be easier for him.

Drew stepped out of the tube car on D Deck, thumbed the enter switch beside the caf door, and stood poised on the threshold, blinking in confusion.

This late at night, the caf should have been empty, or close to it. Instead, the room was full of people, sitting in groups of three and four around Fritz Jensen's round tables. Many of them were holding java mugs. All of them had fallen silent and turned curious eyes on him the instant he appeared in the doorway. For an uncomfortable moment, all he could do was stare back at them. Then one of the dockworkers — Racine? Kowalski? — jumped up and wordlessly offered him a seat.

With a nod of thanks, Drew took it. At the same time, a cup of steaming hot java seemed to materialize in front of him. As he eased himself wearily into the chair, Drew swore he could hear the entire room exhale.

"Any word, Mr. Townsend?" called out an anxious female voice.

Still not daring to believe what was apparently happening here, he replied, "They're on their way home, and so far the Rangers haven't detected them."

"No news is good news, then," declared the man across the table from him. A second later, Drew recalled who he was — Mossman, External Hub Maintenance.

Drew lifted his cup halfway to his mouth, then changed his mind and said, "Don't take this the wrong way, people, but… What are you all doing here at this hour?"

Nervous laughter rippled through the room. Across the table, Mossman flashed him a grin. "Waiting for the young'uns to get home from their date, of course," he said. "We wouldn't be able to sleep until we knew they were back safe."

Of course. He should have known. And if Drew's teen years had included such ordinary things as going on dates and returning home late to concerned parents, he would have known. Mustering a responding smile and forcing lightness into his voice, he asked, "Are you going to do this every time someone goes out on a mission?"

"That depends," came the reply from somewhere behind him. "Are there going to be more missions?"

Drew was spared from having to answer by the sound of the caf door opening. Teri Mintz strolled into the room, fresh-faced and clad in a dressing gown. The entire caf burst into spontaneous applause, prompting her to take a couple of bows.

"Great show, Teri!"

"Encore, encore!"

Beaming, she sashayed over to Drew's table, where Mossman had pulled up another chair for her and someone had produced another cup of java. Teri took and savored a sip of Jensen's brew, then said quietly, "So now we wait. Is everyone all right?"

"What she really means is, is Gavin all right," declared Lu, triggering a chorus of whistles and catcalls as he broke into an off-key rendition of 'That Man of Mine'.

Teri's eyes were dancing. Turning to face him, she got to her feet and, chin elevated in a parody of royal dignity, announced, "The peasants had better be careful what they say about a member of the Fifth Shield."

A roar of laughter erupted briefly and subsided as she sat down again. "So, did you get to watch any of the show?" she asked Drew. "Tell me what you thought about it, honestly."

For the next while, the Daisy Hub crew sat in the caf, chatting and drinking java and losing track of the time until Drew's wristcomm bleeped at him.

It was Lydia. Two words. "They're home."

Chapter 38

Drew went directly to A Deck from the caf, accompanied by as many of his crew as could fit into the tube car with him, and found Doc Ktumba already there. She had brought an anti-grav gurney and all the whole blood Bonelli's stem cells had been able to generate, and was muttering impatiently under her breath as she waited for the archway doors to open.

Finally, they parted. Drew and the others stayed back, allowing the Doc to board with her medical gear. Over the years he'd spent as a field investigator, Drew had seen plenty of broken bodies. When Smith and Holchuk emerged with Bonelli on the gurney and Ktumba right behind, Townsend knew, with dreadful certainty, that the Ranger was near death.

So did the Doc. "Get this man to Med Services right now!" she snapped. Instantly, Hagman and Mossman stepped forward and took over propelling the gurney into the tube car.

Moments later, Drew was barking orders and — miracle of miracles — watching his crew jump to follow them. "I want the mission team in AdComm for debriefing in half an hour and the rest of you either in your quarters or in the caf," he decided. "Lydia, Ruby needs to park *Devil Bug* on the primary landing deck and join us in AdComm as soon as she can."

"I hear you, Chief," called Ruby through the archway. "Okay, everybody out, shoo! And take your toys with you."

Singh and Gouryas emerged, laden down with gadgets and grinning from ear to ear. Clearly, the mission had been a success. Drew waved them impatiently toward the tube car door. O'Malley was the one he wanted to talk to.

The ratkeeper was the last one out. Drew stepped forward and laid a hand on his arm. "I need you to check something in the databases," he muttered urgently. "It's important."

Thirty minutes later, Drew was on his way to AdComm when his wristcomm bleeped at him again. "Drew," said Lydia's voice, "the Doc needs you in Med Services, immediately."

He'd been afraid of this. Bonelli's face had been so pale, his uniform so bloodied.... Reaching for the override button on the tube car's control pad, Drew replied, "Tell her I'm on my way."

"Finally, you're here," declared the Doc as Drew stepped into the Trauma Clinic. "Captain Bonelli regained consciousness once I'd infused him. Now he won't let me anesthetize him for surgery until he's spoken with you."

"Hey, Snooper," said Bonelli, his voice barely a whisper. His color was a little better, but that was all.

"Spike," Townsend acknowledged. "You're in pretty bad shape. What happened over there?"

The Ranger essayed a grin. "The new commander arrived. His creds looked suspicious to me, so I checked them against the database. He didn't like that. Used a lot of body language to make his point. Then you called to invite everybody to the concert. You asked for me, so I knew you had no idea this guy was coming, and you should have, if he was legit. Later, he caught me on the long-range comm, using that."

Too weak to point, Bonelli turned his head and stared at the tray beside his medbed. Drew followed his gaze and saw a familiar looking black cylinder with ridges along half its length. An EIS encryption device.

"He ordered me to turn it over to him," Bonelli continued, "and I refused. Then he mopped the floor with me." Noticing the expression on Drew's face, the Ranger added, "Hey, this was a major operation. You didn't honestly believe they would send you out here all alone, without providing emergency backup?"

Actually, that was exactly what Drew had thought. Correction — it was what he'd been led to believe. But Bonelli's question was rhetorical, so he let it go and asked instead, "Why didn't you say something?"

"Couldn't. Orders. Your response to me had to be genuine. I have to tell you, kid, I had no idea you were still that angry."

"Make it fast, gentlemen," cut in the Doc. "Captain Bonelli has serious internal injuries. I need to get him into surgery as soon as possible." Drew glanced up, startled to realize that Ktumba had been standing there, overhearing their entire conversation. As though reading his mind, she informed him curtly, "Doctor-patient privilege, Mr. Townsend. Nothing you say leaves this room. Unless you talk him to death. Then all bets are off."

Drew faced Bonelli again and said urgently, "You set me up, Spike. Cost me five years of my life."

"I know. That was the plan. Ratting you out wasn't my idea, kid. They wanted you off the street and completing your education. You were no good to them without your Eligibility."

"Them?"

Another faint quirking of Bonelli's lips. "You were hand-picked. So was I. So was everyone on the Hub. And the Zoo. They just don't realize it. On the shuttle, I overheard things. They're good people, Townsend. They've earned the right to know the truth. Tell them what they're doing out here. Then figure out a way to get that ninja off Zulu. Lieutenant Rodrigues is my second. A good man. He'll work with you until the EIS can send a replacement."

"All right, that's enough," said the Doc. "Mr. Townsend, I believe you're late for a meeting…?"

As he walked out of Trauma and toward the tube car, something that Bonelli had said stuck in his mind — for an important operation, there had to be backup. As well, as Townsend had pointed out earlier to Holchuk, tests had to be overseen, experiments observed.

The Meniscus Field generators had been placed on Daisy Hub and on Zulu to be tinkered with. Earth Council had to have placed someone on the Hub to monitor the activities of the engineers and techs. So who was it? If both entire crews had been hand-picked by the EIS, who did that leave? The station manager. And who had arrived on Daisy Hub at the same time as the field generator was being installed?

Karim Khaloub. So the 'unlikely choice' had been working undercover after all. That explained why he'd needed Lydia's surveillance skills.

Bonelli had known from the beginning that Drew Townsend was a fellow EIS operative. Drew went back over everything the Ranger had said to him, recalling:

"If a real threat to security ever arose, I'd say we're equipped to handle it." He hadn't been talking about security around the Meniscus Field generator installation. He'd been talking about anyone who came to the station who wasn't cleared by the EIS.

Pieces were falling into place now. Khaloub's death might have been an accident, but it was a happy accident. Or was it? The entire system was watchdogged — but there was someone aboard Daisy Hub who could get past the watchdogs, who had practiced in the SPA room.

Did Robert O'Malley have an EIS encryption device too?

And if everyone aboard the Hub was there because Earth Intelligence had put them there, and the EIS had ordered the hit on Karim Khaloub, then what about Gavin Holchuk? The Chief Cargo Inspector had spent years blaming the Relocation Authority for his wife's death and his daughter's disappearance. What if the tragedy had actually been engineered by Earth Intelligence?

Ugly questions. They left a distinctly bitter taste in Townsend's mouth. It was too late to ask Bonelli about any of this — the Ranger would be in surgery for some time. Even if he weren't, he might not have the answers Drew needed, since the EIS kept its operatives on a need-to-know basis. Maybe, for the sake of his mission and the ongoing security of Daisy Hub, Townsend should do the same. Bonelli had been right about one thing — it was time to tell the crew of Daisy Hub why they were there. How they had gotten there was another matter, something Drew would just have to keep to himself for now.

Chapter 39

Drew and Ruby stepped out of tube cars on opposite sides of AdComm, and O'Malley joined them a couple of minutes later. Somebody had gathered all the chairs and arranged them in a semi-circle in front of the station manager's desk. As expected, none of the mission team were sitting yet. Drew glanced around, feeling momentarily buoyed by the sight of their beaming faces. Well, most of them. Holchuk stood off by himself, arms crossed, his expression inscrutable. Townsend could feel the Chief Cargo Inspector's eyes on him as he rounded the row of filing cabinets and took his seat.

"Everyone, please sit down," Drew invited them, "and let's begin the—"

Lydia's voice interrupted him. "Drew, I'm getting a commburst from Zulu. It's Major Cisco. He's speaking very quickly and his pronunciation is atrocious, but I'm getting the gist of it. He definitely isn't happy. Something about a missing officer. He's coming back here as soon as possible to search for him. And he keeps repeating the word 'purple'."

"Purple?" Drew echoed. On cue, Gouryas unrolled a bundle he'd brought with him to the debriefing. It was a PLS suit and it was bright purple, right down to the glove fastenings. Drew had to suppress a smile. "You painted Zulu purple?" So much for sneaking aboard and away undetected. No wonder Ruby had referred to the team's technology as 'toys'.

"Not intentionally," Singh explained. "The paint job appears to be a side effect. The paintbrush was obviously set for purple, and—"

"I didn't want to risk turning part of the Ranger station into acrylic by trying to reverse it, so I left it painted," said Gouryas. "We were only on the landing deck, anyway—"

"—which Cisco now thinks you vandalized for fun while rescuing Bonelli," concluded Drew. "But you said it was a side effect. What was the main effect?"

The two engineers exchanged a conspiratorial look. "An invisibility field," announced Singh. In an instant, they were competing to tell the story. Their excitement grew as they relished each new detail, making them sound more like hyperactive children than trained professionals. Drew listened in bemusement, his eyes widening as they swung back and forth. Then, abruptly, the recitation was over. Gouryas and Singh sat back in their chairs, grinning smugly and waiting to be congratulated.

For several seconds, Drew was speechless. He'd sent a team to Zulu to figure out how to shut down a dangerous piece of equipment, and they'd managed instead to turn it into a defensive advantage. And that was a good thing, he told himself. Daisy Hub was an outpost, weaponless and vulnerable. Anything that could protect the Hub and its crew from as yet unknown enemies had to be considered a valuable gift, even one that had come from the Nandrians with some assembly required and no instruction manual.

It wasn't an oversight. The Nandrians loved riddles and puzzles and knew that the Humans did too. So, they'd given Daisy Hub the invisibility field generator in pieces, evidently anticipating that the crew would enjoy figuring out what it was. That meant the security protocols were probably just an empty threat, which would in turn mean that Drew's earlier suspicion was correct — Khaloub's death had been murder, made to look accidental by the only man aboard the Hub who could have arranged it. Drew's report to SISCO had stated categorically that the station manager's death had involved no foul play. If the EIS hadn't ordered this hit, they were all in deep trouble.

Carefully composing his features, Drew turned to meet Holchuk's steady gaze. "Do you have anything to add, Mr. Holchuk?"

The other man shook his head. "Just that the Nandrians will expect the courtesy of a thank you. There's a generosity appreciation script. The next time Nagor boards the station, you'll have to meet him on A Deck and…" He let his voice trail off. "You okay, boss man?" asked Holchuk with a faint grin.

Another speech at swordpoint. Terrific. "I'll let you know," he muttered, then gathered himself and announced to all present, "So, we're now in possession of a stealth cloak, which Earth Council knows nothing about. And the first time we use this field, it's going to paint the Hub purple?"

"Or green, or orange, or whatever the setting on the paintbrush happens to be," Singh informed him.

"Yellow's nice," Ruby chimed in helpfully. "It's a cheerful color."

"Actually," said Gouryas, "we don't know for sure that that effect has to happen. I left the casing open when I activated the field generator and it spray-painted the landing deck. Maybe there's a setting on the paintbrush we haven't found yet. Or maybe we need to keep the generator in a small, enclosed space. We'll need some time to experiment with the invisibility field and figure out how it works."

Drew sighed inwardly. Experiment where, precisely? They couldn't just stage a show for the Rangers each time they needed to borrow Zulu. And what about the damage that had already been done to the bulkheads on the Hub? Twenty-five soft spots, hull integrity dropping — never mind what the effect of painting the shuttle deck purple might be!

Holchuk's harsh voice brought him back to the moment. "Time will be a problem if we can't do something about that ninja over on the Zoo," the Chief Cargo Inspector was pointing out. "He nearly killed Bonelli. Now he knows that we've been there and that Bonelli is over here. And from what I've seen, his hands and feet really are lethal weapons."

Fortunately, Townsend had already thought of that. "O'Malley? What were you able to find?"

"I checked out Major Cisco, boss, as you requested. Bottom line, Cisco's creds are definitely bogus. And they're crude. There's minimal backstory, with no cross-referencing to speak of. Clearly, it's a rush job, and that's not how the Authorities operate. They keep a closet full of ready-made shell identities that their agents can step into and out of. Impeccably crafted."

"You've seen them?" Ruby joked.

Eyes twinkling, O'Malley leaned toward her and intimated, "Seen them? I created some of them." Then, serious once more, he continued, "The only reason I can think of for a government agency to send someone off-planet with creds like this would be to get rid of him. He'd be outed the first time he tried to access a credit account, and people would be lining up to hit him with a baseball bat."

"Except that he knew his creds wouldn't stand up," said Townsend. "That's why he attacked Bonelli — he was checking Cisco out on the database."

"Then the major didn't come from any branch of Earth's government," O'Malley concluded. "He's a freelancer, and I think I know what brought him here." A pause for dramatic effect, then, "You asked me to check for an arrest warrant? There was one issued for Captain Bonelli, time stamped the same date as those creds were entered in the system, but three hours earlier."

"Bogus as well?"

O'Malley shook his head. "I'm not sure. The warrant is thumbprinted by some big-hat on Earth's High Council, but that could have been his secretary doing a favor for someone. It's illegal, but a lot of those high officials get stamps made of their thumbprints so someone else can do the real work while they're off at the sports complex. According to the warrant, Bonelli is wanted by the Space Installation Authority for treason and espionage."

'The people we both work for,' Quan had said.

Townsend swore under his breath. "It's bogus, O'Malley. Cisco had another reason for coming out here, and it's nothing to do with the SIA." He paused, debating briefly with himself. They were good people, Spike had said. They deserved to know the truth. Yes, they did, Drew decided, and the sooner he started telling it, the better: "He wants Yoko. Alison Morgan must have filed her complaint the second she stepped aboard the long-hopper taking her home. That's how Cisco knew to come here."

"He knows about Yoko?" O'Malley demanded, stiffening in his seat.

Ruby pursed her lips tightly, saying nothing.

Drew nodded wearily. "He knows all about Yoko, and he's apparently promised her to a Greater European genetics firm. The arrest warrant was his ticket to Zulu, and the detachment at Zulu gives him something to threaten us with if we refuse to surrender her to him. Needless to say, even if the warrant turns out to be genuine, we are not handing Bonelli — or Yoko — over to that sadistic little privateer."

"I don't understand," said Smith. "What's so special about a cloned white rat?"

Drew opened his mouth to answer, then shut it again. Deserving to know the truth was one thing; breaking the Doc's confidence while she was elbow-deep in Bonelli's innards was another.

Then O'Malley leaned toward Smith and told him in a stage whisper, "Jason, she's not cloned."

Townsend wanted to smack him. Ruby was sitting closer to him — she stretched out a leg and kicked him, hard, in the calf. But it was too late.

"Oh," said Smith. A moment later, as the meaning of the words sank in, his eyes opened wide and he repeated in amazement, "Ohhh!"

Drew got to his feet. If he moved quickly, the situation could still be contained. "Yes, boys and girls," he announced, "Yoko really is the Überrat. And that knowledge, which until a minute ago was a closely-guarded secret, is not to be repeated to anyone outside this room. Is that understood?" he concluded sternly.

Everyone replied at once:

"Yes, sir."

"Absolutely, Drew."

"Understood, Mr. Townsend."

"Mum's the word."

"Of course, Chief."

"Not a word, boss."

Holchuk said nothing, just began to smile and nod emphatically. Drew had never seen him like this. Evidently, neither had anyone else in the room.

"Gavin, what's the matter?" demanded Ruby.

"We're a House!" he declared. "And Yoko is our living staff!"

"And what precisely is a living staff?" Drew asked wearily.

"It symbolizes the power and longevity of the House," Holchuk replied, then explained, "According to legend, Nandor was not the original home world of the Nandrians. When they left it to explore the galaxy, they wanted to bring with them the sacred tree of their ancestors, but it refused to be transplanted. So, each House took a cutting from the tree. The Nandrians believe that the cuttings are still connected to the tree in some mysterious way, and that's why each living staff continues to put out leaves and branches, centuries later. They also believe that if even one staff were to be destroyed, the entire tree back on the original home world would die; so, protecting its living staff — its *tseritsa* — is every House's sacred obligation."

"What you're saying is that if the Nandrians knew about Yoko, then this secret hasn't been as closely guarded as you thought it was," remarked Singh.

"Not true," countered Ruby. "All they had to do was keep their eyes open. We've been going to great lengths to protect Yoko, ever since Naguchi brought her aboard the Hub. And it's common knowledge that live animals are forbidden on ships and hubs, and yet Yoko rides all over the station on Rob's shoulder. Clearly, she's a very special creature."

Lydia spoke up then, adding, "The Galactic database includes information about Earth's fauna. The Nandrians wouldn't have had to look too hard to discover the average lifespan of a *rattus norvegicus*. After that, it would just be a matter of putting two and two together. And the Nandrians are really good at that."

As she returned her attention to her console, an idea began to glimmer in Drew's mind. "So the Nandrians believe that Yoko is our... *tseritsa*?" Holchuk nodded. "And if even one *tseritsa* comes to harm, every House has been disgraced?"

"You getting a brainstorm, boss man?"

"I think I am, Mr. Holchuk. Our first priority right now is finding a safe hiding place for Yoko and Bonelli," he said. "Cisco will be here in a few hours to search every corner of the Hub, and he'll be armed to the teeth, so we can't simply refuse to let him dock." Drew turned his head in Lydia's direction and opened his mouth to speak, but she beat him to the punch.

"I'm receiving another transmission, Mr. Townsend," she said brightly. "It's from the *Krronn*. The *tekl'hananni* scores have been posted, and Trokerk is ahead by twelve. Nagor is requesting docking module one. He'll be arriving in less than five hours."

Drew tried to make his expression reproachful. "You sent that mayday, didn't you?"

She just smiled and busied herself with her communications board.

It was all Drew could do to contain his glee. Cisco would arrive on Daisy Hub to find a Nandrian victory party in full swing. It was almost poetic.

"Mr. Holchuk, is there a script for requesting the safekeeping of a precious object and sanctuary for a wrongly accused man?"

Holchuk nodded thoughtfully. "I'll tack it onto your generosity appreciation speech," he said, then wheeled and headed for the tube door.

"Isn't there something we can do about Cisco, Drew?" asked Ruby, her voice and expression both strained. "He's like a poisonous spider lurking on a web. Is there any way that we can prevent him from returning to the Ranger station once he leaves here?"

"What if we convinced him that he'd killed Bonelli?" suggested Gouryas. "That would take care of two problems at once."

Drew shook his head. "Not really. First, he'd insist on seeing the body. Then he'd insist on taking it back as proof that he'd served the warrant."

"What if we convinced the *Rangers* that he'd killed Bonelli?" mused O'Malley.

Drew considered this for five full seconds and could find no downside. "Keep talking, O'Malley."

The ratkeeper leaned forward, warming to his subject. "We transmit a medical report and death certificate to the Zoo, as soon as Cisco docks here. We let him search the Hub. He finds nothing. He demands to search the *Krronn*, but the Nandrians won't permit it. So he has no choice but to leave, threatening to return with an armed boarding party once the Nandrians have gone. Back on Zulu, he walks, unsuspecting, right into a mutiny."

"Fourteen Rangers against one ninja?" said Smith. "Don't forget, I've seen what a martial arts expert can do. It's entirely possible he'll be able to put down the mutiny. Then what?"

O'Malley was unfazed. "If we also transmit the medical documentation to Earth, Space Installation Security will have to Gatecast an arrest warrant. Rangers will be waiting for him wherever he goes, and they won't hesitate to shoot first and ask questions later. Even if he survives his arrest, he'll be completely discredited. Of course, there is a trade-off: Bonelli won't be able to go anywhere either."

"He can't go anywhere now, with that bogus warrant hanging over his head," Gouryas pointed out.

Drew grinned. "Trust me, people. It won't be a problem."

Chapter 40

The Ranger shuttle *Bonaventure* was still an hour away from the Hub when the *Krronn* requested permission to dock. As it turned out, Trokerk really was the leading House in *tekl'han-anni*. Because the *Krronn* had been in the process of responding to Lydia's distress call, however, the Nandrian ship was much closer to Daisy Hub when the scores were posted than would normally have been the case.

Aboard the station, preparations had already been made. Bonelli was in Recovery, ready to be moved. Yoko was in her cage, on A Deck, beside Drew's left leg. Holchuk had suggested that the station manager carry her on his shoulder, for effect, but neither Drew nor Yoko would have any of *that*. So the Chief Cargo Inspector had quickly added a paragraph of explanation to Drew's speech.

As he watched Nagor emerge from the docking archway with his second and third, all of them seeming to move in slow motion, Townsend had a gut-twisting moment of *déjà vu*. Steady, now, he reminded himself. There was no need to be nervous. He'd already made a good first impression. The speeches were shorter this time and didn't have to be word for word from a script. The downside, of course, was that the Nandrians were carnivores, with sharp teeth and a venomous bite, who had just come off a killing spree. He'd better talk fast, before one of them got the idea that Yoko was an *hors d'oeuvre*.

Carefully, Drew bowed from the waist, then said, "Greetings, Nagor ban Nagoram. It is an honor to receive you on my station."

Nagor bowed as well and replied, "The honor is mine, Drew, son of... *Dammit!* to be so warmly received." Then the big alien made a strange sound, somewhere between a wheeze and a snort.

Townsend glanced sharply, first at Holchuk, then at Ruby, but neither of them would make eye contact with him. In fact, Holchuk appeared to be struggling to keep a straight face.

One mistake and he'd been branded for life, Drew thought disgustedly. Oh, well, may as well get on with it.

"I present to you my second and third, Gavin, son of—"

"We have met," Nagor cut in.

Now all three of the Nandrians were making strange noises.

Undeterred, Drew forged ahead, following the script: "You come here victorious, from *tekl'hananni*. We beg you to tell us of your triumph."

Nagor tilted his massive head and replied, "It was short. We won."

Silence. Now what? Their account was supposed to match. Mentally crossing his fingers, Drew said emphatically, "So did we."

Nagor nodded his head twice, then made that strange noise again.

"And we wish to thank you for your generosity in giving us the invisibility field generator."

There was more to Drew's speech, but the big alien cut it short by leaning forward until his snout was almost touching the Human's nose. "You... are... welcome," Nagor said.

There was a strong citrus smell on his breath.

Clearly, the crew of the *Krronn* had already begun celebrating their victory. If all the Nandrians aboard ship were in this condition, it was a miracle they had managed to dock without knocking Daisy Hub out of orbit.

Holchuk reached out and tapped Drew on the shoulder. "Tell him what we want, boss man."

"What about the protocol?"

The Chief Cargo Inspector uttered an exasperated syllable. "Do they look like they're worrying about protocol? Meanwhile, we're running out of time."

He was right. The aliens were definitely toxed, if not to the rafters, at least within arm's reach. And Yoko and Bonelli needed to be safely aboard the *Krronn* before Cisco docked.

Drew cleared his throat and declared loudly, "Nagor ban Nagoram, we have a problem and we need your help."

Instantly, the Nandrians' merriment stopped. "What is your problem, Drew son of… *Dammit!?*" demanded Nagor.

Drew sucked in a deep breath. "Earth does not wish us to have a *tseritsa*. Earth's High Council has sent an official to take it away from us. He will be docking here in less than an hour. We know that he has no honor, Nagor ban Nagoram. He falsely accused the Ranger captain of a serious crime, then tried to murder him. We have no wish to surrender our *tseritsa* to this official, but if we refuse him, he will try to take it by force. We are not yet ready to defend ourselves against an invasion. If you were to defend us, our alliance would be revealed and Earth would have no choice but to declare war upon us, defeating the entire purpose of the alliance. Our only hope is to conceal the *tseritsa* from the official until he gives up his search and leaves. We also need to protect the Ranger captain, who lies gravely injured in Med Services. Can you help us?"

Nagor tilted his head to one side. "The *tseritsa* is from Earth?"

He wanted to know whether Daisy Hub had stolen it. Unsure what to reply to this, Drew cast a questioning glance at Holchuk. To Townsend's relief and annoyance, the other man immediately stepped forward and answered for him.

"Originally, yes. All Humans came from Earth, Nagor," Holchuk told him, "as all Nandrians came from Serrussha."

"You understand," said Nagor, nodding. Then he turned to his subordinates and spoke to them briefly in Nandrian. "Bring them now," he instructed Townsend. "We will lock them in my quarters. Only I will have the unlocking code. And tell your Doctor Ktumba they will need food for two days."

The three Humans bowed deeply and said in unison, as scripted, "We are honored to receive your assistance."

"I am honored that you would give me the safekeeping of your most precious belonging," Nagor replied, to all of them. Then, speaking directly to the station manager, he added, "You are a gracious host."

So they were back to *that* script. The squirming sensation in his stomach told Drew that he would probably regret this, but he nonetheless replied, "And you are valued and always welcome guests. Please come aboard."

Making even stranger noises than before, the three Nandrians lumbered back through the archway.

"Looks like they've found a way around that five drink limit," observed Holchuk.

Ruby remarked sagely, "I think we've been a bad influence on them."

Chapter 41

Holchuk observed from a distance as Townsend dealt with Major Cisco.

The ninja was not a happy camper. For that matter, neither was the boss man. The last time the Nandrians had come aboard, Townsend had managed to complete the First Meeting ceremony, then had closeted himself on C Deck, refusing to join the party. As long as Cisco was on the Hub, he couldn't do that. Admittedly, these *tekl'hananni* celebrations were very loud. Ruby had once called them "headaches in waiting." But the station manager needed to be a presence whenever aliens were visiting. Maybe the crew ought to give him earplugs as a birthday present — assuming the boss man bothered with such things as birthdays.

Cisco was waving his arms now, and not in time to the music. Holchuk couldn't hear what he was saying, but his expression looked cold and menacing. Townsend had drawn himself erect and was standing his ground. Good. Now he was crossing his arms over his chest. That's it, thought Holchuk. Be firm and rational. Drive the ninja totally nuts.

They were standing in the caf, surrounded by a crowd of drunken aliens laughing at the top of their lungs. The air was so thick with citrus vapor that it could practically be sipped through a straw. The music blaring out of the comm system had already run the gamut from blues to techno-rock and back. Now the Powwow had set up and were jamming, not fifteen meters away, using the speakers they'd built for Teri's show. Everything in the room was vibrating. Holchuk could feel the bass notes throbbing right through the soles of his shoes.

Suddenly there were large hands on Holchuk's upper arms, gently pushing him to one side. "Sorry, Gavin," said Hagman's voice behind him, "you'll have to move. Battle re-enactment."

As if on cue, one of the aliens launched himself from the middle of the room and landed, sprawling, on the deck where Holchuk had been standing. A table and two chairs went flying. And that was just a warm-up. Confident that the boss man wouldn't be hanging around the caf much longer, Holchuk stepped out into the corridor.

"Looking for a swallow of fresh air?" teased a familiar voice. Lu Xensiu drew up beside him, then straightened his back, widened his stance and crossed his arms.

Holchuk followed his gaze and saw Townsend and Major Cisco, arguing as they walked toward the tube car door.

"That's him?" Lu remarked, a disdainful note creeping into his voice. For a moment, he sized up the man everyone had been referring to as 'the ninja'. "I could probably take that guy," he concluded.

Wordlessly, Holchuk shook his head, recalling the fist-sized dents he'd seen in the metal console cowlings on Zulu. "With all due respect for your skills, *sensei*, I have to disagree. He's not only strong and fast, he's vicious. And he doesn't play by any set of rules. He'd probably take you out while you were opening your mouth to challenge him."

"That only makes him all the more deserving of a beating."

A second later, Holchuk realized that he was standing alone in the corridor. Daisy Hub's homegrown ninja had apparently melted into the shadows. Lu watched far too many of those old Asian flat-screen videos.

Meanwhile, Hagman had joined Townsend and Cisco. The major's search had yielded nothing. Now it was time for him to leave. Holchuk watched the burly dock foreman herd the ninja into a tube car while Townsend maintained what could only be described as a forbidding demeanor. As soon as the tube car door slid shut, the station manager relaxed with a huge sigh and a dramatic change of posture. Then, darting a glance in the direction of the caf entrance, he shuddered visibly and took off down the corridor.

Back to his hidey-hole on C Deck, Holchuk thought reprovingly. Definitely, someone was going to have to give the boss man earplugs at the earliest possible opportunity.

Looking up and down the corridor, Holchuk thumbed the tube car button. He had a few more stops to make before his plan would be ready to present to the *Hak'kor*'s representative.

Chapter 42

Lydia greeted Drew with a smile as he stepped off the tube car. "So far, so good," she told him. "Lieutenant Rodrigues has received our message. The Rangers will be waiting with weapons drawn for Cisco to return to Zulu, and Rodrigues has promised to let us know the minute they have him in custody. Also, we have a transmission from the Space Installation Authority — a request for clarification."

SISCO was breaking silence. This could be a warning about Nestor Quan. Or about Steve Bonelli, the alleged traitor. Or maybe someone had confessed to conspiracy in the death of Karim Khaloub. Wouldn't *that* be interesting…

"What's the matter, Drew?" asked Lydia, frowning. "Too much noise?"

On his way to his desk, he nodded glumly. "I'd better take care of this clarification."

While waiting for the decryption code in his biowafer to complete its work, Drew felt the faint throbbing at the back of his head settle in and become a full-blown tension headache as he counted all the crimes he'd committed during his short tenure on Daisy Hub.

He'd probably allowed Robert O'Malley to get away with murder. Literally.

He'd appropriated stolen property and turned it to his own purposes. There would be two counts — one for Yoko and one for the stealth cloak.

He'd misrepresented the Hub as an independent political entity in order to make a secret alliance with an alien race. That was treason, a capital crime.

He was a willing accessory, before, during and after the fact, to InfoComm hacking. Another capital offence.

He'd organized and abetted a break-and-enter on Observation Platform Zulu, resulting in both deliberate and accidental vandalism.

He'd ordered the filing of a false medical report. There would be two counts on that one as well, one for the fraudulent arrest warrant and the other for aiding and abetting a fugitive from justice.

All that in less than three intervals. It had to be some kind of a record.

More significantly, however, it meant that he could never go back to Earth as himself. This was the part that his EIS handlers had glossed over during his mission briefing. He had to remain on Daisy Hub for the duration. If SISCO decided to terminate his assignment prematurely, he would have to call for an extraction and a complete identity change. He had no choice in the matter. The EIS would not hesitate to order the kill if he became even a perceived threat to its security.

Sensing that he was being watched, Drew turned and saw Lydia staring at him sympathetically across the top of a filing cabinet. She leaned forward, rested her chin on her crossed arms, and asked softly, "Is there anything I can do?"

What he really wanted her to do was leave him alone so he could read the bad news from SISCO. But the headache was seriously beginning to bother him, so he said, "Get me some pain medication from Med Services?"

She nodded and disappeared.

As soon as he heard the tube car door sigh closed behind her, he started to call up the decrypted text on his display screen, then changed his mind. Regardless of the content of this message, Nestor Quan had to be neutralized and Spike had to be extracted. And whether or not Khaloub's death was an EIS hit, he had to protect O'Malley, whatever the cost. Anything SISCO had to tell him would only complicate his plans by making him question his own resolve, and he didn't need that right now. Especially when his head was now pounding like a percussion beat from the Daisy Hub Powwow.

Townsend had a good crew. Given time, Gouryas and Singh and their techs would decipher the workings of the stealth cloak and the paintbrush. The Doc would apply her considerable expertise in genetics to the problem of cementing the alliance with the Nandrians. Lydia and O'Malley would top up their databases and complete the Hub's communications network. For weaponry, now that Bonelli was out of the picture, Drew could begin bringing the Rangers, and their ordnance, into the fold. And perhaps, eventually, he would also figure out the best way to tell both crews that they were now working for Earth Intelligence, preferably without triggering a mutiny.

His wristcomm bleeped.

"Drew, you're needed in Med Services right away!"

He'd heard angry voices behind Lydia's, one of them belonging to the Doc.

Dammit! he thought, wincing as he heaved himself out of his chair. *What now?*

Chapter 43

The tableau that greeted Townsend in Med Services today was almost as interesting as the earlier one with Alison Morgan.

Holchuk and the Doc were apparently engrossed in a staring contest, while Lydia stood nearby, one hand at her throat, the other clenched helplessly at her side.

"Drew!" she exclaimed with evident relief as he came through the doorway. "I'm sorry — I know you've got a headache, but I didn't know what else to do. They've never had an argument like this before."

"Over what?"

Doc Ktumba broke eye contact with Holchuk then and drew herself up to her full, imposing height before proclaiming indignantly, "He knows about Yoko, he says the Nandrians know too, and he wants me to clone her!"

Drew swore under his breath. He was no expert, but he knew enough to understand that Yoko was an ongoing experiment. It was the falling dominos all over again. Until she died, there could be no tampering with her, just monitoring and observation. What was more, Yoko was Nayo Naguchi's experiment, one in which he'd invested a lot of time and effort. He'd left explicit instructions with the Doc, knowing that she could be relied upon to follow them to the letter. And now Holchuk was pressuring her to mess with Naguchi's work?

"Holchuk, what the hell were you thinking?" he demanded wearily

"Go on, Gavin, tell him your brilliant plan," the Doc dared him.

The Chief Cargo Inspector stared at the deck for a moment, perhaps thinking things through for the first time and realizing, too late, that it was never a good idea to argue with the Doc.

"It's a way to avoid *ssalssit essendi*," he said at last, "and to speed up the consolidation of the alliance. The ritual is all about trust, about putting our most precious belonging into the safekeeping of our ally. Next to each House's *tseritsa*, that would be offspring. Offspring is problematic for us, but Yoko is our 'living staff', and Nagor was so honored that we let him care for her for a day or two, that I thought—" He broke off, blowing out a frustrated breath. "I still think the *Hak'kor* would go for this."

"Not to mention Teri...?" Lydia muttered, just loudly enough for Drew to hear.

Well, there was that too, Townsend had to admit. Aloud, he said, "Please, tell me you haven't said anything to Nagor yet."

Holchuk shook his head. "I wanted to discuss it with the Doc first."

"And you did, and the answer is absolutely not!" she declared.

But Townsend was getting another glimmer of an idea. "So, let me get this straight," he said. "You figured that if we were to offer Trokerk a copy of our 'living staff', the Nandrians would accept her in lieu of the egg exchange?"

"I've already begun mapping their genome," protested the Doc. "The procedure is doable. I just need a little time."

"This is no reflection on your skills, Doctor," Drew assured her. "But I'm getting the distinct impression, from everything else that's been happening lately, that we may not have the luxury of eight standard years to finalize this alliance. Maybe we should consider Holchuk's alternative."

"This is insane," she sputtered. "Nayo would never approve of—"

"Naguchi couldn't possibly have foreseen the situation we're in right now," Drew pointed out. "Mr. Holchuk, am I correct in assuming that the offerings would have to match?"

"That's right, boss man."

"So, if you're suggesting that we offer them a cloned rat, that must mean they're capable of trading us an exact copy of *their* 'living staff'."

Holchuk's expression, a mixture of surprise and approval, gave him the answer. "You understand," said the Chief Cargo Inspector, bowing slightly from the shoulders.

"They would have to know from the beginning that they were receiving Yoko's daughter, not our actual *tseritsa*. We don't run cons on the Nandrians," Drew warned him.

"Mr. Townsend, I must object," broke in the Doc.

"Noted, Doctor. But for the moment I just have one question for you: if O'Malley were to ask her very politely, do you think Yoko would be opposed to donating some of her eggs to ensure the continued survival of this space station and its crew?"

Expelling an audible breath, she glanced away from his face, then back again. This was the make-or-break moment. Drew looked into her defiantly flashing eyes, saw the stubborn set of her mouth, the tilt of her chin, and recalled: this was the Doc he'd confronted the day he'd arrived on Daisy Hub, the one who could make a charging rhino stop in its tracks. If she stood her ground, they were all back to square one.

Never argue with the Doc, repeated a mocking voice inside his head.

Then, "Ruby was right about you," she declared. "You are a lunatic. However, your other crazy schemes seem to have worked, so if you're determined to go ahead with this one, and Yoko agrees, then I guess I have no choice but to support your plan."

It was all he could do not to sigh with relief. "Thank you, Doctor. Now, could I please have some pain medication for this headache?"

— « o » —

Something drew him back to AdComm, something Bonelli had said that kept looping and repeating in his mind: "They wanted you off the street and completing your education. You were no good to them without your Eligibility."

"They" could only be Earth Intelligence. And since Bruni Patel was the only reason that Drew had worked so hard while in detention to earn his secondary and post-secondary certificates, and had later persevered to qualify for reinstatement of his Eligibility, Patel must have been on their payroll from the beginning. He hadn't befriended Drew out of the goodness of his heart, or because he saw untapped potential in an angry young man. He'd had a job to do for Earth Intelligence, and he'd done it.

As the depth of this betrayal sank in, the strength drained from Townsend's legs, dropping him heavily onto one of the guest chairs in his workspace.

He'd been hand-picked, Bonelli had told him. Drew had assumed he meant recently, for this assignment. But pieces were finally falling into place in his mind, and they were making a very disturbing picture. For the past eighteen years, Earth Intelligence had apparently been grooming him, turning him into something they could use, a tool or a weapon — and Bruni Patel had been Townsend's first handler.

Hand-picked. They'd all been hand-picked, everyone on Daisy Hub, including the current station manager. And what about the previous station managers? As he cast his gaze over the filing cabinets beside him, a bright yellow label caught his attention, on a second drawer from the bottom: Readiness Reports.

Readiness for what?

Curious, Drew reached over and pulled the drawer open. Inside it he found a box of small brown envelopes, each bearing a name and containing a datawafer. Aziz, McCarthy, Naguchi…. There were six altogether. Six former station managers. And underneath the box sat an old-fashioned red cardboard file folder. Drew pulled it out and opened it. It held two sheets of printout, each with the handwritten initials M.R. in the bottom right corner.

He'd seen those same letters before, in the same script, on hard copies of Security documents. Melville Ridout was very fond of paper. But there had been no mention of Ridout serving as station manager in any of Drew's EIS briefings about Daisy Hub. Perhaps the Chief had visited the Hub in his capacity as Deputy Chair of SISCO and had left the file folder behind. Or maybe it had been brought aboard by someone else, with or without Ridout's knowledge.

The first sheet appeared to be a list of requirements: job titles, numbers, desired qualifications. The numbers added up to 53, so this was probably a shopping list. Drew scanned down to the Manager of Hub Operations and read: "Logical, a strategist, able to use psychology to his advantage, street smart, willing to bend rules, trained in security and espionage techniques, risk-taker, able to take charge."

The accuracy of that description put an unpleasant flutter in Townsend's stomach. If Ridout had produced this document, then it appeared that either SISCO and the EIS had parallel plans to make use of the station and its crew, or, even more troubling to contemplate, the two organizations were working together.

With alarms already going off in his mind, Drew turned to the second sheet and felt a chill race down his spine. It was an attack plan, outlining the most efficient way to take control of Daisy Hub, and it listed all the weaknesses and vulnerabilities of the station.

That answered his earlier question about the datawafers. The station managers were reporting on the Hub's readiness for battle. As he sat frozen in his workspace, holding the blueprint for Daisy Hub's destruction in his hand, every instinct Drew possessed was screaming a warning at him. There were bad times coming. Forty-six people were about to become collateral damage. It would take everything he had plus a lot more to keep the Hub secure and her crew safe. And the time to begin preparing was yesterday.

Chapter 44

Day shift was half over when Holchuk received Nagor's commcall. The Chief Officer had just awakened, hung over, had realized what sort of mood the rest of his crew would be in when they regained consciousness, and had consequently decided it would be prudent to move his guests back to Daisy Hub as quickly and quietly as possible. The Nandrians were, after all, responsible for the safety of a *tseritsa*.

Once inside the tube car, Holchuk used his wristcomm to summon O'Malley, Lu, and Mossman to join him on A Deck. Technically, the boss man ought to be there as well, but his official presence would necessitate the sort of scripted ceremony that Nagor was anxious to avoid.

The cage and gurney were already off the *Krronn* and standing in the middle of the deck when Holchuk stepped out of the car. The other three men arrived less than a minute later and took up positions behind him, waiting for his signal to transport Yoko and Bonelli down to Med Services.

Yoko was fidgeting inside her cage, but Bonelli was lying very still. The Nandrians wouldn't have intentionally harmed him. Nonetheless…. Holchuk watched the Ranger for a moment, reassured by the sight of his chest slowly rising and falling. Then he initiated the protocol.

"Nagor ban Nagoram, we are honored that you deemed us worthy of your assistance," said Holchuk, bowing deeply.

Nagor, his skin an alarming shade of yellow, was too hung over to bow. Pronouncing the words with some difficulty, he replied hastily, "And I am honored to accept your gratitude, Gavin ban Samuel. Please remove our guests to safety."

Holchuk waved his detail forward. Within seconds, O'Malley had disappeared into a tube car with Yoko, and the door to another car was closing on Lu and Mossman and the anti-grav gurney.

That should have been the end. As he was about to bow, speak a scripted farewell and get into the third tube car, Holchuk heard Nagor growl, "Please accept this gift." The Nandrian was thrusting a compupad into his hand. Every additional minute spent in the vicinity of a hungover Nandrian increased his peril, but Holchuk didn't get many gifts. He grinned and called up the pad's directory.

"It's in Gally," he remarked.

"I translated it for you. Time is too short," said Nagor.

It was the instruction manual for the field generator. The boss man would be ecstatic.

"Nagor, I'm deeply grateful, and amazed! I am honored to accept this. But shouldn't you be presenting it to Drew, son of... *Dammit!*?"

The Nandrian snort-wheezed softly. "There is no script for helping someone cheat on a test. You may give it to him if you wish. But it would be more useful, I think, to give it to your engineers."

Then Nagor bobbed his massive head briefly and headed for the tube car door.

Holchuk decided to stop in at Med Services to check on the Nandrians' guests. Halfway there he heard his wristcomm bleep.

"This is an all-hands announcement," said Lydia's voice. "By order of the station manager, there will be a crew meeting in the caf fifteen minutes after the Nandrian ship departs. He's got something important to tell us, folks, so we'd better all be there."

Chapter 45

This time, the boss man was the last one to enter the room. He didn't look too happy. So what was the meeting about? Holchuk wondered. Around him, everyone was sitting, chatting quietly in groups of three or four. He looked for Teri and found her surrounded by Ruby, O'Malley, Jason Smith, and Nora Duvall, Fritz Jensen's *sous chef*. Then he remembered what was on the compupad in his hands and looked around the room for Gouryas and Singh. Nagor was right. They were the ones who needed the manual. Let them look like geniuses when they cracked the codes on that damned field generator in a fraction of the expected time — they could use the stroking. They could all use some stroking, come to that.

Lydia slid into a seat directly ahead of him and smiled at him over her shoulder.

Holchuk leaned forward to ask quietly, "What's going on?"

"Not sure," she replied with a shrug. "He looked at something from one of the metal cabinets lined up around his desk, cursed, threw the folder back into a drawer, and told me to call this meeting."

Interesting.

Before he could speculate any further, however, the room went suddenly quiet. Townsend was standing at the front of the caf, looking around expectantly. Counting heads, Holchuk realized. Lydia had been serious when she said they'd better all be there.

"Thank you for coming to this meeting, people. There are some important things you need to know, and we may not have a lot of time.

"First, some bad news. We've heard from Zulu. Unfortunately, Major Cisco managed to elude the trap the

Rangers had set for him. He made his escape on the shuttle *Tripoli*, which had just been refueled. The Rangers suspect that he's heading for a pre-arranged rendezvous point. They are sending warnings to all the colonies within three days' travel of this system, and Lieutenant Rodrigues has confirmed that Earth will be issuing an arrest warrant, based on the documentation and death certificate we've provided for the late Captain Bonelli — but we're not to hold our breath waiting for Cisco to be apprehended in the near future."

Hagman let out a gusty sigh. "So we're in the soup, and he gets away. Slippery little devil, isn't he?"

There was a scattering of mirthless laughter.

"Mr. Hagman is right — we are in the soup. As you've all experienced at first hand, there's a lot wrong with Earth's government right now. And here we sit, three Gates from our home world, unable to do anything about it until we start working together. The mission to Zulu was successful, because we worked together. I know that made you feel good. You told me so.

"Each one of you has a special talent or skill or quality that makes you a valuable member of this crew. Just look at the expertise in this room." As Townsend began singling people out, Holchuk watched for their reactions. He caught the occasional shy grin, and plenty of blushing. The Daisy Hub crew were unaccustomed to being so publicly praised. "Most of you are highly-trained technicians and engineers," the station manager continued. "Ruby, you've been the backbone of AdComm ever since you arrived. Holchuk, you know more about the Nandrians than any other Human alive. Hagman, you and your team are the real Security on this station. Thanks to Jensen, we eat better here than many people do on Earth. And between them, Lydia and O'Malley have given us the best communications and intelligence system anywhere."

Holchuk saw sudden frowns, heard sudden muttering. Okay, he thought, brace yourself, boss man — here it comes…

"What exactly did O'Malley do?" demanded an incredulous female voice.

Predictably, the kid leaped to his feet and retorted, "I hacked Zulu, that's what, Vera. We know everything they do, forty nanoseconds in advance. And they haven't got a clue."

...*yet*, Holchuk supplied, slowly shaking his head. The Rangers didn't know anything about it *yet*. But that would change pretty damned quick if O'Malley couldn't learn when to keep his mouth shut. Would he ever understand?

Now the Doc was on her feet, the picture of righteous indignation. "You mean we didn't have to wait for Alison Morgan to wake up to discover her identity? We could have asked you?"

"Yes, if we'd known," Townsend replied for him. "And that's precisely my point. You've all been following Naguchi's recommendation to keep learning and improving yourselves, but you've been doing it privately, not letting anyone else know what you're capable of. Well, there are big changes coming, and I'm afraid that won't be acceptable anymore. We are going to have to share all of our skills, all of our knowledge, all of our strengths, and all of our talents, if we're going to survive what's ahead."

At the word "survive", there was a collective intake of breath. Then Soaring Hawk piped up, "Can you be a little more specific about these changes, boss?"

"When Mr. Holchuk was adopted by the Nandrians, we effectively seceded from Earth and made a formal defensive alliance with an alien race. When that hits the fan, ladies and gentlemen, Earth will send out a force to retake Daisy Hub. If we have to ask the Nandrians for help, we'll be starting an interstellar war. So, we'd better get busy developing the means to defend ourselves."

You do understand, boss man, Holchuk thought grimly. It was a good thing someone did.

"So, that's why they gave us the invisibility field?" Singh wondered aloud.

There was an immediate chorus of excited voices, echoing, "Invisibility field? We have an invisibility field?"

"Yes," Townsend confirmed, silencing the room once more, "it turns out that the Meniscus Field generator is capable of producing more than one kind of field, when combined with the molecular paintbrush. The one that was discovered over on Zulu gives us a stealth cloak. But I don't believe the Nandrians were foreseeing problems with Earth. Apparently, we have other enemies out there that Earth High Council isn't even aware of. Indirectly, that's why I'm here."

This meeting was becoming more and more interesting. Holchuk leaned back in his seat and crossed his arms over his chest.

"Until there's been a planet-wide housecleaning at all government levels, Earth will remain completely vulnerable. People on our home world have already begun the process. They're targeting the corruption, clearing out the dead wood. They're making a difference. And even though we're stuck out here in the boondocks, we can make a difference too. The other day, someone asked me whether there would be any more missions. The answer to that question is yes, but not until we're ready. Our first priority has to be the defense of Daisy Hub. Once we have those defenses in place, I'll contact the resistance movement on Earth and ask them how we can help."

Hearing that, Holchuk's entire body perked up. There was a resistance?

"I'll bet my brother's neck-deep in it," murmured Smith, shaking his head indulgently.

"I'll bet my uncle started it," countered someone else.

"Drew," said Ruby, loudly enough to cut through the chatter, "what exactly is your plan for getting us ready?"

He sucked in a deep breath. "Okay, people, listen up. You've been working shifts on multiple details in order to learn all you can about maintaining and repairing the Hub. That will continue. But in addition, I'm going to reorganize the duty schedules to give everyone time to attend classes. Ruby, you once offered to teach me how to fly *Devil Bug*. Does that offer still stand?"

Grinning, she replied, "You bet it does, Chief."

"Good. Who else would like to learn?"

There was a clamor of voices. Ruby gazed around the room in astonished delight.

"That's how it works, folks. Ruby is now a flying instructor. The same thing will apply to any skills that might be needed in defense of the Hub or on a mission. Martial arts, for example. Commando strategies. Beginning after the next two station days, we're all going to become teachers as well as students. Ruby and I will set up an interim schedule and post it on the station's InfoCommNet. Each one of us will be expected to take at least three classes per interval, with the following exceptions: Mr. Gouryas and Mr. Singh, your ongoing and only assignment is to master the field generator and figure out the stealth cloak. And I'm ordering the Midnight Muralist, whoever you are, to report to these two gentlemen on L Deck and teach them everything you know about the paintbrush. Are there any questions?"

"Do we have a deadline, Mr. Townsend?" asked Jason Smith.

The station manager sighed. "All I can tell you at this point is that it will probably be sooner than we expect. Major Cisco is at large, and he knows a lot more about what we're doing here than I would like."

Someone made a disgusted noise that carried right to the front of the room.

"And there's one more thing," Townsend added. "We need someone besides the Nandrians watching our backs. Someone close by, and Human."

"And armed to the teeth?" teased Ruby.

"That would be a plus," he agreed, smiling. "Bonelli is officially deceased, so he won't be returning to Zulu. And I couldn't help noticing that without Bonelli around, and in the presence of a common enemy, the Rangers are actually not too difficult to get along with. So, when the new commanding officer arrives on Zulu, I'm going to meet with him and see if we can come to an arrangement."

"You're going to recruit him into the resistance, boss?"

"I'm going to give it my best shot, Mr. O'Malley. Wish me luck."

As the meeting was breaking up, Ruby fell into step beside Townsend. Walking behind them, Holchuk heard her say, "I take back what I said about you earlier, Chief."

"Oh?"

"I believe there's some Naguchi in you after all."

No, thought Holchuk, not Naguchi. Naguchi's mission had been to distract them from their situation by keeping them all busy and useful; Townsend was here for another purpose, which he may or may not have revealed to them today. He was such a manipulative bastard that it was difficult to tell. But one thing was certain: there were some big ugly changes coming down the pipe, and the fact that Townsend was on Daisy Hub meant that someone on Earth must give a damn about the station and its crew. For the moment, that would have to do.

Chapter 46

"Am I too early?"

Ridout glanced up from his paperwork and waved his visitor into the office. "Not at all. I was just about to put this away and break out the bubbly."

"So, Townsend pulled it off?" Barry Novak commented, easing himself into the chair closest to the desk.

Ridout delved into the bottommost drawer of his filing cabinet and brought up an ice-packed wine bottle and four stemmed glasses, which he arranged carefully in the middle of his antique desk blotter. "Don't sound so surprised," he chided. "We chose the right man and trained him well. I've already sent the gatecast confirming his permanent appointment to the post of station manager. The Space Installation Authority isn't happy about it, but it's a done deal."

"What about the murder investigation he was supposed to be conducting?"

"Closed, and the records have been sealed indefinitely. Officially, the death has been ruled accidental. Are you making any progress in the Patel matter?"

"We know who didn't do it, and that's something, I guess. But it's going to take a lot more digging to get to the bottom of this."

"Well, I have complete confidence in you and your team — which, if I may remind you, we also chose and trained well."

Novak nodded his agreement as a third person appeared in the Chief's doorway.

"You're right on time, Nayo," Ridout greeted him. "We're celebrating."

Naguchi sank down with a sigh into the indicated guest chair. "So I hear. I also hear that my old nemesis Nestor Quan has resurfaced."

"On Riviera Hub," said Novak. "I've issued standing orders to all operatives to take him out on sight. He won't be a problem much longer."

Naguchi smiled faintly. "Good. It took Marion a long time to accept my death. I'd hate to have to rise from my grave to settle this."

"Speaking of rising from graves, how is the erstwhile Captain Bonelli doing?" Ridout inquired.

"Bonelli is recovering nicely," replied Naguchi. "Marion did an exemplary job of putting him back together. Of course, I expected no less from my star student."

A rustling sound in the anteroom drew all their attention to the doorway, and a moment later, the fourth member of their group stepped into Ridout's office.

Instantly, the other three rose to their feet.

"Madam Chief Adjudicator, we're honored that you could join us," said Ridout.

She gave them a regal nod of acknowledgement before taking the seat that Novak vacated for her. "I'm always glad to help celebrate the successful conclusion of a long-term project like Daisy Hub," she responded. "How soon before they can be activated?"

"Based on the reports, we estimate one Earth year before we can begin giving them level one assignments," Novak told her. "They'll need another year after that to properly consolidate their own defense systems."

"So," she said thoughtfully, "in another two years we can begin setting things in motion here on Earth. The Reformation is right on schedule, gentlemen. That *is* something to drink to."

* * * *

If you enjoyed this read, please leave a review.

* * * *

Author Bio

Born and raised in Toronto, Arlene F. Marks found her muse at the age of 6 and has been writing and sharing her stories ever since. Her work has appeared in *H.P. Lovecraft's Magazine of Horror* and has been published by *Daily Science Fiction*. Her first science fantasy novel, *The Accidental God*, was nominated for the 2015 Stephen Leacock Medal for Humour. Arlene lives with her husband on Nottawasaga Bay but spends an inordinate amount of time in the Sic Transit Terra universe. She welcomes visitors to her website:

www.thewritersnest.ca.

Read ahead for a preview of the second book in the Sic Transit Terra universe.

THE OTHERNESS FACTOR
Sic Transit Terra Book 2

By Arlene F. Marks

ABOARD THE *MARCO POLO*

Watch Commander Gael Dedrick gazed around the ship's mess, shaking his head in bemusement. Red and green streamers looped drunkenly across the ceiling. Cut-out snowflakes and asymmetrical foil stars were stuck haphazardly to the bulkheads. In the corner farthest from the door sat a metal cone nearly two meters tall, studded with intermittently flashing lights and topped with a figure crafted out of spare computer parts, supposed to represent an angel. A plate of flat cookies shaped like snowmen and bells had been placed on every table. (Some of these 'confections' had tooth marks on them. From year to year, people forgot that the cookies were decorations as well.) And everywhere on the ship, the comm system was sighing out songs about sleigh rides and fireplaces and snow.

All this because it was December on Earth.

Ten standard years earlier, when Ensign Gael Dedrick had been newly assigned to the *Marco Polo*, he had surveyed the crew manifest to see how many Christians were aboard ship and had found nineteen, besides himself. Twenty out of 199. Most of the rest had designated themselves either agnostic or atheist. Only a handful had declared affiliation with one of Earth's other organized religions. Dedrick knew that other faiths observed holy days in the month of December — he had overheard crew members talking about it. These tended to be private rituals, conducted in crew quarters. Christmas, however, was a different matter.

On a Fleet ship, everybody celebrated Christmas, whether they were Christian or not. Christmas was colorful and happy. It was decorations and music and special food served on special dishes. And it was gifts. Once each Earth year, Fleet Control was granted funding earmarked for the transportation of gifts and holiday messages from relatives to the personnel serving aboard Earth's spacegoing vessels. And once each Earth year, over a four week period, the credit units were disbursed. Families in modest circumstances, regardless of faith, were left with no other choice than to send their packages and good wishes in December, turning Christmas on the *Marco Polo* into a month-long, shipwide festival.

Involuntarily, Dedrick sighed. There hadn't been any Christmas parcels or greetings for him for several years now, not since Aunt Emma had died. Abner's mother had been the last Dedrick left on Earth, and even though she knew Gael blamed her for his own parents' death, she had summarily 'adopted' him shortly after they were gone. At that point, there had been no word from Abner for four Earth years. For the next six years, as Gael worked his way up through the ranks of Earth's spacegoing Fleet, he had received Abner's birthday presents, Abner's Christmas gifts, Abner's share of love and best wishes. Then, on the tenth anniversary of her son's disappearance, Aunt Emma had gone to bed with a mystery novel, a bottle of well-aged scotch, and enough sedative capsules to put her to sleep for good. End of story, end of Dedricks.

There probably weren't more than five crew members who knew the Christmas story well enough to tell it. Gael Dedrick was one of them, but he had long ago decided to keep the truth about Christmas to himself. There was no point in spoiling everyone's fun by bringing a doomed savior to their party.

His wristcomm began to buzz. He stepped over to a wall unit and punched in his identification code to access the comm line:

"Commander Dedrick, please report to the captain in his strategy room right away."

"Acknowledged. I'm on my way."

Five minutes later, he was walking through the strategy room door. Captain Takamura was in conference with Doctor Deneuve, the Supervisor of Medical Services. They halted their conversation and looked up as Dedrick entered the room, but only Takamura smiled a welcome.

Hiro Takamura's age was indefinable, but it was common knowledge that he had been out in space for more than thirty years, twenty of them spent in the captain's chair. And, adding mystery to his powerful aura of authority, he had somehow managed while out in space to acquire the tough, weathered look of an old salt who had spent half his life on Earth's oceans.

Deneuve, on the other hand, with her short stature and fair, flawless complexion had the smooth, polished appearance of a porcelain doll. Seen side by side, they made an odd pairing.

"Commander Dedrick," said Takamura, waving him closer. "The *Marco Polo* is about to receive a singular privilege. An alien has asked to join our crew."

A guerrilla memory sent Dedrick's heart crashing down into his stomach. "Please, tell me it's not a Nandrian."

"No, it's not a Nandrian," Deneuve cut in. "It's a Dimmlesi. At least, that's what the individual claimed who replied to my posting."

"Claimed?"

Takamura nodded. "According to the Great Council's database, there is no such race in our arm of the galaxy."

"Is Fleet Control aware of this?"

"They are, and I've been informed that our orders stand. We're to add Doctor Minegar to our ship's complement." Takamura shifted his stance and folded his arms thoughtfully. "I don't believe this is a practical joke, although it may be a test. Or a confidence game of some sort. Or possibly an attempt by a fugitive to elude pursuit. Whatever it is, we have no choice but to deal with it. Doctor Deneuve and I have been attempting to formulate a plan. We decided to ask for your input as well, since you're the one who will be making first contact."

"Me? I—" For a moment, the watch commander couldn't trust himself to speak. Sending a subordinate ranked officer to make first contact was what had triggered the incident with the

Nandrians one year earlier. Three crew members had ended up in Trauma with serious injuries. Surely they didn't want to go through that again! Finally, Dedrick cleared his throat and continued in what he hoped would be a calm, professional-sounding voice, "I'm honored, Captain, but with all respect, wouldn't it be more appropriate for the highest ranking officer on the ship to deliver a formal greeting to the alien first?"

"Doctor Minegar has requested that we forego all ceremony and let her come aboard quietly," explained Deneuve.

All the more reason to wonder about her motives, Dedrick realized.

"Your recommendations, Watch Commander?"

Dedrick sucked in a breath, feeling two pairs of eyes resting expectantly on his face. "Foregoing ceremony doesn't mean we forego security," he decided. "Where are we meeting this Doctor Minegar, exactly?"

"Zekaris Station, just outside Earth space," replied Takamura. "The High Council has forwarded me the coordinates — it's a two-interval journey from here. I've been assured that the only ships docking when we arrive will be the alien's and our own. You'll have to cross the landing deck, meet our new crew member and escort her onto the *Marco Polo* and into this room."

Dedrick nodded. It was doable. "I'll take a security detail with me. Assuming she's traveling alone, two men should be enough."

"Dress them as ordinary crewmen," Deneuve advised, explaining to Takamura, "We don't want to risk frightening her as she steps through the docking portal. They can carry her bags while Commander Dedrick accompanies her on board."

"And have a second security detail waiting just this side of the airlock, to escort us to the strategy room," Dedrick continued. "I'll tell her it's an honor guard."

"Tell her whatever is necessary to avoid the sort of debacle that occurred last year with the Nandrians," said Takamura sternly. "The High Council has indicated that it is willing to forgive that unfortunate misunderstanding, provided we are successful at integrating Doctor Minegar into our crew."

"Aye, sir."

"And, Commander? We know nothing about this alien's culture. Anything at all could be interpreted as an insult, so I want you to be extremely careful around her. Your wording, your body language — everything must be calm and neutral."

"Understood, sir."

Takamura bowed slightly to each of them in turn, murmuring, "Doctor Deneuve, Watch Commander, thank you for your time." Then he spun and headed for the strategy room door.

When it had sighed closed behind him, Deneuve sank into a chair and said wearily, "A moment, Gael, please."

Curious, Dedrick sat down beside her. Deneuve reached a hand into the pocket of her lab coat and pulled out a datawafer. "This message arrived earlier today, from Leslie Eberhart's brother Sam. You were right — once the diagnosis of cancer was confirmed, they tried to rescind his Eligibility for medical reasons."

"They tried," he echoed, "but...?"

She smiled. "Whoever your contact is, he's got pull. Once the cancer is cured, Sam gets to stay Eligible for purposes of financial security, consumer options and health care priority. That's the good news."

"And what's the bad news?"

"They're keeping him on Earth, indefinitely. Leslie doesn't know yet, and I dread having to tell her that her brother will have to watch his kids grow up on a commscreen from now on. You know how strongly she feels about family."

Dedrick sighed. Yes, he knew. Eberhart's fierce protectiveness towards those she cared about was the thing that had first attracted him to her. This wasn't a perfect situation, admittedly, but it could have been a lot worse, for both Leslie and her brother. If Sam carried a genetic predisposition for cancerous growths, then Leslie might be carrying it as well. Once the Authority stripped someone of his Eligibility for medical reasons, they could use the rescision as grounds for reviewing the status of *all* his blood relatives. Entire families had been recalled from off-planet postings and restricted to Earth until either their bloodline was cleared or their Eligibility was revoked...

…which, now that he thought about it, might not be such a terrible thing, Dedrick mused. Interplanetary travel was one hell of an adventure. However, families *needed* to gather in times of stress, to support and comfort one another, and that was hard to do when the Relocation Authority seemed bent on scattering Eligible Humans all over the galaxy. Leslie's two brothers had been posted to colonies at opposite ends of Earth space, where they'd married and were raising broods of little Eberharts. As long as Watch Commander Eberhart wore a Fleet uniform, she would remain, like Dedrick, a singleton, in transit. By some miracle, the Eberhart clan had come through Angel of Death almost unscathed. But once all those nieces and nephews had grown to adulthood, the Relocation Authority would separate them and start moving them around, strowing Eberharts across Earth space like seeds blown by the wind. Thanks to Abner, Dedrick would never again know the pain of that kind of separation. It was the only benefit, he reflected sadly, of not having any family at all.

"Are you sure you don't want me to tell her what you've done for Sam?" Deneuve asked, breaking into his thoughts.

"Positive."

Deneuve's expression became the portrait of incredulity. "You want her to go on thinking you're a coldhearted bastard who wouldn't lift a finger when she asked you for help?"

Dedrick blew out his breath in a sigh. What he wanted was to remain an anonymous benefactor so he wouldn't end up like Uncle Dennis, constantly pursued by 'friends' with ulterior motives. He was already regretting having confided in the ship's Supervisor of Med Services, but what was done couldn't be undone.

"Until I'm ready to tell her myself, yes, that's exactly what I want. And I don't want anyone else aboard to know about this either. I want your word, Doctor," he added, holding eye contact with her until she finally, reluctantly, nodded assent.

— « o » —

Need something new to read?

If you enjoyed The Genius Asylum
Sic Transit Terra Book 1, you should also
consider these other EDGE titles:

~ ~ ~

The Rosetta Man

By Claire McCague

Wanted:
Translator for first contact.
Immediate opening.
Danger pay allowance.

Estlin Hume lives in Twin Butte, Alberta surrounded by a horde of affectionate squirrels. His involuntary squirrel-attracting talent leaves him evicted, expelled, fired and near penniless until two aliens arrive and adopt him as their translator. Yanked around the world at the center of the first contact crisis, Estlin finds his new employers incomprehensible. As he faces the ultimate language barrier, unsympathetic military forces converging in the South Pacific keep threatening to kill the messenger. The question on everyone's mind is: Why are the aliens here? But Estlin's starting to think we'll happily blow ourselves up in the process of finding that out.

Praise for The Rosetta Man:

"The cover and synopsis had me expecting a light-hearted comedy. I didn't realize I was getting a geopolitical first contact thriller that somehow still managed to be a light-hearted comedy. I really enjoyed this book! The characters are rich and diverse. Estlin and Harry are great, Beth and Bomani made me cry. The story is fast paced and engaging and again, completely unexpected. Great book for fans of first contact scifi, but also fans of thrillers and mysteries. And so well-executed that I give it a solid 5 stars."
> — *Scott Burtness, author of Wisconsin Vamp (Monsters in the Midwest)*

"This book ranks up there with many of the classic sci-fi "first contact" stories and Claire McCague's scientific background comes through in waves."
> — *Cameron Arsenault, Amazon Reviewer*

"A completely enjoyable read. Good action, lots of humor, and a global setting. Strongly recommended."
> — *Diane Lacey, Amazon Reviewer*

— « O » —

The Triforium:
The Haunting of Westminster Abbey

By Mark Patton

After Butterfield Senior's death, 'Butterfield and Son Architects' becomes, for all intents and purposes, 'Son — Newly Graduated — Without a Clue — Architect — Maybe'! With his inheritance sold to get the architectural business on its feet, Wallace Butterfield eagerly hopes to add a major architectural project to his curriculum vitae. (Critics describe his previous project, le Mareschal's Supermarket, as a large and unimpressive glass and chrome rectangle — though some shoppers have told Butterfield that they appreciate the large inventory of groceries and home products...) When Butterfield gets a call from the Reverend Poda-Pirudi, chairman of the Westminster Abbey Foundation, he overlooks the fact that the Reverend can only meet with him in the middle of the night — in an office located in the dark and cluttered attic of the Abbey itself. Butterfield thinks he's finally moving up in the world. However, the interred ghosts of Westminster Abbey haven't yet weighed in; and a local group of WITCHes (Women In Therapeutic Chemical Healing) have also taken a special interest in the architect. And unfortunately for Wallace Butterfield, these particular WITCHes aren't above kidnapping.

Set inside Westminster Abbey, England's enduring symbol of unity and crowned culture, a community of ghosts, whose remains rest inside the iconic building, arise at the bidding of a strange cleric. A series of adventures come into play as a hapless architect is dogged through the streets of London by a coven of drunken witches and illustrious but dead personages.

Praise for The Triforium: *The Haunting of Westminster Abbey:*

"As I finished the book and put it down with a very contented sigh, my first thought was "Why have we not previously heard the name Mark Patton in the realm of fiction writing?" If this is the author's first publication, it bodes well for what may yet come. 'The Triforium' is a superb piece of fiction that provides the main ingredients to satisfy me: humour (I laughed aloud several times, startling my partner and my dog), a good plot, detailed research, and some very intriguing thoughts on the genesis of souls, ghosts and gods."
— *Christopher A. Smith, Amazon Reviewer*

"A very well written fantasy, entwined into the incredibly interesting history of Westminster Abbey. I thoroughly enjoyed this bizarre, extraordinarily entertaining tale. Well worth a read and I highly recommend it."
— *S McDermott, Amazon Reviewer*

"Thought provoking humor: " You need your good dreams to make you want to go to bed and some bad ones so you don't grow overly fond of being there." The author's accurately detailed description of Westminster Abbey and London had me searching the internet for further historical insight on many of the facts included in the telling of this unusual story. Fascinating and entertaining!"
— *Amazon Reviewer*

"Parts had me laughing out loud and the story line is really well thought out and worked through. It's a fun, wild, ghost story that I was sorry to see end. I really enjoyed it quite a lot. 5 out of 5 stars."
— *Emily, Amazon Reviewer*

— « o » —

The Milkman:
A Freeworld Novel

By Michael J. Martineck

In the near future, corporation rules every possible freedom. Without government, there can be no crime. And every act is measured against competing interests, hidden loyalties and the ever-upward pressure of the corporate ladder. Any quest for transparency is as punishable as an act of murder. But one man has managed to slip the system, a future-day Robin Hood who tests dairy milk outside of corporate control and posts the results to the world.

When the Milkman is framed for a young girl's murder and anonymous funding comes through for a documentary filmmaker in search of true art beneath corporate propaganda, eyes begin to turn and soon the hunt is on. Can the man who created the symbol of the Milkman, the only one who knows what really happened that bloody night, escape the corporate rat maze closing around him? Or is it already too late?

Praise for The Milkman:

The Milkman won the Independent Publisher Book Award (IPPY) as the best science fiction novel at the national level. The novel was also a finalist in the Eric Hoffer awards, given each year for salient writing from small presses.

"Reminiscent of the novels of Michael Coney, Frederik Pohl and Cyril Kornbluth as well as Terry Gilliam's Brazil, although with less bitter humor and more outrage than those

luminaries, the work is a reductio ad absurdum examination
of the increasingly corporatized world in which we all live, an
impressive demonstration of the author's skills."
— *Publisher's Weekly*

— « o » —

For more Science Fiction, Fantasy, and Speculative Fiction titles from EDGE and EDGE-Lite visit us at:

www.edgewebsite.com

Don't forget to sign-up for our Special Offers

www.ingramcontent.com/pod-product-compliance
Lightning Source LLC
Chambersburg PA
CBHW031954120726
47898CB00002BA/446